GW01071855

Sleepers Publishing
PO Box 1204
Collingwood Victoria 3066
Australia
www.sleeperspublishing.com
sleepers@sleeperspublishing.com

The Sleepers Almanac 4
ISBN: 978-1-74066-610-7

This *Almanac* was produced with the fabulous support of Arts Victoria. And
this project has been assisted by the Australian Government through the
Australia Council, its arts funding and advisory body.

Distributed by

Hardie Grant Books

Sleepers Publishing is a proud member of the Small
Press Underground Networking Community (SPUNC)

The
Sleepers
Almanac
No. 4

Edited by Zoe Dattner and Louise Swinn
Sleepers Publishing, Australia

In memory of Jack Ames.

Contents

First things first:

Thanks to copyeditors Olivia Mayer and Kate Freeth.
Thanks to Fran Berry and Emma Schwarcz at Hardie Grant.
Thanks to Arts Victoria and the Australia Council, without
whom this would have trouble existing in a physical sense.

"IT'S TERRIFIC..."

A fourth wedding anniversary is traditionally celebrated with gifts of linen. It is appropriate therefore that the floral motif on the cover of this fourth *Almanac* is taken from the upholstery of my couch. OK, upholstery is not linen exactly, but I'll bet you can get a doona cover by the same designer to match my couch. Then this *Almanac* would go wonderfully beside your bed, and if you live in one of those open plan, New York-style apartments (I think they call them 'lofts') then you'd have a very tasteful ensemble indeed, and perhaps then the short story and independent publishing will catch the idle eye of the Reading Masses when it appears on the cover of *Vogue*. How's that for a series of segues? Now you can see the strange string of logic an editor such as myself follows when designing a book. Let's hope it works.

You've bought this book (I hope) for any number of reasons (and I encourage you to let us know why). And now that you have it you've put yourself in that category of People Who Read Introductions at the Beginning of a Book (a fine club to belong to; in fact, I think you can even join one on Facebook). This means that you are interested in actively forming a relationship with this book, the stories, and the writers who have contributed. This is ultimately our intention with producing the *Almanac*. We don't solely exist to provide opportunities for writers, or to make money (ha ha ha). We simply love making books, just like somebody else might love building mudbrick houses, or constructing model airplanes, or creating Youtube videos. So when people ask us: does the world need another literary journal? I find myself thinking of the baker in Carver's short story *A Small Good Thing*, of how much he enjoys baking, of the simple pleasure he gets from putting a fresh, still-warm bread roll in front of a hungry person and watching the look on that person's face as they breathe in the possibilities contained in this perfect offering of sustenance. How could the world ever cease to need or desire such a thing?

This *Almanac* is a small good thing. The world is a richer place for the words it contains. And if nothing else, it makes the perfect gift for anyone you know celebrating a fourth anniversary.

Zoe Dattner

"AMAZING..."

Despite the fact that we have the highest per capita number of literary journals in the world (don't take that as gospel) and we are always reading short stories in some form or another, there are inordinately few places to publish stories of 10,000 words. Even if we agree that there was a gap that needed filling then the question remains, why did we – that is, Sleepers – take it upon ourselves to fill it?

Were we: a] qualified (almost certainly not) – as if that alone would have done us any good – b] ready (perhaps) c] funded (negative) d] unemployed (no) or e] under the misapprehension that doing so would render us financially secure (on the contrary: we knew it would be worse even than miserable assistant-to-the-assistant-salaries, rents would go unpaid, beans stretched, T-shirts turned to nappies) but still, we did it instinctively. I think we had no choice.

This book contains our favourite pieces, collectively argued over. I won't give too much away right now, but I will tell you that when Liv came in the morning after reading 'Dingbats' she was stark raving high, and when Zoe finished '365 Birds' she breathlessly put it on my desk saying, 'you HAVE GOT to read this one', and when I read 'Best Medicine' I was so excited I was almost sick.

It's our fourth *Almanac* and we've gone down $5. We've reduced the page size to better fit in handbags, halving the printing costs; and we've increased the page extent. This is our first non-themed collection, despite the fact that our last one, 'The Family Affair', was the theme best kept to. In general, the themes were a stretch, in all honesty; they didn't quite work. Live and learn. Thanks for being part of Stage One. The fourth *Almanac*, announcing us as it does into the mass market and therefore preparing our authors for infamy, for multiple quotes, for wikis and profiles with headshots, is the start of Stage Two.

It's more than forty years since Barthes announced the death of the author but these ones are very much alive and working hard. However, right now it's just you and this book; and you are, suddenly but definitely, of utmost importance. It's you who is alive, and we know you're alive because you're reading this *Almanac*.

Louise Swinn

A Shade Less Perfect
Max Barry

'It's not that I don't *like* him. During that mess with the Baker account, Dave was a rock. As far as bosses go, he's great.' I squinted ahead. 'Is this it?'

'Hmm? No. White picket fence, Julie said.'

I pressed down on the accelerator. Oak trees, high hedges, and trim, vibrant lawns slid past. 'Ninety-five per cent of the time, Dave and I get on great. It's just—'

'That's it,' said Elizabeth. 'White picket fence. Go up the driveway; she said there's enough space for our car.'

I blew air between my teeth. 'Of course. See, this is what I'm saying. *Naturally* their driveway has plenty of space for cars. You know?'

'No.' Elizabeth turned around in her seat to inspect our cargo. 'I don't know what you're talking about.'

'He's *competitive*. He has to have the best of everything, all the time. God forbid Dave has a house with a tiny yard like the rest of us. Because what if one of us *didn't*? He can't stand to be second best. That's what I'm saying.'

'If you can stand it at work, you can stand it for one afternoon tea. I want to see Julie.'

'But that's the thing. At work, he's my superior. I *acknowledge* he's my boss. *Outside* of work, though, he's supposed to be my equal. So outside work, him telling me about his stock portfolio or how his golf handicap is down to eighteen is *obnoxious*.' I pulled up and gestured over the steering wheel. 'You see? Look at that. He could have parked that in the garage. Why is it out in the open?'

Elizabeth looked forward. 'Ooh. Convertible.' Then she saw what was behind it. 'Oh my *God*.'

I peered up. 'They probably don't even use half the rooms. How could they? It's just two of them and the baby.'

'It must have cost a *fortune*.'

'Oh, by the time we leave, I'm sure Dave will have told us exactly how much of a fortune it cost.'

'Not jealous, are we?'

'No! I couldn't care less if Dave wants to mortgage himself up to his eyeballs to have a, what, eighteen-bathroom house in the most expensive suburb in the city. What annoys me is that I know the whole time we're here, he'll be thinking how *impressed* we must be with his house, how much *better* it is than ours. Because *that's* all he cares about: being *better*.'

'Your paranoia is showing, darling.'

'You wait. Because you know what he's worst about. What he *never stops going on about*. Not the house. Not the car. Not the stock options.'

'They're just proud.' She unfastened her seat belt. 'So are we.'

'Proud is one thing. This is *obsessive*. You'll see.'

Elizabeth twisted around again. 'He's asleep.'

'For God's sake, wake him up,' I said, alarmed. 'If he's drowsy, Dave will think he's *slow*.'

I pressed the doorbell and took a step back. Elizabeth was cradling Charlie, who, thank God, had not burst into tears the moment upon waking, but rather was looking about with clear, interested eyes. I was carrying the bag of nappies, wipes, bottles, favourite toys, books and the thousand other miscellaneous items vital to a successful outing with a ten-month-old. Deep in the house, I heard chimes. Through frosted glass panels in the front door, vaguely human shapes began to resolve themselves.

'Relax,' Elizabeth said. 'You're standing there like a robot.'

'I am not.' I unclenched my hands. 'Just one thing. I told Dave that Charlie could walk.'

Elizabeth's mouth dropped open in outrage, but the door handle was already turning and suddenly there was Dave in his cream sports jacket and open-necked shirt and Julie cradling their ten-month-old son, Sebastian. We were a mirror image of each other (only Dave with no bag), so spontaneously we all burst out laughing. Then Elizabeth and Julie both went, '*Ahhhh!*' and rushed forward to coo over each other's babies. Dave and I shook hands and grinned at each other while I noticed that Dave had apparently spent Saturday having his teeth whitened.

'I can't believe how *big* he is,' Elizabeth said, and Julie said, 'Look at all Charlie's *hair*,' because the last time Elizabeth and Julie saw each other was in hospital, shortly after each had given birth.

'Yes, the little man's up to nineteen pounds,' Dave said. There followed a pause, during which he was clearly waiting for me to tell him Charlie's weight. I declined.

'Charlie's seventeen-and-a-half,' Elizabeth said. 'Aren't you, little guy?'

'He's *adorable*,' Julie said.

'Well, come in, come in.' Dave stood aside and swept an arm grandly out, inviting us into the mansion. He planted a kiss on Elizabeth as she passed, and I went to smile at Julie but she leaned forward expectantly, so I kissed her cheek. During this manoeuvre I got my first look in ten months at little Sebastian. He was chubby, with dark, wet-looking hair and skin like fresh plaster. He was also asleep and drooling down one cheek. I was surprised; following Dave's tales at work, I had been expecting a muscular, thirty-inch Adonis, with lightning crackling in his eyes.

When I pulled back from the kiss, Julie was looking at me with a smile. Julie is very attractive – Dave never settles for second best, of course – and this smile made me say something stupid; in fact, the last thing in the world I wanted Dave to hear. But for a second it was just me and Julie and her ten-month-old baby, so I said, 'He's a perfect little boy.'

Julie's smile wavered. 'Well—'

'Yes,' Dave said. 'He is.' I turned to see those newly-whitened teeth shining at me. 'Would you like the tour?'

This was about as mind-numbingly boring as you would expect, the tedium moderated only by intense irritation as Dave made overly jovial interjections about the expense of various items of furniture and the appalling amount of space they simply couldn't find a use for. Elizabeth, naturally, gushed over everything, but knowing that Dave was waiting for me to do likewise, I restricted myself to grunts. When the torture finally ended, Dave said, 'Well! Shall we adjourn to the sitting room?'

The sitting room was, of course, enormous. It was lavish. It offered a view over the vast expanse of their magazine-quality gardens. And in the middle of the floor were two baby rockers, side by side. They were positioned so we could insert our babies and compare them accurately.

'Tuck little Charlie into a rocker, if you like,' said Dave, slipping into an armchair.

'No, I'll hold him,' I said, but Elizabeth was already in motion. She slipped him in and fastened his straps while, beside her, Julie did likewise with sleeping Sebastian. Charlie bounced and gurgled. I felt as if I'd betrayed him.

We settled into the sofas. 'Would you like a beer, Jonathan?' Dave asked. 'Or something more serious? I have a Scandinavian malt you might like.'

'Whatever's going is fine.' Scandinavian whisky. Honestly.

'Anything for you, Elizabeth?'

'No, thanks. I'm still breastfeeding.'

Dave nodded. 'Sebastian's mainly on formula now. Julie was breast-feeding, of course, but Sebastian has… special needs.' He and Julie exchanged a look, and there was an odd pause. Then he smiled at us. 'Amazing how ravenous they are, isn't it? I'd swear Sebastian drinks his own body weight every day. Of course, he needs the energy. I tell you, sometimes he's crawling up the walls.'

'He's walking?' Elizabeth asked. I groaned inwardly.

'Since six months! Now he *runs*. Sometimes we have trouble catching him.'

'Goodness.'

'Unfortunately, though, you may miss the show. He usually sleeps until six or seven.'

Elizabeth's face fell. 'Oh, no. I want to see him properly.' I was thrilled. It meant I wouldn't have to tell Dave how wonderful his kid was, and know he was hearing: *better than Charlie*. 'He's sleeping well, then?'

Julie said, 'Ah, during the day, yes. But he hasn't worked out what nights are for yet.'

'Huh,' I said. 'That's rough. Charlie's slept through since he was three months.'

'Yes, we'd be totally sleep-deprived, if we didn't have Nicola,' Dave said. To Elizabeth's confused look, he added, 'The nanny'.

'Oh.'

Julie said, 'Dave tells me Charlie's walking as well?'

'Sure is!' I said.

'Well,' Elizabeth put in, '*walking* could be a bit of an exaggeration. He pulls himself up on things.'

'And *walks*,' I said.

'He *staggers*.' Dave laughed at this, and, irritatingly, Elizabeth turned to laugh with him. 'He staggers when aided by *furniture*.'

'He doesn't need furniture.'

'He does, Jonathan.'

'I've seen him walk plenty of times. You must have missed it.'

'I am *with* him ninety per cent of the day, and I have *never* seen him walk without hanging onto something.' She looked amused. 'For God's sake, you don't need to exaggerate. Plenty of kids aren't walking by ten months. There's nothing wrong with it.'

During all this my eyes were fixed on Elizabeth, because I couldn't bear the thought of turning to see Dave's smug expression. But finally I couldn't hold out any longer. And to my surprise, he didn't look smug at all. He looked relieved.

'He crawls,' I admitted. 'He crawls like the wind. But he can't walk yet.'

Dave and Julie laughed. Again, it wasn't what I'd expected: they weren't patronising but open and friendly – almost grateful. A second passed, then Julie said, 'Oh, tell them'. Dave shook his head slightly. '*Dave.*'

He sighed. 'Well… the thing is…'

'Sebastian's a *lovely* baby,' Julie interrupted. 'He really is. We adore him. But…'

'This is just between us,' Dave said. His voice was hard. 'This can't get around at work. You understand, Jonathan.'

'Of course.'

Elizabeth said, 'Julie, if something's worrying you, please, you can tell us. It's perfectly natural to worry about every little thing. And if there's anything I learned from Charlie, it's that babies are individuals. They're not always like in the books.'

Dave nodded. He rested one hand on his wife's knee. 'I know. You're right. It's just… well.' He laughed. 'I should just say it.'

Julie nodded encouragingly.

He said: 'Sebastian doesn't reflect.'

There was silence. I said, 'Reflect what?'

'In mirrors,' Julie explained. 'He has no reflection. You can't see him at all.'

Elizabeth said, 'What…'

'I'll show you.' Julie abruptly stood up and disappeared into the kitchen.

'I know,' said Dave. 'It really threw us, too. Well, still does. There's nothing about it in any of the books.'

I said, 'I'm sure it's just…' But I had no idea what it was just. 'I'm sure it's…'

Julie returned with an ornate hand mirror. She knelt beside the rocker and held the mirror near Sebastian's head. 'Can you see?'

I craned my neck, because the mirror was only showing the blanket Sebastian was wrapped in. Then I realised this was not because of the angle. The angle was fine. The problem was Sebastian.

Elizabeth's hand flew to her mouth. 'Oh dear God.'

Julie rocked back onto her heels, pressing the mirror to her chest. 'You think it's terrible.'

'Oh, *no*,' said Elizabeth. '*No*, Julie. It's just… what did the doctor say?'

'Well,' Dave said, 'the thing is, we haven't talked to the doctors. We haven't talked to anyone. We didn't even notice until he was a few weeks old. I mean, in all other respects, he's fine. He's a perfectly normal baby boy. In fact, he's very advanced. You know, Jonathan, I've bent your ear enough times about how quickly he's developing…' I waved this away. 'And he's *healthy*, I don't need to see a doctor to know that. He just has… this odd problem.'

'Is it *all* mirrors?'

Dave nodded. Julie said, 'And cameras. He doesn't come out on film.' She bit her lip, suddenly close to tears. 'That's how we first discovered it. When our photos came back…'

'We thought it was a joke,' Dave said grimly. 'I was going to drive down to the photo place and tear strips off them. Then… well, there's a mirror above the mantelpiece in the dining room. We must have walked past it a hundred times with Sebastian, but you know how it is when you have a newborn; you don't look at anything else. But this time…'

'You can't imagine how scared we were.' A fat teardrop rolled down Julie's cheek and spattered on the mirror. 'And all the family want photographs, and we don't know what to tell them! What can we tell them?'

'Oh, Julie…' Elizabeth sprang from the sofa and threw her arms around her. Still, I saw her glance down at Sebastian: at sleeping, silent Sebastian.

'I've been trying to research it on the Internet,' Dave said. 'To find other parents with the same problem. But all I can find is…' He grimaced. 'Well, you know.'

I did, but didn't want to say it. 'What?'

He forced the word out. 'Vampires.'

'What?' Elizabeth said, honestly confused.

'Vampires don't cast reflections,' Dave said, reddening. 'According to myth.'

'Well, that's ridiculous,' I said.

'Of course.' He glanced at Julie. 'But… that's where we got the idea.'

Julie sobbed. Beneath her hair and Elizabeth's arms, I couldn't see her face. 'He was always hungry! No matter how much he drank, always hungry!' Her body shuddered.

'We only give him a little. Just a few drops, mixed in with the formula. I doubt he can even taste it. But he started putting on weight. Now we're afraid to stop.'

I said, 'You're talking about blood?'

Dave nodded, his face a mask of strain. 'It's… I mean, the thing is… we didn't know what else to do.'

I stood, walked across the carpet, and knelt in front of Dave. I put both my hands on his. 'Dave. You did the right thing. Both of you. You're wonderful parents. There is nothing wrong with Sebastian. It's like Elizabeth said: each kid is different. That's the way of the world. So Sebastian doesn't reflect. So what? It doesn't make him any less of a beautiful little boy. It doesn't make you love him one single bit less. Does it?'

Dave was crying now. He shook his head. I did something I hadn't done in ten years: I hugged another man.

I found myself facing Elizabeth over Dave's shoulder. She raised her eyebrows. I shook my head.

It was almost six by the time we left. We were exhausted. And, to be honest, I wanted to be out of the house before Sebastian woke. I didn't want to see him running along the hallways. What had Dave said? *Sometimes he's crawling up the walls.*

Charlie had fallen asleep and didn't stir as Elizabeth strapped him into his car seat. She climbed in the passenger side and closed her door. As I reversed down the long driveway, I began to hum a tune.

Elizabeth sighed, exasperated. 'Sometimes, you are too much.'

'What?'

'You know very well what.'

'I comforted the man! I was sensitive! I *helped* him!'

'You could have mentioned what happens to Charlie every full moon.'

'Oh, shush,' I said. 'There's nothing wrong with that.'

Jam is for Amateurs
Rose Mulready

In the afternoon I make butterfly cakes, the phone to my ear. It's Max's sixth birthday. He's at school and the house is very quiet. The only sound is the ting of the fork against the bowl and the purr of the fridge. Jan's voice, low and squeezed, asks me what I've never done.

I think about it. 'I've never gone down on two men at once.'

'You mean a swordfight?'

'I guess. I've never done it. I don't know what they call it.'

'You don't have to have done something to know what it's called. You know what murder's called, don't you?'

'How do you know I haven't murdered someone?' I smile. The phone shifts against my cheek.

'I know. Miss Snow White Hugger-Bunny Butterfat. Don't think I can't hear you creaming that mixture by hand. You're disgusting. Use electricity like the rest of us.'

'It affects the texture. It isn't as light.'

'Who would know, if it weren't for people like you?'

'Grandmothers would know.'

'Grandmothers. Who listens to them? Tell me what else you haven't done.'

'Um. Amputees.'

'Duh. And?'

'I don't know. Dwarves.'

'Now you're just groping at clichés. Tell me really. Have you and Craig ever filmed yourselves?'

I watch slick bubbles form in the mixture. That means there is sufficient air. I reach for the tin and rub butter in the hollows.

'You're not saying anything. How many bottles do you have for this party?'

'How many bottles will six-year-olds drink?'

'Come on. You've been to kids' parties before. You know what the mothers get up to in the kitchen.'

I sigh. 'I don't want them all staying forever. I'm tired.'

I can hear Jan yelling at Tamsin, her four-year-old, to stop eating mascara. She comes back on the line sounding ruffled. 'I just weaned her off lipstick.'

I am absently licking the bowl. 'Do you know what I wish?'

'No, honey lamb. What do you wish.'

'I wish Craig would do something bad to me. Really bad. So I could leave.'

Jan pauses delicately. 'I think I'll just come over now. I have a bottle of Stoli in the glove box. Are you putting jam in those butterfly cakes?'

'No. Jam is for amateurs.'

'See you then.' She sounds relieved.

I am picking up Max's Lego piece by piece. Every time I bend over my back aches so I lay down on the floor and start throwing the Lego into the box. The floor looks dirtier from down here. I turn my head and look at the ceiling. Plaster roses. I drift off to sleep.

When I wake up Jan is lying next to me, propped on her elbow. She shakes the glass in her hand so the ice jingles. 'Wakey-wakey, Princess.'

I wipe off my mouth with the palm of my hand. The spit feels like something left by a snail.

'What time is it?'

'Three or something.'

'Where are Tamsin and Tyler?'

'In the kitchen I guess. You want an Alabama Slammer? I found Scotch in your pantry.'

I struggle upright. 'That's Craig's.'

'So what's he gonna do? Throw you out?'

We look at each other. I reach over and take a gulp of her drink. Jan looks around at the room. Lion balloons are tethered onto the chairs, moving gently in invisible breezes. There are tulle bunches filled with freckles and those headachey banana lollies. A bright, conical hat sits on each plate. I lie back and press the back of my wrist to my eyes.

'All set then,' says Jan.

Bullock Max, rocket Max, careening meteor smashing my atmosphere Max, smelling blamelessly of crayon. I named him after the hero of

Where the Wild Things Are. Craig wanted to name him after Jackson Pollock but he relented in the thirty-eighth hour of the labour. When they told us they'd have to do a caesar.

Max hits my midriff, playing grenades. He makes the sound of an explosion in his throat. I touch his sleek hair. 'Good day at school?'

He shrugs. 'I got to be Harry. Tom had to be Hagrid. Everyone sang.'

Jan comes into the room, eating fairy bread. 'Happy Birthday, Maxim.' He looks at her warily. I give Tom's mother a drink. 'Thanks for picking up Max.'

'No bother, no bother at all. You had so much to do!'

Jan widens her eyes at me. She thinks Cynthia is a dolt.

Everything starts happening at once. Mothers, small boys, music that starts and stops, paper that tears. I carry platters of food. The room unreels before me in stop motion, the trays of vol-au-vents emptying, children painting themselves in blurs across the furniture, a vase shattering slow and beautiful. All the women shriek, plucking their kids out of the way of the glass. Cynthia shows me a dustpan full of shards. 'Now don't worry. Don't worry about a thing. I got every last bit. Where shall I put this?'

'You're an angel,' I say, pointing to the kitchen.

Jan, propped on the piano keys, folds her arms and snickers. 'Yes, an angel, an angel,' she parrots.

I go over and sit beside her. The piano squawks softly. 'You're not being very nice.'

'Well, I don't be nice.'

'You do. I've seen you.'

'When?' She feigns outrage.

'After Max was born. You held my hand. You said he was beautiful.'

'Even though he looked like a bald weasel.'

'It was nice of you.'

I remember the day, the moment. Craig had gone to call his mother in Broome. I couldn't feel anything below the waist. Jan put her cool hand in mine and gave me a smile like a wrapped present. 'You'll get to like him, you know,' she said. 'He's beautiful.'

Tamsin is the only girl here. She moves uneasily between her brother and Jan, who finally lifts her on to her hip and gives her a freckle. She sucks it, whimpering.

'She's tired,' Jan says. The boys are howling, blindfolded, thumping the piñata. No one can get a clear blow in. The piñata is a yellow fish with a mouth that looks surprised. I watch it swing, hit the roof, lurch on its string.

'Why do children get so tired?' I ask. 'They never do anything.'

'They run around experiencing emotion all day,' says Jan. 'It's tiring as hell. They don't pace themselves.'

I press a black note on the piano. 'Do you pace yourself?'

'I break up the day.' Jan examines Tamsin and puts her on the ground. 'You're sticky,' she says. Tamsin looks bewildered, wanders off. Jan pinches my wrist. 'Let's go and sit in my car.'

'I can't.' I gesture at the party.

'Come on. Ten minutes.'

The piñata's belly splits, disgorging bright lollies. Max bellows. He holds up a fist crammed with cellophane. Jan's nails dig into my wrist. 'Ten minutes,' she says.

I haven't been outside all day. Tepid sun leaks through my eyelids. Jan's Audi is warm. It smells of mandarins and spit. She rolls a joint on the roadmap. I close my eyes again. 'This is bad.'

Jan scrabbles in the glove box for a lighter. 'So. What *do* you and Craig do? Is it all missionary and two veg? Twice on a Sunday?'

'Of course not.'

'Well?'

'We've been through this.'

'I forget.' Jan waves the joint in my face. 'We do it to forget. Remember?'

I take it from her. The tobacco tastes sour. I watch the prism hanging from the rear-view mirror, the way it quivers, shaking the sun into pieces. I think of Craig's tongue. It's a long tongue and he's very proud of it. Once he asked me to measure it. I remember my fingers feeding in the tape measure, the feel of his soft palate.

'Wake up.'

'I am awake.'

'Barely. You and I need a holiday. Let's go to the sea.'

'With the children.'

'No.' Jan is eating the last butterfly cake. She holds up a wing. 'This is good. Light.'

I dip my finger in the well of cream. Too much vanilla. I think about the sea, the way it rolls. The sound of it rolling. I start the car.

'What are you doing?'

'We can buy toothbrushes. Which coast?'

Jan swallows the wing. She looks proud of me at last. 'The closest.'

I pull out from the curb. The moment reminds me of dressmaking. You grab the satin where you've cut it and pull, and there's a sound like a snake's hiss and two clean pieces.

Jan makes me stop for chicken. She leans over me and breathes into the speaker until the cars behind are hooting and the attendant is restless and afraid. Then she orders a family barrel.

'That's too much,' I say.

'Do you know how far it is to the coast?'

'Yes.'

'Well then.' She settles back into her sheepskin collar, gnawing. Jan is thin. She burns food in minutes.

We are actually driving into the sunset, a Hollywood fondue of colour that turns our skin tenderly orange. Jan finds this hilarious. She wants to take a polaroid of us and throw it into the wind. 'You can be Geena,' she says magnanimously.

'That means I have to fuck Brad. I can't do it. He sickens me.'

'Me too. He's too perfect and girly. Those cushiony lips.'

We shudder.

'Who would you fuck?'

'You mean actors?'

'I mean in general. What's your perfect type?'

I try to think. It's hard because I don't fantasise. Jan called me still-born when I told her that. She was furious. She actually hit me with a rolled-up magazine.

'I like men who are passing by.'

Jan throws a slick bone out the window. 'What, like backpackers?'

I shake my head. I was thinking of Craig: his gym muscles, his laundered smell, his calm face planted in my landscape, there whenever I open my eyes.

Jan is driving. The lights blink green as she approaches. I am half-sleeping against the window, dreaming in patches. I see Max with his hand full of cellophane. I sit up.

'This is bad.'

'Of course.'

'What if they hurt themselves. Knives. That glass.'

'Cynthia is there. Craig will come home.'

'But Max.' I blot tears on my cuff. 'It's his birthday.'

Jan does her funny, sideways smile. 'You can get him something. A fur seal. A pail.'

'Shut up. This is real.'

Jan pulls the car over and parks in the emergency lane. She leans into my face. '*This* is not real. This is driving into the sunset. *That* is real.' She points behind us. 'Craig. Tennis whites. The house. Little Athletics. Will Brooke marry Thorne. A fuck on your birthday.'

We are breathing together. 'OK,' I say. 'This was my idea.'

'Exactly,' says Jan, looking out into the traffic.

We pull into the motel car park. Little stones crackle under the wheels. Jan comes back from reception carrying keys and scratchy towels. She swings the door open like a magician. I recognise the scent of Pine Fresh. There's a picture of the sea on the wall.

'Check for Bibles,' says Jan. She rifles the drawers, a cigarette clamped in her teeth.

She finds it in the bedside cabinet. We sit on the rigid sheets, taking turns on the Stoli. Jan clears her throat and opens the Bible at random. 'He who is often reproved, yet stiffens his neck, will suddenly be broken beyond healing.' She shrugs.

'Jan.'

'Ahuh.'

'It's not Craig's fault.'

'I know. Have a slug of this.'

'It's my fault.'

'I know. Deeper, sunbeam. Finish it.'

'I can't feel anything.'

'Mission accomplished,' says Jan. She wipes her lipstick off.

'I'm not joking. I smell Max's little neck. I see him run out of the house in the morning. I love him. It rises up in me but it doesn't reach me. Like with Craig. I wake up and he's there and I'm not. I'm outside it all.'

'Honeybubble.' Jan takes my hand and looks at it. 'There's nothing to feel.'

'Other people feel.'

'Or so they say.'

'Children feel.'

'Until they work it out.'

I go to get up, get caught in the blanket and fall on the floor. Jan would usually laugh but she doesn't. I guess she's being nice.

The sea is completely flat, soundless. I sit on a rock. I'm thinking about the first time I met Jan, at some constipated party in the suburbs. She was in the kitchen eating the hors d'oeuvres straight out of the oven. I spent a long time watching her, studying the angle of her earrings, the way she talked through a mouthful of cheese, the disdainful way she examined ornaments. She saw me watching and came over and began to teach me how to be careless.

She saved me, I'd always told her that.

Tentatively, I say Max's name. I wait.

The Miracle of the Beer and Tim Tams
Jeff Hoogenboom

Jesus stood on my doorstep wearing a white robe, sandals and a Nike puffer jacket.

'I got your invitation,' he said. His English was perfect, with a slight accent that was hard to place. I'd been worried, having not been able to find an ancient Aramaic phrasebook.

He stuck out his hand. In it was one of the photocopies I had put up at the local churches.

Dear Jesus, it read. *You are invited to my house for pizza and videos. No heavy theological discussion.*

Date: This Friday night.

Time: 7:00p.m.

Short and to the point. I'd agonised over what else to add, specifically the phrase, 'I bloody dare ya', but in the end I left it off, along with my address. This was half as a test, half because I wasn't really sure I wanted him to come.

I let Jesus into my house. He wiped his feet carefully; it wasn't raining outside but his feet left wet prints on the spiky grass mat. His hair smelled like incense.

'You could be some kind of kook,' I said.

'So could you,' he replied. I shrugged and took his jacket. His fingers brushed mine and I felt something spread through me, filling up dark, empty parts of me that I had never realised were empty. I gasped, and Jesus raised an eyebrow at me but said nothing.

I turned away from him and hung his jacket on a spare hook in the hall, using the time to take a few deep breaths. There was a long, brown hair stuck to the nylon collar of his jacket. I wondered if it was worth anything.

I turned back to Jesus who stood in my hall in just his robe, which was spotless except for a large rust-coloured stain that spread down one side.

'You should try Napisan,' I suggested, nodding at the stain.

'I'd need a miracle to get this out,' Jesus replied.

I led him to the lounge room and told him to sit down. I let Jesus have the good chair – the one with the footrest, the one that faced the telly straight on. I looked at him, as he looked around the room and then at me. He smiled at me in a way I could only describe as beatific. Either that or it was the smile of someone trying to humour another person who has possibly lost his mind.

'Hungry?' I asked. Jesus nodded. I picked up the phone and dialled the pizza place. 'Do you like ham and pineapple?' I asked as the phone connected.

Jesus gave me a funny look. 'I'm the King of the *Jews*,' he replied.

'Right.' I looked at the menu; everything had ham except for the Vegetarian. Jesus had Vegetarian, I had Meatlover's.

Jesus's table manners were very impressive; he'd obviously been brought up well. A credit to his long-suffering mother. He picked the olives off his pizza, making a small pile on the side of his plate. Once he had finished his pizza, he popped them into his mouth one by one. I watched his hands out of the corner of my eye. Each palm had a small round scab, like a slice of Cabanossi sausage was resting there. I picked the Cabanossi off my pizza, making a small pile on the edge of my plate.

I offered Jesus a drink. 'All I have is water,' I said. 'If you want anything else you will have to change it yourself.'

Jesus laughed. 'There's a new one,' he said. I went to the kitchen and got a couple of VB's.

'Do you like VB?' I asked. Jesus said he did, but I think when I wasn't looking he changed it. Into what, I don't know – something imported and expensive. I wouldn't have minded having mine changed, but I didn't like to ask.

We watched the Simpsons on TV. Jesus said he knew people just like the Flanders'.

'Do you like those kinds of people?' I asked. He just shrugged. I wanted to ask more but I'd promised there'd be no theological discussion. I did ask Jesus if he would prefer discussing politics or philosophy but he said he was happy just to watch movies.

I had spent a long, agonising afternoon in the video shop. Who knows what the Son of God likes to watch? I decided against *The Passion of the Christ,* certain it would only have brought back bad memories. I had a decent pile of weeklies to rummage through. Jesus chose *Reservoir Dogs*.

'I'm a big fan of Steve Buscemi,' he told me.

'You look a bit like him,' I said.

'He looks a bit like me actually,' Jesus said, finishing his first beer. I got more beers and turned the movie on. Jesus watched the movie and I mostly just watched Jesus. I thought his beard could use a trim, and he had spilled pizza topping on his robe – so much for his table manners. Otherwise he seemed in pretty good shape for a two-thousand-year-old dead guy. On the screen, Tim Roth was bleeding to death.

'Are you really here,' I said to Jesus, 'or are you a vision?'

He looked down at his stained robes. 'Do I look like a vision?' he asked.

I told him he didn't.

After the movie, Jesus burped and stretched. He looked around the room. 'Can I ask you a question?' he said.

'Anything, my son,' I replied.

Jesus didn't laugh. I worried that I was being sacrilegious.

'Why did you invite me here? There's none of the usual religious paraphernalia that I've come to expect.' He motioned to the walls, which were free of pictures of him, but covered in pictures of my friends, some of whom had long hair and beards and, to be honest, thought they were God's gift. 'You haven't even asked me the meaning of life.'

'What's the meaning of life then?' I said.

'God only knows.' Jesus was sitting in my easy chair cracking jokes.

'Someone at a party was asking who we would invite for dinner if we could invite anyone at all,' I said. 'A lot of people picked you.'

'Yes, my appointment book is very full.'

'Others picked Michael Jordan or Leonardo da Vinci.'

'Dan Brown has a lot to answer for. Who did you pick?'

I paused, remembering the feeling when our hands had met. 'I chose myself,' I said finally. 'Myself when I was about five years old.'

Jesus leaned back, put his feet on the coffee table and stroked his beard. Steve Buscemi playing Sigmund Freud.

'Go on,' he said.

I showed him a photo. A young boy smiled back at him. The boy was surrounded by the ocean; it spread across the horizon and covered his body. His head had turned back toward the camera as if to say, *look what I have discovered.* His delight had always intrigued me. It intrigued me because I was certain I would have remembered this moment of such pure joy. For me, however, the moment existed only in this black and white photograph.

'Sometimes I look at this photo and just wish I could go back and tell myself what to expect, what to look out for,' I told Jesus. 'I want him to be prepared for those things that come out of nowhere and strip you down to your bones.' I looked away, realising I was complaining about my life to the Son of God. 'Most of all, I want to ask him whether he – we – had ever really been that happy,' I finished quietly.

Jesus had looked at me with those same eyes that my friends had looked at me with. There was pity in his eyes. Even after being nailed to a cross to atone for the sins of mankind, Jesus still pitied me.

'I knew that was impossible so I decided to invite you. Just to see what would happen,' I said. 'Why did you come?'

'Because you invited me! I get asked for a lot of things, but I don't get invited for many relaxing dinners.'

'What if I was some kind of weirdo?' I said.

'My dad's tougher than your dad,' Jesus replied.

We watched another movie – *Indiana Jones and the Last Crusade*. Jesus scoffed a little at some of the claims relating to the Holy Grail but kept any comments to himself. I made coffee and offered Jesus Tim Tams. He had never eaten Tim Tams before and vowed to pick some up before he headed home.

'Make sure you go to the all-night supermarket,' I said. 'The convenience stores are a rip-off.' He stood up and got ready to leave. He asked me if I would really want to speak to a younger version of myself. I wondered whether he was offering to organise it.

'Probably not,' I said after a moment. 'Even though I don't remember that picture being taken, that kid is still me. I don't want the easy answers now, so I'm pretty sure I didn't want them then. Doesn't seem fair, you know?'

Jesus nodded and looked around the room. I followed his gaze, taking in the clutter and accumulated stuff of everyday life.

I nodded toward his Cabanossi palms. 'Was it worth it?' I said. 'All the suffering, all the sacrifice?'

He looked down at his palms then leaned over and picked up the photo of my happy youth. 'It was worth it for this,' he said and handed me the photograph.

I looked down at the face beaming back at me. 'Thanks,' I said to Jesus. It was the first time I had ever said that to him. Jesus picked up the last Tim Tam and handed it to me. An image of his face had appeared in the chocolate.

'Here,' Jesus said to me. 'Sell this on eBay.'

'Great,' I replied. 'For sale: One Tim Tam emblazoned with an image of Steve Buscemi.' Jesus laughed. I followed him down the hall where he put on his puffer jacket.

'Do you look the same to everyone who sees you?' I asked.

'I don't know,' he said. 'Do you?'

'I probably don't look how I want to look,' I admitted.

Jesus shook my hand. I could feel his scab, rough against my palm, but that was all I felt this time.

'Thanks for stopping by,' I said.

'Thanks for inviting me,' Jesus replied. He walked down the path and got onto a moped. I had expected him to disappear in a blaze of light. Instead he just putted off down the street, robe flapping in the wind, and turned left into High Street.

As I Was Saying
David Gibb

The bay was hot and so was I. But the heat I was feeling wasn't from the searing slant of the early sun. It was from my messy assortment of relatives. They'd gathered for their traditional alcohol-fuelled summer break at the bay and, according to them, I was the biggest no-hoper the family gene pool had ever produced.

They claimed I was the first Miller kid ever to fail the Intermediate Exams and the blistering sneers started the moment they read the results in *The Advertiser*. Apparently it was going to be the end of the world as I knew it and they delivered their views with all the subtlety of a bag of bricks through a deli window.

'Next stop for you is sweeping the streets,' claimed Toby, my smug and loathsome cousin. He was a medical student who believed that a tertiary education meant you automatically inherited the earth.

You might have brains but you're a complete tool, mate.

'You'll never afford a wife and kids,' contributed my grandfather, a reptilian criminal lawyer with bloodshot eyes, flaky skin and the vile habit of hawking up gluey gobs of smoker's phlegm.

Bewdy, gramps. Just what I'm thinking about right now, getting myself a wife and kids.

'Suppose I could give you a job driving one of my trucks,' muttered Uncle Arnold. He had a hauling company and a peculiar muscular tic that prompted his head to snap violently to the right when you least expected it.

Yeah, and that'd be the first thing you ever did *give me Arnie, you tight wad.*

Even my grief-stricken father, an architect who designed some of the ugliest houses on the planet, lined up to sink the boot in. He'd been loudly lamenting my academic failings ever since my mother had died the year before. I missed her desperately because I knew she wouldn't have let him get away with it.

'What sort of job do you think you'll get if you can't even pass Intermediate?' he whined. 'Miller men only have professions, lad.'

Gee dad, think I'll just drown myself and save you the embarrassment.

It was all just another variation on the family's constant carping question: How come I was so hopeless at school when I came from such an impressive line of engineers, doctors, lawyers, school teachers, dentists and other assorted clever dicks?

The barrage of belittlement reverberated around the family's haphazard arrangement of swanky caravans, imported luxury cars, camp chairs and a steadily growing stack of Southwark Bitter empties. The trouble was, I was starting to think they were right; that I *was* useless, that I *would* end up in some deadbeat job. 1968 was only a few days old and already it was a lousy year thanks to the rising tide of doubt flooding my brain.

To make matters worse, I had this family flotsam all to myself. My brother had escaped the torment of another aimless holiday at the bay by landing his first job just in the nick of time. The lucky bastard was back home basking in the glorious title of Understudy To The Manager of a pharmaceutical company. If he'd been here he would've given the family the finger and reminded me that they were nothing more than Olympic-standard bullshit artists.

To escape the aggravation I drifted down to the beach and did what I always did when I needed to clear my head. I started jogging. That's when, in a blur of tanned legs and a shower of swishing sand, a girl in a blue one-piece swimsuit sprinted past. With the day already well on its way to a typical January scorcher, pushing myself and getting all hot and bothered wasn't on my agenda, but instinct kicked in. I gave chase, not so much because I liked the shape of her, although I admit it was pretty impressive, but more because I was a crash-hot middle distance runner at school and being passed by anyone always gave me the screaming irrits.

Reckon you can run, do yer? Well getta loada this, cute bum.

I gained on her pretty smartly, but not nearly as easily as I should have. It took me a good 200 yards to get on her heels and that really got my goat. By then my calves were tightening and my lungs heaving, but the view was certainly worth the effort. Her legs were shorter than mine, but more uniformly powerful and definitely better proportioned, athletically speaking of course. Her waist seemed impossibly narrow and, courtesy of the plunging back of her swimsuit, I could follow the rhythmic ripple of her spine right up to where it disappeared beneath a short blonde ponytail. I was close enough to smell her suntan lotion, feel the damp sand from her feet flicking onto my shins and hear her steady, controlled breathing. The girl was cruising and, whoever she was, I didn't like her.

Who the hell do you think you are, Raelene bloody Boyle?

Suddenly I regretted all the nights I'd skipped training in favour of hanging around with my mates at the Arndale Shopping Centre, perving on the dolled-up shop assistants, and chain-smoking Rothmans filter tips. Keeping up with her was making my throat fizz. But it got worse.

Suddenly she took a quick glance to her left and, in the space of a couple of lung gasps, the gap had widened. I didn't even see it coming. The funny thing was, she didn't seem to be going any harder but was easily pulling away. So I responded with a quick burst of my own and there I was again, right on her heels. My thighs started to blaze.

How do you like them apples, darling?

But she immediately did it again. Quick glance, effortless spurt, widening gap. I didn't want to keep doing this, but I had no choice. I gave her the same back, and it hurt like hell. She responded in kind, and so we went on chewing up the beach until we'd run close on half a mile. We were halfway to the jetty before I twigged. She was pacing my shadow. The sun, still low over the water, sent our gangly shadows stretching up the beach. All it took was a casual glance and she had me in her sights. She was racing with contempt, toying with my pain, without even the slightest hint of stress in her stride. Every time I got on her heels her effortless breathing ridiculed me. I felt like I was sucking on a blowtorch.

Just what I need today, to be shat on by a sheila!

Then, inexplicably, she slowed slightly. I eased up beside her and there we were, running side-by-side. That's when she decided to have a casual chat. I could hardly breathe, let alone talk, but there was no stopping her.

'Your stride's too short,' she said.

'Oh… yeah?' I managed. I was staring straight ahead, focusing on the jetty. It was going to be my finish line whether she liked it or not.

'You're trying to go faster by taking more steps.'

'So…?

'Not very efficient.'

Now she's my friggin' coach!

'This is… how… I run.'

'Step longer.'

'Get… lost!'

'Try it. You'll beat me easy.'

The jetty was a hundred yards away, maybe more. My legs were pleading for mercy, my lungs begging for oxygen, but stuff it, she was enjoying this a bit too much. So I gave it everything I had and, wouldn't you know it, I left her chewing my sand by doing exactly what she'd suggested. I strode longer, went faster and reached the jetty a clear winner. In its wet shadow, hands on trembling knees, I gulped hot air. It tasted like seaweed. Eventually, with my lungs heaving grateful thanks, I looked up to find my school's pin-up girl.

'Bloody hell, I know you,' I said. 'Well, know who you are, anyhow.'

'Snap,' she said.

'You're Sarah Sheerwater, right?' Every boy in my school knew who Sarah Sheerwater was, only they didn't call her that, they called her Sarah Sheer Pleasure. Not from any personal experience, mind.

'And you're Roddy Miller.'

'Yep.'

'Told you so.'

'What?'

'That you'd beat me.'

'Betcha didn't even try,' I said, then immediately cringed. Faking a bit of modesty to impress her was pathetic, but she either saw right through it and decided to ignore it, or just didn't notice.

'You won fair and square,' she confirmed, and the way she held my gaze with her startling taupe eyes made me believe her. 'Longer strides. Works every time.'

'Longer strides. My New Year's resolution,' I said, trying to calm my breathing. I didn't want her to know how much the run had hurt.

To beat Sarah Sheerwater at running, in fact to beat her at anything, was as good as winning the lottery. She was one of those annoying students who could do everything better than everyone. She seemed to be in charge of the entire world: captain of girls' athletics; leader of the inter-school debating team; president of the science society; first singles seed in the mixed tennis squad; photography club founder and, just to fill in her spare time, girls' head prefect. She'd been dux of her year ever since starting high school and there were always more photos of her in the school magazine than anyone else. The running joke around the classrooms was that if you told Sarah Sheerwater you'd climbed Mount Everest on the weekend, she'd casually mention how she'd done it last month, but without oxygen. And to top it all off, she was dangerously good looking. And there I was, alone with her on a beach, the generous contours of her breasts plainly visible through her swimsuit.

I must've died and gone to heaven.

'You staying in the caravan park?' she asked.

'Yep. The Millers make camp in the same spot every year and everyone else gives us a wide berth if they know what's good for 'em.'

'Why's that?'

'My family comes here to drink, brag about how much money they earn, what school they went to and how many letters they have after their names. I can't stand the sight of them.'

'That's not a nice thing to say about your family.'

'I haven't *got* a nice thing to say about my family.'

'You'll have to introduce me.'

'Like hell I will!'

'If you don't, I'll go and introduce myself.'

'Take a crash helmet.'

She giggled at the suggestion as we started back along the beach, walking slowly against the frantic tide of our own footprints.

'You're a terrific runner, Roddy,' Sarah said.

'I'm OK, I guess.'

'I watched you last sports day. First in the 200 final. First in the 400. Second in the mile. That's not just OK, Roddy, that's amazing.'

Sarah Sheerwater – the *Sarah Sheerwater* – *watched me run!*

'Yeah, well…'

'Junior School Champion.'

''Spose I am.'

'Congratulations.'

I looked sideways at her, battling not to stare at her figure as we walked, wondering if this was how she mocked people who weren't as good as her. But she turned to me and smiled in a way that lit a slow-burning fuse in my stomach, and I knew she meant it.

'Thanks,' I muttered, embarrassed and strangely elated at the same time.

'How old are you?' she asked.

'Fifteen.'

'By the time you're seventeen, you'll be Senior School Champ.'

'Doubt it.'

'Doubt it and you won't, believe it and you will.'

For a strangely suspended moment my brain completely stalled. Her praise and certainty were right out of the blue, something I wasn't used to, and I couldn't conjure up a single thing to say.

Doubt it and you won't, believe it and you will. Strewth, maybe she's some kinda religious nutter.

I walked with my head down, my mind a hopeless void. Her toenails were polished a faint pink and her legs belonged in *Australasian Post*. My chest was thumping again, but this time it wasn't from the run.

'Won't still be at school when I'm seventeen,' I eventually blurted. I was shocked at how pathetic my own self-pity sounded.

'Why not?'

'I'm hopeless at exams.'

'Who says?'

'Everyone, including today's paper.'

'Oh, not good news?'

'Nup. I'll have to repeat the year.' I didn't fancy telling her exactly how badly I'd done, that I'd sat seven subjects and only passed two. 'What about you?'

'I went alright, I suppose,' Sarah said.

'Come off it,' I scoffed.

'I'm so nervous before the results come out, I can't eat for days.'

'But you always get straight A's.' She was a year ahead of me, so I felt pretty safe in assuming she'd romped through her Leaving Exams, but she just shrugged and didn't volunteer her results.

'Did you swot hard?'

'Nup,' I said. 'No point.'

My miserable admission plunged us into another awkward silence, which we filled with the sound of our bare feet slopping on slick sand as the morning tide ran out, leaving behind a pearly sheen of exposed cuttlefish. My throat was tight from the anxiety of wanting to tell her things about myself and not having a clue how to go about it. And right there and then, as salty heat wafted on a lethargic breeze, I decided that I wanted Sarah Sheerwater to be my girlfriend more than anything else in the world. I was sick of feeling useless, of not amounting to anything, of not having a future, of getting the idiot treatment from my smart-arse family. If Sarah Sheerwater was my girlfriend, I'd show the whole bloody lot of them.

You're a peabrain, Miller. As if that's going to happen.

When we drew level with the caravan park, Sarah nodded towards an old white plywood van hunched under a stand of she-oaks. It had a red, hand-painted cheat line and a faded striped annexe. An FJ Holden nuzzled up to it.

'My place,' she said.

'Thanks for the race.' I fought off a looming panic that this was as close to her as I was ever going to get.

'Look Roddy, if you promise to stop feeling sorry for yourself I'll make you breakfast.' A hot flame of embarrassment licked up my neck and I was startled to feel tears prickling my eyes.

'I... dunno,' I faltered, looking away, afraid of seeming too puppy-dog eagre.

'I don't bite, you know. Peaches and cold milk OK?'

'Sounds alright.'

'Come on then, I'm famished.'

I couldn't drag my gaze from the subtle sway of her hips as I followed her up to the lawns of the caravan park.

No one'll bloody believe this.

The Sheerwater's campsite was as orderly as the Miller's was chaotic. An assortment of leather sandals, Dunlop Volleys and rubber thongs were neatly lined up on a squeaky-clean tarp at the entrance to the annexe. The ground around the caravan had been carefully cleared of she-oak needles, the tidy tracks of a leaf rake still visible in the dirt. The annexe guy ropes were perfectly spaced and uniformly tensioned. A makeshift clothes line strung beneath the trees displayed a precise parade of brightly coloured shorts, shirts and underwear. A lacy pink bra hung lazily among them. I wanted desperately to believe it was Sarah's.

'This is Roddy Miller, a friend of mine from school,' Sarah told her parents when they emerged from the annexe. 'He's a brilliant runner.'

A friend of hers? Did I hear that right?

'Pleased to meet you, Roddy,' her father said with a no-nonsense, finger-crushing handshake. 'What's your best event?'

'I like everything up to the mile, but my favourite's the 400, Mr Sheerwater.'

'What's this Mr Sheerwater business?' he said. 'That's my father's name, Roddy. Just call me Vern.'

'Righto, Vern,' I said, but it seemed disrespectful somehow.

'And I'm Jules,' said her mother. I smiled as a smart-alec comment leapt to mind, but a razor look from Sarah pulled me up short.

'Roddy, they've heard all the jokes about Jules Verne, so don't even think about it!' she said.

'It didn't occur to me.'

'Liar, liar…' she began.

'… pants on fire,' her mother finished, and as the four of us laughed easily together I felt an unexpected elation at being part of their intimate family banter.

We ate Sarah's promised peaches and milk sitting at an ancient camp table in the cool canvas breezeway of the annexe. She sat opposite me, next to her father. Every now and then, as light-hearted conversation tumbled easily around the table, our legs brushed together. I knew it was accidental but wished otherwise. Then she disappeared inside the van to make toast and instant coffee. I could hear her bare feet padding about in between the homey clatter of plates and cutlery. I badly wanted to be in there helping her, to be right beside her like I'd been on the beach.

'What exams did you sit, Roddy?' Jules asked.

Why does everyone want to talk to me about the bloody exams?

'Intermediate.'

'How did you go?'

'I failed. Pretty badly, actually,' I told her.

'There's no shame in that,' Vern put in quickly.

'Not at all,' Jules confirmed. I was expecting them to start telling me about Sarah's results, but they didn't.

'Crikey, I didn't even *get* to Intermediate,' Vern said with a dismissive shrug.

'Neither did I,' his wife chipped in.

'Don't get your knickers in a twist about exam results, Roddy. Bloody overrated they are, take it from me. Matter of fact, I'll bet my last dollar that when you eventually leave school and start applying for jobs you won't meet one boss who'll ask to see your school reports. And you know why?'

'No.'

'Because they'll all be worried that you got further in school than they did. It's a dead cert, Roddy. And besides, there are more jobs out there than you can poke a stick at.'

How come the family know-alls never mentioned that?

'You won't have any worries,' Jules said.

'What profession are you in Mr Sheer-er Vern?' I ventured.

'Horticulture.'

'That's plants and things, isn't it?'

'Too right.'

Jules chortled softly, and when Vern began to laugh in my direction I figured it must've been a dumb thing to say, that horticulture was plants and things.

'Vern's pulling your leg, Roddy,' Jules explained eventually. 'He mows lawns.'

I was relieved beyond measure that I hadn't made an idiot of myself. 'What's that like, being a lawnmower man?'

'Best job in the world. An absolute corker.'

'Dinkum?'

'Too right. Doesn't matter what you work at, as long as you give it everything you've got and it makes you happy.' That was news to me.

We were interrupted by the caravan door swinging open as Sarah reappeared carrying a tray precariously stacked with toast, honey and Vegemite jars and over-filled mugs of coffee. She offloaded it all onto the table, set the tray aside and sat down next to Vern, ruffling his hair playfully.

'I can't believe you're still using the old horticulture line, Dad,' Sarah said.

'When you're on a good thing, princess.'

She gently elbowed him, then gave me a mischievous wink. I tried to swallow, but couldn't.

Sitting opposite Sarah and her father, watching their good-natured teasing, I could see that her athletic litheness came from him. She had his sinewy strength in her arms and legs, the same streamlined face and the brown, well-polished skin that spoke of a healthy way of living. But her blonde hair, feminine shapeliness and full-of-life eyes were obviously bestowed by Jules who, I pretty quickly worked out, was a head turning middle-aged beauty. I suddenly understood the blokey saying I'd heard bandied about; if you want to know what a girl will look like in twenty-five years, have a good gander at her mother.

We crunched on toast and sipped coffee between idle chat about the changing colours out in the bay, the likelihood of a sea breeze springing up and whether or not there'd be a dodge tide that night. I decided that this was the best breakfast I'd ever had. It had nothing to do with the food and everything to do with the realisation that Vern and Jules and Sarah were people at peace with their lives and themselves. It created in me a sense of comfort, a quiet pleasure that had somehow eluded me until then and I came to the sudden conclusion that I would rather belong to Sarah's family than my own. That unexpected awareness both thrilled and shocked me all at once. Then, as Sarah and her mother began clearing away the dishes, I felt such a searing guilt about disliking my own family so much that I got up in a stumbling hurry.

'I'd better get going.'

'Righto then, Roddy. Good to meet you,' Vern said.

'Thanks for having me.'

'Drop in any time,' Jules offered. 'We'd be pleased to see you again.'

'Says who?' Sarah asked.

'Says all of us,' Vern said.

Smiling at her own cheekiness, Sarah walked with me to where the lawn ended and the beach started.

'As I was saying, step longer,' she said.

'OK. I like your Mum and Dad.'

'So do I.'

'Lucky you, I reckon.'

I was unfairly jealous of her good fortune and didn't want to leave their little sanctuary beneath the she-oaks, but I knew I couldn't hang around like a pathetic stray. I took a deep breath and put my neck right on the line.

'Can I see you again?'

'Yes.' She answered so quickly I almost missed it.

'Oh, gee, that's good.' I practically choked with relief.

'What say we go swimming after lunch? I'll race you out to the pontoon.'

Please, not another race!

'You're on,' I said.

It was stifling in the phone box, which stood like a sentry post at the entrance to the caravan park. I propped the door open with a foot, hoping for a skerrick of fresh air while the ring tone *brrrd* in my ear.

'Speak up, it's your money,' my brother said as the coins clattered. It was his standard phone answering repartee.

'It's me.'

'How's it hangin' Squirt?'

'Pretty good.' The sound down the line was hollow and hissy. I thought I heard a girlie giggle mixed up with it. 'You've got a bird there, haven't you?'

'No way. You know me, pure as the driven snow.'

'Don't bullshit me. Who is it?'

'No one you'd know.'

'Anyhow, guess who's staying here in the caravan park?'

'No idea.'

'Sarah Sheerwater.'

'Sheer Pleasure is there?'

'Yep.'

'Bloody hell.'

'And I'm going out with her.'

'Ah, take yer hand off it, Squirt!' I didn't blame him for not believing me. I hardly believed it myself.

'Swear to God. We've been for a run, she's just made breakfast for me and later we're going swimming. Just thought I'd let you know.'

'Betcha can't even get to first base with her.'

'I might.'

'She's worth a shot, Squirt, but I don't like your chances. Better men than you have tried and failed.'

'You should see her in a swimsuit.'

'Bloody hell, I'm crackin' a fat just thinkin' about it.' I heard the girlie giggle again.

'Sounds like you're getting all the help you need right there.'

'Piss off. Tell the family I miss 'em.'

'Yeah, the same way you miss food poisoning.'

'Got it in one, Squirt.'

I laughed and hung up.

The pontoon was a lopsided, jerry-built affair anchored out among the fishing boats. Sarah swam to it backstroke, barely disturbing the water, while I chugged along, spitting and gagging, in my interpretation of freestyle. She beat me by a good minute, but I didn't care.

We sat out there for ages, talking quietly, our legs dangling in the water while the sun dried our hair in no time flat and baked scaly white salt circles on our too-hot skin. As the pontoon rolled lazily on the swell, our shoulders and arms occasionally touched. I pretended not to notice, but I noticed so much it was painful. Every now and then we slipped into the water feet first to cool off and each time we climbed back, cooled and dripping, I wished I could heat up and cool down and heat up again with Sarah Sheerwater forever.

'I looked up your results in the paper,' I told her. 'Five subjects, five credits.'

'It's no big deal,' she said and quickly changed the subject.

After a time we noticed someone on the beach waving their arms, trying to attract our attention.

'It's Dad,' Sarah said.

'What's he want?' I slightly resented the intrusion.

'I'll go see.'

She swan-dived off the pontoon with barely a splash and morphed into a silky, blue-clad shape against a waving bed of seaweed ribbons. When she surfaced she transitioned effortlessly into a stylish breaststroke and reached the beach in no time at all. She ran to her father and flung herself at him in a deliberately soggy hug, her shrieks of boisterous laughter coming to me clearly across the water. The joy of it lodged in my chest. Then she swam back, lifting herself onto the platform next to me as if she'd just strolled to the corner to post a letter.

'He's got a new lens on his camera. Wants some shots of us diving.'

And so we skylarked about for Vern's benefit. We leapt off the pontoon holding hands, piggybacked each other crazily over the edge, sat on each other's shoulders and, staggering wildly, bombed into the water in a tangle of arms and legs. The feel of her wet skin was intoxicating.

Much later, as we swam back to the beach, she eased herself in beside me, analysing my stroke.

'Roll your body more as you lift your arms out,' she said.

Now she's Dawn bloody Fraser!

'Why?' I spluttered.

'You're too flat in the water.'

'What's wrong with flat?'

'Too much drag.'

'Silly me.' But I started rolling with each lift and, you guessed it, I felt myself slicing the water more easily.

We came ashore and sat on the beach to let the sun dry us once again, and without even thinking about it I said: 'That was my best swim ever.'

'As I was saying, roll your body more.'

I feared she'd missed my point.

Sarah and I became inseparable, and with our friendship came an electrifying new awareness; the bay had never seemed more inviting, its water never bluer, the salt-thick air never more delicious, and Sarah never more beautiful. My exam miseries rolled away on a wave of euphoria. I was permanently light-headed.

I ate exclusively with the Sheerwaters, only returning to the Miller campsite to sleep. No one asked were I was going, who I was seeing or what I was doing. Hopelessly footloose and absorbed in each other, we walked, ran, swam, held hands and finished each other's sentences. We debated what'd really happened to Harold Holt just before Christmas, whether Ronald Ryan should've been hung and if America would beat Russia to the moon. Sarah knew I was in the school cadets, so we argued about conscription and Vietnam. We licked double ice-creams sitting on the seawall under silent Norfolk pines. We played fierce tennis matches on the sportsground courts; she was always Margaret Court and I was Rod Laver. We told ridiculous knock-knock jokes, acted out silly scenes from *Get Smart* and broke into Beatles songs at the drop of a hat. I was desperate to kiss her, to taste her lips, but chickened out every time I thought I had a half-decent chance.

You're hopeless, Miller. Absolutely friggin' hopeless.

Every morning, our conversation picked up precisely from where we'd left it the night before.

'As I was saying…' Sarah always began, and it became our running gag, a comforting confirmation of a seamless friendship.

'You planning on going to uni?' I asked.

'Yes. I'll do Leaving Honours this year, then try to get into law.'

I screwed up my face. 'My grandfather's a lawyer. You sure you want to be one of those?'

'Yes.'

Her certainty confounded me because I wasn't certain about anything. 'Dunno what I'll end up doing,' I said.

'You'll shine at something. Everybody does.'

'Dunno what I'm good at. Running maybe.'

'Actually, I think you've got a way with words.'

'I've got away with more than most,' I said.

'I rest my case,' she laughed. 'And you've got a very sexy voice, Roddy Miller.'

'Fat lotta good that'll do me.'

Our idyllic days ended in the middle of January because I'd signed on for a cadet camp to qualify as an NCO. Before Sarah had raced into my life I couldn't wait to escape to this tough, two-week spell of military life, but now the prospect of it pressed in like the looming gloom of a storm.

On my final night at the bay we walked hand in hand through warm, velvety darkness along the beach. Reflections from the esplanade lights performed a jittery fluorescent dance out in the bay. Anchor chains rattled against wooden hulls as the ghostly wings of late-settling gulls whispered overhead. Sarah was saying less than usual and I was struggling to speak at all. I didn't want our time together to end, even though I knew I'd see her from afar most days at school. It wouldn't be, couldn't be, the same as this ever again.

'Race you to the jetty?'

'Don't feel like it.'

'Only joking,' she admitted and squeezed my hand.

We climbed rickety steps onto the jetty, which was already hosting the night statues of silently hunched fishermen. Rods flicked and reels spun out with sharp, whirring cries. We went to the end of the jetty and sat with our legs swinging over the edge. Across the gulf, the lights of Adelaide smeared a yellow smudge on the horizon.

'I'll come out here tomorrow night and think of you over there,' Sarah said.

'Thanks,' I answered, not for the first time feeling pin pricks of tears at something she'd said.

'Please don't leave school until you're senior champ, Roddy.'

'I dunno.'

'I'll be your tutor. You know, in maths and physics and all the other things you say you're no good at.'

'You'd do that?'

'Yes.'

'Why?'

'Because you're much smarter than you think,' she said with a certainty that astounded me. And then, very softly, she added: 'And because you're the only boy I know who hasn't tried to grope me.'

'Don't think I haven't wanted to.'

I turned to her and without any warning she kissed me on the lips. I could tell straight off that she'd done that before, and I'm sure she could tell that I hadn't. She tasted of strawberry lipstick.

'I promise I'll stay at school if you promise *me* something,' I ventured.

'What?'

'That you'll also be my kissing tutor.'

'Okey dokey,' she agreed brightly.

'Good,' I said.

Hells bells, I've just done the deal of the century!

Early in the new school year, still burning with embarrassment at having to repeat Intermediate, I received a large envelope in the post. Inside was a colour photo of Sarah and me, frozen forever in mid-air, holding hands and laughing wildly as we launched ourselves off the pontoon in the bay. The attached note said:

> *Dear Roddy,*
> *As I was saying, I'll be your tutor (!!) How about Wednesday nights at 6.30, my place? Mum said to tell you that dinner is included.*
> *Heaps of kisses,*
> *Sarah*

Something shifted inside me. I wasn't sure what the feeling was, but I knew for certain that things were about to change. I couldn't have imagined how much.

At first I went to Sarah's weekly tutoring sessions for the kissing practice that came with them. A deal was a deal, after all. Then I found myself going for the kisses and her mother's meals, because Jules knew how to cook wog food like spaghetti bolognaise and ravioli, which were a complete revelation to me. A bit later I went for the kisses, the food, some interesting yarns with Vern about photography and also to improve my results at school because that's what Sarah wanted. And, later still, I went simply because I began to get A's and distinctions in subjects I'd never even passed before. This, I eventually realised, was what I needed more than anything. The kisses and the wog food and the yarns with Vern were handy fringe benefits.

Sarah was a demanding tutor, but she revealed the mysteries of maths and the finer points of physics in a way no teacher ever had. Gradually I became inspired, as much by the possibilities of success as by her constant closeness and the scent of lavender in her hair. I swotted so hard that a persistent hammering developed in my temples and a permanent knot of anxiety pulled tight in my stomach. But in ten months I went from being the idiot kid who couldn't even pass Intermediate first time round, to that clever young Roddy Miller, the most improved student of the year and the winner of the Intermediate Maths Prize. On top of that, I walked off with the Best All-Rounder Trophy at sports day.

'As I was saying,' Sarah reminded me, 'believe it and you will.'

But all that was nothing compared to being known around the school as Sarah Sheerwater's boyfriend, that lucky bastard who ran, studied and pashed and God knows what else with her. Except there was no 'what else'.

My father, preoccupied as always with designing his lousy houses, didn't even notice the change in me. I felt like belting him one, especially because he now had an added distraction – an expensively clothed, mean-lipped optometrist who peered with disdain over evil black-rimmed glasses at my brother and me as she wafted in and out of our home like she owned the place. One well-chilled glare from her made me as nervous as a butcher's thumb.

'What happens if that bitch becomes our stepmother?' I asked my brother.

'I'll be off like a shower of shit,' he said.

'Easy for you. You've got a job and money. I've got two-fifths of bugger all.'

'You could live with the Sheerwaters. You just about do now.'

'Fat chance.'

'You done the deed with Sarah yet?'

'I wouldn't tell you if I had.'

'Which means you haven't.'

'So what?'

'So nothing. Like I've told you before, better men than you have tried and failed. Jesus, Squirt, how do you control yourself around her? Those legs and those bouncing…'

'Just belt up about Sarah, OK?'

My blood boiled at the thought of anyone else perving on her, my brother included.

Sarah finished Leaving Honours as dux of the school – as everyone except her knew she would – and the next year she went to Adelaide Uni to start her law degree. She threw herself into it with the same focus and energy she put into everything else. I understood when she told me she didn't have time for our Wednesday night tutorials, but it left me moping around with a gaping hole in my weeks that slowly filled with cold, trickling dread. She'd graduated to a world I wasn't part of.

We still ran, talked endlessly on the phone and went to movies together, but more and more often she'd arrange things so that we'd go in a group with her uni friends. They were always beautiful young women who swarmed like bees around their queen and looked at me with undisguised annoyance as if to say, what the hell are you doing here kid? Except, that is, for a strikingly angular music student called Clarissa Delandre, who treated me as an equal and laughed at my increasingly desperate jokes. I began to notice that Sarah often touched her in a delicate, tender way that was indefinably different from the way she touched me. I tried to ignore it but it felt like a bullet had lodged in my guts.

She began kissing me on the cheeks instead of the lips and, although she didn't say it, I knew what it meant. She just wanted to be friends and I couldn't disguise my misery. Jules tried to comfort me in her kind, motherly way, but seemed awkward and uncomfortable.

'Roddy, her life is changing.'

'I can see that.'

'In ways that even Vern and I don't quite understand.'

'I love her.'

There, I've said it, and I don't give a fiddler's fart who knows.

'And she loves you, believe me when I say that, but as the brother she never had.'

'I see.'

I wasn't really listening and was too naive to recognise her confusion over her own daughter. I simply didn't get it, not then anyway, and so steadfastly pretended it wasn't happening. I hit the books and the running track harder than ever because that was the only way I knew how to show Sarah my worth and to repay her for the time and faith she'd devoted to me.

Soon enough, just as she'd predicted on the beach that day, I was holding aloft a trophy that said I was Senior School Athletic Champion and reading about a cocky kid called Roddy Miller in the school magazine. I barely recognised him. But even better was the fact that I passed the Leaving Certificate with five subjects and five credits. In a glorious, gloating moment, I clipped the results from *The Advertiser* and sent them to all the relatives who'd given me stick about being dumb Roddy.

Shove that where it won't fit, you morons.

Sarah Sheerwater and I have been friends now for close on forty years, a constant presence in each other's lives. It hasn't been hard to keep track of each other through the decades, given the way our lives turned out and how our paths kept colliding.

Sarah, with her usual certainty and stellar ability, became a lifelong collector of causes and I eventually came to understand that I'd been her first. At the height of the Vietnam Moratoriums she could often be seen on the TV news services, spruiking through a megaphone at the head of battalions of protestors, arms linked with the likes of Jim Cairns and other prominent anti-war figures. In turn, she became a strong, reasoned voice for feminism and equal opportunity for women, a formidable advocate for Vietnamese boat people and something of a celebrity activist for Greenpeace. Later still, with her trademark single-minded purpose, she became a campaigner for the preservation of Aboriginal languages and art, and chaired powerful committees that looked into issues as diverse as youth unemployment, road safety, drug abuse and the amalgamation of suburban councils. Photos of her cropped up in magazines and papers with stunning regularity and they never failed to take my breath away.

I went through most of this with her because of who and what I became. By the time I left school my confidence had undergone such a transformation that I was convinced I could do anything. I found that Vern had been right, that there were more jobs than you could poke a stick at. I dabbled in printing, drafting, selling and carpentry. For a time I even thought I'd make a good airline pilot, but a trial instruction flight turned me to jelly in the first five minutes. Then, with the possibility of conscription looming, I decided to confront the situation head-on and volunteered for the army. Everyone, including Sarah, suggested I was a couple of snags short on the barby. Fortunately, the Duntroon selection board wisely rejected my application, which briefly punctured my ego but probably saved my life. As it was, I didn't get called up and got doggedly drunk for a week to celebrate the lucky escape.

Eventually I stumbled into advertising, copywriting for a radio station. I felt right at home; it was like Playschool for grown-ups. I won Golden Stylus awards for my writing, did voiceovers for some of my own commercials, started acting a little, and rapidly became convinced I was a genius. Then, on a fraught night in 1973, I was propelled into the studio to fill in for the radio station's midnight-to-dawn announcer who'd turned up for his shift so legless he couldn't speak. I didn't have a clue what I was supposed to do but, with nothing to lose, just played at being Roddy Miller for five hours. Something clicked. I was an instant hit and the first person to ring when I came off air was Sarah.

'As I was saying, you've got a sexy voice Roddy Miller.'

Within two years I was hosting the station's new morning talk show, earning an obscene amount of money, interviewing everyone from the Prime Minister down and, in a moment of media insanity, was hailed as Adelaide's most influential man.

'The moment you start believing that,' Sarah warned, 'I'll have you locked up.'

I'd accidentally become one of the country's first shock jocks and no one was more shocked than me. Suddenly, I was everyone's mate. People claiming to be old friends from school crawled out of the woodwork, and young mums pushing strollers in Rundle Mall started asking for my autograph. My cousin Toby, by now a successful doctor, began nagging me about getting reacquainted. I told him I was too busy sweeping the streets.

The only person I allowed to shamelessly use my celebrity was Sarah, who became something of a regular guest on my show as she sought free publicity for her causes. I didn't mind a bit. Movie stars, politicians, trade union firebrands and any number of rebels had nothing on Sarah Sheerwater for on-air conflict and quotable quotes. We sparred furiously and my listeners would've been forgiven for thinking we hated each other's guts. But in the commercial breaks we just about wet ourselves laughing, safe in the knowledge it was all good for business and that nothing could shake our friendship or stop our rising stars.

Every Saturday morning we ran together on Glenelg Beach in a decades-long, head-clearing ritual and even when Sarah hit fifty, unashamedly clad in tight shorts and a meagre bikini top, she still turned more heads than women twenty years younger. Often, as we ran barefooted on cool, wet sand, she'd say wistfully: 'Take me back to the bay one day.'

'Yeah, we should do that. I could still beat you to the jetty,' I'd taunt.

'I wouldn't bet on it, mate,' she'd counter, knowing full well that, with my buggered knees and cigarette-tarred lungs, I wouldn't stand a chance.

The intensity of my passion for her never diminished, but by necessity it matured and mellowed, finally settling into a heart-filling platonic love because of the other constant presence in her life, Clarissa Delandre. Clarissa is now an acclaimed singer-songwriter and ten years ago she and Sarah were famously married in a very public ceremony that made headlines and raised ire as well as eyebrows. It was the most beautiful wedding I'd ever been to. I was their best man and it became a constant source of amusement that their marriage outlasted all three of mine put together.

Last year, it was Clarissa who broke the news to me in a desolate phone call from London, where they'd gone for an extended holiday.

'Sarah has lung cancer,' she told me with a fearful tremor. 'How cruel is that, Roddy? She's never smoked a cigarette in her life.'

After the initial jolt I collected my thoughts and said: 'If anyone can beat it, Sarah can. How soon can she start chemo over there?'

'Roddy, it's beyond that. She's dying.'

I flew to London the next day and was profoundly shocked by the Sarah I found. She was grey and staggeringly gaunt. I sobbed as I kissed her.

'As I was saying,' she whispered. 'Take me back to the bay.'

So I did.

In the late afternoon, as the tide rippled in and the boats swung gently on their mooring lines, more than 400 people whose lives Sarah Sheerwater had enhanced assembled for her funeral service on the sand in front of the caravan park. Clarissa, unaccompanied and with unfaltering dignity, sang the love song she'd composed on the flight back to Australia. There wasn't a dry eye on the beach. Jules and Vern each honoured their daughter, speaking with haunting courage through their frail, trembling grief. Then it was my turn.

'The bay was hot and so was I,' I began.

Listless?

Phone numbers of friends you can ring up for a pint

Days to go before you're on the road again

How many pints you're up to

How many dollars you've spent versus how many dollars you had

How many extremely naughty meals you've been eating

Places in Paris your French friend Laurence has told you to go to

Chopin Liszt

Things that need mending

Things to do on your birthday

Things not to do on your birthday

Baby names

First sentences

Titles for your book

Names for your band

Number of caffeinated drinks over the last 24 hours

Places that will let you put up a poster advertising your garage sale

Unacknowledged food groups (eg, biscuits)

Places you might have left your sunglasses

Annoying bumper sticker slogans

Car registrations of mobile-phone-talking-drivers

Places for rent

People you admire that you'd never want to be like

Nicknames you had when you were a kid

People you forgot to add to the list

Favourite sandwich fillers

Favourite grammatical errors in signage

Pompous long words

Favourite bildungsroman

Moments in time you'd go to if you had a time machine

Dream jobs

Ideas for lists

Scar Tissue
Patrick Cullen

Paul woke to find his wife sitting on the end of the bed again. When he asked what she was doing there in the dark Carol said that she couldn't sleep and that instead she was going for a walk.

He rolled over to where she'd been in the bed and found the last of her warmth there. He eased his head off the pillow so that he could see the alarm clock on the small table beside the bed. 'You can't walk now, though,' he said. 'It's four o'clock in the morning. Come back to bed. At least for a little longer.'

'No,' she said, pulling at the laces of her shoes. She got up off the bed. Paul stretched out, folding his arms up behind his head, and saw her silhouette against the back of the door.

'Where are you going anyway?'

'I don't know. The beach, maybe.'

'It's too dark.'

'I'll be alright,' she said as she opened the door, the handle making a slow grinding sound. He listened to her footfalls on the stairs and then reached out and turned on the bedside light. He squinted, scratched at the side of his face, and swung his legs out over the side of the bed. The floorboards were cold beneath his feet.

'Give me a minute,' he called out down the stairs. 'I'll come with you.' He pulled on a pair of shorts and a shirt and got his shoes out from behind the bedroom door. He went downstairs and sat at the kitchen table and laced up his shoes.

Carol came out of the bathroom, pulling her hair back off her face. Paul yawned, cupping his hand over his mouth. 'I can't sleep either,' he said as he went through to the bathroom. She tied her hair back and went out to wait on the footpath.

When he came out of the bathroom and made his way down the hallway to the front of the terrace he saw how the light spilled out around her and he stood in the doorway a moment until she looked up at him and smiled. He pulled the door closed behind him, the sound stirring fruit bats in the trees overhead, and they flapped and jostled and settled again. Carol reached for Paul's hand. 'Thanks for coming with me,' she said.

'We're in this together,' he said, tightening his grip on her hand.

They walked to the end of their street, turned towards the beach and kept going. They passed a row of shopfronts, only glancing in the windows until Paul stopped in front of a secondhand bookshop. He pressed his forehead against the glass and pointed into the window, tapping his fingertip against the glass. 'Didn't you want to read that?' he said. '*Love in the Time of Cholera?*'

Carol looked into the window and nodded.

'We should come back later and get it.'

She shook her head. 'It's no use,' she said, crossing her arms against her chest. 'I've already got two books beside the bed. But I haven't been able to read more than a page at a time since the operation. You could read it, though. You might even learn something.'

'About cholera?'

She shook her head and laughed, backhanded his chest. 'About love,' she said, and rubbed her palms together.

He pulled her to him. 'You're cold,' he said, running his hands over the small of her back. 'We could go back to bed.'

Carol shook her head. 'Let's keep moving,' she said.

A short way along the street they heard someone coming up behind them. They stepped aside as a man jogged along the footpath towards them, his shoes slapping heavily against the bitumen. Paul nodded and lifted his hand a little. The man said, 'Hey.'

'Good morning,' Carol said as he passed and slipped away into the darkness ahead of them.

The car park above the beach was empty. Ships waited offshore, their lights pale amber in the darkness. The movement of water was only a sound beneath them. They followed the concrete pathway through the bitou bush and paused to take off their shoes at the top of the long flight of stairs that led down onto the beach. From there they could see the water rising black and grey and breaking white as it slicked over the sand. Beneath their feet, sand worked its way into the grain of the timber treads. The white paint had been worn away by the procession of bare feet.

They walked a short way along the beach and sat. Carol pulled her knees in against her chest and breathed heavily. Paul dug his fingers into the cool sand and let it slip through his fingers. He looked out toward the horizon and neither of them said anything.

* * *

Months before, in the first week of summer, they woke before dawn to the sound of rain on the iron roof. They moved into the middle of the bed together and made love and slept and woke again when a wedge of sunlight fell across the bed. Traffic began to move out on the street. Carol got up and went down to the shower. The water shuddered in the pipes. It took a while for the hot water to come through and when it did she turned the taps on a little further, and then she stepped in beneath the stream.

Paul came and stood at the sink, lathered his face, and began to shave.

'I have the day off today,' she said. 'We could go out.'

'My interview is this morning.'

'I forgot,' she said. 'Maybe we can go out this afternoon.'

He nodded, swept his palm back and forth over the mirror to clear the steam. He had been out of work since he quit his teaching job. At first he hadn't even looked for another job, he had just finished off some work around the house. For a while he wondered if teaching was what he really wanted to do but he now felt ready for it again.

'Do you want me to leave the water running?'

'Uh-huh,' he said as he ran the razor down over his throat and tapped it out against the edge of the sink. 'I'm almost there.'

She turned the water off.

'I'm almost there,' he said again.

She pulled back the shower curtain. She had one hand on her breast and her other arm up behind her head. Steam rolled out around her. 'Paul,' she said. 'Paul, I think I've found something.'

'What is it?'

'Whatever it is, it doesn't feel right, Paul. It doesn't.' She held out her hand to him. 'Can you feel it?' He put his hand over hers and she slid her hand out and moved his hand around a little.

'I can't feel anything,' he said.

'It is there,' she said. 'It's right there. Push down a little.' He moved his hand and looked at her and shook his head. She pushed down on his fingers and moved them around again. She stopped and looked at him. 'There,' she said. 'Can you feel that? Can you?'

He nodded and her arm fell against her hip. She leaned over like she was going to sit and he got her a towel, put it around her and held her up. 'It's probably nothing,' he said.

Paul waited at the kitchen table while Carol called the clinic. She talked quietly on the telephone, saying that she needed to see a doctor, that she needed to have something looked at that day. 'No, I can't wait. There's a lump,' she said. 'I can feel it. There's definitely a lump.' A space opened up and she made the appointment. She sat opposite Paul at the table and stared at something across the room until it was time to go.

At the clinic, she got changed into a pink gown and the doctor did a breast exam. 'Here?' the doctor asked, pressing down with the tips of his fingers. Carol nodded. The doctor finished the exam and washed his hands at a sink in the corner of the room. He threw the paper towel into the bin beneath the sink, stepping onto the pedal to lift the lid. The lid slapped against the plumbing beneath the sink.

Carol sat up and the doctor led her to another room where a young woman used an ultrasound to guide a needle in for a biopsy. After she was dressed she and Paul sat in the waiting room. They didn't talk. People came and went and, after the doctor came out and said that he'd call them if they needed to see him again, they went too.

They waited three days before the call came saying that she would have to go back in. The doctor came out into the waiting room and led Carol and Paul back into the room where he'd examined her. The room had no windows. Carol drew breath as the doctor pulled his chair out from behind his desk and began to speak. 'It's not a good one to have,' he said. 'Not that any of them are. But at least we're onto it.'

Paul reached his arm back over Carol's shoulder as the doctor talked them through options for surgery. He said, 'We'll need to take all of the breast to be sure we get it.'

Carol left hospital two days after the operation. Paul drove home past the beach and they stopped in the cliff-top car park. A sheet of rain hung dark beneath the clouds to the south and the wind came in hard across the water. Surfers did what they could with the swell. Gulls lifted off the railing, falling away to fight the invisible forces they live their lives by. Paul looked out into the water.

'I could still die,' Carol said. 'You do know that, don't you Paul?'

He nodded and looked over at her. 'I do know that,' he said and she put her hand on his arm and they sat in silence as the rain closed in around them.

'Your interview,' she said. 'I'm sorry, I haven't even asked. Were you able to arrange another one?' He shook his head. 'Paul,' she said. 'You could've been working again.'

'I couldn't face it.'

'I thought you wanted to get back to work.'

'I do, but I just can't face it now.'

'But it was a good job. And you had a good chance,' she said. 'Now you might just have to take whatever you can get.'

He tapped his knuckles against the steering wheel and reached down to turn the key in the ignition. 'I'll make some calls tomorrow.'

'Today,' she said. 'Can you please make the calls today?'

At home, Carol went up to the bedroom to lie down and Paul sat beside the telephone in the lounge room. He called friends from teachers' college and people he knew from schools where he'd taught before. When he had finished on the telephone, he went upstairs where Carol was lying on top of the bed. She turned away from the wall, rolled onto her back and wiped the corner of her eye.

'Do you want to talk?'

She shook her head and sat up on the edge of the bed. She eased off her pants and started pulling her shirt off over her head but her mouth drew tight and she stopped. She still had the drains in and she couldn't raise her left arm. She let her shirt fall back down. Paul pulled back the bedding, Carol moved in beneath it, and he sat on the end of the bed until she was asleep.

* * *

Carol got up and started walking away along the beach and after a few steps she stopped and looked back at him. She said, 'If we're in this together, how come I feel so alone?' and started walking again. Paul brushed the sand from his hands and got up and jogged after her. She was crying and he held her as they stood on the beach in the half-light.

After a while he suggested that they should go for a swim. She leaned back in his arms and looked up at him. 'It's almost winter,' she said. 'It will be too cold.'

'Come on,' he said, grabbing the hem of his shirt and pulling it over his head. Then he pulled his shorts and boxers down, let them fall around his ankles and stepped out of them. 'Come on. Before it gets too light,' he said and ran naked into the water.

She watched as he dived beneath a breaking wave. He surfaced in the whitewater and waved for her to follow. She shook her head. He went under another wave and came up again. He cupped his hands around his mouth. 'I won't look at you,' he called.

She looked up and down the beach. She took off her pants. She slid her underwear off onto the sand and stood for a while running her thumb around the hem of her shirt. She looked up and down the beach again, took off her shirt and bra. She folded her arms across her chest and walked quickly down into the water, turning her back to the waves. She swam out beside him, bared her teeth at him, let them chatter. 'It's too cold,' she said and laughed.

'That's it.'

'What?'

'That's the laugh I fell in love with,' he said. 'You haven't laughed like that in a long time.'

She laughed again and turned to face the horizon.

'Why don't you let me see you?'

'I don't know how long I can last out here,' she said. 'It's too cold.'

'Carol,' he said. 'Why won't you let me see you?'

'I'm getting out,' she said, turning back toward the beach. 'It's too cold.'

He floated on his back. 'Stay with me anyway,' he said. The stars were fading overhead. His body rose and fell as the water moved beneath him.

'What do we have, Paul?'

He righted himself in the water. 'What do you mean?'

'After all that we've been through – what do we have?'

He looked straight at her. 'What do you mean?'

'I mean, do you still love me?' she said as a wave came through. They disappeared beneath it. Paul came up first; looking back in towards the beach he saw someone run along the cliff-top. Carol came up in the water behind him. She was a little further out, treading water.

'It's too cold,' he said and turned away from her. He swam a few strokes toward the beach and stopped. He looked back and wiped water away from his face. 'You're my wife,' he said. 'Of course I still love you.'

Carol laughed. She lay back in the water and he saw how they had taken his wife's breast. A scar ran from her armpit, curving around to the middle of her chest, the scar tissue a crimson arc on her pale skin. Her other breast moved freely about on the surface of the water.

She drifted on her back until another wave came through, then they were both beneath the water again. Paul let it carry him along until his breath ran out and then he came up in shallow water and waded in to the beach. He walked quickly up to where they'd left their clothes and pulled on his boxers; they clung to his body and he teased them away from his skin.

A man came around the rocks at the southern end of the beach and began running towards them. He had his head down and was running close to the water's edge. Paul waved for Carol to come in to the beach and she began swimming, moving slowly, keeping her arms low in the water. Her strokes were uneven; he now saw how she favoured the right arm.

The sun edged over the horizon and he lost sight of her in the glare. When he saw her again she was standing in waist-deep water with her arms held across her chest. The man was almost between them; he looked at Carol out in the water. She hesitated for a moment then let her arms fall to her sides. The man looked back at Paul and then, after a few more steps, glanced at Carol. 'Good morning,' she said and laughed. The man opened his mouth as though to speak but said nothing and ran away along the beach, his shoes moving heavily through the sand.

Good Morning Mrs Edwards
Virginia Peters

Morton and I are to stay with his parents at their new country home, Saint Cloud, in the Southern Highlands of New South Wales, until we sort ourselves out – this is the plan. As we drive into their road he reaches across and squeezes my knee, but I'm too preoccupied to react. Too apprehensive.

We've just been honeymooning in London for a year – technically speaking. We were actually working to help an old uni friend of Morton's set up a new business, our desks jammed together like twin mattresses. The business failed. Sometimes I thought we might too.

Morton's parents have never fought. Morton has never seen a woman shout, hit and hurl insults and consequently he is under the impression I'm mentally unstable. Mostly we fight about fighting. I tell him, me giving him hell is part of the attraction. I'm helping him access his emotions. I yell at him and he yells back, and when we are finished I fall into his arms, completely sated. He thinks he is forgiving me.

He has been so excited at the prospect of going home, in that anxious way, singing loudly at pedestrian crossings, jiggling his leg under tables in cafes. His exuberance has been making me nervous.

As we drive up a short incline and onto the property he toots the horn repeatedly. It's a fairground sound, like someone's won first prize on the big hammer. I flex a smile.

'It's a big bastard, isn't it?' he says with a laugh. He's right. The new house rises large on the paddock as though it has descended from the wintry sky, white paint glowing with opalescence, grey roof looming like a mountainous rain cloud. Newly planted trees are staggered over the paddock – many of them looking like skeletons.

'You have to envisage it,' Morton says. 'Three years from now it'll be beautiful. They're experts at getting the foundations set in place.' I nod, as if I can see this.

We follow the red paving around the back. Alerted by the horn, Marian and Harvey are already scissoring across to meet us. Harvey is gesturing to where we park with a flamboyant sweep of his arm. Marian is in tartan pants. Harvey is in a tartan bush shirt. I have to smile – they are highlanders now, albeit Australian ones, and are dressed accordingly. Harvey waits with his hands behind his back, his stomach projected like a little boy's. Marian's arms are rising from her sides, preparing to engulf. Mama and Papa Bear. It's as though their fleecy stuffing has been completely renewed with this move to the country – all this rosy fresh air. What have I been so worried about?

Before I know it I'm sinking onto Harvey's fuzzy front. He feels warm and I feel a moment of contentment as I lie against his chest, my chin on his shoulder.

'Well, well, well,' he says, pressing his lips together as though he might cry. Marian, I see, is in fact crying. We hug silently.

'That's lovely,' I say, grinning at a brooch she has fastened over her top button. I think it looks like a piece of toffee, swirly with cream, and I would like to pluck it from its filigree surround and pop it in my mouth.

I stand back, smiling as they embrace Morton. Biscuit, the family terrier, joins in, yapping madly under Morton's arm.

Breaking their hug, Harvey looks serious as he turns to me. 'Now, this is your home,' he says. I see Biscuit is looking at me too, with equal intensity.

'For as long as you need it to be,' Marian adds, with one distinct nod. She stretches a hand out to include me in their group. The effect of her touch on my shoulder causes a fleeting abrogation of responsibility. A fleeting abdication of doubt; I have to square my feet on the ground.

'You got that?' Harvey says.

'Yep,' I nod, and I have to gulp. This is what Morton wants. For us all to love each other. I hear him say 'Thankyou' quite solemnly, as though terms have been reached and set. Darling Morty. I sometimes have an incongruous reading of reality, but I'd swear I've just been made their daughter. I'm flattered, amazed at how they seem to like me so much when they know so little of me.

We walk across the cobbled patio to the house together, with Morton telling them how wonderful the house is.

'It reminds me of an American homestead,' I say, and Marian laughs, doubtfully.

Harvey is pulling my ponytail as I walk through the door, saying, 'as if you can't tell'. I have no idea what he is talking about, but I take it as a compliment.

We sit on cane chairs, improvised thrones with their high fantail backs. These are arranged in a circle around a coffee table that reminds me of an African drum. There are large urns like Ming vases bearing palms, their great long arms reaching out to stroke us. Here we sip tea and nibble on butter cake from the highland bakery, while discussing the business in London. Morton gives a precis of the events in setting up the business, detailing all the negotiations and the reasons for its failure. Despite this failure I can't help but feel proud and pleased by their intense interest. Harvey is thrusting questions and Morton is responding with respect, like a military officer in a congressional inquiry. Unsmiling. Slightly flushed. His sentences slow but so carefully constructed. I've got a smile pushing up my cheeks as I look from father to mother – as if to say, *Come on, don't you think he's just wonderful, don't you think he's fabulous?*

'And what did you do with your time, Jacqui?' Marian asks when Morton slaps his thighs to finish.

'Oh, um, I ran the business with the boys. Morton and I shared an office.'

Morton leans in. 'Jacqui was very good at handling the promotional side of things with the advertising agency.'

'We both were,' I say as I reach across to squeeze his thigh.

Harvey is saying, 'Well, that's terrific, terrific,' but he wants to talk more about our future plans – 'More importantly, Mor-*ton*, your legal career'. He says 'legal career' so nasally it saws right through my eardrums. But Marian is telling him not now – we are tired and she is going to show us our room in the attic.

When Marian suggests one of the men take my bag, I insist on hauling it up the stairs myself, much to her surprise.

'I really think you shouldn't. It's far too heavy for you to manage,' she says.

So I force myself to carry it with a straight back, determined to impress her with my strength.

It's hardly an attic. It's enormous – broad and airy, with dormer windows cut into its low sloping ceiling. Just as I go to place the bag along the skirting board, she warns us to be careful not to hit our heads on the sloping ceiling. Too late – I hit mine on the unrelenting board with a thud.

'Oh dear, are you alright?' she cries.

'Yes, I'm fine.' I suppress my desire to hiss *shit* and laugh, in a manner that I'm sure indicates a mild nature.

'Silly duffer,' says Morton.

Marian is explaining the under-floor heating to us and how they are able to isolate those sections of the house in use, but I'm more fascinated by the light filtering through the window; soft pink drapes tinge it with rosiness to create a peaceful air. It has the light and dimensions of a chapel. Adding to the atmosphere are two convent chairs flanking the dormer window on the far side, their upright backs impressed with the crucifix. No one would sit like that of course, up against a wall, on either side of a window, nor at such unrelenting right angles, no one but penitents.

Marian indicates the ensuite. Through a crack I see the stark white tiles – it sparkles like an igloo. Everything is white. There are white guest soaps in a white china dish on the vanity, and fluffy white towels and slim white cotton ones that are more like hankies, embroidered with white flowers; I can't imagine wiping my hands on those, they're so clean and ironed flat. Marian seems to be treating us with undeserved reverence, I think, but later Morton would explain it's just the way she does things.

'Now why don't I leave you two to nap,' she is saying, her hands on her hips.

Morton has already collapsed on the bed. He has sunk into the middle of four enormous frilly white pillows. The bedhead rises like a steep bell curve behind him – blue peacocks on a pale yellow within a rich mahogany frame. The bedspread is in the same fabric. It's very exotic. I imagine all the public seats Morton's pants have rubbed over during our thirty-six-hour journey from London; planes, transit lounges, toilets too I imagine, as he's not very careful about that sort of thing. But Marian looks happy to see him luxuriating and I must say he looks perfectly at home. So I kick off my shoes and lie down next to him.

'Here,' Marian says. She lifts the satin eiderdown at the foot of the bed and drapes it over us until it reaches up to our chins.

'Thankyou, Mummy,' Morton says in a baby voice.

'Thankyou, Mummy,' I say, equally baby. They laugh – and for a moment I feel we're as thick as thieves.

When she has gone I close my eyes. But they won't rest beneath my lids. The nerves are jumping like spawning insects. I have so many questions. Like what's going to happen next? Because it's not up to me anymore. He *says* it's up to us, but that's a laugh – how long will we lie here for, for instance? He could sleep for hours. I breathe deeply, forcing the country goodness to swell inside me then drain like a slow leak. But it's no good. Out the window all I can see is cloud, long frays of faraway cloud.

'It's a Quaker's sky,' I whisper to Morton in a haunting voice, but he sighs his head the other way.

Finally I close my eyes, but a dog barks. Probably Biscuit. The sound cracks like ice in the thin air.

Duncan's wives. Where are all Duncan's wives? Are they in a box somewhere? Will I end up in a box too, despite it being Duncan's little brother I've married? I am in the green room, standing in front of the china cabinet. It's made from dark bowed wood, a formidable piece carved with inflexible garlands and ribbons, and upon its top is a collection of silver frames.

Duncan's wives have been replaced with Duncan grinning into the face of a rainbow trout, Duncan in a snuggly argyle knit, leaning with the mainsail and laughing into the wind. There's Morton and me on our wedding day – a hesitant smile frozen on our faces.

There is another frame that I pick up for closer inspection. It's an extraordinary photo: Duncan, Morton, their sister Elizabeth, and Harvey, all in wig and gown, outside the Supreme Court – Admission Day. What a feat for one family. They look like wizards. I have seen a similar one where they all stood smiling next to Morton in the grounds of Trinity Hall in Cambridge, in his cap and gown, the last in the line to graduate there. Marian is not in this photo though. I imagine her hunching over a camera, the only one in civvies – she would have spoiled the legal flush.

Morton has found a Burt Bacharach recording and we lay back on cream sofas covered with cabbage rose cushions, a fire spitting savagely between giant slabs of pale stone. Harvey stands next to the fire with a poker and a wine glass.

'Sit down, Dad. Relax.'

'I'm just fine as I am,' he says, and he moves his hips to *The Look of Love*. 'I'm admiring my beautiful son and his lovely new bride,' he grins. 'It's really hard having your kids out of the country, you know that?' he says, looking at me. I nod and smile, warmed at how pluralising 'kids' seems to include me.

'Sure I can't help?' I say, as Marian puts blue cheese and crackers on the coffee table.

'No,' she says, 'I want you to totally relax and enjoy yourself.' How irresistible it is to be so utterly cared for.

'This house is far too big for you, you know,' Morton is saying to Harvey. 'You'll go mad rattling around in all this.'

'Well, you know, we've bought it for *you* guys, so you can get away from all that rat race. You'll *all* be here in a few weeks. Duncan, Elizabeth, Rick. We've planned a weekend.' *Why can't it just be us?* I think. It's so nice, just like this. 'And you'll all come down for Christmas, no doubt,' Harvey is saying.

'Well that's *lovely* of you,' Morton replies, 'But I imagine we'll still be here, anyway.' Morton laughs cunningly, and I join in with Harvey. Now we're all barking like otters, our heads thrown back for sardines.

Over dinner we discuss Duncan's new relationship.

Harvey says, 'Jesus, the last one was a real psycho.' His voice can be so nasal at times, it almost rings in my molars. 'You're not going to turn psycho on us are you, Jacqui?' he teases. I smile brilliantly at him, as I'm unable to think of a response, and they all laugh as though I've said something extremely clever. I have to take a mouthful of red. *Ahhhh* – it descends like a ribbon. I sink back, my bottom sliding over the velvet of the dining chair. This psycho talk is making me feel slightly woozy.

I have told him it's his parents who are not *normal*. Everybody fights in the real world.

'No, I suspect it might be you, darling, who's not normal.' I didn't like this, especially the word 'suspect'. I suspect I am still under suspicion. I have told Morton this is not good. It's not good for my confidence – it's suggestive and detrimental – which at the time I thought sounded very balanced and self-possessed.

Sometimes he says, *But that's the thing about you, darling, you have no confidence* – and he looks into my eyes and says, *I believe in you. I only wish you did too. You could be anything,* anything. I love it when he says this. He looks into my eyes with such a deep longing, and I feel as though I've already won some race without running or hearing a shot being fired. I adore his belief in me. I adore him.

In the latter stages of the meal, Harvey draws Morton into a serious discussion about prospects while Marian engages me. She is saying, 'I want a donkey. I've always wanted a donkey with a big loud eee-aw and lots of cherry trees.' It's the glass of wine, I'm sure, and I titter with her, as though we women are filled with quite silly propositions. But I'm listening to Morton. He's talking in first person, about us – *I this, I that.* I have to swallow.

'Why do you say "I"?' I ask Morton, in bed. 'You should say "we". What *we* are going to do.'

'I don't know,' he says, looking perplexed.

'Well don't. It makes me *sick.* It's as if I don't exist.' I feel quite invigorated, having spent the evening with my mouth in the shape of a gentle crescent. My lips are flexing and stretching in all sorts of directions.

'I'll try and remember,' he says softly. 'It's not personal. I do it to protect you, I think.'

'Protect me? From what?'

'My parents are very demanding, in a quiet sort of way. And I guess if things don't work out, I want any mistakes that are made to be *my* fault, not yours.'

'What do you mean, *fault?*'

'I don't want them to be critical of you; I want to protect you from being judged,' he says. But I don't believe a word of it. *I this, I that.* What a blowhard.

The following week, I come across an art supplies shop in one of the towns that circle Saint Cloud. The idea of painting fields and skies suddenly becomes a necessity as I stand looking through the window, hot plumes of breath between me and this diorama of possibilities. The Chinese easels are cheap and the canvasses are on sale. I enter, question the old man on the cost of setting up with a small range of paints, and tell him to wait – I'll be back.

Morton frowns. 'I suspect this is an aberration,' he says.

'It's not. I swear. I have nothing to do at bloody *Saint* fucking *Cloud* – no offence,' I add softly. I can see him thinking, feeling a bit guilty, perhaps, about the time it is taking for him to sort out his affairs. Finally he agrees to the old man's seventy dollar quote.

'But not a penny more,' he says, knowingly. My arms open like a cape and wrap round him.

'Thankyou. Thankyou. Thankyou.' He shakes his head, his smile dubious – as though he's been swindled. And of course he has. It comes to seventy-eight dollars.

I work on my canvasses from first light to sunset in our bright white bathroom. I've never painted before, but now everywhere I look my heart swoons with pigment and light. My head is filled with marigolds. My eyes are torch beams. Black trees are electrified with lime, I see red polka-dot toadstools everywhere, inexplicable purple shadows – I'm a spinning top streaking with colour.

Another week passes and Harvey and Marian have begun talking to me about the importance of a good breakfast. I'm getting too thin. Thin is good, I'm flattered. At lunchtime they holler up the stairs, 'Jacqui. Luuunchhh.' Every day. Breakfast, lunch, dinner, breakfast, lunch, dinner. And it takes so long. I'm beginning to resent them eating up so much of my time. All I want to do is paint in my igloo.

'Why can't I grab a couple of crackers?' I ask Morton.

'You can't.'

'Why not?'

'They would find it disrespectful. It's just the way they are,' he sighs.

'You treat them like a king and queen.'

'Well they are, of sorts,' he says with a snort.

Lunch is set under the pergola, beneath the soft leaves of a grapevine, unless it rains. We sit around a chunky cast-iron table that resembles lace, with placemats, wine glasses, linen napkins and condiments. We could be in Italy. We all talk, back and forth, experimenting with cross-ways too. But Marian and I have found our place is with one another, and Harvey's is with Morton. The latter discuss law, politics, money-making.

Marian seems to have less to say about things. She listens to me traversing a wide range of topics, as serene as a Brahman cow in the way she stares and moves her head from ten-to-two to ten-past-two, her eyes slightly crossing over the tip of her nose. It's hypnotising. My language is boring into the middle of her face, way beyond its normal speed. It's as though the world is going to end and I have less than twenty minutes to explain myself to her. She has to tilt to help me, twisting this way and a little that way to help me get the words inside her head, but I'm still not sure she understands.

When lunch is over I watch Morton slump, allowing his food to digest at an obtuse angle. His arms hang over the sides, thighs apart. He'd be prostrate but for the chair. '*Relax*,' he mouths. *Relax?* Fuck you, I think.

'Now Jacqui, sit down. Let *me* do that.' Marian's voice admonishes as I leap up to clear the table.

'That's OK. I'm fine. You sit down. Really. I insist.'

Marian gives in with a little satisfied smile. It's a minor struggle now, I notice. She's cornered me. The alternative is to sit on my chair, indifferently, like the men.

Morton kinks his head to watch as I retrieve the plates. He reaches out his hand and runs it over my behind, gripping a handful of flesh to finish. Harvey snickers and Morton smiles up at me. *Lazy prick*, my eyes gleam. But I'm obliged to smile, as Marian is laughing a falsetto of little haha's.

Later. In the bedroom.

'You're such a dickhead. *Some*times,' I say, as a small consolation. 'You know that? You can be so *fucking* infuriating.'

'I beg your pardon. Jesus. Pull your head in. How *dare* you speak to me like that.'

'*Dare? Dare?* Just who do you think you are?'

'Good morning Mrs Edwards,' Marian says when I arrive in the kitchen. She says it every morning like a schoolmistress introducing the day's lesson.

And I say, 'Good morning Mrs Edwards' back. I go to her and press the corner of my mouth on her cheek. Harvey and Marian kiss Morton on arrivals and exits. Now it's customary they do it to me. But Marian is already busy at the stove, and I feel she treats this kiss as bit of a chore this morning. Where's that encouraging little *schmuck* she makes with her lips? She stands with her back to me, now. I hang at the edges of the bench. Heavily.

I notice her elbow is cranked up like an axle, twisting and turning the spitting rashers. I pick up a cloth and wipe a dead moth into the sink. I drop the cloth back into the sink. I fold my arms. I unfold them.

'So, what are your plans today, Jacqui?' Marian calls out over the ruckus in the pan. Plans? Oh please. I think this is pretty obvious. Why is she asking me this?

'I'm painting,' I say, a little unsurely.

'Righto,' Marian replies. 'Now, *you* like your bacon well done. Don't you?' she says.

'*Actually*, would you mind if I just had toast? I find it a bit rich…'

It's a retaliatory gesture I suppose, but why should I have to eat everything they eat?

'Oh.' Marian says. 'Righto, then.'

'Sorry, it's just my tummy… it feels a bit funny. Maybe I could set the table.'

But Marian says, 'No. I've done that,' throwing her voice over her shoulder. 'But you could make the toast. That would be a big help.' *Really?* It doesn't sound like much help, I think. My hand rummages in the bread bag – moving beneath the sweaty, soft plastic it looks about the size of a rat, and I shiver as though it is not my hand, but in fact a rat, trying to find its way out the sealed end of the bag. I whip my hand out with a bundle of bread. As I line the white slices up in the toaster I wonder if painting a picture is actually 'a plan'. Harvey and Marian had shown tentative curiosity the other day, asking what my expectations were as though I was Margaret Ollie. According to Morton's elaborations last night, although my painting gives me intense pleasure, unless I become serious, practically speaking, it's unlikely to provide such a benefit for others – especially the graveyard scene I'm painting up there at the moment.

'They believe in setting goals,' he explained firmly when I became exasperated. 'They're just trying to help.'

The thought that Marian might consider me too ephemeral, too self-absorbed, too odd perhaps, is scratching back and forth in my mind when Harvey walks in.

'Good *morning*, Jacqui.' Harvey moves smoothly and lightly across the black and white check floor towards me. Although top-heavy, he walks in full possession of his girth, a little spring off the top of his toes; there's theatre in the way his hands turn at the wrist, too. He's almost feminine. I feel his cheek press into mine. I sink into his face slightly, and it's as though beneath the skin he is filled with cold water.

'You smell nice,' I say.

'Yerse. I know. It's my ablutions,' he says, borrowing from Morton's bag of funny accents, or perhaps they were his in the first place. I hate that word, 'ablutions' – it makes me think of watery bowel motions. He grins, cunningly, as if he knows this.

'And how are we today?' he says. 'Good… and where is that gorgeous son of mine? You *do* think he's gorgeous don't you?' He leans into me and bares his teeth like a rabbit.

'Oh yes, he's very gorgeous,' I say.

'Oh, *dear*. That doesn't sound very convincing. What's the matter eh?' He rubs my back to jolly me up. 'Are we getting ready for the arrival of *la famille* this weekend? You haven't seen them for a while have you? Happy? Good on you.'

We sit in the sunroom next to the kitchen, awaiting Marian's arrival with the plates. Morton is so sweet to me – *darling this, darling that*, as though nothing harsh was said last night. Funny Morton, not the tiniest bit of a grudge. I don't know whether to feel slighted or relieved.

'You're not having bacon and eggs?' Harvey asks – it's a wild exclamation.

'She's not,' Marian answers for me.

'Good, well that's more for us,' Morton adds helpfully.

I munch in discreet circles on my piece of white toast while the others clack about with their knives and forks. Morton is feeling optimistic about a partnership opportunity with another solicitor. I know all about that. I know every little detail – I make it my business to discuss these things in bed every night. The men speak between mouthfuls about the pros and cons of such a move while licking their teeth, and the women listen.

'Why don't you buy brown bread?' I ask Marian. 'My mother bakes her own lovely wholegrain loaf.'

Marian responds, 'Oh, I don't think brown bread is all that good for you. We've always eaten white.'

'Oh but it *is* good for you,' I smile.

'No, I don't think so,' she says, shaking her head. 'My doctor has told me it causes polyps in the bowel.' I can't believe she has said this while her plate is still covered with yolk and bacon.

I swallow my mouthful of dry paste.

'My understanding of it,' I say, 'is that it has completely the opposite effect. They have found that the grains in brown bread *clean* the bowel by gentle exfoliation.' I run my fingers across my palm to demonstrate.

'Well that's not my advice,' Marian says with a shrewd laugh.

'Well, I'm sure that's what the latest gastroenterological studies have found.' That was quite a mouthful. I feel my face begin to prickle for I'm not sure I've said that word properly. I have to take a breath before making my next move. 'You wouldn't mind if I get a loaf, would you?'

'Not at all, Jacqui,' she cries. 'You can have whatever you want.' Head lowered, I imply my pleasure with a single nod.

'What does she want?' Harvey calls.

'Wholemeal bread,' Marian says, flatly.

'Actually it's wholegrain.' I look up and pull my lips blandly across my teeth.

'*Wholegrain?* It's bad for your gut.' Harvey screws up his face.

'She's read somewhere that it *cleans* the bowel.'

'Oh please Marian – do you mind not talking about bowels while we're eating? *Really. Dear oh dear.*' He looks at her with disgust. Then at me. The 'dear oh dear' is belittling – Marian shrugs and I raise my brow, and for a moment we are allies, cast off to some scullery quarter in our minds.

'Hey tell me,' says Morton, cutting through the slightly thickened atmosphere. The 'hey' sounds so exciting. Harvey and Marian's ears have become pricked. So have mine. 'Have you two seen Jacqui's latest painting?' They look quite startled. They shake their heads vigorously as though disguising an involuntary shudder. 'It's bloody good.' I gather he is referring to the yellow-brick cottage dwarfed by giant sunflowers and bumblebees, as it turns out he has not seen the current effort modelled on the local cemetery. 'She's got a real talent. I take my hat off to her. She only just picked up a brush a week ago.'

'Is that so?' they chorus.

Oh, what a dear boy. I don't know whether to laugh or cry.

Later. In the bedroom.

'You're a cunning fox,' I tell him. 'I don't know what had them gagging more at breakfast – the talk of bowels or my painting.'

He is lying on the bed with his hands behind his head.

'What *are* you talking about?'

I roll onto my elbows and grin at him.

'What am I *talking* about? I'm talking about "*Oh*, you really ought to see Jacqui's painting – *oooo* she's *so* good."' I'm wobbling my head at him, four-four time. 'You nearly made them *sick*.'

'What on earth are you talking about?'

'Oh, come off it. You were protecting me. You know they don't like me painting. They hate it. They can't *get* at me up here.'

'I swear I have no idea what you are talking about. *Dear oh dear*, what goes on inside your head?' He makes a prim line of his mouth. This is Harvey. Harvey says 'dear oh dear'. Harvey does the same thing with his mouth.

'I'm not stupid. They hate me. OK, maybe they don't *hate* me, but they hate the fact I'm not going to be what they want me to be. And they know it.' I leap up onto my knees to get closer to his face. 'They can't corner me into being a doormat. I'm a free spirit. And, by the way, I know *exactly* what they're up to. They want another *Marian*. I know it. They're as cunning as can be.' I've been swivelling above him like a lasso, but he doesn't move. His hands remain clasped behind his head, intransigent, elbows and biceps protruding from the sides like large antlers.

'What an odd girl you are. You've got *real* problems. You *do* know that, don't you?'

'Why did you marry me?'

His eyes roll. 'You have to understand my parents *only* want the best for you. You have to stop this dangerous nonsense. You have this shocking habit of twisting everything. *Everything*.'

'Don't muck with my head.'

'No, darling.' He looks at me with sad love. 'You're doing a good job of that entirely on your own. You *see* things that are not even there.' He wipes a tear falling from my face. 'This is your *modus operandi*. I've been observing you for a while now.' I look at him, puzzled.

'Maybe I *see* things that you don't see,' I suggest.

'No,' he says, 'I think you *think* you see them.' I stay with this for a moment.

'Do you really think I'm deluded?' I'm curious now, for I'm thinking I will be anything. Anything at all... *anything* but Marian.

'I think there may come a time when you may need some help. In the meantime you have to try and modify your behaviour.'

Modify? This word makes my face twitch.

'Do you love me?'

'I don't change that quickly.' His voice is cautious, as though it toes a tightrope. This is my fault – I threaten his balance. His equilibrium. Oh God, what am I doing to this man?

I must look sad, for he says, 'Come down here and lie next to me'.

Harvey and Marian are seated in the carvers at either end. Rick, their son-in-law, is opposite me, with Duncan and Elizabeth on either side. There is a white platter in the centre of the table, covered with the broken carapaces of bright orange crab. I'm grateful that Morton is at my side, his hand on my thigh – although he still seems so far away. Maybe it's just the wine mixing with the antibiotics, doing things to my eyes. My head feels like a hot air balloon. I've been sick with a throat infection for the last few days.

Duncan looks clean, scholarly too with those Einstein glasses on the end of his aquiline nose. I've been watching him speak, wondering: if I could fall in love with one brother, could I fall in love with the other? He's certainly more attentive than Morton, smoother, asking me about my family and how I enjoyed England – fascinated and cheered by my responses.

'And how are you settling into Saint Cloud?' he asks with a slow rumbling laugh.

'I feel very at home,' I lie.

'Well that's terrific. Here's to you, Jacqui,' he raises his glass. 'Or should I say, Mrs Edwards. You're one of us now.' I smile, thinking of past brides as I watch them toast me and swallow their wine. 'We're not perfect, but we do our best,' he adds with a smile.

'Yes,' says Harvey, 'we *do* do our best.'

'Who says we're not perfect?' This is Elizabeth. She pulls her head in, mockingly.

'Yes, speak for yourself Duncan,' says Harvey. Morton's hand squeezes my leg.

Rick sits up in his chair. He looks every bit a Kennedy in his navy blazer and polo shirt. He's just thought of something. A joke. I re-member now – Rick fires jokes, one out after the other. I gather we've reached the punchline as the others are sighing in appreciation. Rick nods furiously, egging me on to the same.

'I'm sorry,' I say, putting my hands to my cheeks when I fail to laugh. 'I think I'm a bit hot.'

'What you need, Jacqui, is another glass of the falling-over water,' his face serious. He picks up the bottle. 'There you go, that'll fix the bugs,' he winks. He misses my smile of appreciation, for he's off onto the next thing.

Down the other end, Elizabeth's hands are twisting at the wrist as she describes something to Marian. She reminds me of her father, but she wears heavy rings on her fingers, and has false nails which she has been using to tweeze the meat from the crab claws. There are a variety of bracelets on one wrist that have been crashing up and down since we sat down to lunch, and a thick gold chain around her neck, weighted by a large pearl; it sits just above her powerful chest, her cleavage a deep wedge as she leans in to Marian.

'It was absolutely divine.' She speaks in sighs, swirling her de-scriptions around her hands like plumes of chiffon. Marian's lashes are quivering with concentration.

'We're talking about a party I went to,' she says, sensing me watching. 'I was just telling Mother that the detail they'd gone to was *extraordinary*. You would have loved it. I imagine you'd be good at planning that sort of thing – you've got a good eye for detail, haven't you?'

'Me?'

'Well, you've worked in that *world*,' she exudes, as though my world is a mystery to her. 'You're a creative type.'

I giggle. 'I've only worked in sales.'

'Yes, but it's that magazine world,' she persists.

'She's been painting, you know,' Marian says.

'Yes, I've heard. Look, I think it's wonderful. Really, I do. It's about time *someone*' – she roars this down the table to the others – 'demonstrated some creative talent in this family.'

'Absolutely,' agrees Rick. 'If you'd been another lawyer, Jacqui, I'd have gone out and shot myself.' Elizabeth rolls her eyes at her husband.

'I have to say, I believe I am as much a creative person as I am a tactician.' This comes from Harvey.

'What rubbish,' someone says. Another calls for a definition of creativity and as if this is his cue, Rick leaps out of his chair, reaching for my plate.

'Oh no, Rick, please I'll do that.' It's Marian, calling from the other end of the table.

'No, no. I've got it,' he calls back. 'You just stay there Marian.' I watch Rick as the others deconstruct creativity. Marian gets up to help him, but he is making such quick work of it, head down as he rushes back and forth. This is the first time I have seen him look serious; there is something lugubrious about his handsome face that reminds me of a faithful bloodhound. I'm watching, warily.

'Oh – what is creativity?' I say, when I realise they are all looking at me. 'Um. Well, I guess it's self-expression, isn't it?'

Duncan rubs his chin. 'I think it has to be more than that, Jacqui. It's a good point, but I think you'd have to narrow it down to expression through an accepted artistic form.' I feel myself slightly bristle at his pedantic tone.

'Why?' demands Elizabeth, with operatic force. 'I might be expressing my creativity through forms outside those commonly accepted.'

'Like what? Creative spending?' Morton jibes. She pretends to look affronted.

'Oh thankyou, Rick-ee darling,' she says as he takes her plate. 'Now,' she says, 'let me take issue with you, Morton.' Minutes later they are still at each other, Elizabeth booming, Morton and Duncan outwitting each other. The debate has moved beyond me into the merits and misuses of creativity in the law – or something like that.

'Hey.' It's Harvey. He beckons me closer. I lean in so our heads are a hand span apart. 'That's what a *Cambridge* education does for you,' he says, nodding at the three. His eyes twinkle with pride and I smile warmly at him before taking another swallow of wine.

My head is getting lighter and lighter. I look for Morton. 'Love you,' he whispers. 'Me too,' I whisper back.

We eat lamb cutlets next. At least they do. 'It's this bug,' I say flippantly, flapping my hand about my throat as I dump them on to Morton's plate. Too bad. Too spaced out to care.

Morton tells them all about England and I listen, happily sipping on my wine. There are questions flying back and forth. Opinions. They speak with volume, gravitas. Marian, Rick and I, we watch more than we speak. Rick is pouring me another glass, barking, 'Do yor want another?' I notice he has adopted the voice of a drunken aristocrat.

I don't know how we've got on to drugs, but Duncan is admitting he has puffed on a reefer. He calls it '*mara gee wana*', in a silly voice. 'I didn't inhale though,' his laugh rumbling again.

It seems dope is the worst misdemeanour of all three. Marian raises her eyebrows and Harvey makes a horseshoe of his mouth as each describes the circumstances of their experience. It's ridiculous – I can feel my throat tightening, for if there is an area of worldliness I have dabbled in, *it's this*. They all seem so naive.

Now Duncan is saying that if any child of his came home with drugs he would throw them out of the house.

'Well that's a bit hypocritical, I have to say,' says Morton.

'Seriously,' Duncan says, his head driving an arc. 'Zero tolerance. I just wouldn't stand for it.'

'I'm sure that would work,' I add, quietly. It's a facetious remark. It dangles. I'm surprised they even heard it.

Harvey looks up as though he has seen me for the first time. Duncan touches his fingertip to the bridge of his glasses. I feel everyone is looking at me except Morton beside me, whose hand rests on my thigh.

'Yes, I have to say Duncan,' Morton says, clearing his throat, 'Your views are rather extreme.' Morton, my darling Morton. Everyone is back looking at Duncan now, and I take this opportunity to take a slug from my glass.

Duncan ignores this. 'I think Jacqui was about to say something… weren't you Jacqui? Go on, I'm interested to hear what you have to say. What's your angle?' Everyone is looking at me once again.

'Angle? I can't say I actually have an angle. I just think you can't stop kids, or anyone for that matter, from doing things by using *force*.'

I have read snippets in the newspaper. I know terms like rehabilitation, decriminalisation, prohibition, supply and demand, but I forget them all. My argument runs along the lines of getting your kids to share a few low-impact drugs at home in a family environment, such as over a game of Scrabble with your mum and dad. It's not good, I can't think straight – alcohol, antibiotics, lack of legal training.

'Non sequitur,' Duncan says when I'm finished.

I would have said, 'I beg your pardon', but nothing comes. I'm thinking, *What do hedge clippers have to do with drugs?*

'Duncan, she doesn't know what "non sequitur" means.' Morton sounds unimpressed.

'I think what she is saying is—' Duncan begins, but I find my confidence and interrupt him.

'Actually what I'm saying is… what I'm saying, Duncan, is…' I can't think of anything. I start to laugh. 'What I'm saying, Duncan, is that *you are*… a fuddy duddy.' My voice is teasingly high. I've not heard this word for at least a decade and it has amused me.

'A *fuddy duddy*? Excuse me?' Duncan has stiffened.

'Jacqui. I'm sorry, but that is totally uncalled for. Duncan is not a fuddy duddy.' Elizabeth looks at me, truculent.

It's not a rude word. It's a harmless word. It comes from the same barrel of friendly words as 'silly ninny', 'ning nong', 'wally woofter'. My family used to use them daily, with affection. I'm completely confused and now they are all staring at me with their eyebrows raised. I don't know what to say. It certainly won't be sorry. I react, I suppose, as most people do in a panic situation – completely on reflex, and I do something I have not done since I was a child. I stick my thumbs in my ears and wiggle my fingers at them.

'Darling, please.' It's Morton. 'Stick your tongue back in. Come on.'

It's a new day. Morton has brought me into his parents' bedroom, *So we can get this all sorted out before people start forming opinions.* I feel sick. Hung-over and beaten. Harvey is in a singlet leaning up against the bedhead, pink skin and fuzzy chest – he's like a peeled crustacean. Marian, next to him, looks like a reprint in a faded papery nightie. I'm sitting on the edge of the bed in a borrowed robe. Morton, curled at their feet.

'Don't you worry. We perfectly understand what you're going through,' says Harvey. I fist my eyes and wipe my nose with the length of my index finger.

'Thankyou,' I say, lifting my head for a moment to look at him.

'I think it's those bloody awful antibiotics,' says Morton. 'My poor darling's not been feeling well for days. And it all got a bit much for you. Didn't it chooky?' I nod and give him a pitiful look as I wipe my snot along the length of my robed leg.

Morton says, 'Why don't I make us all a milk coffee?' and Marian and Harvey say that'd be lovely.

'You stay here,' he says, as he bounces off the bed. Now is not the time to appear disagreeable, so I do as I'm told.

'Hey, come here,' Harvey says, in a playful voice, patting the mattress. I give a little smile and shift closer towards him up the bed.

Marian smiles, and Harvey smiles as he rests his arm on my shoulder. 'Between you and me, Jacqui,' he says, 'I have every faith in you.' I nod, meeting his intensity by looking him in the eye. He holds the look and I feel so grateful to him for this sign of mutual respect, considering my escape across the paddock and the lengthy disappearance that followed.

'You know, a lot of people have a thing about us. We know that. We know that.' I nod. 'They've got chips on their shoulders. You know what I mean?' I nod, again. 'They can't handle our success. But I know you can work through it.' I look at the sheet and inhale fragments of them, breath, cotton, their skin. 'You're a great girl. Isn't she Marian?'

'She certainly is.'

'You're smart. You look good. You've got a good sense of humour. You'll work through it. I have every faith in you. In fact, you remind me a lot of Marian. And I thought she was so good I married her. She was just like you. You'll make a great wife and mother. Morton's a very lucky man. So don't worry about those couple of big gallumfas of mine, eh! Cambridge wallies, eh!' He's rubbing my back, so hard that it stimulates the stunted sounds of laughter. When he has finished he plants a kiss on my forehead. Then I lean across so that Marian can give me one too. I'm so filled with relief I nearly faint.

Later. In the bedroom.

'They think I've got a chip on my shoulder,' I tell Morton. He is sitting on the edge of the bed holding my hand on his lap.

'Did they actually say that?'

'I think so.'

'Mmmmm. Do you think you do?'

'Do *you* think I do?' I look at him closely.

'I think they may have a point,' he sighs.

'Jesus.' I can't look into his eyes; I have to lower my head.

'Don't worry, don't worry,' he's telling me. He cups my face in his palms and lifts my gaze. I look out the window at a long streak of pale cloud. 'You've apologised to everyone and that's what counts. You've done the right thing.' His thumbs wipe away at my cheeks.

'But I'm so ashamed,' I say as he crushes me to him, the pressure making me wail. Snot loops like yolk from my nose and runs into my mouth. I nuzzle his woolly shoulder, rubbing my face into its soggy fuzz. I can feel all the bones in my body. I'm a bundle of sticks he holds together, and it's only morning.

FUZZY REAPER

A cat called Oscar has developed an infamous reputation at a Rhode Island, USA, nursing home where he resides. He has revealed an uncanny ability to predict when residents are about to die, and has presided over the demise of more than 25 of them, according to an article in the *New England Journal of Medicine*. Oscar makes his rounds, jumping on and off beds and deciding whether to curl up beside them or continue his patrol. "His mere presence at the bedside is viewed by physicians and nursing home staff as an almost absolute indicator of impending death," said David Dosa, a medical doctor with the Rhode Island Hospital in Providence. "Oscar has also provided companionship to those who would otherwise have died alone. For his work, he is highly regarded by the physicians and staff." Experts continue to attempt to explain the cat's mysterious abilities, but are reluctant to spend too much time with him.

Cosmos Magazine, Issue 17, 2007
(www.cosmosmagazine.com)

The Aunt's Story
Steven Carroll

I see it like this. The woman is elderly. She has a woolly head of thick, white hair. It is uncombed and wild. Her eyes are large, her eyebrows black, her cheeks high and her jawbone strong. She is a big-boned woman and she is walking across her block of land in what is now the outer-Melbourne suburb of Nunawading. It is winter, the ground is wet and slippery, and she is wearing boots. The tent that she lives in is pitched behind her and she is walking across her block of land, up an incline, towards an intruder, waving her left fist in protest.

To this woman virtually anybody is an intruder, an unwanted presence, a pest. This particular intruder, a young painter, is calling something out to her but she doesn't hear. Not because she can't, her hearing is very good. But because she doesn't want to.

He has time to call out to her once more. He is making a request, but by now, after less than a minute of contact, it is clear to the young man that this woman has only limited tolerance of the world and other people. Her stride hasn't slowed. She is walking straight towards him and he backs off to his parked car.

The intruder dispatched, the woman turns back to her tent. It is a cold mid-July day, 1946. The young man stands beside his car, mulling over the brush-off. By the time he leaves, the woman is back inside her tent, annoyed by the second intrusion in as many days. Only yesterday a journalist and a photographer approached her from the road and tried to talk to her. That night an article and photograph had appeared on page three of the city's evening newspaper, the *Herald*, with the headline 'Old Pensioner Has Pioneer Spirit'. This second visitor is an artist and he wants to paint her portrait, after having seen the article the previous evening. But having failed to engage her in conversation he jumps in his car and drives back to his current lodgings in Heidel-berg. The next day his painting will be complete, and will be exhibited at the Contemporary Art Society, in Melbourne.

The woman was my great-aunt Katherine Carroll. She was one of four sisters, the Irish Catholic daughters of John Carroll, a police constable in the tough inner-Melbourne suburb of Collingwood. Aunt Katherine was born when he was serving as a mounted trooper in Kapunda, South Australia. None of the sisters married. Agnes became a nun and painting teacher. Mary-Anne (my grandmother), Frances and Katherine more than likely worked as housekeepers throughout their lives.

Katherine was the most idiosyncratic of the sisters and much of what is handed down about her is unreliable, to be looked upon as most family mythology should be, with a sceptical eye. But one thing is certain, those two days, the 16th and 17th of July 1946, contained a jigsaw of events that eventually gave her a kind of immortality, ensuring that her name and her image were preserved in the art of the country.

The young painter was Sidney Nolan. He was twenty-nine, brought up in St Kilda by working-class Irish immigrant parents. He was not well known at the time but was part of the Melbourne-based group of writers and artists known as the Angry Penguins. He was living at 'Heide', the house of art patrons John and Sunday Reed (the name was a contraction of their suburb, Heidelberg), and he was working on the paintings that would establish him internationally – the Ned Kelly series. During this time he did a few paintings on the side, and one of them was *Woman and Tent* – Aunt Katherine. It was painted in one day, and exhibited on 17 July 1946 at the Contemporary Art Society, run by John and Sunday Reed.

The *Herald* photographer was not named in the paper, nor was the journalist who wrote the article. *Herald Sun* archives do not keep negatives as far back as 1946 and because reproductions must either come from microfilm or the printed page, it is impossible now to get a clear shot of Aunt Katherine. Photographic reproductions, like the circumstances surrounding both the article and the painting, are blurred.

The painting now hangs in the Nolan Gallery, Lanyon, Canberra – part of a permanent exhibition, a gift to the country, personally selected by Nolan. The painting has been there since 1972 and, before that, was part of Nolan's personal collection.

It was clearly an important painting to him and remained so throughout his life. Why was Nolan so drawn to the subject? She was,

after all, only Aunt Katherine, regarded as something of a family odd-
ity, an eccentric, an embarrassment – especially when she went around
getting her picture in the paper. Yet, somewhere in the figure of that
rebellious or cantankerous old woman – depending on your point of
view – Nolan found something of a cultural emblem.

The sequence of events would presumably have worked like this.

Nolan, working on the Ned Kelly series which he began while he
was still a conscript during the war, would have been deeply immersed
in the past – albeit a relatively recent past. All of his artistic efforts
would have been geared towards recreating the final days of colonial-
ism, when phenomena like the Kelly Gang were still possible, when the
country was in the first serious throes of robustly asserting its separate
cultural identity, when rebels and outlaws like Kelly were seen as em-
blematic of some essential, national quality.

With poet and critic Max Harris, Nolan travelled extensively through
Kelly country during much of 1946. He would probably have examined documents, newspapers, photographs and literature of the time,
as well as interviewing and talking to people who still might remember
something that just might spark an image or provoke a theory. During
this process, the material remnants of the world the artist is seeking to
recreate – buildings, sites of significance, artefacts – all become gateways
into the past. The process becomes all-consuming. So much so that this
imagined world can become more immediate than the real one. But this
evocation of a past world must also have contemporary resonance – not
only for the viewer/reader, but for the artist too.

So Nolan picks up the paper one morning and there it is. It may
be that what he found in this defiant, white-haired old woman living
in a tent on the fringe of the city was a figure who corresponded with
the mythic types in his Kelly series, a confirmation that the spirit he
saw embodied in the Kelly Gang was indeed an enduring part of the
national spirit.

The painting – done in quick-drying Ripolin, a kind of house paint
used by Picasso, among others – was ready for hanging the next day.
Family folklore has it that Nolan drove to Nunawading that day and
tried to talk with Aunt Katherine. He might have wanted her to pose
for him, either at the tent site or in a studio. He would have got nowhere
– and fast.

But did he? There are memories of Katherine visiting family members and complaining about a cheeky young man, saying that he had

been prying into her private life and how dare he! Perhaps this cheeky young man was just the *Herald* photographer. Perhaps she was visited by both, and both were given their marching orders in quick succession – one day after the other. Perhaps, in the end, Nolan simply painted the work from the photograph and never met Aunt Katherine.

An incident during a visit by Sidney and Mary Nolan to Orkney in 1989 would seem to suggest this. The couple was there for an exhibition which included *Woman and Tent*. At a question-and-answer session after the opening, Nolan was asked about the painting. The question launched Nolan into a passionate account about how to make fresh statements in painting. It emerged that Nolan had originally chosen a completely different painting for that mixed exhibition in Melbourne in 1946, but the evening before the exhibition opened he saw the *Herald* photograph of Aunt Katherine and apparently worked all night on a painting of it. The next day he took down his original exhibit from the wall and replaced it with the still-wet *Woman and Tent*, to the outrage of both his fellow exhibitors and the general public.

Certainly, Nolan did get into hot water over the painting when it was first hung because he deliberately put the photograph of Katherine on the wall beneath the painting, presumably to show that the subject was real and contemporary. But in some minds it raised an important aesthetic question. The photograph and the painting are extremely close, the only major difference being that Nolan added a bold strip of blue sky. If Nolan simply reproduced the photograph, and if he never met the subject – could it be 'art'? Isn't it just a picture of a picture? A case of the 'original' being the photograph, and the painting a poor imitation that adds nothing to what the photograph already gives us? Today, it might not be such a debated point, as 'originality' and 'authenticity' in art are no longer such sacred concepts.

Indeed, it may have been a deliberate strategy to annoy the traditionalists. Painters have used photography since its invention, but have usually hidden the evidence whenever a painting was exhibited. Nolan didn't. In fact, Nolan used photographs frequently. The 1952 painting *Carcase* is clearly taken from a private photograph *Carcase in Tree*. The difference with *Woman and Tent* is that the painting is quite a literal rendering of the photograph.

In one of his few recorded references to the painting and that exhibition, Nolan said, 'I wanted to show how immediate art can be, so I hung the painting with the press clipping below it'.

Nolan experts suggest it would have been consistent with Nolan's approach that he would have tried to meet Aunt Katherine. He was a frequent traveller and a short trip to Nunawading from Heide would have been nothing to him. We not only know that he travelled extensively through Kelly country, he went to Fraser Island to learn more about Mrs Fraser, up to Cooktown and Port Douglas. He was not a painter who confined himself to the studio.

Another interesting aspect about the painting of Katherine is that it is a one-off. At the time he tended to paint in a series. It's possible that what he saw in 'Mrs Carroll', as she was originally referred to in the catalogue – she always insisted on being called Miss Carroll – was an early version of the Mrs Fraser and Daisy Bates paintings that he went on to produce afterwards. That is, portraits of tough women, living on the edges of society, suspicious of society and always guarding their independence of spirit against intruders. Katherine, again, became a contemporary focus that helped illuminate the past for him.

So, whether she liked it or not, whether they ever met or not, Katherine was transformed in Nolan's imagination into an archetypal figure with national and historical resonance.

If Katherine were alive today she'd be taking camels across the Simpson desert and writing books about it. As it was, she travelled through much of southern Australia, nearly always by train, but nearly always with a small tent which she pitched in the evenings. Without knowing precise locations we know she travelled extensively throughout the Victorian, New South Wales and South Australian countryside. The *Herald* portrayed her as an old-age pensioner who couldn't find appropriate rooms to rent and lived in loneliness and solitude in a tent hopelessly inadequate for the winter rain and occasional flooding. She may have had the 'pioneer' spirit, but she was a battler, a sad and lonely figure. This is, in fact, far from the truth. Katherine was certainly no poor old lady. If Nolan had sought a contemporary version of the pioneer woman he found one. Aunt Katherine was ripe for mythologising.

Nor was she dumped by her sisters. She lived in a boarding house in the Melbourne suburb of Surrey Hills – on the corner of Union and Canterbury roads – with one of them, Frances. Her other sister, Mary-Anne, my grandmother, was employed to clean the place. But Katherine got sick of it. She felt too confined, and walked out one day and bought a block of land with her savings. It was close to the Nunawading station, which apparently suited her, for she could take off on a train trip when she felt like it. The tent was temporary accommodation and she planned putting a small cabin on the land. She was happy, apparently – except when intruders disturbed her.

She died in nearby Blackburn in 1949, at the age of seventy. On the death certificate she is 'Catherine' Carroll. The death officially occurred between the 21st and the 24th of July, which suggests that the body remained undiscovered for four days. It is not known if the planned cabin was ever built and it is quite possible that she died in her tent. By then she'd already found a kind of immortality. She'd brushed with the art of the country, only she didn't know it. Nolan, for his part, had brushed with the very stuff of his mythology and may have been surprised to learn that he'd actually stumbled across the 'real' thing.

A few years before Nolan died, I saw him at an exhibition opening in Melbourne. By then I was familiar with the story of Aunt Katherine, and was tempted to approach him and say, 'Hey, you painted my great-aunt, she lived in a tent...' But I didn't.

Perhaps it was because I'd started out as a painter and had spent a year training to be an art teacher, before I realised I couldn't paint. During that time my idols were the Angry Penguins – especially Nolan and Tucker – and perhaps I didn't want too close a brush with my mythologised figures.

I also had an uneasy feeling that he wouldn't remember the painting. Of course, he would have. It is only recently that I discovered how special the paintings he bequeathed to the Nolan Gallery in Canberra were to him, and that whenever he visited Lanyon he would linger in front of Aunt Katherine and her tent. Perhaps remembering the muddy slope she tramped up to tell him to get lost, if she ever did.

A restless spirit in life, Katherine has since toured Australia extensively, especially in 1967–68 when she had a busy time as part of the Nolan Retrospective of paintings 1937–67. Hers was among the images touring the Art Gallery of New South Wales, the National Gallery of Victoria and the Art Gallery of Western Australia. *Woman and Tent* was catalogue No. 30, and toured with 143 of Nolan's paintings. Katherine would have liked the travel, but not being dragged about with a crowd the whole time. It's also likely that when Nolan moved to England, Katherine went too. The painting's brass framing was made in England and we know that Katherine was exhibited at King's College, Durham, in 1961. And, although hard to verify, it's also quite likely that she toured Europe. Furthermore, when Nolan made the selection for Lanyon, Katherine would have been flown back to Australia in 1972 on Gough Whitlam's plane, with Whitlam as her escort. Which would have suited her nicely, being Irish Catholic and Labor down to her muddied bootstraps.

She has also become part of biographies and art history. In one 1961 publication, *Sidney Nolan*, with an introduction by British art historian and critic Sir Kenneth Clark, Aunt Katherine occupies a prominent position as No. 2 on the list of selected plates. In another, a biography of Nolan by Brian Adams called *Such is Life*, Adams refers to the 'idiosyncratic' *Woman and Tent* when speaking of the Nolan bequest to Lanyon. The painting is a favourite among the older visitors to the gallery, especially women.

There are no family photographs of Aunt Katherine. She apparently had no close friends. The only surviving images of her are the *Herald* photograph and Nolan's painting.

Sidney Nolan *Woman and Tent*, 1946
Enamel on composition board, 919 x 1220mm
Collection: Nolan Gallery, Cultural Facilities Corporation, Canberra

In Hell With Al (Travels to Die for)
Russell McGilton

'Just throw the dice, Alan.'

'It's *die*. I've only got one in my hand now.'

'Alright. Die. The *die*! Just throw the bloody die!'

He threw the die on the ground. It skittled across the marching feet of shoppers, bounced, then stopped next to the other fallen cube. 'Seven. What's that?'

'Let's see…' I scanned the choices in my notebook. 'Go west.'

'I don't like the feeling of this. Why did I ever…' Al mumbled, as he picked up his backpack.

Inspired by Luke Rhinehart's famous, but fictional, story *The Dice Man* (about a psychiatrist who lives his life according to throws of dice and eventually goes insane), we had given ourselves over to the flick of the wrist, out of the palms of decision and into the loose, unfolded sheets of chance: we were going to attempt to travel around Victoria for the day by dice.

But rather than follow the questionable choices of Rhinehart – 'Should I sleep with my best friend's wife?' – our options were mostly navigational: for example, a dice roll of six would mean go south-west, a three go by bus, a nine travel ninety kilometres. Arriving at our destination, we would ask six people six different things to see or do and, when the moment took hold of us, something silly to do (usually after a number of fat pints).

This experiment was all in the hope that we would get some kind of interest from publishers or indeed short-sighted producers to take our half-baked idea. Fame and fortune, I believed, were in our grasp. Except for one thing. Alan.

Quite frankly, I was surprised that we'd got this far at all, here in Melbourne's Bourke Street Mall. Alan, you see – my bumbling, clumsy friend – had nearly closed the door on our grand dice adventure altogether. Literally.

When I had rocked up at his place, all packed and ready for our big trip, I noticed that he had left the front door ajar – a sign, I presumed, for me to walk in when I arrived. However just as I walked up onto the porch and got in reach of the doorway, the door snapped shut in my face. I heard a muffle of laughter.

'What are you playing at, Alan?'

I tried looking through the opaque glass door. He kept laughing then suddenly stopped.

'Oh, shit.'

'What?'

'I've locked myself in.'

'What do you mean you've locked yourself in? It's your house.'

'Well, I've given the keys to a friend of mine – political activist, great guy, you'd really like him—'

'Get to the point, Alan.'

'Oh, right. Of course. Well, you see I gave him the keys to look after the house while I'm away.'

'But we'll be back by the weekend. That's only three days.'

'Yes, but I need someone in the house... for security, you understand.'

'Oh, Christ. Not *this* again.'

'Yes, yes, yes, it's *this* again,' he sighed, his balding head blurring into long, fuzzy spikes as it slid down the channelled glass of the front door. 'It just keeps me less paranoid.'

'*Less paranoid?*'

In the twelve years that we have been friends, Alan has demonstrated an unfailing ability to be fearful, scared and downright paranoid about everything. And I do mean everything: Armageddon Gulf Wars, peak oil conspiracies, millennium meltdowns, testicle-shrinking oestrogens in plastic bottles of water, rising sea levels and brain-cancer-causing chemicals in tofu, not to mention capping my mouth with his hand every time I tried to eat over 'the seven almond limit'. 'They'll kill you if you have one more!'

This latest, shall we say, 'Alanism', was probably his most enduring. Some time ago, Al had been absolutely convinced that a music arranger, Helfman, whom he'd worked with on a feature film, had broken into his house and stolen an important contract – a contract that would show Helfman to be lying and forfeit any claim to Alan's APRA royalties.

For months Alan burned up in his own bile, stewing sleeplessly over Helfman's criminal act and attacking those who did not believe him (usually me). One day he rang me up with 'He's been back in here again! He's taken another contract! I know it! I know it!'

'How… how do you know?'

'You've got to take me seriously, but I know you won't.'

'No, I will,' I lied. 'I promise you.'

'Well, I went out for the afternoon and came back and found – and you won't believe this – a shit in the toilet.'

'What?'

'There was a turd left in the toilet!'

'OK,' I said, taking a deep, deep breath. 'Let's get something straight here. You're telling me that Helfman somehow broke into your house, stole another contract and hey, in the excitement, couldn't contain himself and took a dump?'

'Yes! Exactly!'

'You're insane! Haven't you thought that it could've been *you* who left the shit in the toilet?'

'No, I'm sure.'

'How do you know?'

'It didn't look like mine.'

I took another long, long breath.

'*What do yours look like?*'

'Er… mmm… you know, that's a really good question.'

'You're insane!'

I hung up. Some months later Alan sheepishly admitted he'd found the contract – and it was where he'd left it all along, in his filing cabinet.

'Was it filed under 'C' for *CONTRACT*?'

'You bastard, McGilton! You *bastard*!'

Still, this didn't stop him from thinking Helfman *could* break into his house, and now Al never leaves home without the contract: up to the video store, a friend's house, the cinema, the milk bar and even at parties (odd to see him drunk off his head with a courier satchel still slung round his neck, contract presumably safe and sound inside it).

So there I was, left to wait on Al's porch on a cold winter afternoon while we waited for his activist friend to turn up with the key. I couldn't help but think that this was already turning out like my last grand adventure where everything had gone wrong: malaria, caught in Pakistan during September 11, a stack with a yak, robbed, splitting with my girlfriend…

Thankfully with the dice I couldn't stuff up my plans, because I didn't have any. And that was the exciting thing about it: Who knows where we'd end up? Who knows what strange and amazing people we'd meet on our chaotic journey because of a flick of the die? Who knows what stories would come of this, what publishing deals?

'Who knows,' I began to shout, as it dawned on me that I was going to be travelling with someone even more unpredictable than two dotted cubes, 'WHEN BLOODY AL WILL OPEN THE FUCKING DOOR!'

In *The Road to Gundagai* (London: Hamish Hamilton, 1965), Graham McInnes wrote of Ballan in the 1920s:

'Ballan itself was ungracious and unlovely… The prevailing impression was of openness, dissonance and a ramshackle unplanned confusion as if the town had been thrown down in a hurry from a passing aircraft and somehow taken root.'

Looking at Ballan now as we hitched up our packs after getting off the train, nothing, it seemed, had really changed here in the intervening eighty-odd years. It was still a small country town and a place that defied imagination because imagination, apart from a nearby house with a front lawn filled with crockery sculptures that whistled an eerie tweedle-dee to Willy Wonka, had skipped town.

Why had the dice sent us here, of all places? It was a disappointing entrée into the dice world and already Alan was moaning about going back home (something about forgetting to lock the back door and rambling about Helfman again). I suggested we meet the local fauna at the watering hole and garner our six options of places to see here and something silly to do. Al rolled his eyes at the thought.

Inside the town pub, the Hudson Hotel, a group of workmen in overalls wrestled over a pool table, swearing loudly at each other. As we ordered a beer they gave us a look that suggested the words 'dumbbell press' were not in our vernacular.

My throat tightened and an alfalfa male voice squeaked through my teeth, 'So gentlemen, what six things would you suggest to see in Ballan… *mmm*?'

Someone grunted behind me. A large man was sipping from his froth-webbed schooner. He offered choices that seemed to suggest the town was suffering from either a short-term memory or a crippling identity crisis.

'Well,' he said, rubbing his expansive belly, 'you could try the Ballan Video Store, the Ballan Friendly Grocery Store, the Ballan Bakery, the Ballan Pub, the Ballan Hairdresser or even the Ballan Sock Factory.'

Alan crept up behind me and seethed into the froth of his beer, 'We have got to get out of here, Russell! The stains in this beige carpet are more interesting!'

I wrote down the choices and threw one of the dice.

'Number six.'

'The sock factory?' Alan groaned. 'Nooo!'

'You must obey the die!' I raised my finger, putting on a Yoda voice. 'The die speaks the truth. The die knows. It is your *destiny*.'

'Alright, alright,' he sighed heavily. 'Let's just get on with it.'

'We also need something silly to do. You know, something that will get a reaction, something that'll be great to film.'

'Like what?'

I wrote a list of possibilities:

1. *Go into the sock factory with my Indian guidebook and ask for directions: 'How do I get to New Delhi from here? I'm a bit lost.'*
2. *Pretend that it's a condom factory and offer to try one on;*
3. *Ask where the Oompa Loompas are;*
4. *Pretend to be German tourists;*
5. *Walk in with open mouths and ask repeatedly 'Can you put a sock in it?'*
6. *Use our own socks as hand puppets to try and interview the owner.*

I read them out.

'You're not really going to go ahead with this, are you?'

'Alan, my dear stalwart of support, yes. Whatever is rolled we must do.'

I threw the die again. 'Four!' I said, then checked the list. 'Pretend to be Germans!'

Alan closed his eyes then put his palms over them.

'I want to go home.'

We found the sock factory down a side street. It was a corrugated building, rusting away in the fresh country air. A sign above it read 'JOHN BROWN HOSIERY – QUALITY SOCKS FOR MEN'.

'Now let's get our stories straight.' I turned to Al, stopping him in his tracks. 'What's your name?'

'Alan.'

'No! I mean a German name. Think of a German name.'

'Alink?'

'Come on!'

'Hans. And you?'

'That was mine! Let me think. Oh, I know. Helmut.'

'Hans and Helmut. Isn't that a little too obvious?'

'It'll do. Here. You film.' I gave him the video camera.

'I don't know if I can do this, Russ. My hands. They're really shaking.'

'Well then, get them out of your pockets!'

'Stop it! Russell! Russell! Listen to me. Are you really happy with my hands *shaking* and *filming*?'

'Are you really happy with leading us through as a pretend German?'

'Ahhh…'

'Look, you'll be fine. Just breathe deeply.'

Alan flicked on the camera and in we went, backpacks and gear bouncing and scraping through the narrow door of the factory.

Inside was a small office with mock timber walls and threadbare rainbow-coloured carpet. Two squat women, their grey hair puffing around them like Columbus clouds, sat behind computers while a white-haired man was slumped over, talking into a phone. One of the women got up.

'Can I help you?' came a flat voice.

Here we go. I took a breath.

'Yes, vee are from Germany and vee are vanting to do a program on your factory. Is it OK if vee film?'

'What's the program?' Her eyes were going up and down, scanning us like The Terminator.

'Vee are doink a program on throwing zer dice und it ended up here as a choice.'

'Oh…' She seemed nonplussed, as if German tourists came in here every day with video cameras. 'Wait a minute.'

She turned around to the white-haired man, who had just got off the phone.

'Charles. We've got some Germans to see you.'

He shot up. 'Bloody Krauts?! We'll have little Hitlers running around here next.'

I snapped a look to Al but he had already drowned in front of me.

Charles walked toward me. Was he going to throw us out?

'Where ya from in Germany?' he said, with a friendlier tone.

'*Err…*'

'I said "Where ya from in Germany?"'

I had gone completely blank. Unfortunately, Alan hadn't.

'Venice,' he blurted.

'*What?*' Charles blinked.

'Er… Prague?'

I jumped in front of Al just as he seemed to turn into a tumble dryer.

'Vee took a flight from Prague. Vee were in Venice but vee are… originally from Frankfurt.'

'Oh, right. Yeah,' he held out his hand. 'Charles.'

'Helmut,' I said, shaking his hand. 'And zis is my friend Claus.'

'Hans.'

'Hans-Claus,' I threw a razor look to Al. 'Is his full name.'

'Ah, right.' He put his hands on his hips. 'So ya wanna have a look at the factory?'

'Ja.'

'Five minutes.' He held five of his fingers in my face so I'd understand.

'Ja, five minutes.'

'Come with me.' We followed him down the hallway with the fake veneer panels into the factory, when he said something that made me totally shit myself.

'My co-partner in the business is from Germany,' he said. 'You should meet him.'

'*Ah-HA! Vell…*' I tapped my watch rapidly as if I was sending out a help message in morse code '… vee can't stay very long. You know us Germans and time!'

'Too bad. I was gonna say if you were here till Monday you guys could have a chat about lederhosen! Haha!'

'Haha! Goot joke.' I relaxed.

'Though his wife is around here somewhere.'

'OH!' I broke a forced smile. '*Riiiighhht!*'

'But I think she might be on her lunch break.'

'Zis is too bad,' smirked Al, watching me squirm again.

Charles took us around the factory, a place full of needles and complicated machines and women bent over sewing desks and baskets. I stopped by one and said, 'Ah, goot job'.

'Yeah, right, mate.' She raised an eyebrow then stitched another sock and threw it into a long production bag filled with other socks.

Around the factory we went while Charles spoke to us, glasses perched on his nose and talking over them as if we were completely stupid.

'Uber,' he said and pointed to some boxes that burly men were packing. 'They're German. Ha!'

He slapped me on the back.

'Ja, ja. Goot. Goot.'

Of course, with all this manufacturing going on Al had to bring up some obscure left-wing politics that only a local activist like him would know about, and in the worst German accent I've ever heard. He sounded as if he was in a *Carry On* film.

'Is da bi-lateral agreement wiz American affecting the price of cotton wiz competing OECD nations?'

'What?' Charles grunted.

'Nosink. Nosink,' I stepped in. I turned to Al and grabbed him by the arm as Charles turned back to showing us around the factory. 'What are you doing? Cut that shit out, man!'

'Oh, yes. Right.' And his hands began to shake even more.

On and on Charles went about how they made the socks, where the material came from, how many units this machine made.

'Kevlar.' He held up a sock. 'No slippage, ja?'

It was becoming so tedious, so boring that I wished I really wasn't able to understand English.

'Right, boys. That's all the time I can spare,' he said, showing us to the door. 'Oh, one more thing…' He tapped me on the shoulder just as I was almost outside.

Oh, no. This is it. He knows we've been faking it. He's gonna beat the shit out of us for wasting his time.

'Put these on where it fits,' and handed us two pairs of black socks.

'Sank you!' I said, then hurried out the door, Al bouncing after me.

When we got around a corner and safely away from the factory we burst out laughing, falling about against a corrugated fence.

'I can't wait to see this footage, Al. It's gonna be a scream.'

And it was. On the train back to Melbourne I was indeed screaming.

'What the hell is this, Al?' I blasted him as we watched the footage on the tiny LCD screen. 'This is like some kind of fucking weird cubist art!'

'What?'

'You've got a shot of my shoulder for most of the time we were in there.'

'Well, it's very hard to shoot and talk at the same time you know.'

'Yes, but you weren't even *talking*!'

His eyes flipped to the ceiling, thoughtfully.

'This is true.'

I looked through the rest of the footage of the trip.

'I can't fucking believe this. We've got nothing. I can't use any of this. I can't use this to pitch the book. You've fucked it up.'

'If someone,' Al rose up, 'had trained me to shoot then it might've been a better recording.'

'*Trained*? Fucking *trained*? How hard is it to point the goddamn camera at someone's face?' I flipped the screen shut. 'I'd hate to see your photo album. It'd be just full of body parts. "Look, here's me in Egypt by the pyramids" and they'd be just an ankle or an ear lobe. Christ! I don't fucking believe this.'

Alan was silent for a moment. He looked down at his shoes.

'Look, Russ. You really are a good friend and I am really sorry for fucking up. But all I ask is for you to look at it in a different way. You see, artists are frequently misunderstood and what you have there is quite groundbreaking, quite confronting, quite—'

'Incompetent.'

'Er… yes,' he sighed. 'Look. All is not lost. W-we couldn't just throw the dice again?'

I let my head fall into my hands, trying to wish it all away.

'Russ? Russ? Why aren't you talking to me? You're not crying are you? Come on, it's not that bad. Russ… hello, Russ? Let's throw the dice again. Eh, good buddy? Let's just throw the dice one more time. What do you say?'

I slapped a cube into Al's palm. The train had stopped and people were getting in.

'Alright,' I said. 'Evens we do this dice trip again. Odds we don't.'

Al threw the die up with great force, whereupon it bounced off the ceiling, ricocheted off the train door window and scuttled over an old lady's muddied shoe before escaping out the door and into the unforgiving chasm between the platform and the train.

'Odds!' Al yelled after it. Our eyes met and we burst out laughing as the train took us back to Melbourne.

Front Steps
Grace Goodfellow

The concrete steps out the front of my house are a perfect place to eat ice-cream.

I can see the entire street from here without even having to move. I can watch old Mrs Witherby nearly run over her tabby cat, Thomas, as well as laugh at Bindy chase her little sister up and down the footpath.

A whole little world – right here on my front steps.

I can watch the ants go marching, one by one, hurrah hurrah – and smile quietly to myself as a beautiful lorikeet flies into the jacaranda tree, which is situated slightly to my left.

I can sit here and think about my day, and wave shyly to Bodhi who lives three houses down from me. I can be amazed at his absolute gorgeousness and wonder if we'll ever end up being together.

I can stretch my legs out and think, *Probably not going to happen.*

My lazy street tumbles down to the sea. On a hot day I can smell the salt in the air and run as fast as I can down my steps to the beach. I can race across the road to Bindy's house and almost break her door in. She can open the door and grin wildly, nod her head and skip to her room to grab her bathers.

After the beach, we can sit on my steps and talk about when we were little and what our favourite colour is and what the best flavour of ice-cream is and how good or bad it is to have little sisters and whether aliens actually exist or not.

We can sit there and watch the sun go down, just behind the jacaranda tree. The concrete will start to go cold and we will run inside so we don't get varicose veins on our bums.

The sun will slowly set, and I'll know that tomorrow, I can open our blue front door, and the steps will be waiting for me.

Leopards
Jessica Au

You open your eyes as the ground beneath you begins to shake and roll with life. It's the heavy grind of the machinery as it bites and rows into the dirt, the hot scream of the engines as they churn and guzzle oil. The shadows of the scaffolding, the thin timbre frames that they throw to the floor like warping skeletons. The cold tight around your shoulders like a strap.

Vater.

The boy at your side nudges you back from the brink. Your eyes swim as you look for him. Always too tired these days, but aware that the foreman is watching from the shady cab of his truck.

Carefully, you take the warm bricks in your hands. The toothy corners nip at what softness remains on your palm. You can almost smell the roaring fire of the kiln on them, and the wet, dark clay robbed from the earth before that. The boy bends to mix the mortar for you. And, for the first time, you're surprised to notice the snare of muscles suddenly there in his wiry, brown arms.

Lay the bricks, build the wall. That is what they said to you, the first day, that first cold labourer's morning.

You came with your hat in your hands, your heart in your mouth and the boy at your side to translate. The strange hulk before you, blond-haired and pink-faced like a baby. There were no names, no passports, no contracts to sign. Just these orders and a small, folded wad of notes into your hands at the end of the week.

Build the wall, set the bricks. And so you do. Day after day. Mixing up a grainy paste of sand, cement and lime, a mortar that claws your hands and cracks your skin like burnt bacon. This you trowel onto the bricks like butter to lay a simple running bond. Nothing but twine strung between two mason pins and a chipped gauge rod to remind you of balance, of geometry. During this time you seal your mouth and eyes shut against the fine cloud of dust that washes over you like silt.

The sing of the shovel against a bed of nails is exactly the sound you hear before you fall asleep at night.

Throughout, the boy remains with you. Striking the bricks in half with a bolster and hammer so that you can set the corners. Rubbing over the joints with a small piece of copper tubing to finish. In the white, almost fluorescent, morning light his eyes are dark and raccooned. Blacker, brighter and angrier than you ever remember being at that age.

At lunch, the other men shore up together with their backs to the old wooden fence, which is rheumy-green and oystery with rot, slouching into the gravel. They eat beef sandwiches and meat pies soured and sodden with tomato sauce, drink from hipflasks that smell as leathery and warm as old boxing gloves. The paint-speckled radio spurts static and bush rock. They are mostly young, these men. Arrogant, wolfish and shameless in a way that only the young can be. The muscles, the skin on some of them, is almost obscene. They rollick and spar, shamble and growl in packs, speaking fast and thoughtless about things you do not know or understand.

And all the while you sit in the distant shade with your *pastrami* and *matzo*, a small thermos of sweet, strong tea. Aware that your prayers, your strange cleanliness, casts you apart. You hear them talk, feel the hot wash of their eyes over you, their prickly laughter at your back. And somehow you know that it's you they sneer at, your name they slur. But still, you say nothing. Bow your head and pretend not to understand. Your boy sees this and in his tense silence, his hard, dark eyes, he despairs of you and your meekness.

There's a quiet when it happens. Sore, your spine splitting, you rock back on your heels and rest for a moment. The boy casts a half-worried, half-exasperated look at you but carries on, gritted and determined in your absence.

You end up dozing, so that when the foreman comes up behind you, you start and scramble messily sideways. He speaks but you can barely catch anything of that quick blurry of words. It's only when they steer the boy away and saddle him up with a new pair of goggles and a workman's saw that you understand.

Among the other apprentices, you can see that he is tense and unsure. But already he has something of their slack arrogance, their cool pride. And there in his face, you see it. A raw, new joy growing as he begins to work the blunt, heavy instrument in his hands. As he finds a place among them.

In the last sack of light at the end of the day, the men uncurl their fists, shuck their tools and loosen the laces of their boots like belts. Rest a moment to survey their work, what foundations they have laid, what rents they have covered in this turning body of land. Open up their throats like gullets and toss back drams of whisky, capfuls of sweet bourbon. Necks flexing thirstily as they swallow.

You are not part of it.

On one of these evenings, you'll come back from a piss to see the boy among them. Him and two others surging up the scaffolding hand over hand with a grace and power that churns your gut and cinches your chest. Wrestling themselves three storeys high so that they can stand on the topmost shaky wooden plank, throw up their arms and crow into the bare, stripped world before them. The light burning on their skins, the wind loving up their loose shirts. Stamping out dust showers and sucking up the air from that height as if it were ether. The other men laughing and hooting back from below.

Just seeing him up there sends a black jack of fear right down your spine. Alive and untouchable in a way you could never be. Even from such a height his dark eyes find you, love you and defy you. And just like that, you know how things have changed.

In your small house by the railway, the light from the thirty-watt bulb rocks, shrivels and dies. You have nothing to replace it with, so you and your family eat in silence to the flickering bright white of the TV on mute. You cannot stand that pale nimbus on the bodies of your wife, your daughter, your son. Like the quiver of ghost lights. The shadows suck and heave on the peeling walls.

Opposite, the boy wolfs down his food like a man starving. You recognise this new hunger in him. You had it too, decades ago when you first became apprenticed. But now, everything holds the floury taste of raw cement mix, the sourish warmth of brass, and some nights your gums bleed as you bite into the hard crust of your bread.

Outside, the trains clatter and bump their way along the tracks, scattering the spill of the streetlights like a film reel. Your wife clears the plates and brews *kafé* black and sweet. The boy reaches across the table and turns the volume of the TV up and over the silence pouring between you.

Later, he comes out of his room in dark jeans and bomber jacket. In his hands, a black leather wallet, faded knapsack and your tarnished car keys.

Quietly, you ask him where he's going, and, quietly too, he answers. He explains about his friends – the other boys, the builders. The ones who you saw shimmy up the ladders like shadows and, with your son, roar deeply into the throat of the world. The ones who almost made you sick with their bravado, their youth. They have plans to meet tonight, he says, things to do. Gestures to the door.

Slowly, you shake your head. No.

The boy mouths a protest but you slice across it.

No. Not this night.

But, *Vater*—

No!

Your fists slam onto the table before you know it. The coffee pot skids over and spills a violent, thick glut of dark liquid over the wood like oil. You feel the burn of a bruise in your reddened knuckles, your spraining wrists. Your ribs almost moan with the effort of holding your heaving chest in.

The boy only waits a second before he hoists the knapsack and bangs through the door. You feel the hot blast of his fury rolling on after him, the hard smack of your silence in the air. And the words he throws over his shoulder – they surge through the house like an after-shock and leave you beat and windless.

Get *fucked!*

Outside, a car engine burrs to life, the boom gates sing, and tyres ride high and reckless on the wet, barrelled road. These sounds slip into darkness.

Then, nothing.

Soon, it will be morning. A blackbird morning, with the sky high and purple and the bricks red and dulled like old blood. And the dark will thaw, the wind turn.

You push your breath into the palms of your hands to warm your fingers, lean your back against your perfect, unharmed wall. Old depressions in the earth, like sown fields, stretch out before you.

It's been three days since your boy slung his curses at you, and you have not seen nor heard from him since. At home, your rage is soft and full. It burns your quiet wife, your lovely daughter. You can see the fear and distrust in their eyes as clearly as the hate in his on that scarred night. And at work, you say nothing. Alone, you build the wall.

The men, they lay like leopards in the shade and watch you, wordless.

Game
Jo Bowers

They were in her bedroom because she'd seized an opportunity, earlier in the evening, to engage him in a word game. Its purpose had been to resolve the sexual tension that had built between them as they sat at a bar, drinking beer and nibbling pizza. So engaged had she felt, from the moment he stepped into her space, that she'd hardly noticed their temporary posting at the bar turning into a three-and-a-half hour seduction. It was their second meeting and it had been six months since the first, yet every part of her was present before him. She'd laid everything out, all her vibrant fabrics and fragrant spices, like a shameless third-world street vendor.

'What will we do now?' he had said as he showed her the time on his watch, a glint in his eye hinting at a past full of easy women.

'I'm terrible at decisions,' had been her reply, although she knew she must get to his skin before the night was through. 'Let's decide together... I know, I'll say a word and then you say a word until we've made a sentence that tells us what we're going to do. I'll start: I.'

He paused.

'Would?'

'Like.'

'To.'

'Maybe.'

'Uh. Think.'

'About.'

'The.'

'Possibility.'

'Of...'

'Going.'

'Somewhere.'

'With.'

'You.'

'And.'

'Umm… sinking.'

'Into.'

'Your.'

'Sunset.'

It was his turn but he paused again. He was a poet, she knew, and she waited in sweaty anticipation for something brilliant.

'Clause.' He smiled broadly, revealing a set of teeth fit for an advertising campaign.

From there they'd walked to his car through air that pressed against their skin. He'd kissed her on his bench seat and driven them to her house. She'd sized him up along the way, imagining how their bodies might fit together. He was in the six-foot category with a footballer's build – thick arms, narrow hips and that slight gorilla slump – but the way he walked suggested a different game.

In her bedroom she took those meaty forearms in her hands and tried to make sense of him. She felt him up and down, probing his flesh for something sure that she could grasp, a search for something familiar, but he was all new to her.

'It's funny, isn't it?' she whispered, allowing her hands to settle loosely around his wrists. 'How you can't just pick up where you left off with the last lover. You have to start all over again. Just when you thought you were becoming expert at body parts.'

'How many lovers have there been?' he asked.

She slipped out of her sandals while she thought how to respond. 'Oh, you know, lots and lots.' She smiled and shook out her hair defiantly.

The look he gave her told her he was paying attention.

'I'm hopeless at holding onto them though,' she said. 'I reject them without sort of meaning to. In fact, let me say up front, if I do anything that seems like a rejection, it probably means I really like you.'

'What would a rejection be like, coming from you?'

'Oh, I might make you go down on me and then kick you out into the gutter.'

'Are you kidding? Would you let me back in again? I'd love that!'

She slipped her hands beneath the short sleeves of his shirt, up into the hot space where shoulder muscle dips into collarbone. 'I usually act tough and like I'm just using the guy for sex. I don't want them to think I have any needs beyond that. I don't want them to think that I want anything. I like to present as contained. Intact.'

He looked at her so long and close and steady that she had to look away.

'You paint little pictures of yourself,' he said, gently.

'Ha! Painting myself into a corner, more like.' Her tone was brash, but she liked what he had said. He was listening to her. He was interested.

They kissed then, and she ran her hands down the broad reach of his back, slipping her fingers under the waist of his jeans. His skin was sweet-smelling and tacky from beer and heat.

'I really like you,' he said, 'but I need to be honest with you.'

She felt her throat contract and her stomach shrink and knew what would come next: a qualification of his feelings. All men got around to it eventually. She counted herself lucky that this time it wasn't going to be sprung on her late in the piece.

'Tell me.'

He sighed. 'I'm not capable of giving a whole lot at the moment. I like being with you and I'd like to be with you again, but I thought I should let you know where I'm at.'

She recalled, then, that he was not as new to her as she'd tried to kid herself. This was, after all, their second date. They'd been out six months earlier, something that he'd insisted on calling a 'catch-up' and she'd written off as a dud. Back then he'd seemed too earnest, too intense, lacking in humour, and, worst of all, he could not manage to move very far from the topic of his ex-wife and his life 'post-separation'. Just the way he'd said it – *post-separation* – made her weary.

'I have just decided,' she said, 'that I am not going to have sex with you.'

'Should I take that as a rejection?' he said. 'In which case I don't really know how to take it.'

'And I don't really know what it is.'

'You do know that I really like you?'

'Yeah, I heard all that.'

Then things turned robotic, like they were stepping over lines they'd drawn in front of themselves. He kissed her again but her nerves wouldn't carry the kiss to any meaningful place. When she touched him it was as if his contours had sunken into a flat sea of featureless flesh. She finally let her hands, her face, fall away from him.

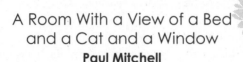

A Room With a View of a Bed and a Cat and a Window
Paul Mitchell

He lay on Mia's bed, a simple one, covered by a white doona with red patterns, ever so light in hue, dotted around its inviting expanse. He lay there, naked in the yellow light seeping from her lamp, and explained to her that several months earlier he had taken an hour to get out of his own bed.

'I don't mean I was lying there, tired, or not wanting to get out of bed or anything. I really, *really* wanted to get out of bed, but I couldn't raise myself up. Not because there was anything physically wrong with me, just that the mental effort was beyond me and I gripped the sheets and pulled at them and couldn't get out. When I finally did, I raised my fist in triumph and said, "Yes, I did it!"'

It was difficult to tell, but he thought she smiled at him. Naked too, she turned onto her side and he saw again her 'ripe' breasts. Why couldn't he find another word for them? Why weren't there more words? he thought, as he put a hand on one of those breasts. Then he remembered there *were* more words. They were called Languages Other Than English.

He must learn one. Maybe more than one. He must, in fact, learn every word for beautiful breasts in the world's languages and say them to her. With the correct pronunciation.

Mia started talking about the Deborah Eisenberg book of short stories she'd been reading. He took his hand from her breast as she explained that Eisenberg had written about the same terrifying ennui he'd experienced, her character having endured it after quitting smoking.

'But I think it was something much bigger,' she said.

They were silent. Outside, a cat, just visible in the streetlight, crawled to the window, meowed, then disappeared. This time Mia definitely smiled.

'He's a crazy cat.'

She got up and he watched her back and bottom, supple in the half-light, blending with the dark cupboards and moving to the window. She knelt at the opening and the cat returned.

'Hello you,' she said. 'Come in.'

'What's its name?'

'Murakami,' she replied, raising the window.

'After the author?'

She feigned a scowl.

'I take it, yes?' he said, but she ignored him. The cat hauled itself inside with a jerky movement that ended in a sprawl at the foot of her bed. It arched its back and sat down, padded in front of itself, then rested its pointy head on its paws.

Mia lay down again, kissed his cheek then nibbled his ear. His cock announced its enjoyment of his ear's saliva bath and he reached down to feel it hardening. He allowed this development, grabbed at her bottom and curled his arm around her side. He kissed her lips, brownish in the light, but red, he knew, full and red. Their heads pulled apart, they looked at the ceiling and he hoped that all this touching signalled the start of sex.

'Did you really *try* to get out of bed?'

He heard his quick breaths and steadied them.

'Yes,' he said. 'I *really* tried. But I couldn't do it.'

'But you must have done it eventually?'

She was right. He was here wasn't he?

'I don't know how,' he answered, scratching at his thigh. 'I suppose I just wore myself down.'

She gave a quick laugh which he mimicked but didn't mean to. Then, also involuntarily, his head shot up. He stared at her.

'Do you think I've got an unbalanced personality?'

She was quiet for a second, her eyebrows fixed.

'How am I supposed to answer that?'

He lay back down, but kept his eyes on her.

'Yeah, I know… Sorry.'

'I mean, OK, I go out on this second date with a guy and he asks me, "Do you think I have an unbalanced personality?"'

She was right. What could she say? To say 'yes' would offend him, unless she managed to perfectly construct a tone of irony or humour. To say 'no' – well, why would she *need* to say no if there wasn't some element of imbalance?

He raised himself from her bed.

'I'm going to go.'

'Why?' she asked, straining the word. 'Stay…'

He lay back down. He got back up. He lay down.

Murakami ran for the window.

The White Day
Paul Morgan

Ursula sat back in her favourite chair by the window of the school staffroom. She was often the only one here at this time of day and it was usually a chance to get on with some marking. But the stack of classwork lay untouched beside the chair, and in front of her, a mug of coffee had gone cold while her hands repeatedly folded and unfolded a letter in her lap. The movement of her fingers was unhurried and almost sensual. At each unfurling she felt an echo of the delight she had experienced on opening the envelope for the first time. The letter was typed and brief, a note really, but this only exaggerated the pairing of her name and that of the Great Writer which topped and tailed it in the flowing cursive of a fountain pen.

She had hardly even expected a reply. Her request had seemed an act almost sufficient in itself, a celebration. Less than a year before, the unthinkable had happened. A great wall had been pulled down, almost, it seemed, with the bare hands of thousands demanding freedom. An empire had fallen. Already there was talk of perhaps ridding the world of nuclear weapons. The times demanded some response from her, it seemed, and one morning she woke knowing with quiet certitude what had to be done. She would suggest to the headmaster an annual prize for the best essay on peace. One of the rich parents could be cajoled into donating a prize each year (a $100 book token would do) and she would send a letter to the Great Writer who had campaigned so long for peace on so many marches, his noble head towering over the untidy crowd and capped by the unmistakable black beret. She would ask to name the prize after him and – if it weren't too inconvenient, and all expenses would be met of course – the school would be honoured if he would present it to the very first winner. The headmaster saw the fervour in her eyes, decided there was no great expense involved (and possibly some good publicity for the school), and agreed she could go ahead. The letter had been written.

Ursula unfolded the letter one more time. She would donate it to the National Library one day, she supposed with a sigh. Once more she read the words.

Dear Miss Morrow
I should be delighted to present the school's inaugural Essay on Peace Prize on September the thirtieth. Please telephone my agent's secretary nearer the date to confirm details (5550 1476). My health is not what it was, but I make a special effort to support this sort of initiative, which is so important for the youth of our country. I look forward to meeting you.
Best wishes
Patrick White

'I look forward to meeting you,' murmured Ursula, lying back in her chair. She smiled as she imagined the headmaster's expression when she told him. And then there were the others. Mrs Caudell, the French teacher, would be so annoyed, she thought pleasantly. After almost twenty years, Ursula was the longest-standing member of staff, and had been senior English teacher for the previous five. Not that she was some dry old Jean Brodie type, she often told herself. She had the one-bedroom apartment in Sydney, bought years ago, and she stayed there most weekends. She was a subscriber to the Sydney Theatre Company, and caught up regularly with friends from student days. There had been a time when she was an especially welcome weekend guest, being able to babysit for one evening. There had been a time when she was the odd one out at dinner parties. Well-meaning friends had tried to pair her up with unattached brothers-in-law or, once, a boring friend-of-a-friend with a red face, huge hands and a property in the Hunter Valley. She had drunk more than her fill that night. But lately when they all met up, she and the others would go bushwalking or treat themselves to a spa together, while their husbands (divorced, dead or merely playing golf) were rarely or never to be seen.

Ursula always looked forward to meeting up with friends on her visits to town, though none of them was especially close, even after all these years. Sometimes she caught herself thinking that every one of them had a particular best friend, but that she was never one of those. They had all marched together at university against the Vietnam War, listening to speeches by student firebrands, union leaders, politicians like Jim Cairns and, of course, her hero, the Great Writer. What ridiculously short skirts we all wore in those days, she thought, though she had to admit she had enjoyed the attention when she started at the school – from older students as well as the other teachers. She remembered once deliberately perching on a desk and crossing her legs, letting the grateful seventeen-year-old boys gaze dry-mouthed at her thigh for a while as they attempted to answer questions about iambic pentameter in *The Taming of the Shrew*. Well, those days were gone, she sighed to herself ruefully, taking a sip of the cold coffee. Nowadays the boys were more likely to give each other puzzled smirks as she threw open a classroom window, muttering, 'Gosh, it's warm in here…'

Ursula's excitement mounted as the weeks went by. The winning essay had been chosen (by a panel, it was agreed, of the headmaster, the history teacher and herself): 'Two Germanys, One Peace'. It argued forcefully that a united Germany would be too powerful, and would endanger Europe again within a generation, that the cause of peace would be served by keeping East Germany as a separate state. Though submitted anonymously, she had picked the author immediately as that Jewish boy, Damian Bloch. A shock of blond hair but, as always, she had been able to tell straightaway before she even knew his name. Well, it was far and away the best essay. And, really, what else could you expect? (She had a vague memory that his grandparents had died in a concentration camp, or was that the Bloom boy three years ago?)

As the date of the presentation approached, Ursula began to have trouble sleeping, lying on one side and then the other, going over endless variations of the big day. She imagined entire conversations between herself and the Great Writer. When she made a witty remark that was all prepared for the right moment, he laughed loudly, throwing back his head, and all the other teachers looked towards them in envy of her. Ursula also had a first edition of his novel, *Voss*, with the original dust jacket design by Sidney Nolan. She had bought it years before at Berkelouw's, and was determined to build up the courage to ask him to sign it, with a special personal message perhaps. She saw herself walking him to the waiting car, slowing her stride to his as he leaned on a walking stick with every other step. How gentlemanly he is, she thought, and how much they had in common.

'I'm so glad I made the effort to come,' she heard the Nobel Prize-winner say, one hand resting on the open car door. 'And it's been such a pleasure meeting you.' He paused to give a warm smile. 'If you're ever near Centennial Park when you're in town, why don't you call by for tea?'

The day of the prize-giving came at last, as all days do. In final preparation, but really for something to occupy her nerves, Ursula went
over the running sheet one more time. She made sure the parking place
near the main door was reserved. She checked that there were enough
chairs in the school hall, that the PA system was working satisfactorily
and that the microphone cable was safely taped down. The staffroom
had been set aside for a modest reception after the speeches. Here a
trestle table had been set up along one wall and covered with a crisp
linen tablecloth. Pyramids of neatly-quartered sandwiches lay trapped
beneath cling wrap until the appointed time and exactly two dozen
cups and saucers sat obediently waiting to be filled. (Cook had put out
the everyday brown earthenware set at first, but Ursula had insisted on
the school's best china, a delicate white porcelain that you could almost
see through.)

It was here in the staffroom that the headmaster found her at last.
He had been looking everywhere and rushed up in a flustered way that
was most unlike him, she thought.

'It's White,' he said. 'They've just announced it on the radio. He
died this morning.'

'Died…?'

'He's been unwell for some time, it seems, but soldiered on. His
heart, I think… but we shall have to cancel the prize-giving of course.
It can't possibly go ahead, even without him. Out of respect. Next term
possibly, and I think you should present it yourself. That would only
be right.'

'He died this morning?' repeated Ursula softly, staring out of the
window.

'Perhaps I should leave you alone for a while. It must be a shock.'

'Died this morning,' she repeated again when she was alone. 'How
could that happen? And he was going to invite me to tea…'

Her fingers tightened around the first edition of *Voss* which she had
carried around all morning with the reverence of a prayer book. He
must have over-exerted himself, reaching for a high shelf or something,
she thought to herself. Really, how careless, how stupidly careless when
he had an important meeting that day. 'You stupid man!' she hissed out
loud. 'You stupid, stupid old man…!' And a wail of anger and despair
came out of her mouth, for which there was no word.

She looked at the book gripped in her hand, and with the obscene
deliberation that anger sometimes takes, she flung it across the room
towards the table. The dust jacket ripped and, pages fanning open, it

landed on the crockery, sending the last row of cups flying through the air. They hit the floor like china bombs, with explosions of fine white dust and chunks and slivers and tiny particles of cup spinning in every direction. The cleaners would be finding fragments beneath bookcases and under the carpet for months to come.

But just before they smashed into the floor, it seemed to Ursula Morrow that the row of exquisite porcelain cups paused for a second above the hard parquet surface – delicate, neat and glowing white, their handles all pointing in the same direction – as though to taunt her with a vision of everything that might have been.

They Shoe Horses, Don't They?
Kalinda Ashton

We sit out on the porch on two wooden rockers that Simon's mother gave us. The sky's swollen and glum. I tell myself when I've creaked back and forward ten times I'll have to say something. Simon is looking into the wind, blinking so slowly it seems mechanical, inhuman.

'It's not like I want the entire suburban nuclear package. I don't want stretch stirrup pants and a bungalow and a matching-shoes-to-handbags wedding.'

Simon pats me on the hand. 'Stretch stirrups I'll negotiate on. Viva la eighties.'

I take a breath in. Exhale. 'I think I'd like to have a baby.'

'What for? All they do is shit and vomit and sleep.'

'They don't,' I say. 'They cry too. And scream.' Simon doesn't want to have children. He's afraid they'll be anxious and terrified of life. He's begun to say they don't fit into his life plan. He's never had a life plan before. His desire not to have children is giving him a future.

I dream that I am pregnant. My stomach bulges and clothes don't fit well but I walk around the city wrapped in my own smug assurance. I'm warm and protected. It's not until I wake that I realise I was imagining *myself* enclosed and safe, somehow cordoned off from the world at large and in retreat. I'm not dreaming about having a baby, I'm dreaming about being one.

I'm in the bathroom at the mirror, perturbed by the faint lines of mould growing on our walls in the winter damp. Soon, I think. I will do something about this. I rub tinted moisturiser into my face. My eyes look peculiar: the eyelids stretch and the skin below distends oddly as if my face is too big for my eyes. I'm aware that the fashion is to have things the other way around. In modern commercial novels or interviews with pop stars, women are described as having eyes too large for their faces but never faces that take over their eyes, eyes disappearing amongst flat, droopy skin.

I'm wearing my red glass beads, that black dress the cost of which could have fed a family in the Third World for a week, my boots with heels, lipstick. I comb my hair, spray on perfume. He comes in to collect his towel. I wait for him to say, 'You look nice' or 'All dressed up and somewhere to go?' but he doesn't. He potters about filling a Thermos of hot water to take to his desk and chats to me from the other room. I think about performing the little routine I enact when I've had my hair cut – a small dance on the spot and '*Notice* something? Something different?' but I can't be bothered.

By the time the Turkish coffee arrives we've eaten couscous with roasted eggplant and tomato paste, chickpea salad fragrant with lemongrass and Moroccan spices, and some dish with toasted corn chips buried in rich yoghurt that I carefully hoard at my end of the table, gobbling with the kind of urgency that once caused by brother to spit on the meal with the most roast potatoes when we were kids. Our friends line the table, mostly couples, two by two. I'm sitting next to a friend's son, who is inordinately well behaved. He doesn't interrupt or whinge but plays quietly and entertains himself. The friend is reflective and composed, a careful person. I have told my boyfriend that I think if I had a child it would be bossy and infectious, not respectful and calm. It will shriek, 'Look at me' and demand to be entertained. My nephew is only seven and has already learned to adopt a sarcastic drawl. '*Really? I didn't know that. How interesting.*' Seven-year-olds should not be droll, even when being lectured on the problems of capitalism, one of my sister's favoured topics.

The room is crowded, painted in warm orange, and has a cabinet containing a glass display of tagines and tureens, ceramic, with glowing shiny finishes and sensual curves. We are served by a young woman wearing a hijab. The waitresses are dark-eyed and voluptuous and they grin at each other as they work, flashing smiles over their shoulders as they carry out trays and dishes. I gulp down my coffee and yawn. I've been too greedy and the grounds are not wet enough to make any patterns at all, except for the dried sludge in the bottom of the cup pattern that doesn't tell me anything I didn't already know.

I drink another cup. 'What do you see? Can you see a dog?' I ask Chris, tall and pale, who assumes a knowledge of such things. I swill the grounds and tip the excess liquid onto a napkin.

She squints. 'I see a star pattern.'

'A dog,' I say firmly. My boyfriend groans. 'He doesn't want a dog because he thinks first it's a dog then a baby,' I tell the table. He's drifting.

At the other end of the table, Tony and his boyfriend pretend to see a baby in their coffee grounds. I've known Tony more than half my life. His new boyfriend is very pretty, earnest about horoscopes, employed in advertising. He litters us all with compliments until I begin to detect an ironic echo in his approval of my hair and shoes.

My boyfriend looks at my cup. 'Yeah, I see a dog with a baby riding in on its back,' he prophesies. I laugh but I am tempted to see in his cup a lonely life brought to an end by a sudden death in a small flat no one visits, in which he ends up getting his face eaten by the cats he keeps. This is the threat that single women try to keep at bay. Why shouldn't he fear it in his future? Except he wouldn't have the cats. Possibly not even the flat. And he won't let us read his coffee grounds.

He always has four almonds with his muesli at breakfast. Each and every time exactly four. I love him. He has a jumper that is so old I can't pat him on the shoulder when he wears it. The wool has so disintegrated it has unravelled and there's a huge hole up the arm and over the shoulder. If I touch him when he wears it, he fears I'll be the final trigger for its collapse into jumper Armageddon.

He's too scared to wash this jumper in case it falls apart. I say when things get like that they ought to be thrown out. He has another jumper that is knitted pale salmon with a rollneck.

He goes to bed very early and gets up early. We eat well and don't watch much TV. I say we live the life of retirees. There have been times when we have gone to sleep when I know for a fact my friend's two-year-old daughter is still awake.

He puns without mercy and this even when we are arguing. Though I've told him it makes me feel as if I am living with a seventeen-year-old, even this produces more lame humour. 'Half your luck,' he says.

He has had one shining success with his jokes. We were talking about horses, and an old friend said she didn't know what a farrier was. 'They shoe horses, don't they?' Simon asked. I hold this up as a beacon of light, a standard of pun all others should aspire to.

I have noticed how intractable my thoughts about children are even though my good friends think that I am a pushover and malleable.

Tricia corrects me, 'Just very suggestible,' she suggests. They say this because I am prone to taking advice.

Also because once, years ago, I went through my wardrobe, putting clothes in piles to give to the Op Shop, to repair or to keep. My friends frowned and shook their heads at nearly every item. They told me that the cut was weird, or that it didn't fit properly, or that the dress was horrendous, or that the eighties were over. When I became anxious and downtrodden they admitted they'd done it on purpose just to see what I would do. There was nothing wrong with most of the clothing – they'd just dared each other to see how long they could keep it up. The heap of clothes to throw out was very large.

Yet I come from a long line of bossy people. The word that isn't said is *gullible*. What sort of prospects are there for a gullible, assertive, suggestible, bossy person? Could I make a career out of this unusual combination of attributes? PR? Counselling? Journalism? No. I need a bustling, organising sort of role where mindless good faith isn't a drawback. I could run school fetes or play the Julia Roberts character in a stage version of *Pretty Woman*, and a B-grade copy of Richard Gere would climb up my balcony with roses and offer me the world.

My art teacher doesn't think I am suggestible. He is certain that I am stubborn but this is meant as praise. He leans in close to whatever I'm making and says, 'You'll get there. You won't give up. Too stubborn.' At least I think it's praise. It might mean that I should be doing new work; that I cling like a limpet to the styles and forms I know.

I come to my evening class from a long talk with Simon and think I want to begin again. I'd like to be the sort of person who would shred the old collages I'd spent months making and toss them out the window. But we're on the ground floor and it's winter so I just take them down and place them against the wall in the studio that's being renovated. I start to compile fabrics and textures. I glue a snip of patterned paper napkin onto glass. I've cut out pieces from the table cloth, the candy-striped small dress my friend Julie's daughter's grown out of. I paste the teeth from a comb.

My art teacher frowns. 'That's very... domestic.' He chews on his lip. I show him some sketches where the pastiche forms the outline of a woman from a fifties horror film. My teacher pauses. 'I'm sensing ambivalence about the responsibilities thrust on women. The realm of the home as the site of anxiety.'

Leo, the man who works next to me, hovers about, muttering in a vexed way. I can't figure out whether he's summoned up the accent to

suit his notions of himself as an artist or if it's the other way around.
'You have children?'

I shake my head.

'Then perhaps you want?' The accent's not French or German or
Italian – just a weird, off-key imitation of soulful characters in a late
night SBS movie.

'I don't want a baby,' I announce. But I do.

'It is the clock of the body, as they say.'

I paint a red square onto the glass.

'Goes tek tek tek.'

I would like to bite him hard. I think about sinking my teeth into
his forearm and I am laughing then weeping a little. Chris says that
she has been so vulnerable at times that she's cried at the slow motion
replays of athletes in the final mile of the marathon on Commonwealth
Games re-runs. I told myself I was preserving some dignity by only allowing myself to sob helplessly in front of the TV to the soft unravelling of
angst-ridden marriages on quality HBO productions with good reviews.

Turning back to the layers of fabric, I know what I need to complete
the picture. A piece of the salmon jumper.

At home my boyfriend is holding our tablecloth, stretched out
where the pieces of fabric are missing. 'Please explain,' he Hansons.

'It's the new me.' I sweep past him.

He calls after me. 'Why does the new you so resemble a moth on
steroids?'

On Tuesday I stroke him in bed. I press closer and kiss him. 'Do you
know that sometimes when you're doing that you accidentally close off
my nostrils and I can't breathe?' he asks. I sigh and roll over. He spoons
me. 'What is it?'

'I want sex,' I say.

'You are so mysterious and enigmatic,' he says as he gently turns me
back towards him.

At the end of the week I walk home from work in the rain. My coat gets
soaked and begins to give off that damp-wool scent of school locker
rooms and musty blankets at the back of the cupboard.

When I get home I find I don't want to ramble up and push open
the gate, unlock the door and dump my bag in the hall, toss wet clothes
and hair bands in my wake as I head for the shower. So I stand in the
downpour and lick the rain on my face. I'm thirty-five. I've told Tricia

that my life is settling into its own shape. 'Like being halfway through a novel. There might be a redemptive ending or a horrific surprise but some parameters have already made themselves at home, some conventions can't be reversed. A lean, French literary tragedy won't become a fantasy novel at this point. If it's chick lit, the woman won't spurn her offer of marriage for exploring the jungles of Borneo.'

Tricia had frowned, crinkled up her face. 'Couldn't you always... you could read another book.'

I have been with Simon since I was just on the wrong side of twenty-five. Now I'm on the wrong side of thirty (but perhaps the right side of forty?) Our miserable neighbours are playing a Radiohead CD loudly in the car as they pash in the front seat. They mash their faces together earnestly to the wails of longing and despair. It's easier to cry in the rain, it seems almost polite, blending in, like walking in the same direction as a crowd leaving a train station.

Simon stands in the doorway to our house, one elbow propped against the frame. We both wait.

His Other Master's Voice
David Astle

I'm standing in the playground with Abo down the other end. The rest of 3W make a tunnel between us, waiting for the show I promised, a little bit of loyalty to prove I wasn't lying.

That off-lemon smell is Miss Wakelin standing next to me. She opens her Nokia and says, 'Are you ready?'

I look down the tunnel at Abo and can't really give an answer. How can I? Abo stares back, his tongue hanging out, waiting for me to speak.

My dog is half kelpie, half German shorthair, and loyal as they come. You fill a bowl with chicken scraps and he won't go near it unless you say, *Eat Abo.*

Oppa, my granddad, called it respect, what every dog should have and then some. Oppa was Abo's first master, the bloke to name him and raise him and teach him what he knows. Though right now, all my mates in a line, I wish I could change that. See the dog down the other end as a mutt and not the history he comes with.

'Abo the name is wrong,' says Mum. Like smoking cigarettes or shooting parrots, she says. Oppa did both. He'd sit on the veranda with a Winchester repeater, smoking, while he waited for the parrots to lob. When the birds came he took his time aiming then bang, a puff of feathers, a dead lump dropping in the crop. Oppa would lean his gun on the rail and say, 'Fetch Abo'.

Mum grew up in Myrtleford too. The river was bigger when she was younger. Back then, when smoking wasn't bad for you, the whole valley was filled with tobacco, just like Oppa's place, green as far as the eye could see. At night when rain fell the whole town sounded like an umbrella.

My first memory of Oppa's farm is that scratchy wool-feel of Dad's arm still holding me on the back of the tractor. We packed the crop into bundles, lying the leaves crisscross in the trailer. We drove the load to the shed and hung them like washing on the drying poles.

Myrtleford was part of every Christmas. Me and Dad and Oppa would jam rocks into wombat holes and fix up fences. We put sheep guts into pantyhose to catch yabbies in the dam. His dog back then was Bingo, a nutcase kelpie who'd end up being Abo's mum. Don't ask me who the Dad was.

Oppa's real name was Ernst but no one called him that. He came from Holland on a ship when he was little. He didn't go to school. He learnt everything from his parents and the farm was all he knew, said Mum. But Oppa was smart. The snake skins and the fossils along his veranda were a home-made museum. He knew about medicine as well, like the time Tegan fell in a ditch and Oppa used his grappa to clean up her knee.

Tegan's my sister. She's twelve. The week Oppa had his accident she got the front seat and I got the back to spread out my X-Men and Justice League Unlimited. Tegan listens to music on her iPod shuffle and I don't like talking to her anyway. Mum drove quiet most of the trip, only talking when we were getting in range.

Our main job was saying hello and making Oppa soups until we drove to the farm the next weekend. My granddad had poisonous blood thanks to a generator falling on his foot. His toes turned black. His leg got septic. His knee went blue. The doctor said he had to stay in bed until he could walk. No matter what part of the house you went all you could smell was old singlets.

Mum filled a bowl with warm water. She put it down near Oppa's head and straight away the language came flying her way.

'Do I look like a vegetable?' asked Oppa. 'Last time you did my face I bled like a fucking river.'

Mum tested the razor on her own skin. She said the day was lovely, why don't we kids take the chance to explore. 'Pick me a flower,' she said to Tegan. To me she said, 'Find El Dorado'.

I took a shortcut through the vegie patch where Abo was dozing. I bent to pat him and he scrunched his body, shivering like I'd come to belt him. Just so he'd know we were mates, I scratched his belly and flopped his ears and dragged my nails across his scalp and he was fine after that. We spent the day together.

Abo's black from snout to tail. I think he was two back then, two-and-a-half. He didn't have papers or any particular birthday. He raced around my legs, a kid in human years, busting to show me the farm like I'd never set foot in the place.

We picked out lemons as hand grenades and blew up the windmill. We hunted lizards. I'd need the plank to cross the irrigation ditch but

Abo could jump clean over. He knew the hidden ways through the leaves. He'd bolt ahead, just flashes of black in the crop, then circle back around to check I was following. Deep down he knew I was the next master like that's a superpower dogs have.

Obviously, if you want to find El Dorado you fly to Peru or follow the Amazon to the place where it starts. I know about mysteries like monsters and aliens and the various lost cities. Did you know the Sulphur Queen went sailing into the Bermuda Triangle with thirty-five crew and was never seen again? I told this to Abo inside the tobacco, our own private jungle, and I swear he was listening.

'Come on Ben,' says Miss Wakelin. 'We don't have forever.'

'I'm waiting for the right moment,' I tell her.

She looks through her Nokia. 'This is it.'

I look dead ahead. Sitting in the key of the basketball court, not thirty metres away, Abo is 110 per cent focus. My dog is a spring waiting for his master's voice.

'Miaow,' says Duleep, and most kids laugh. Normally I'd laugh too but my guts are a Slurpee machine and I wish Pet Week was never invented.

On Monday, when Gary used his lunchbox to transport his guinea pig, I thought I was safe. Noah had a mouse and Mia had a schnauzer, which left a puddle in the Discovery Corner. Li Nah comes from Vietnam but her cat comes from Egypt and has no hair. Miss Wakelin let us touch him and it felt like warm potato.

That was Thursday, the second-last day. 'Any more pets?' asked Miss Wakelin, doing the roster. And Duleep pointed to me.

'Ben has a dog,' he said.

Duleep is easily my best human friend. We play together heaps. He knows Longshot and Dazzle and all the other obscure X-Men. We're both into spy stuff and taking turns destroying the cities we build with Lego. Duleep can count to fifty in Tamil and turn his elbow inside-out. We don't have many secrets left to trade. He even knows the story of where my Dad went.

'He's sleeping with another woman,' I told him.

'Sleeping?'

'You know,' I said, 'like sex. She lives in Canterbury.'

'Hot sex?' asked Duleep, and we couldn't stop laughing.

Duleep's got an older brother called Ranil who uses the net for homework but we can't except for Club Penguin where you make seaweed pizzas because we're nine.

Duleep eats weird stuff too. You walk into his house and you're entering another kingdom, the kitchen smells, the cushion covers, the fluoro way his Mum dresses. One night she made a thing called a stringhopper, which sounds like a bug but looked like a noodle and tasted like glue. But I ate it.

Apart from our skins you'd say we're brothers, the way we speak, how I start a sentence and there's Duleep filling in the end. We know each other's bike locks, their combinations, and what dream jobs we want. (I'm going to be a polar explorer and Duleep will be an X-Box tester.) Duleep's allergic to bees and I can't stand sultanas. His skin is the colour of Nutella and when he laughs his teeth are enormous.

On spare weekends, when Mum isn't driving me to Myrtleford, or me and Tegan aren't spending time with Dad, I'd be sleeping at Duleep's house or he'd be over at mine. By sleeping I mean sleeping – and talking. After lights out we'd blab till dawn. I'd prop my pillow the perfect height to watch those giant teeth talking in the dark as if the night itself was chatting away. Even silent we knew what the other one was thinking. Like the crush he's got on Hazel Medhurst who owns a corella, and he knows I like being chosen in Amy Bartoli's team but so what? That's no big deal. It doesn't mean I want to marry her.

Duleep knows Tegan is into bangles and he knows about my dog. Obviously. Why else am I here, the last day of Pet Week, wishing I was on the moon? He knows about Oppa but not the whole story. Same goes for Miss Wakelin and the rest of 3W.

A Monday in Myrtleford, we have the graveyard to ourselves. The priest came from a town starting with B and was called Ernst, Ernest, making us wonder who was in the box. Mum didn't cry. She breathed aloud instead. Dad stood in hugging distance, in case Mum wanted holding, but she didn't want a bar of it.

If I can't explore Antarctica I want to drive a bobcat M400. 'Check out the cylinders on that baby,' said Dad. We hung around the gate to watch the driver fill the hole.

'You been keeping OK?' he asked, heading back to the farm.

I nodded.

'That tie makes you look older.'

'I am older.'

Felicia was there. She complained about her heels sinking into the ground. My stepmum I guess, Felicia has her hair pulled back like she wants her face to seem more important. Every time I see her freckles I want a texta to see what picture I could draw on her skin. The rest of the crowd were farmers, not too many, nowhere near the size of 3W.

'Oppa was a piece of living history,' said Alan, a milk truck driver, speaking on the veranda after the sausages. Then Mum stood up, saying Oppa was ten times larger than life. But both things sounded wrong to me. My granddad was dead for starters. And if life was smaller, how come life won?

Tegan and me had jobs to do. We picked up cups and put them in the sink. We collected plates and napkins. We moved around the yard giving out tobacco in special-made pouches and tried making small talk, which was murder. I wore a tux jacket and Tegan wore a black floppy hat. 'You look like a scarecrow,' I said, and she put me in a head-lock until I took it back. Tegan's strong. She does gymnastics.

'Any projects?' asked Felicia.

'Sorry,' I said.

'At school,' she yelled. 'You doing anything?'

'Tornadoes,' I said.

'Fascinating.'

'Except Australia gets cyclones which spin the other way.'

'I never knew that.'

'You need two forces to crank them up,' I shouted. 'When the cold and the hot meet together they make like a spiral.'

We had to shout thanks to Abo. He was tied to the lemon tree and pulled the rope full-stretch, barking or whining or digging little holes as if his boss might pop out.

I stole a sausage from the table and threw it on the grass but Abo was way too schizo to be hungry. He rolled on his back and showed me his belly. Maybe the quiet made everyone look our way. Before too long, me and Abo were stars of the funeral, me rubbing his guts and Abo almost purring at the feel of it. I heard one bloke say to Mum, 'There's that problem solved'.

Tegan wasn't fussed, dog or no dog. Mum said Abo was a piece of continuity, whatever that meant. Dad said adoption was good in theory but his new house had a Zen garden. 'Not ideal for animals,' he added.

Mum collected plates. 'For dogshit you mean.'

The farm was empty. The crowds had gone. Now the place was family, including Felicia the Geisha as Mum says behind her back, and Abo in the yard.

'As chief caregiver,' said Mum, 'I get the casting vote.'

'Suit yourself,' said Dad. 'We're making tracks.'

'The kids should have the dog,' said Felicia. 'To help with the processing.'

'Processing?' Mum laughed. 'I think you're getting confused with tobacco.'

'What about the fossils?' said Tegan. 'Who's getting them?'

Abo and me shared the backseat the whole way down the highway, his skull on my lap, his breath kind of ticklish on my legs. The only time he got rowdy was a sheep truck in Euroa until I said, 'Quiet Abo.' And sure enough he quit.

'We'll need to change the name,' Mum said.

'What's wrong with it?'

'Times have changed,' she said, looking in the mirror.

'Changed into what?'

Mum focused on the road for a while as if I was the one talking nonsense. She said, 'Thankfully your generation is putting the past behind it.'

I looked to Tegan in case she got what I was missing but my sister was lost in *The Best of Pink*. I had no choice but to ask Mum about the so-called problem.

'Remember the girl in the superhero costume?' she said. 'What was her name? Cathy Freeman. She ran like the wind. Another term you hear is black Australians.'

'Is Duleep Abo?' I wanted to know. 'Cause if he is then he's not that fast.'

Mum tried to cover a laugh. I could see her shoulders shaking and the wheel flinch a little. 'He's from Sri Lanka,' she said in the end. 'That blob beneath India.'

'Do we know any Abos?'

'Aborigines, Ben. And no.'

'So what's the problem then?'

'It's the impact,' she said. 'People hear the word and it sends them a message.'

'What message?'

'Jesus, little man. Why do I feel like a dog chasing its tail?'

'You started it.'

'If I didn't,' she said, 'then your granddad did.'

Whatever his name, my dog loved chasing planes across the sky. He didn't like the leash but that was part of life, I told him. He lay on the deck and chewed his favourite towel to a pulp. Because I fed him and threw the ball and groomed him and picked up his business in the garden I was like his master and that's the way we did things.

After the sheep truck, the only other time Abo went ballistic was hearing the front gate squeak. Mum called it instinct. 'A dog needs to protect its ground even if that ground has changed,' she said.

The first squeak belonged to Duleep. He came the Tuesday after Oppa carrying a kilo of mango chutney. 'To cheer you up,' he reckoned.

Duleep saw Abo and broke out in a grin. 'What's his name?' he asked. And I felt this sort of freeze-beam inside me, like the gamma ray in Dr Doom. If Abo was a name we'd buried at the farm then what was the sequel? Me and Mum never worked it out. My dog was a spy with his alias missing.

'Arrow,' I said, and Duleep said, 'Cool.'

'Well,' said Mum. 'That's the name we're stuck with now.'

Talk went dead for half a second and I knew something big just landed. Two, maybe three – I could count on one hand the times I'd lied to Duleep and even then he usually picked it. That was his power. 'Divine,' said Mum, licking her finger. 'How does your Mum do it?'

We went outside. Duleep got on his haunches to call this make-believe Arrow but my pet didn't move. In fact his hackles went up like triggers and two fangs jutted out. 'Car sick,' I said. 'He misses the river.' But the problem didn't go away.

Abo's heart was set on being Abo and no amount of second choices would change that fact. I took him to the oval when Duleep wasn't round and tested out Zorro, or Hoover, or Rocket, even Arrow, to see what name might fix the situation but nothing else did the trick.

I ordered him to stay – without a name – and he'd wander off like I was talking to a brick wall. 'Sit,' I said, using his real name – *Sit Abo* – telling him to wait until I walked backwards to see if the command kicked in.

Under Abo he'd wait. But when I tried the other names – telling him to come by random stuff – Abo got creepy. He'd sink in the grass in that classic kelpie style, not knowing if he was part of my game or being ignored. Now and then he'd shiver like that time at Oppa's farm as if I might walk back and whack him round the ears but I never did. Even if his first boss had a lousy temper, I was different. What we needed, me and Abo, was a lie we could settle on.

Down at the oval, Duleep on his bike and Abo chasing the ball, I had to whisper his name in case the truth leaked out. Or skip the name altogether with Duleep up close.

Not that it mattered, I told myself. Big deal if Duleep got wind of the real name, I thought. Probably Abo meant as much to him as it did to me, driving home in the car, another way of saying nothing, but that chance had gone and my dog meantime was busting to run.

I threw the ball with the flinger. 'Fetch, Arrow,' I said, and Abo would stutter instead of race away. He'd slow, then stop, and look back over his shoulder as if to say, Me? He gave up the chase to face me square-on, his head cocked and his brow this fuzzy kind of galvo. Fetch what? he asked. Go where? Who's Arrow?

'Bit slow,' said Duleep. 'For an arrow I mean.'

'He's learning,' I said.

'I thought you said he was smart.'

'My voice sounds different from my granddad is all. He's taking his time adjusting.'

Duleep laughed. 'He's taking your Mickey you mean.'

Every night I hated Tegan and her pissy fossils. I wish they were mine to look after instead of something living with big brown eyes and a pea-sized brain. Being ancient, the little fish seemed a million miles from Oppa. With Tegan at netball I'd sneak into her room to look at the tiny skeletons, how they swam left to right inside the rock, moving forever in the one direction no matter what name you called them.

A week went past. Then a few more, getting to the night before my Pet Week test. I felt like a prisoner lying in my bed. When Dad was still home he stuck Jupiter and Venus and every other planet on my ceiling. The galaxy glowed above my head, watching me twist in the sheets. I prayed for flu. A mean case of laryngitis. Or better yet a meteor the size of a Volkswagen to land on my school and change the afternoon's schedule.

I got out of bed when the house was dark, looking to borrow Tegan's iPod in case music could wash the problem away, and that's when I saw a firefly dancing on the deck.

If not a fly then a min min light, those alien reflections you get in the outback, but it was neither. Mum sat alone on the barbecue chair, smoking a cigarette.

I know Mum pretty well and she doesn't smoke full stop, not since I've been around. Or not so you'd notice anyway. Back in the old days, when smoking was the fashion, she said she tried a few. Growing up with Oppa, surrounded by tobacco, I guess smoking was just what people did. In black and white movies, the type Mum loves to watch on weekends, people spend the whole time puffing away. And then there was the cigarette butt Tegan found in the basket fern near the back door. There one day, gone the next. (Tegan wants to do CSI.)

She said the week after Dad left, January 12, a Sunday night, just after lights-out, the butts started breeding like rabbits.

'Hi Mum.'

'Jesus, little man, you scared me half to death.'

'That smells like Oppa's stuff.'

'It is.'

The timber was cool on my feet. I noticed a funeral pouch sitting in her lap, and the red spark-gun from the oven there too. Standing up close, tasting the smoke in the air, I suddenly realised Abo lay between us, dark and long like a mountain ridge across the deck.

'I can't sleep,' I told her.

'Aren't we the pair?'

Her arm snaked around me. It pulled me closer and I didn't mind that night. The smoke took me back to the farm, which also helped. The garden was full of shapes. We clung together like a statues game seeing who'd be the first to move.

'Pet Week,' said Mum, sounding like a question, and I nodded.

She slapped the chair's arm where I perched on the wood. For a time I watched the fire breathe. I liked the idea of us three in the open – no Tegan, no stepmum – even if I couldn't explain what was bugging me.

To put the problem in a word it was 'loyaler', which sounds made-up, not a word you'd say out loud, not with anybody listening. Can you be loyaler to a dog versus your family, versus your best mate ever? Even if 3W could laugh at Abo, the name, I knew it lay at the bottom of everything.

Unsure where to start I said nothing. Mum rested her spare arm on my sleeve and read my mind like Duleep used to.

The night was peaceful under the real planets. Mum tapped her ash through the cracks in the deck, and after a while, wetting her fingers, she snuffed out the spark with a pinch. 'I'm tempted to roll a freshie.'

'Pretend I'm invisible,' I said.

'Like Abo,' she said. 'Black as night.'

'Yeah,' I laughed, not really sure why.

'So long as I know you're both in reach.'

For some weird reason the picture in my head was Hazel Medhurst's corella. I said nothing to Mum but that was the image I kept seeing, this pinky-white bird that Hazel let loose on Tuesday, the second round of Pet Week, opening the cage and letting her corella fly around the school.

'Leroy's got a built-in radar,' Hazel told us, not worried a bit. 'Let him go and he never strays too far. You watch.'

We all stood staring at the parrot shape bobbing on top of the music hall. Hazel zinged her nails against the bars and Leroy dropped like an angel, screaming its song straight back to the perch. All of us cheered like we'd seen a magic trick but Miss Wakelin said it was Mother Nature. 'Once a place feels right,' she said, 'there is shelter and nourishment, then that's where an animal will call its home.'

'He's good to go,' says Miss Wakelin. 'I promise you.'

'Must be stage fright,' I said.

'His or yours?'

My big mistake was promising anything. Back in the classroom, talking the talk, as Tegan would say, I said Arrow was loyal and you can't rewind words once they leave your mouth. 'Arrow will come when I say Come,' I said. 'Just like he's done a thousand times before, you watch. Not running but slow, the only way he knows.'

Except Arrow's name is Abo and miracles like that don't happen in 3W, not with my dog's breeding, not the way he understands the world. I want to blame my granddad's blood, how the poison in his system put this problem at my feet, but the chance has gone, if the chance was ever there. I want to clear my throat and say how loyalty is a two-way street, like Mum put things last night, but every face along the line is begging for action.

Duleep starts a slomo handclap and Noah joins in. Soon 3W is clapping in sync, daring the demo to start. I wait for Miss Wakelin to order shoosh but she's getting tired waiting too. Everyone is. Even Abo.

I wave and act like the pause is part of the show. Right now, if I could be an X-Man I'd be Storm in the DC version. Open my arms and start a blizzard, all of us needing to scatter and forget whatever loyalty was coming our way.

But I'm not Storm. My name is Ben. Of all the heroes inside me I carry a bloke called Mr Vogelaar, alias Oppa. His trace is the smoke that stank my clothes when we shared a veranda, waiting for the parrots to lob.

The clapping is dying out. I look down the court and see a mutt not thirty metres off, lurching in the key, staring me down, spoiling for the word that lies ready in my mouth. But my tongue is cotton and I've got no air.

At least my teacher's phone is good for pictures not sound, I'm thinking. Not that Abo could care. He'll bide his time all day. So maybe if I whisper his name, like that Chinese game we play at camp, soft enough for super-hearing only, giving the class what I promised but minus any damage. In weeks to come the Pet Week scrapbook will show a black dog marching to his owner. *Ben and his kelpie cross*, says the caption, and nobody my age will tell you anything different.

Instead I crouch and try to whistle. Abo's ears prick up. I drop to eye level and yell what never worked in the park. 'Come boy,' I say. 'Come on Arrow.' But Abo doesn't budge. He's not made that way. His only move is a slow half-tilt of his chest as if to will us closer together but not until I say the truth out loud.

'Arrow, please.' But my dog is a rock. A rock who grinds me down and in the end I walk to him, loyaler than any master could wish for, taking my time like this is how I planned things from the start. I'm a man who's pacing a map and I hear every step scrape across the asphalt. Every eye is watching me until slowly the tunnel breaks apart. But Abo still waits. He stays like he was told, swelling to his height as I get nearer. One by one the class goes separate ways and Miss Wakelin shuts her Nokia.

A Short Story
Ryan O'Neill

This story is 2,034 words long. Most of it is written in the past tense, and in the first person. It is a true story, but the direct speech is approximate. I've read too many books where the writer claims to remember every word that happened seventy years ago.

There are two main characters in this story. Firstly, there is myself, the unreliable narrator. And then there is James Gibbon. On a character questionnaire he would be described as:

1. Scottish.
2. 42 years old.
3. Atheist.
4. English lecturer at the University of Newcastle.
5. Stoutish, with greying brown hair and a slight squint (which he claimed was from eight years of working in a bank and a lifetime's suspicion of counterfeit banknotes, so that it seemed he was straining after the watermark in the world).
6. Unmarried.
7. Wry, melancholy, intelligent.

It was James who taught me that a good short story should have no more than three main characters. He also taught me that all stories follow this structure:

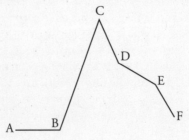

We are at point A. The story is just beginning.

A

I was literally run off my feet. It was a muggy day, but hot only because it was hot. The weather was not symbolic of anything. And though I had dreamed vivid dreams the night before, they were not symbolic of anything either, as they always seem to be in stories. I caught the bus to the university. On the bus I read Faulkner, and looking out the window I found myself comparing everything to everything, gutting every metaphor and simile. My thoughts were incomplete and mixed-up, like a book's burst appendix. (James once crossed out these last two sentences from an old story of mine with a red pen. If you don't like them, you can do the same.)

I was late for the seminar on 'The Short Story', which took place in James Gibbon's dim and stuffy office on the university campus. I remember that you always had to blink away the world when you went in. On the walls there were unframed photographs of Defoe, Dos Passos and Dickens, and a large map of the world in which Australia had almost faded with the sunshine. There were also several (at least five and no more than twelve) rough wooden bookshelves in the room, containing a hundred or so short story collections. The walls were either green or yellow or red. (Proust would be ashamed of me, I know.)

On top of the bookshelf under the window was an issue of *Meanjin* from 1979, which contained James Gibbon's only published story, 'The Sleep in Her Eyes'. I was in the middle of writing an essay contrasting it favourably with Chekhov's 'Lady with Lapdog'. There were several of us waiting for the tutor to arrive. I suppose I should describe them, but in truth these characters are entirely peripheral. I sat by the window and watched out for him. James Gibbon was a large man and proud, but with something beaten down inside of him, and sad and ridiculous in his pride, like a circus bear. He walked everywhere slowly. He had trained his feet to follow iambic pentameter (so he said) in order that he might think in blank verse. He wore clothes that said nothing about his character, and today his right arm was in a cast. When he came into the classroom he told us how he had slipped on a paperback Patrick White he had been reading the night before and fallen heavily to the floor, breaking his writing arm.

'I seem doomed to be a metaphor for Australian literature,' he said.

I volunteered to write his notes on the board for him. He spoke for twenty minutes about Carver and Flaubert, and if someone whispered he would cry out, 'Will you please be quiet please?' He swore often, and because of his Glaswegian accent, even when he did not swear, it seemed like he had. For the last half of the class he asked us questions.

'And you, Molly, how does Salinger's style compare to Maugham's?' he asked me. He called me Molly Bloom for the habit I have of answering any question two or three times, 'Yes, yes, yes.' The class discussed Nin's *Delta of Venus*, and he told us that when he was a boy in Scotland he had been too poor and frightened to buy pornography so he had written his own. He made us laugh. At the end of every seminar I would ask him about his book of short stories. He had been finishing it for ten years. I would ask if I could read it, and he would always say no, for I was the kind of woman who read *Finnegans Wake* just to say she had read *Finnegans Wake*.

'But I haven't read it,' I protested.

'You will, Molly. Probably twice, to look at you.'

We all of us signed his cast. I waited until the others had left, then I wrote 'Molly' and my phone number.

B

James called me two nights later and we went out for dinner. When we sat down in the restaurant, I noticed that my message on the cast had been doodled into nonsense. James drank a lot of wine and stammered odd words.

'Forgive me. I've been speaking English all day. It's a difficult language,' he said. He told me how much he enjoyed watching me read in class, and that he had noted that my face changed on coming upon certain words. Adjectives raised my right eyebrow, he was sure, and a plot twist had me stroke my cheek with my knuckles. He said that he liked to imagine sitting before me, watching my face as I read Thackeray or Tolstoy, so that he could read the novels again through me, and they would be new and beautiful to him once more.

'More' is the 1015th word of the story. We have reached the middle. According to the graph, there should be a climax now.

C

Reader, I fucked him.

D

Often after that first time, we would lie in bed and he would tell me all the sad things that had happened to him in his life, and I would cry, though I hadn't wept non-fiction tears since I was a child. He read all my stories and criticised them. He told me that I aspired to the elegant style of a traveller in an African train writing in her journal, but instead resembled a boarding school girl crying on headed notepaper. He told me I should put my stories away in a drawer for a year and then return to them, and then I would know if they were worth keeping. James abhorred incorrect punctuation.

'There is a special providence in the fall of a full stop,' he would say. He read Borges and Updike to me. When I asked him questions about the women before me he sat in a calm, neutral posture and said nothing. He easily defeated the knowledge of body language I had acquired from psychology textbooks. On my birthday, he gave me his only copy of the *Meanjin* with his story in it, and dedicated it, 'For Molly, with love and squalor'. In April his cast came off, and I told him I was falling in love with him. But he wouldn't answer me.

'Tell me! Do you love me?'

He only smiled.

'Don't be so cruel,' I said.

'April is the cruellest month,' he muttered, and kissed me. He was always restless. Every time he thought of a new thought, he ran to a different place.

E

And then one morning, I found his wedding ring, a piece of plot that had rolled under the bed. All those months and I had never known he was married. I consoled myself; neither had Jane Eyre. Still, I was furious. James had turned me into a cliché. (Later I discovered it was his wife that had broken his arm, in a fight over his last affair. I saw her once, shopping in the supermarket. There is a word for her between cunning and cup in *The Macquarie Dictionary*.)

That same afternoon I went to a drama lecture, 'Feminism and *Hedda Gabler*'. I took a lot of notes, and thought about what I should do. When I saw James again, I begged him to let me see his unfinished book. He said that it was close to completion, and was apprehensive about lending it. There was only one copy, handwritten and hand-corrected on several yellow legal notepads with a fountain pen that had (he maintained) once belonged to Henry Lawson. He reminded me what had happened to the first draft of Carlyle's *French Revolution*. But I pleaded with him until eventually he agreed to let me borrow his book for one night, if I promised to be truthful about his female characters.

'I can't write women,' he said. 'I don't understand them well enough.'

'Women are meant to be loved, not understood,' I said.

He brought the manuscript to me at 7:00 on a Friday evening. I had matches and paraffin hidden, and a copy of *Hedda Gabler* open in front of me. Before he left he paid me a compliment about my eyes that I had read the night before in a Tolstoy story. When he came back I was going to quote to him in return – the same thing Hedda had told her lover after destroying his book – 'I burned your baby'.

But I was curious. I read the titlepage on the first notepad, *Novocastrians*, and the date at the bottom of the page read 1982– . I decided to read the first story. I read it twice, and then I read the second story, and the third. By then, I couldn't stop laughing. The best that could be said about the dozen stories in the manuscript was that James's handwriting was very neat. The plots were either predictable or non-existent, the characters were simply a few proper nouns bumping into each other and shrilling 'Fair dinkum!' and the style was all at once Carveresque, Kafkaesque, Joycean, Borgean and Chekhovian. I recognised several half-plots he had stolen and at least thirty direct quotes from various short stories he had given us to read in class. I wondered if he even knew he had plagiarised them. The stories were completely unfit for publication, and would likely remain so even with another ten years work. I held the unlit match between my fingers. After all, destruction was also a form of creation.

I was startled by his sharp knock on the door, in the rhyme pattern of a limerick's first two lines. I lit a cigarette and let James in.

'Well?' he said. 'What did you think?'

'Quite frankly, I think it's a brilliant collection,' I said.

'Really?' he smiled at me, and for a moment I felt sorry for him.

'Yes. I loved all of your stories. They just need a little more polishing.'

'I love you,' he said.

'You should work on your dialogue though,' I told him. 'Sometimes it isn't very convincing.'

I let him come inside. I let him make love to me, though it was an awkward and embarrassing sex scene. The old writers were correct. It is better just to conceive of sex as three stars on a page.

* * *

F

A week later, after a class on Conrad's short fiction, as we stood under the gum trees in the warm rain, James confessed to me that he was married, and that he could not see me anymore. He had a black eye.

'I'm sorry. You're a nice girl,' he said

'No, I'm not,' I told him. 'And don't look for me in a drawer in a year's time. I won't be there.' He stared at me, puzzled, and then turned away. He attempted to saunter, but all his walking involved effort – even his stroll showed strain. I closed my eyes. My soul swooned slowly as I heard the rain falling faintly through the universe.

The End

Saints in Hell
Tony Wilson

This letter was first broadcast as one in a series of 'Letters That Didn't Need to be Written', on radio 3RRR's morning show, Breakfasters. At time of printing, Tony has received no reply.

His Holiness Pope Benedict XVI
The Vatican,
Vatican City
Rome, Italy

16 April 2007

Dear Your Holiness,

I have only written previously to one Pope, your predecessor John Paul II, who responded to my question, 'Is there a God?' with a pithy two-paragraph letter about faith, love and the ultimate sacrifice made by Our Lord and Saviour Jesus Christ. I still have the letter.

I'm writing to you with a more specific question. I've noted in recent weeks that you are moving forward with the beatification of John Paul II, having authenticated his intercession in the miracle cure of French nun Sister Marie Simon-Pierre of Parkinson's disease. I'm completely in favour of this decision, because this does seem to me to be a genuine miracle, even if it could be argued that a more selfless move from the late Pope would have been to intercede in some diseases with which he is less personally involved like, say, my psoriasis. This is a joke, by the way. There are certainly other afflictions much more worthy of papal intercession than my damned psoriasis! My keratoconus, for example! (Another joke!)

Also, this week you have stressed to an audience in Rome that Hell really does exist, despite being largely overlooked in today's society. Again, I thought your point was both timely and well made, because sometimes in the hurly-burly of buying ingredients for a seafood pappadelle or remembering to empty the vacuum cleaner bag, or complaining to the bank about fees, one can forget about eternal damnation and how hot and uncomfortable it must end up being.

My question combines the two things you have been talking about this week. It is simply: are there any saints in Hell? What I mean is, has there ever been a situation where the Church has authenticated miracles, gone through the process of beatification and then canonisation, whilst not being aware that the would-be saint has done something truly terrible, perhaps in his private life? But God, being all-knowing, would judge that person to be Hellworthy, and would quite correctly condemn him for his sin(s). Basically, I'm talking about a blue on the part of the Church. A time when you think you've got a good'un, but God and Jesus and St Peter know that he is a rotten apple.

I should stress that I'm not thinking about John Paul II here. I doubt anyone who is as generous, kind and diligent at answering mail as the late Pope could be bound for anywhere but Paradise. I'm thinking more of some of those Middle Ages saints – churchmen who might have grovelled their way into the papal good books at the time of the Inquisition, but who history might regard as bloodthirsty executioners. 'Thou shalt not kill' is, after all, a tricky one, and God is surely super strict when He comes across a transgressor.

It's true that I've just finished reading *The Name of the Rose* and my head is full of evil inquisitors, but is it not possible that politically savvy cardinals, who played a key role in the deaths of thousands of so-called infidels, were beatified and canonised here on Earth while simultaneously they were yoked-up and cutting ruts through fields of fire for all eternity in Hell?

I shouldn't name names, but these are some of the saints that I've had question marks over, and wonder whether they might not actually be in Hell:

St Bruno the Carthusian (died 1101)
St Gleb of Russia (died 1015)
St Isidore the Farmer from Spain (died 1130)
St Celestine V of Italy (Pope at a very bloody time; died 1296)

And surely there is still a question mark over St Charles the Good of Flanders (died 1127)? He seems very keen to say that he was good. Maybe too keen.

I'd appreciate your thoughts on this question of saints in Hell. At the moment, when I search 'saints in hell' on Wikipedia, most of the references refer to the Judas Priest song of the same name. This hasn't proved to be of much help.

Sincerely,

Tony Wilson
cc: Father Bob Maguire, South Melbourne parish priest

Russell Barling,
Advertising Man
Scott McDermott

1.

The call that he was expecting from Human Resources came a little after 3:30p.m. From the comfort of a plush Italian chair, he feigned what he considered to be the appropriate amount of shock and disappointment. He heard out the proposed course of action, contributed a fatalistic sigh and agreed that the relevant policies and procedures must be applied. Within the hour his personal assistant had collected her belongings in a cardboard box, was stripped of her magnetic swipe card and escorted from the building.

His name was Russell Barling and he was an Advertising Man.

His departing PA was a smattering of offensively unremarkable traits lolling about in a wrinkled sack of skin that smelled of age and talcum powder and went by the name of Nora. While her sins were numerous, they included nothing that might be considered a sack-able offence in the traditional sense. Be that as it may, she had to go. She was old and ugly and given to wearing a variety of unpleasant cardigans, which were generally accessorised with one of a large collection of garish brooches varied in style but united by a common bad taste.

Having the workstation immediately outside his door occupied by this human monument to decrepitude was a serious impediment to Russell's projection of a dynamic persona. In his capacity as an Advertising Man, he appreciated better than most the importance of maintaining equity in his personal brand.

In truth, Russell's relationship to advertising was marginal. He worked for a small city council and was responsible for the public notices, which were placed in local newspapers to advise of road closures and revisions to the waste collection schedule. He spent his days drafting notices and signing off on layouts that came back from an agency. He also composed text for council signage, including the plaques that were affixed to buildings of historical significance, but since this aspect of his role didn't fit with the image that he cultivated as an Advertising Man, he seldom mentioned it.

Russell took his responsibilities as an Advertising Man very seriously. He had long since dispensed with the traditional notion that shirts should be white or blue and matched with a tie. Instead, beneath his suit jacket, he had taken to wearing a variety of colourful shirts, many without collars much less the accompaniment of a tie. These illustrated amply his preparedness to fly in the face of convention and he considered flying in the face of convention a duty of the creative and intellectual types that populated the world of advertising. It was one of Nora's further failings that she had declined to voice support for this obvious challenge to the corporate orthodoxy.

In his quest for justifying Nora's dismissal there was one detail Russell could use. For some weeks she had been extending her lunchbreaks beyond the hour allowed. When challenged on her absences, Nora had suggested, with no hint of an apology, that perhaps Russell had been looking for her when she had popped off to the loo for a moment. That she would use an indelicate phrase such as 'popping off to the loo' in a professional environment only cemented in his mind the necessity of her departure. And of course it was a lie. He knew very well that she spent her lunchbreaks attending the city's overburdened public hospital where her husband was being taken from her in increments by cancer of the something-or-other. He further knew she could not possibly make that trip, spend any reasonable period there, and be back at her desk at the required time.

In fairness to her, it was a sad state of affairs. If only she had confided in him, he would have been perfectly amenable to negotiating an arrangement whereby, for example, the extra twenty minutes or so by which she extended her lunchbreaks daily could be made up by a half-day worked on Saturday.

But of course she had not and he felt compelled to act.

By week's end, he had the two things he required. The first was a timesheet, completed and signed by Nora, indicating that each day she had worked the standard seven hours and thirty-five minutes, commencing at 9:00a.m. and concluding at 5:35p.m., with a one hour lunchbreak from 12:00p.m. until 1:00p.m. The second was the knowledge that the latest IT user logs would show that for approximately twenty minutes each day that week, commencing at 1:00p.m., a series of hardcore pornographic websites catering to 'the mature lady' had been accessed from Nora's terminal.

2.

On the day that Russell conducted interviews for his new PA he wore his orange shirt.

The first applicant suffered the disadvantage of some similarity to Nora herself insofar as her shrunken form struggled for definition within a wrinkled hide evocative of scrotum. She had an impressive CV that he dismissed based on a conviction that the advantage of experience bestowed by age is more than offset by a diminishing of vigour. He wrapped up the interview quickly, tapping his pen impatiently on his desk.

The second applicant was infinitely more promising. Her name was Leda and she wore a scarf over her head from which thick braids of blonde hair escaped. Russell noted that she had fine full breasts, not at all old and saggy like those belonging to Nora or the previous applicant whose name he had already forgotten.

'I see from your CV – and let me just commend you on your penmanship – that you haven't worked in the last twelve months,' he said.

'I spent some time in the bush – sort of a commune – deciding what to do with my life. I think it's important to do something important, you know? I couldn't just work at KFC every day and be happy that that was my contribution to the world. And the clothes you have to wear there are kinda ugly.'

'I see,' he said, nodding encouragingly, understanding about ugly clothes and confusing Leda's interest in *doing something* important with his own interest in *being* important. He considered her intently. She looked a bit like a hippy. Not to the point where he wouldn't bend her over his desk and have his way – he couldn't abide hippies – but there was some trace of hippy influence about her nonetheless.

'What do you think you might like about working here?' he asked.

'Well, your ad talked about a creative and dynamic environment and I'm, um, like, creative. I used to do sculptures from found objects and grow my own vegetables, which is not, um, creative but, you know, shows that I'm resourceful because our dole money didn't go very far and I used to model for life drawing which is creative I guess because it's, you know, art.'

At the conclusion of the interview Russell offered Leda the job and was rewarded with a tight hug that caused his penis to swell nicely inside his Y-fronts.

3.

Leda wore the scarf, or another like it, every day. Russell encouraged this as a similar challenge to the corporate orthodoxy in which he himself was perpetually engaged, and he would proudly recount for her his history of minor dress code infringements.

Leda found that she liked working at the council very much. The work, if not as creative as the advertisement had led her to believe, was at least unchallenging and afforded her the opportunity to engage in pleasant daydreams and generally explore the wide terrain of her imagination.

Russell was a constant presence, always hovering about her to provide guidance and reassurance. She was not completely oblivious to his nature though and realised that he took these opportunities to peer into the recess of her cleavage.

If that made him happy, she reasoned, then it all contributed to workplace harmony and couldn't be such a bad thing. It was not that she ignored the dissenting voices in her head that warned he was a shallow and unprincipled man – it was just that she considered that, if he were, there must be something in his history that made him that way. She resolved that she would do her best to help him. She was that kind of person.

4.

Nerida was the Personnel Department's legal clerk. This meant that her time was almost entirely consumed by assisting the council's parking inspectors, or next of kin, to lodge the necessary compensation and insurance claims that followed the assaults that the PIs inevitably attracted. She sat in a dark corner of the council's basement parking bay and took a deep drag on the joint between her fingers.

'I could not work for that man in a million years,' she said.

'Not in a million years,' echoed Griff, a junior accountant that Nerida was fucking on a semi-regular basis.

Leda took a toke on the joint and nodded as she held it in her lungs. 'It's not so bad,' she said by way of invoking her philosophy that all things were connected and that to denigrate part of a system was to denigrate the whole. In her view, each of the universe's elements had to be nurtured – even those elements that talked about themselves too much and stared at your tits. She passed the joint to Griff.

'You know,' said Nerida, 'his wife is dead. Hit by a train.'

'No shit,' said Griff, 'probably threw herself under. He could drive you to that.'

'Hit their car,' Nerida said. 'He was driving.'

Oh my, thought Leda, *that poor lonely man.*

She checked her watch. It was time to get back.

'Jesus, what a hippy,' Griff said when Leda had disappeared into the stairwell.

Nerida held up what little remained of the joint, offering Griff a last drag. When he shook his head, she crushed it under her heel.

5.

Russell stood at Leda's shoulder, granting himself a tremendous view down the front of her blouse. He thought that he might, very soon, have to risk a wank in the staff toilets. Ostensibly, he was bringing to Leda's attention a misplaced comma that she had failed to notice in a proof that had come back from the agency.

'Just think of it as a pause. If you say it out loud with the pause here,' he said pointing to the offending comma, 'then it changes the meaning completely doesn't it?'

'Uh, I guess. I'm sorry about that, Russell. I must have been distracted.'

'Don't worry too much,' he said. 'Just keep your eye out. Attention to detail is important.'

'OK,' she said. 'Um, Russell, I was wondering if you have any, you know, plans for Saturday night.'

'Nothing set in stone,' he said, deciding that, on balance, a vague intention to debase himself in front of pornography did not constitute an actual plan. 'One or two tedious invitations that I hope to decline if the right excuse presents itself.'

The way he talked, so serious when he oughtn't be, puffed up and ridiculous, made her smile.

'Well, would you like to come to a club?' she asked.

'That might be just the thing.'

It never occurred to him to ask what kind of club.

6.

Russell had murdered his wife, Amanda, very early one morning in the March of 1997.

'Alright dear?' he enquired as she sat at her dressing table applying makeup.

'It's five o-fucking clock in the morning, Russell. I don't see why we have to leave so early.'

'It's going to be a hot one today. You'll thank me when you're on the beach by eleven instead of still cooped up in the car.'

He had booked a long weekend at the Diamond Bay Resort and had been unwavering in his insistence that, in order to make the most of their time away, they should leave as early as possible.

'Besides,' he said. 'You can sleep in the car on the way up. I'll drive.'

'You know that once I'm fucking awake I can't get back to sleep.'

Over the course of their marriage he had come to know this very well.

His wife was widely and accurately considered an intolerable woman. Outside of her immediate family there had been, throughout her life, a protracted debate as to whether her talent for casual cruelty was attributable to genetics or to having been brought up in an environment of ridiculous and unappreciated wealth. Amongst family, a parallel debate raged as to how she might have developed this spectacular talent *in spite* of her genetic heritage and upbringing.

She was, all agreed, splendidly well-rounded in her ability to cause offence.

'If you're all packed, I'll take the luggage out to the car,' Russell said cheerfully.

Taking his cue from a grunted reply, he collected his wife's suitcase with some difficulty and beat a path to the garage via an obstacle course of furniture sourced from Eastern European workers' canteens and state-run dormitory housing. The furniture had been one of Amanda's whims, informed by some magazine or other, and in this, as in all things, Russell had indulged her, partly because their money was really her money anyway, and partly because his disagreeable wife was even more so in the face of opinions contrary to her own.

Clumsily, he bundled the heavy suitcase into the boot of the Vänkerauto. He considered for a moment just tossing it into a corner of the garage, given that she would never have the opportunity to rummage through its contents anyway. He quickly quashed the thought, reminding himself that it was the details that matter in situations such as this.

The car, like the house, had been a gift from Amanda's parents, though Russell had been instrumental in the selection of model and vintage. Among people that take these things seriously, the Vänkerauto was something of a collectible; the model had introduced airbags to the modern motorist – driver's side only at that point – and was painted in a discontinued hue known as Harlean Rose.

Amanda's parents had suffered greatly at their daughter's hands. She was loud, rude, obstinate, a drunkard and completely oblivious to the feelings of others. Accordingly, it had caused them much anxiety to reflect that, notwithstanding the improbable prospect of marriage, Amanda was in no hurry to leave the family home. Their gratitude had been considerable when Russell stepped into the breach. Specifically, Russell and his bride had received the Vänkerauto, the house, a substantial sum in cash and investments, and a clear indication that they should not feel compelled to visit too often.

Russell went back upstairs, excitedly taking the steps two at a time.

7.

Leda wore a beanie, as did the majority of people in the queue. In fact, Russell noted, each of the beanies that he could see was identical.

'Should I have one of those?' he asked.

'Not your first time. You'll be given one when you leave. It's kind of your membership.'

By way of illustration, at the head of the queue, a barrel-shaped bouncer turned away two athletic but beanie-less young men, who appeared to have sprung from the pages of some fashionable magazine. One spat a prissy insult while the other admonished his companion with a muttered, 'I told you'.

'You either have to be a member or the guest of a member, and then after your first visit you *are* a member. It's exclusive,' Leda confided.

This pleased him. Membership of exclusive clubs was an important trait of successful people. He noted also that he was clearly older than the others around him. He drew additional satisfaction from this, as it is well known that creative types have a tendency to gravitate toward younger people and their pursuits.

'What is this place anyway?'

'It doesn't really have a name,' Leda said.

The queue stood in a poorly lit laneway. To reach this location they had negotiated a succession of similar laneways, the effect of which had been to leave Russell more than a little disoriented.

As they shuffled through the door, he braced himself for an assault of bass-rumble and pounding beats. It never came. In fact, there was no music.

'Well, this is it,' said Leda.

The club was dark. Or not dark exactly, just dull. Like the few moments before the summer sun has set completely. There were few features to distinguish the space from a warehouse floor or community hall. There was a small bar to Russell's left, tended by a dreadlocked young man. He wore the same beanie as the club's patrons and appeared in earnest conversation with an angular, bony woman in a singlet and loose-fitting pants. She too wore the beanie. In the room's centre, winding its way up to another floor above, was a spiral staircase.

'Not quite what I expected,' said Russell leaning, unnecessarily, toward Leda's ear to speak.

'I'm glad you're surprised. The best bit is that there is more to come.'

In a wide arc around the spiral staircase, a circle had been painted on the timber floor. In the half-light Russell could make out swirling patterns painted within its circumference. This was apparently the dance floor, for despite the absence of music a number of people had taken to this area and were moving to rhythms only they could hear. It was the kind of hippy-ish dancing that reminded him of seaweed moving in an ocean current. With the spiral staircase rising out of the group's midst they might have been Indians dancing around a totem pole. He made a note to himself to use the term 'Native Americans' if he shared this thought.

'Should we have something to drink?' he asked. He'd already made up his mind to order an organic New Zealand beer, imagining that anything organic would be useful currency for gaining entry to Leda's panties.

'There's only water, I'm afraid,' Leda said apologetically.

'What do you do here then?' asked Russell leaning in closer this time so that he might press himself against Leda's breast.

'Let's show you,' Leda replied, smiling.

8.

'Almost ready, dear?' Russell enquired of his wife, anticipating an expletive-laden rebuke before the words had yet chance to form in her mouth.

He stood at the window that looked down at the river. A hint of morning diluted the darkness outside. The silhouettes of trees were beginning to distinguish themselves from the empty darkness. He consulted his watch. There was still time.

He had chosen the house with his father-in-law. In addition to the view, it was large and boasted a fashionably impractical approach to architecture. Mr Hodgman, who had never invited his son-in-law to address him as anything other than Mr Hodgman, noted that the railway line that separated the house from the main road might be a noisy inconvenience. Russell, however, to allay this concern, pointed to the extensive use of double glazing and the fact that the house sat well back on the block, some distance away from the railway line itself.

Amanda's reflection appeared in the window. Russell turned to face her with a smile. While he had put on weight since their wedding, she had remained slim. Her only real concession to ageing was the accumulation of lines around her eyes that she referred to, without irony, as her laugh lines.

They were atypical of wedded couples in that their marriage continued in precisely the same vein as their courtship. Unhappily for Russell, this meant a continuous barrage of demands, abuse and threats to which he duly prostrated himself.

They did, however, maintain an active and even vigorous sex life. This was not so strange, for there was no genuine malice in Amanda's behaviour; she was simply oblivious to the harm that she inflicted on others, least of all her husband. For his part, Russell would sustain his erection and propel himself to orgasm with thoughts of the physical tortures that he should very much like to visit on his wife, lashed to one of the cold steel chairs that she had sourced from a munitions factory outside Kuibyshev.

He looked at his wife.

'OK then,' he said.

9.

Leda led him up the spiral stairway. Facing the landing was a ring of cubicles. Several had curtains drawn like department store change rooms.

Browsing for a possible explanation, Russell's mind trailed a forefinger along the few shabby volumes that constituted his mental library of preoccupations until he reached Sex. He wondered whether they were going to fuck in one of these cubicles. They weren't terribly private with just a curtain to hide them from view, but he imagined that might be part of the thrill.

10.

In the car, Russell consulted his watch again. They were a few minutes early.

'Be right back,' he said.

His wife grumbled a brief curse upon him.

When he returned he had the stainless steel travelling mug from which he would normally drink his coffee on the way to work. He handed it to his wife.

'I thought if you weren't going to be able to sleep, you might want a coffee on the way.'

He backed the Vänkerauto out of the garage and closed the door with the grey plastic clicker. He could see the early morning freight train approaching as he eased the car down their driveway.

Driving into the path of a speeding train was not a task to which he addressed himself lightly. He had given the endeavour much thought and concluded that a less clever man could be killed in such an attempt.

The secret, he determined, was not to allow the train to plough into the car at right angles where it might be carried along and crushed against who knows what. Rather, the angle between the car and the train should be at something like forty-five degrees, with the front passenger door at the point of impact. This, he had deduced, should inflict maximum damage to where his wife would be seated and at the same time ensure that the car would be thrown clear of the tracks.

With the train approaching, he gathered speed. It was a tricky business driving into trains and he was glad for the assistance of a precision automobile like the Vänkerauto.

'Slow down, Russell. You're not going to make it. Let it past.'

'Just relax now,' he said patting his wife's knee.

With the train now sounding its horn, he gently depressed the accelerator further.

'Russell!'

He wrenched the wheel to his right. The impact was an explosion of white as the driver-side airbag pinned him in his seat. He felt the car take flight and became disoriented as it rolled. The adrenalin that flooded his system drew time out like a stretched rubber band. Then he blacked out.

He was ushered back into consciousness by the screams his wife gurgled through her shattered face.

'Fuck. Fuck. Oh, Jesus, Russell. It hurts.'

He hadn't expected her to survive the impact. When he managed to remove the airbag from his view he was reassured to see how broken she was. Her legs were crushed. The jagged point of a fractured femur pierced the light cotton slacks that she wore. Her chest was caved in and her summer clothes were dark and heavy from the gore that poured from the borders of her body like a refugee populace. He had no doubt that she was dying.

Through the spiderweb of the Vänkerauto's shattered windscreen he could see the train's driver wandering in circles, shaking uncontrollably. He would look up at the car, shake his head and resume the motion that carried him nowhere. All the while he muttered to himself words that Russell could not hear.

He closed his eyes and listened to his wife scream herself to death for the longest fifteen minutes of his life. It was the most terrifying sound he had ever heard.

Then she was silent and a murder that he had planned even before their wedding was concluded.

In the distance, sirens could be heard approaching. As husband to Amanda Hodgman he had been granted some wealth and status. As her widower he would have the freedom to enjoy them.

11.

The screams of his dying wife, never completely forgotten, had at least dulled over the years. He still couldn't be in the house without having the television or stereo on, but he harboured no regrets.

It was only in rare moments now that the contemplation of his success and its attending comforts was interrupted by a dull pang that questioned, however timidly, whether he had done the right thing. In those moments, his wife's screams, for a time, would become a little louder.

12.

Leda led him to an unoccupied cubicle. Inside, two stools flanked a chair. The stools were of the type where you could spin the padded circular seat to adjust the height. The chair looked to Russell like a dentist's chair.

'Sit there,' Leda said, indicating the dentist's chair.

He sat, which was of course not so much like sitting at all as reclining in preparation to be launched through the ceiling.

'Do you trust me, Russell?'

Perhaps not sex at all then, he thought. Regardless, he answered quickly in the affirmative without troubling himself to consider the question. Trust, in this instance, was simply an investment he was prepared to make in anticipation of reaping a return, preferably at his place, preferably a number of times.

'Have you ever been hypnotised, Russell?'

'No.'

'It doesn't matter. You'll be fine. And I promise you that after this, everything is going to be much better.'

'OK,' he said, a little uncertainly.

A black man with a broad, flat face stepped into the cubicle and closed the curtain behind him. He approached a stool and gave its seat a spin. When he sat he looked down at Russell from above in the manner of a god looking down from the heavens.

13.

There was nothing; a vacuum of thought and feeling. Slowly the nothing began to resolve itself into something – several somethings. The somethings became shadows. Dark shapes moving. The shadows became figures; human figures. They danced around him ceremonially. They had broad, flat faces like he'd seen somewhere before. He could hear now also. Drums, and feet stamping the earth. The beat was too insistent and his heart struggled to mimic its uncomfortable pace. There were other things too. Crackling. Like a fire. That must be where the light came from. Light danced above the figures. Not like light though; not linear and predictable. It swivelled and writhed like a snake or a flag in the breeze.

Then there was nothing again.

14.

'Did you see them, Russell?'

'Huh?' He felt like he was talking to Leda through a glass tunnel. Strange light swam around the periphery of his vision. It was as if Leda were a television channel that hadn't been tuned correctly. Other signals – noise and voices – crept in.

A black face joined Leda in his field of vision. It smiled at him.

'The tribesmen – did you see the tribesmen?' Leda asked.

He recalled the dancing figures.

'Uh, yeah,' he said. He tried to get up but it made him dizzy.

'Don't get up yet, Russell. Just take your time.'

'Who were they?'

'They are my ancestors,' said the black face.

'Michael is descended from the Kisii of Kenya. You're lucky; not everyone sees the tribesmen when they have it done.'

Russell found that he had to concentrate very hard on what Leda was saying. There were other voices vying for his attention.

'Have what done?' he asked.

'Trepanation,' replied Leda, smiling at him sweetly like at any moment she might tell him he was a brave soldier for not crying while the doctor tended his boo-boo.

'It is a custom of my people,' the black face called Michael said.

'Trepanation?'

The voices were growing louder, angrier. Russell thought for a minute that there might be others waiting behind the curtain, impatient for their turn.

'OK, you have to promise not to freak out,' said Leda.

'What?'

'Well, trepanation is... Michael is an *omobari omotwe*. It means head surgeon. We've made a hole in your head – your skull anyway.'

'What?' Russell said, reaching instinctively toward his scalp.

Leda took his hand and drew it back down to his side.

'You mustn't touch it. You mustn't allow it to infect. Look,' she said and removed her beanie. She moved aside the tangle of her braids to reveal a small hairless patch of scalp crossed by dissecting lines of scar tissue. It was flat where it should have curved over bone.

He thought he might throw up the oysters he had downed earlier as fuel for his sexual ambition. The voices had grown louder still and, where previously they had blended together, each was now becoming more distinct.

'It promotes oxygen to the brain. It, like, unleashes abilities that we forgot we had. We, people I mean, haven't been very good at nourishing our potential, Russell. Trepanation provides that nourishment and gives us back abilities we had lost,' Leda said.

'What abilities?' he asked, now desperate to examine the mutilation wrought on his head.

'The ability to truly know our place in the world. We lost our ability to see and feel our connection to everything and then we forgot that we were connected – connected to the environment, connected to our ancestors, connected to those we love and whose lives we shape. You don't have to feel so alone anymore. All you need do is listen. You won't have to wonder whether you make a difference, you'll be able to feel your influence on everyone around you. You're part of a common whole.'

'Common?' he asked, a quiver in his voice.

'It's a wonderful thing, Russell. You're more than just this body. You're energy. We're all energy – and none of us ever truly dies, we just shed the body. Nobody is lost to us.'

Nobody is lost to us.

His head was a shrieking mess, the screaming voices stripping the defences from that part of him where his sanity hid, and prominent among them was his wife, screeching and wailing and hurling great molten fireballs of abuse.

He knew that voice would be with him now, forever.

Small World 2001
Andrew Preston

Flying back to Melbourne from overseas, and getting close, I see what I think is my hometown but later realise is only mottled clouds. (I may be delirious after the long flight, or perhaps it is wishful thinking.) I imagine a story about a man flying home who sees various shapes in the clouds, including what he thinks is his city. But later I see an ad about a man who looks into the sky and sees shapes made from clouds. My idea suddenly seems a bit derivative.

My partner and I have broken up again. This time is the last time. But I said that last time, and the time before that. I think of a story title: 'The Eternal-Making Up, Breaking-Up Machine'.

The dry leaves in the driveway of the block of flats I live in creep across the cracked concrete as if they were pulled by an invisible string. Sometimes I think that if I followed them to get to the source of the string, I would be trapped, I would have gone too far into an underworld, a dark, murky inner-surburban underworld, unable to escape. Then again, I'd probably just be in the drain, along with all the other garbage, and I'd simply roll into Port Phillip Bay.

I email a woman I met overseas. We spent a day together in Aix-en-Provence, making a magical visit to Cezanne's studio, seeing the tools of his trade and his beautiful, peaceful garden, and the locales that he made into transcendent art. When we parted, she said she was going to go to London to try and get work, after a brief trip to Spain. But in her reply she says she is in Portugal: Sagres, the most southwesterly point of mainland Europe. Land's end, Europe's end, the end of the world. Emails have no postmark, so I just have to take her word for it. She could be anywhere. She left her husband after being married for twelve years and now has almost no possessions. They were in business together and owned a house and a boat. He now says there's no money left, he is broke. She is trying to negotiate with him back in Australia through her lawyer, by email from Europe. I tell her I'm envious that she is still travelling, and in such an exotic location, but I say she probably needs it more than me.

Sitting in my flat I hear noises. The sound of a window closing says someone's home next door. I think it's a woman who lives in the flat next to mine. So far I've only seen an arm and some dark, curly hair. That is all I could see of her on her balcony watering her plants, from my couch. She enters from a different stairway to me. Even though her flat and her balcony are next door to mine, we have never met.

Trying to find ways to make money from writing, I do a course in copywriting. The course lecturer says, 'Listen to what people say and note it down. It's great material for advertisements, especially the headlines of print ads.' The next day I overhear two guys walking down the street.

One guy says, 'Since we're guys we see it from a guy's perspective'.

The other guy says, 'She's gorgeous but I'm too young for her'.

I think that both of these lines could be used as a headline in a print advertisement. But in my fiction writing classes, the lecturer says the same thing: listen to what you hear, note it down. You might be able to use it in a story.

There is a toy bear named Edward at the Bean Bag Store, just down the road, with the same birthday as me – June 12 – but born thirty-nine years after, in the year 2000. He has his birth date on his tag.

I phone a woman from Citibank. After I have completed my transaction she says, 'If you hear really weird noises on your street tonight, please forgive me'.

'Why?' I say.

'Because my friend lives near you.'

It is becoming less and less necessary to live our lives. They are being lived on television for us. We get home from work and turn on the TV and watch ourselves, watch our lives, not even realising it is us we are watching. The people on the screen are us. The secret life of us. 'Reality television'. Relationships, share households, home repairs, money management. I compare myself unfavourably with characters in *Sex and the City* – my former girlfriend and I have broken up four times and reunited three times, but I think Carrie and Big did it several times more. I have written her out of my life now, and it's unlikely she'll come back, even as a guest star, but who knows what God the scriptwriter has in store.

The birds in the trees above our driveway shower my car, baptise it every day, with their turds.

A dream. I ask a woman to be the pilot of my light plane. She's not sure whether to resign from her job at a major airline. It gives her job security, which I might not be able to provide.

Dana waits till the ad break before she takes the dishes back into the kitchen. They will not be washed tonight. After the show there is the other show, then the other other show. You know, it is one of those nights when all the shows she likes to watch are on. In the flat next door, Des does the same. He is home alone too and will be watching TV. His dishes will also begin to pile up, as they do periodically. Dana and Des don't know each other but they are living next door to each other and living very similar lives.

A copywriter gives a talk at our course. He says advertising tells the truth these days and newspapers tell lies, giving the example of the 'children overboard affair'. There are so many regulations now that advertisers have to tell the truth, he says. 'The truth well-told', is the line the advertising industry uses about itself. But advertising has nothing to do with the truth. In fact, in some ways, copywriters have actually taken over the role that fiction writers once had. There is little left for fiction writers to fictionalise. The world itself is becoming a world of fiction.

At one point in our relationship my former girlfriend cut off all her hair and shaved her head almost bald. I was really pissed off with her. She had shoulder-length hair when I met her, which I really liked, and I had seen photos of her with short hair when she was with her previous boyfriend, so I associated her short hair with him and their time together. Anyway, I was overly critical of her new hairstyle and it led to a crisis that almost led to her breaking up with me. Other people really liked her new look, and once her hair grew a bit I started to like it too and it seemed natural, and preferable, to me. I wrote a story called 'The Tail', about a woman who attaches a tail to herself. All her friends and relatives think it's great but I, her boyfriend, don't like it. I showed her the story and she asked me if it was actually about her cutting her hair off. I said that I hadn't consciously planned to write a story about that (which was true), but it may well have been about that underneath it all.

A guy I met in Avignon, a Malaysian who studies Law at Cambridge, had been through eight countries in three weeks. He had a four-week Eurail pass and wanted to squeeze as much out of it as possible. But nothing lived up to his expectations. 'Stonehenge wasn't much, was it?' Rome and Florence also weren't up to scratch. 'What are the Spanish Steps? Just steps,' he said. 'I expected more, more old buildings, more old paintings, more grandeur, more history.' So he kept on moving.

I overhear a mobile phone conversation. 'Every morning I think of you. There's an ad near the station with a guy in it that looks just like you. It's an ad for food, a butcher or something. Every morning I see it and say, "Hi, Colin".'

Someone puts a slip of paper on my car in the driveway of the block of flats. It's been printed out on a computer to make it look like a mock parking ticket. At the top it says 'Parking Violation', then it's got spaces to fill in for 'Street', 'Make/Model', 'Rego. No' and 'Time'. Below that it says:

> *This is not a ticket. But if it were within my power, you would receive two! Because of your feeble attempt at parking, you have taken enough room for:*
> - *2 elephants and one goat*
> - *a 20-strong mule team*
> - *a safari of pygmies from the African interior.*

The reason for giving you this is so that in future you may think of someone else other than yourself. Besides: I don't like domineering, egotistical or simple-minded drivers & you probably fit into one of these categories. I sign off wishing you an early transmission failure (on the freeway at about 5:30p.m.). Also, may the fleas of a thousand camels infest your armpits!

I have no idea who the person is that put this 'ticket' on my car, or which flat they live in. Previously, I have both had my car crashed into from behind and been asked to allow more space by a driver in front of me in our driveway. With this and the bird turds, it's not worth the trouble of parking there. From now on I will park on the street and leave the driveway to the leaves and birds (and other cars).

'No Name' sees 'No Logo's' profile on the Internet Personals website. He sends her an email.

'Hi, No Logo. I liked your profile. I like Dean Martin and DJ Shadow also. Get back to me.' A series of emails follow, as they discuss their lives, their views about the world and their tastes in movies, television programs, music and books.

When I got back from Europe I couldn't get used to living at home again. I saw the backpackers in the hostels near where I live. They could have been the same backpackers that I met when I was overseas. Melbourne was just another city, just another destination on the backpacker route. I thought that I could pretend to be a backpacker in my own city. I could sublet my flat and begin staying at the backpacker places in my city, hoping to see it as a tourist would. My tourist days would never have to end. 'At home he feels like a tourist' – an old Gang of Four song.

Quote from *The Age*: '"This is not a television show," says executive producer Peter Abbott who also provides the voice of Big Brother. "It's a number of big deals which create a phenomenon and one of the side-effects is the TV show – the deals construct the framework in which the show is made."'

This is not a short story. It's a number of big deals, which creates a phenomenon and one of the side effects is the short story – the deals construct the framework in which the short story is made. I had to move heaven and earth to get it up. There are a number of cross-media tie-ins.

During one of the periods when my girlfriend and I had broken up, I tried to meet women through Internet dating. One of the women I contacted lived in the block of flats next to my girlfriend's block. Another one was actually a woman I already knew, through other mutual friends.

The people from market research companies, who want to ask you questions about this or that product, always seem to call at dinnertime. I guess they know that that is the most likely time to catch people at home. I generally say I'm busy but I feel a bit sorry for the people calling. They're just trying to make a living and probably don't like what they're doing. But I prefer the ones who just say, 'Hello, I'm doing some research for such and such company, would you mind answering a few questions?' to those who begin by saying 'Is that Mr (my surname)?' With the latter there's always a silence after you answer the phone, probably because it takes a while for their system to kick in. They've obviously just got your name out of the phone book but that false intimacy is very off-putting.

I notice a woman I met briefly years ago. She's leading a tour group through the Balaclava shopping district, talking about the Jewish history of the area. It reminds me of walking tours I did in Paris and New York. I imagine myself leading a tour group of my neighbourhood, not talking about the cultural or ethnic origins, but simply about banal or mundane details of everyday life, including my own.

For the copywriting course I had to create an advertising campaign for a dummy client. Our course convener said we are, in a way, like lawyers. We don't have to believe what our client says; we just have to write a campaign according to what the client says he wants. My client was a distributor for software used by accountancy firms, so that was appropriate advice.

We watch. We sit and watch. We see ourselves on the screen – we are applauding. We are on the screen and we are applauding, applauding ourselves. We have given the correct answer and we are applauding ourselves, along with the studio audience, who are also applauding us. We watch ourselves applauding ourselves. And we applaud. We applaud ourselves watching ourselves applauding ourselves. We sit and watch and applaud.

My story, 'The Tail', about my girlfriend attaching a tail to herself, ends like this: 'I went down to St Kilda Pier and I looked towards the horizon. Surely there was an answer there, where the sea meets the sky. I thought of my ex-girlfriend's niece's painting, which we have on the wall. When her niece came around to our place she said we had hung the picture upside down. We thought it was an abstract, with wavy blues, greens and yellows. But yes, we turned it the other way up and it was a landscape. The sea, sky and sun. How could a kid have tried to paint an abstract, how could we have thought it was an abstract? I tried to turn the picture in front of me upside down – make it an abstract. The sea fell down into the sky, the sky got wet. Blue and green and yellow got mixed up – just a mess, a liquid mess. Tears formed in my eyes. Everything was wet. Everything was a mess. But suddenly I liked it. The tears made everything runny, gooey. The world was an abstract and it was alright.'

I ride my bike along my street and hear a quick intake of air behind the screen door of one of the houses opposite my block of flats. What could this breath mean? A gasp. Laughter. Crying. But no more information than that. I just hear the intake of air then I'm gone. I'll never know what it was about. There is a story there, in that breath, there is a character behind that tiny sign of life. I just have to imagine it.

A radio documentary about the new face of marketing. It says that brands are 'lovemarks'. Marketing is not about selling products but about creating a relationship with the public. Lovemarks should have three elements: mystery, sensuality, intimacy. These elements are needed for all satisfying relationships. Brands are just like people – they have personalities. And we can break up with brands and find a new brand that is more satisfying for us.

I thought I remembered having a telephone call but it was actually a talkback call on the radio I had heard earlier.

I walk down a street I've never been down before, even though it's very close to where I live. There are flats and houses I've never seen before, and different people, yet they are strangely similar to the ones in my street and other streets nearby that I regularly traverse. Everything is so different and yet so similar.

Eventually 'No Name' and 'No Logo' meet. Their real names are Dana and Des. When he sees her, Des thinks, *Hey, you're just like you said you were in your profile: 'Blue eyes, brunette, five feet five'. Truth in advertising.* They discover, amazingly, that they actually live next door to each other, in adjoining flats, but they have never met. After having a coffee, they walk along St Kilda pier. They hear a buzzing above them. Looking up, they see a light plane doing some skywriting. What will the writing say? Will it be a message of love, or something like, 'Jesus Saves'? No, nothing of the sort. It says 'Agfa Film'. They continue walking towards the horizon. Classical music plays. It might be Mozart, or perhaps Chopin. They think they've heard it somewhere before. Maybe in an ad.

Sunburn
John Burnside

Every year, on the first really hot day of summer, I get sunburn. I go out into the garden, or I'm sitting on a beach, and I take off my shirt, just for a moment, to cool off, or to feel the year's first warmth on my back and shoulders. All the time, I am planning to cover up after fifteen minutes, or at most, half an hour; all the time, I know exactly where things are headed. I am fair-haired and light-skinned and I burn easily. I should be using a high-factor sunscreen; better still, I should keep my shirt on my back, where it belongs, because I know, from years of experience, that as soon as I feel the heat beating down on my neck and arms, I fall asleep. I drift away, I dream, the dreams are complicated and utterly compelling, tiny myths unfolding in my head. Then I sleep for an hour, or an afternoon and, by the time I realise what has happened, my back is red and my arms are already tingling. When I pull my shirt on, an exquisite shiver runs across my skin, part-pleasure, part-pain, fleeting and dark, like the wind on a field of ripening corn. An hour later, I am raw.

The sad thing is, I know why this happens, but I keep on doing it. Whenever I hear someone say that self-knowledge is the key to a happy life, I have to laugh. It's not that I'm against self-knowledge, as such; but, for me, it's just a hobby, like every other form of knowledge. Whatever we need to do, we do it, again and again, once the pattern is established. We can go to therapists, we can read self-help books, but we either continue doing what we have done all along, or we become something less than we were. Like Cindy, for example. Cindy has read every self-improving book under the sun and, as a result, she spends most of her life as a shadow of her real and inevitably mysterious self, doing what she thinks she ought to be doing, practising reiki and emotional intelligence, eating food from a book and asking for help from her peers when she feels a little fragile. She's like a well-tended suburban garden: a little too tidy, a little too well managed. Meanwhile, I go about my business, doing what I have to do and, beyond that, as little as possible. Every year, on the first really hot day of summer, I get sunburn. Some years I burn quite badly; others, only a little. It doesn't matter, though; it has to happen. It's how I remember the story that my body is telling, a story that, for much of the time, is really rather pleasant, in spite of how things sometimes appear.

The story begins late in my fourteenth year. From the off, I was one of those reclusive, moody children who lie awake at night and wish they had a talent of some kind, cryptography, say, or music. At some point in the not too distant future, I thought, I would learn something that would mark me out from my peers. I would speak six languages, or I would be the one person in the entire world who could tell the wealth of some ancient civilisation from the random contents of an earthenware jar or some arcane system of knot-work and braiding. At school, I would sit at my desk and think about the future, which was coming any day now. Meanwhile, I was alone. I didn't talk to anyone, not even my parents – especially not my parents – and I didn't know anyone because, like any teenage philosopher, I didn't believe it was possible to know anyone. Not, you know, really know. I was more or less contented with this state of affairs, or I would have been, if other people had just left me to it, but the worst thing about being almost fourteen is that people expect you to have friends, and if you don't, they worry. At fifty, say, a man can be the quiet, studious type, something of a night owl, fonder of his books, or his cat, or a good single malt than he is of company. Like my father, for example. So why was it that he, of all people, kept trying to get me to do something? Why did he think it was so unhealthy that I preferred not to go out and meet kids my own age, when his idea of human contact was listening to the radio? To be fifty and have no friends is a sign of thoughtfulness; to be in the same condition at fourteen is a sign of failure, if not now, then soon. If I could, I would go back and tell that almost fourteen-year-old that it was all nonsense, all that talk about going out and meeting people, and I would tell him to think less about the future and take more notice of what's passing him by, because I like that boy, now that I no longer have to be him.

I never think about the future now. A time comes when the only meaningful work is to forget about the future altogether and return to the one thing that's always there: the present, the incalculable. A time comes when the present is all there is, and it goes on happening, as opposed to melting away, or fading into the past. The past remains, of course, as an idea; but the future is nothing at all. It's not even the source of tomorrow's, or next year's, fleeting present, the way it once seemed. A time even comes when things forget their names, when the figure you know from an old painting is crossing a street in the everyday world, an angel from a Duccio Nativity, or one of the lesser apostles in a fresco that some fifteenth-century master left to a bemused posterity. The time comes when nothing is other than it seems, when there is nothing to calculate, nothing to figure out, nothing to measure yourself against. If I could go back, I would tell that almost fourteen-year-old boy this, and a good deal more besides, though it would be ridiculous of me to expect him to listen.

The past remains, and it does no harm to visit it from time to time. Mostly, it isn't what it seems; almost all of it shifts about as we try to navigate our memories, but there are places that stay constant, whole hours at a time that never fade or alter. Like that day, when I found myself alone at home on a beautifully hot afternoon and rushed outside to sunbathe, a book in one hand, a stolen gin and tonic in the other. I didn't much like alcohol, but I felt it was my duty to drink whenever my parents went out for the day, announcing as they left that they wouldn't be back till after midnight so I should help myself to food from the fridge, and not stay up too late because I had school in the morning, or music, or whatever else I was doing to improve myself. Even at that age I ought to have known that alcohol and hot days didn't go together; my Dad had got sunstroke once from sitting in the garden all day drinking beer, and my mother was always telling him to cover up because, like me, he had pale colouring. It always felt like a failing, that pale colouring. Not an accident of nature, but something that we, the two men of the Williamson household, had not quite managed to get right.

I have no memory of falling asleep, or of how much gin I drank before I did, but I do remember our neighbour, Angela Mathers, leaning over me suddenly, her hand on my back, her voice arriving from the perfect distance of sleep. 'Hey,' she was saying. 'Wake up. You're going to fry here.' She touched me again, and I started up, electrified. She pursed her lips. 'Whoops,' she said, 'looks like you already did.' She straightened up. 'Where's Caron?' she said. 'Where's David?'

'They're out,' I said. I looked at her. At that moment the heat in my back and arms wasn't that bad, just a pleasant hum, really. The difficult fact to take in was Angela Mathers, in a short lemon-coloured summer dress standing over me with a half-worried, half-amused look on her face. 'Gone away for the day,' I added, to keep the conversation going. I didn't want her to abandon me.

'Well, I'll have to see what I can find to fix you up,' she said. 'You come indoors to the shade and I'll see what there is in the medicine chest.'

I was a little worried by this. I didn't think we had a medicine chest, as such. Still, I rose slowly, the heat in my back suddenly stinging as my skin crinkled and buzzed, and I followed her into the house.

I had been in love with Angela Mathers for three years, ever since I'd seen her walking to work one morning in a dark blue winter coat and navy gloves. She worked at a place that people referred to mysteriously, with a hint of knowing secrecy, as the vet lab. I had no idea what they did there, and I suspected nobody else did either, but I liked to picture her up there, in the low, thirties-style buildings that stood at the edge of the woods, conducting tests or making long, complicated calls to scientists and technicians in Denmark, or Manitoba, her soft voice fusing in the telephone lines with snowfalls and birdsong and the wind over the North Sea. Inside the vet lab, it was always evening and when Angela Mathers emerged at the end of a long, important day, she was touched with the shadows of elsewhere, even as she walked home in the sunshine of late afternoon. She had perfectly blue eyes that couldn't be compared to anything else I knew, and she wore her dark, not quite black hair in a tight bob, which made her look confident and deserving.

Inside I sat down in the dining room while Mrs Mathers disappeared in search of medicaments. I had no idea what she intended, but the possibilities suddenly appeared terrifying and miraculous at the same time. I remembered her cool fingertips on my shoulder, and I thought the only thing that could possibly cure me of my ills was that coolness, that smoothness, stroking the hurt away. I felt a little dizzy. My mouth was parched. I thought of going into the kitchen for a glass of water, but I didn't want to move. Finally she reappeared, all reassuring smiles like a television nurse.

'Just the ticket,' she said, producing a large blue tube that I had never seen before. She unscrewed the lid. 'Now this may smart a little,' she said. 'Just you sit still.' She pulled a chair up next to mine and studied my left shoulder. 'OK, you'll live,' she said brightly. 'Here we go.' With which she set to work, and the room vanished around me, and then I vanished and all that remained was the cool lotion, the light pressure of her hands and a voice that I could barely follow, guiding me into the darkness.

I imagine some time passed then. I have no memory of that but, sadly, time never stops. She talked, asking me questions, drawing me out of myself, and I did my best to sound normal and grown-up and casual in my replies. We talked about school, and books, and she asked if I had a girlfriend.

'No,' I said. 'There's a vacancy there.' I had no idea where this came from. Maybe the last of the gin.

She laughed. 'Well,' she said. 'If I wasn't already spoken for, I'd consider applying.'

'The job is yours, should you choose to accept it,' I said, right back at her. I couldn't believe it: I was flirting with Angela Mathers.

She laughed again, an unbelievably musical sound, but she didn't say anything, she just kept on working the lotion into my shoulders. There was a longish, though not particularly awkward, silence before I began to realise that she was almost finished and that I was about to let her go without another word. I cast around desperately for some way to detain her, but my sudden flash of confidence had faded, and now I couldn't think of anything to say.

She patted me gently on the back, and stood up. 'There you go,' she said. 'You'll be right as rain.'

'Thanks,' I said. 'I feel better now.' I stood up too, and turned towards her, but she had already moved away. 'Can I get you something?' I ventured. 'A drink? Or something?'

She laughed again and shook her head. 'You're incorrigible,' she said, as she headed for the French windows. 'Stay inside, and stay cool,' she sang out in parting; then, with a knowing smile, she added: 'And no more mad dogs and English gin, alright?'

I nodded and, with a last, glorious smile that was meant only for me, she vanished into the sunshine. I wanted to go out too, just to watch her cross the lawn, and see her back safely to her own garden, but I stayed where I was. There was something about that parting smile that made me want to do exactly what she'd told me to do.

Later that evening, before my parents got home, I woke up. I had gone upstairs to lie down for a while, and ended up asleep on my stomach. I was thirsty again, though not for gin. I had no idea what time it was, but I knew the house was empty by the stillness from below, and by the way the sounds from across the way drifted in through my window. Mr and Mrs Mathers were having dinner in the garden with friends; I could tell from the sounds I could hear: Angela Mathers's bright laugh floating through the dark, the other voices deeper and heavier, like the background characters in a radio drama. I got up and went to the window, still half-naked, the chill of the cool air on my skin, not hurting now, though I knew it would later. From where I stood, I could see her, though she didn't see me, and I watched for as long as I dared, as she talked with her husband and their guests: a grown woman, far away and impossible, just beyond the cherry laurel hedge. For a moment, I let myself imagine an impossible future, then I went downstairs and fetched a long cold lemonade from the fridge, with plenty of ice.

I saw a documentary once about a group of scientists who spend their entire lives drilling deep into the polar icecap and analysing the rope-thick, silvery core of it to find out what the atmosphere was like hundreds of thousands of years ago. They were, in the main, cool, soft-spoken creatures, those Arctic scientists, but you could see in their eyes that something unexpected about their work had touched them deep in the quick of their imaginations – a distance they hadn't anticipated in the ice when they started, a sense of something urgent besides the cold they endured on a daily basis or the results they were compiling, building theories of global catastrophe that, for me at least, seemed almost incidental. The ice had affected their bodies, too, making them still and dense, adding a gravitas that I have only ever seen in old black-and-white films. It had something to do with eternity, and with the cold, this sense I had that each of them was keeping his own secret, not because he wanted to, but because the deeper, more physical knowledge he had achieved, through his work and through grace, could not be put into words. I have never forgotten this program, though it was, on the surface, a routine science feature on television, Horizon, say, or Equinox. I remember it for those scientists, for their stillness and for the darkness in their eyes, and I remember the desire I had, watching them handle those beautiful cores of ice, a desire that was as urgent, in its own way, as real and desperate thirst, a desire to drink that cold liquid as it dripped from the melting ice-strand, and taste the air of long ago, a trace of prehistory, the cold minerals of origin. What could be more tempting than this, I thought. What could be more necessary than this longing to drink from the purest cold, to gulp down the salty essence of a world before time? As I sat watching them, I could see that these scientists, each in his own way, had tasted that original ice. That was what showed in their eyes and in the way they held themselves. It was a special kind of knowledge they had, a secret that went beyond even the desire to tell. It was the knowledge of ice, the secret of the eternal.

I didn't know, when I was fourteen, that what I loved most was the cold, just as I didn't know, until much later, that the future wasn't really what I was after. Yet what I want most is more than just ice: I love the cold, and high winds, and the first snows, but more than that, I love the chill shiver that fever reveals in the flesh – and so, every year, on the first hot day of summer, I get a medium to bad sunburn. Usually, Cindy is out when it happens, or she's busy with something indoors, so she doesn't catch me out till it's too late. I suppose I shouldn't be surprised that she gets annoyed. She stands looking at me, holding a paintbrush or a bag of groceries, while I sit sheepishly in the kitchen, my shoulders bright red and tingling. Usually I feel a little feverish, as if my whole life is flickering at the border between the real and the imagined but, after the first few minutes, this isn't as unpleasant as Cindy thinks it is. All the while, I want to tell her that I can't help myself, that all of this happens for a reason. I want to say that, somewhere in the back of my mind, I let it happen. I let it happen for love and eternity and a long kinship with the cold. I let it happen for the sensation of putting on a clean white shirt and feeling the shiver run across my back, for the fever that will possess me later, when she is asleep, and for the minutes when I stand awake, half naked at the window, feeling the cool of the night on my skin, and listening to the dark, for whatever is there in the quiet of the eternal, millimetres away.

POURING COFFEE OVER
MY HEAD WAKES ME
MORE QUICKLY THAN DRINKING IT

Darby Hudson

Old Friends
Andy Kissane

Paul took her order and brought the Portuguese tart and skim latte back to her table. There was something familiar about her, though he wasn't sure what. She was wearing dark sunglasses, her hair was cropped short and her head was buried in the newspaper. It was hard to tell if she was someone he knew or not.

'Thankyou,' she said. He should have recognised her voice, he thought afterwards, for he had heard it so many times before, had marvelled at the timbre and colour of her vocal range. But it wasn't her voice that triggered his memory, but the way that she moved her hand to pick up the Portuguese tart. The ease of the movement and the way she spun her wrist reminded him at once.

'Ursula?' he asked. It has to be her. It has to be, he thought.

'Paul? Paul Somerville. How wonderful… I'm sorry I didn't—'

It was good to see her smile, this woman he had trained with at the National Institute of Dramatic Art when they were both in their twenties. If only he had known then what he knew now about acting. But Ursula had made it – in film and on stage – at least for a while. Though he hadn't seen her name around lately – perhaps for the last five or the last ten years. He imagined it was just the shortage of decent roles for older women, for Ursula had talent and undeniable presence. Even the way she sat down at a table seemed to draw other people's attention.

Unfortunately, he had customers to attend to, so he excused himself and hurried over to a large table to take their lunch orders. Whenever he could, he glanced back towards Ursula, hoping that she wouldn't leave before he had time to catch up. But The Last Drop filled up with the usual lunch crowd and he didn't get another chance. It must have been fifteen or twenty minutes later when he looked down to see that Ursula was gone. He was surprised at the disappointment that rose in his throat. He might have talked to her, but he had been too busy with the rush, with complaints about lukewarm food or requests for more bread or water or coffee.

Then he heard her voice, right behind him.

He turned and Ursula took his elbow warmly. 'I have to go,' she said. 'But we must find time to talk. Have you heard about Julian?'

Paul frowned. 'Julian. Julian Rhodes?' Back at NIDA, Paul and Julian had been 'this close'. Until they asked Julian to leave in third year – the last one to be thrown out of their group, the last to be told that in the opinion of the staff he didn't have what it takes. Not that having it necessarily got you anywhere, as Paul now knew. 'No, I haven't,' he replied.

He could see from the expression on Ursula's face that she was hoping he knew, hoping she wouldn't have to say anything.

'Julian's sick. Very sick. He's in Prince Alfred Hospital. I'm sure he'd love to see you.'

'I'll look him up. I'm sorry, I'd love to talk, but— ' Paul said, aware that the barista was motioning to him, and that there were three plates of food waiting on the counter.

Ursula nodded, gave him a quick hug and kissed him on the cheek. He said he hoped she'd drop in again, suppressing a groan at how formal he sounded. If only he wasn't busy and they could relax and talk. But the lunchtime rush had begun and he put his energy into serving his customers.

On the way home he remembered how funny Julian was, how much they had kicked around together at NIDA, how they had supported each other. Julian had been particularly good with Jack, Paul and Leeanna's baby son, a fact that Paul had managed to keep from the NIDA staff for the whole of the course. It wasn't that you couldn't have children, that they could have made any logical objection. But NIDA wasn't the sort of place where logic held sway. They wanted commitment, a total all-consuming commitment to developing your acting skills, and leaving classes early to change nappies or feed your son pumpkin mash was not the sort of commitment they were looking for.

Paul had managed to get by on the days when Leeanna was working, with lots of help from Julian, Ursula and the others. They would take it in turns to miss Theatre History or Movement Studies or Voice and the whole thing was such a well-kept secret and so well-organised that the staff never suspected a thing.

Then their third year started with that fateful production of *A Midsummer Night's Dream*. Paul had played Lysander and Julian had played Demetrius, the two Athenians who were vying for the affection of Ursula's Hermia. The director had been young and brilliant and his ideas shaped the whole production. As Paul remembered it, he put a lot of emphasis on the rude mechanicals and their play within the play. He had an obsession with space and height and had set the wood above the audience, in mid-air. Oberon and Titania swung through the air on small seats suspended by ropes, while Lysander and Demetrius chased the girls up and down ladders and along these thin platforms high above the stage. Then the girls chased them. One wrong step, one mistimed push could have resulted in a sickening fall to the floor below. It was Shakespeare for acrobats. It might have turned out fine if Julian hadn't been desperately afraid of heights.

It was a stressful time, yet in the end neither of them fell. Julian's performance was the best that could have been expected, given the circumstances. It had been nuanced, honest, truthful. They were always going on about truth at NIDA – the importance of truth in acting, how you had to think and feel your way into a character's world, how you had to find the truth from within and not fake it.

Even when you produced your best work, the Head of Acting was rarely impressed. Your truths were his lies. You were labelled a fake, a deceiver. There was no point defending yourself. Nothing to be achieved by arguing back. There was nothing to do but go to the pub, get drunk and start all over again.

Unfortunately, Julian never really learnt how to keep quiet. He challenged their authority, he justified his decisions. Even in *Dream*, when he'd been too scared of falling to really get it right. After the last performance when the director gave out his notes and everyone was glum and dejected, they took Julian aside and asked him to leave.

It had happened in first and second year, but hardly anyone made it to third year and was told to go. Julian was shattered. He had no idea it was coming and tried to change their minds. He went to see everyone to plead his case, but they refused to budge, then they altered the security code you had to punch in, so Julian couldn't even get into the building.

Of course, Julian asked Paul for the new code. He couldn't believe that Paul wouldn't give it to him, didn't listen when Paul tried to tell him to let go, or to get back at them by making his own way in TV or film. No one could argue with success. But thinking back, it was probably inevitable that they drifted apart. Paul didn't blame Julian. After all, in Julian's eyes, Paul had succeeded while Julian had failed.

* * *

Paul went to visit Julian that afternoon. Rather than turn up empty handed, he stopped at the bottle shop of the Marlborough Hotel and bought a hipflask of whisky. He also purchased a box of Maltesers from the hospital gift shop, remembering how they had eaten a box religiously when they went to the movies every Friday night through first and second year. It had been their way of winding down after the week's stresses. They alternated between Hollywood schlock and art house movies, then went for a drink afterwards to dissect the acting, often talking into the early hours of the morning about acting, life, and anything, anything at all.

Paul rode the lift to the eighth floor. His stomach seemed to be travelling faster than the rest of him and he could feel sweat collecting on the back of his neck. He was nervous, more nervous than he'd ever felt before going on stage. He didn't know how Julian would react to him, didn't know if he'd embrace him, yell at him or snub him.

He asked a nurse for directions and found Julian's bed by the window in a ward of four. Julian's face was a dreadful shade of yellow and although he was propped up on three pillows, his eyes were closed.

Paul stood awkwardly for a moment, then put the Maltesers and the whisky down on the bedside cabinet. He felt as if he had entered a crowded room and could not find a single familiar face. He gazed out the window. When he turned back to the bed, Julian had opened his eyes and was looking at him.

'Paul?' Julian said, in a voice that did not sound the least bit sick.

'Hi, Julian…' Paul began, then abruptly stopped. What else to say? He could hardly tell him how sick he looked. He didn't want to apologise, he didn't want to dredge up the past. 'Here, I brought you these,' he finally muttered, gesturing at the whisky and chocolates.

'Thankyou,' Julian said, picking up the whisky and laughing. 'But I can't touch this stuff, so why don't you keep it.'

'I'm sorry, I thought you might be hanging out for some hard stuff, like in those movies where hospitals seem like prisons…'

'Yeah. Would be nice. But my liver's shot. Can't drink a drop. Hep C, you know.'

'Shit, Julian. I'm sorry. Ursula didn't say—'

'So that's how you found out. You know when I opened my eyes, I thought for a moment I was back at NIDA rehearsing that two-hander. Can't think what it's called… the Albee play?'

'*Zoo Story?*'

'Yeah. You had to beat me senseless.'

'No. You beat me up. I was left on the garden bench, pretending to be dead.'

'Trying to look like you weren't breathing.'

'If the director tells you to stop breathing, you stop breathing,' Paul said, suddenly uneasy about this reference to death in front of an obviously sick man.

'I hate directors,' Julian replied. If he was affected by the subject matter he showed no signs of it.

'You haven't changed, then.'

'I have. I have.'

Paul waited for Julian to elaborate, but he offered no explanation. Two nurses had walked over to the bed opposite and Paul glanced in their direction. He was always looking at women. Sometimes he pretended he was studying their posture or the way they walked as a preparation for acting, but he knew it wasn't true. Women magnetised his eyes and he followed their movements for no reason at all, just because that's what he did. He had done it for as long as he could remember. The nurses pulled the curtains around the bed and stepped inside them. The tenuous privacy of hospitals.

Paul turned back to Julian. He thought he detected a flicker of amusement in Julian's eyes, as if Julian had been watching Paul and not the nurses. Paul wanted to ask about the blonde one, but held his tongue. He didn't know if he could joke around with Julian or not. So many years had passed since they were twenty. It was like a pause in Beckett that's hard for an actor to hold, especially when the audience starts to cough and fidget.

Julian sat up in bed and reached for the Maltesers. 'Remember that code?' he said. 'The one you wouldn't fucking give me.'

Paul nodded.

'It didn't matter, mate. Ursula coughed it up. I went in one night after everyone had gone home. I wrote "The Truth Sucks" in white paint on MacPherson's door and signed it "Number One Fake". I was just looking for somewhere to stash the tin and the paintbrush when MacPherson came sauntering down the quadrangle towards me. I panicked. I thought he'd probably punch me out or something. But I was past caring too, so I stood by my handiwork and didn't flinch. MacPherson took one look at the graffiti and at the paintbrush in my hand and burst out laughing. I was stunned. I hated him so much I had dreamt of killing him, and here he was laughing at my vandalism.

'But then I realised he wasn't laughing at me, he was laughing at himself, at how he used to go on and on about the truth. I was ready for the customary abuse, but instead he put the key in the lock, opened the door of his office and asked me inside. He got a bottle of whisky out of the filing cabinet and poured two glasses. He gave me one and I took it and drank it straight away to make sure I wasn't dreaming. Then he told me I was lucky to be out of NIDA, that acting was a hell of a life and that he agreed with me, the truth really did suck. I didn't know what to say. It's as if he drew the venom out of me, turned my fangs into harmless white prongs. He actually listened to me – my confused wanderings, my hopeless ambitions. Then he told me about his career, how his marriage had broken up, how he'd never achieved what he wanted, how he'd taken this job for the money and how he'd come to believe that teaching was what you did if you were a failure. Those who can't act, teach, he said. He told me to just get on with being a failure – that you could learn to live with it. He said other stuff too, but somehow that night turned it around for me. I found a way of letting go. I found I could get on with things as long as I didn't see you guys… '

'So you weren't angry at me for not catching up?'

'Angry? Sure. I hated you for it.'

'I'm sorry.'

'Are you? It's the easiest word in the world to say, but who means it?'

'You mean who says it truthfully? As opposed to faking it?'

'Yeah. The old NIDA mantra.'

Truth sucks. Part of Paul wanted to apologise again, truthfully, but it seemed pointless. He didn't know if he was sorry, anyway. Ashamed perhaps, but not sorry. He could do a performance of sorry, but he wasn't sure he could do a truthful performance. So instead he asked, 'Can I do anything to help?'

'No.'

They looked at each other. Paul was no longer nervous. The visit had gone better than he could have hoped – except for how sick Julian seemed. But it wasn't something you talked about.

Julian offered Paul a Malteser and Paul took one gratefully. They talked for a while about old friends, those they'd bumped into and those they'd heard about.

Julian looked exhausted, so Paul got up to leave. 'You gonna be in here for long?' he asked.

'Yeah. More treatment. More tests.'

'Mind if I come in again?'

'Yeah. Sure. Keep me in Maltesers.'

Paul touched him on the shoulder and turned to go.

'Don't forget this,' Julian said, motioning to the whisky.

Paul picked it up and smiled at Julian, then turned away. The nurses had left without him even noticing. He felt that Julian was watching him leave, and although he wanted to check, he made his exit without looking back, like a trained, disciplined actor. Walking to the lift Paul felt sad, sadder than he'd felt for years. As empty as when his marriage had broken up. As empty as an out-of-work actor can feel after another unsuccessful audition. He knew that if he went home he'd drink the whole bottle of whisky and he didn't want to do that. I need to be with people, I need to talk, and I need to talk about Julian, he thought. And the best person to talk to would have to be Ursula.

Alone in the lift, he watched the lighted numbers cascade down. Why is your cheek so pale? he said to himself, remembering a line of Lysander's. How chance the roses there do fade so fast? But if he remembered rightly, he delivered the line to Hermia, not Demetrius. Yet it was Julian who had pale cheeks, who was literally fading away in a bed above him.

Paul walked out of the hospital doors into the late afternoon heat. He wanted a beer not a whisky, so he headed for the Marlborough, deciding as he sipped on his ale that he'd borrow the White Pages and try to track down Ursula. He quickly discovered that Ursula wasn't in the telephone book. Maybe she lived with a friend. She could be married or she could have a silent number. After all, she had been famous for a while, ten years ago, the sort of magazine-cover-talk-show-fame that only a few Australian actors achieved. There was nothing he could do about it. He didn't even know anyone who might know where Ursula was living.

He finished his beer, thought about another and decided against it. He realised he was the only one who was drinking on his own. A group of women, twenty-somethings, were partying at a nearby table. Their talk was loud and ostentatious, as if everyone had to know how much fun they were having. He was alone, but he wasn't the only one. What about Julian, yellow and out of it, too sick to appreciate the beauty of the nurses as they checked his pulse or wrote on the chart that clipped onto the end of the bed?

Staring at the ring of water his beer-glass made, Paul saw himself as a pathetic miser, a miser out of a Molière play who couldn't stand other people being happy. He wondered if other people saw him like that. There goes Paul Somerville, the miser, the giggling women whispered as he passed them, clicking their gin and tonics in glee at his hunched shoulders and slow shuffle to the door. He knew they weren't saying anything of the sort, but he was glad to get out onto King Street and wait at the bus stop. At least now he wasn't conspicuously alone.

As much as he tried to distract himself, the image of the miser wouldn't leave him, and he caught himself checking that his wallet was safe, or calculating how much money he had left that week. He had to be careful and scrupulous with money or he wouldn't survive. It was just part of being an actor. No point complaining about it. No point living on credit either if you couldn't pay it back eventually. It was the life he had chosen; no one had forced him into it. But he didn't want to be frugal with people as well. OK, he wasn't a scrooge who hoarded gold in a shoebox. But what scared him was the idea that he might be the sort of scrooge who had forgotten how to love.

* * *

A box of Maltesers in his hand, Paul stopped at the entrance to the ward. Ursula was sitting in the chair near the bed, talking to Julian. Instead of a hospital gown, Julian wore a white singlet, and he looked a little healthier than Paul remembered. The two of them were deep in conversation. Occasionally Ursula's hands flashed out, her long elegant arms and theatrical wrists reminding him of Meryl Streep. When Julian spoke, Ursula rested her hand on the white sheet in a manner that appeared to Paul to be proprietary, not just friendly. Every so often Ursula laughed, a spontaneous and very musical laugh that seemed to clang and bounce off the curtain rails and sweep through the room. Why was he here? Julian didn't need him. Whatever Julian had with Ursula, whatever form of friendship or love they shared, it was more than Paul could ever hope to offer Julian. Paul wanted to leave then, but before he could do anything, Ursula noticed him, said something to Julian, and the two of them waved him in.

Paul greeted them both and gave Julian the Maltesers. Ursula moved her chair back and Paul sat between them.

'I'm sorry if I interrupted anything,' Paul said.

'Not at all,' Julian replied. 'I'm through with whingeing about hospital food. That and the 5:30 wake up call to see if I want a cup of tea—'

'When he doesn't drink tea,' Ursula added.

'And the barbarity of daytime soaps. We were just starting in on the screen kiss.'

'Do you have a favourite?' Ursula wanted to know.

Paul shrugged. He felt that he was expected to come up with something captivating, but could only think of James Stewart and Kim Novak in *Vertigo*, and he wasn't sure if they had kissed or not.

Luckily no one else seemed to remember either.

'What about stage kisses?' Paul asked. He had kissed on stage and loved it – the silent attention of the audience, the way the actual kiss was different each night. He always looked forward to the kiss, was always aware that he was kissing a woman, and always slipped out of character in the process.

Ursula mulled it over. She laughed and said, 'Yep. I've done that. Even though I told myself it was just work, there's something about kissing a man, or a woman… It puts ideas into your head.'

'Like Daniel Day Lewis playing Hamlet and seeing ghosts,' Paul suggested.

'Yes,' Ursula replied. 'It gets personal, kissing someone. You tell yourself it's just a physical action, but it still messes with your mind. I guess it's not possible to keep things in neat little compartments. And I remember one play where I had this urge to slip my tongue in… it was a long passionate kiss and one night we bumped teeth and it happened and we had such a hard time suppressing our giggles and keeping the scene together.'

'That's exactly it,' Paul said. 'Except I never pretended it was professional. Usually I couldn't wait to go mouth to mouth.'

Julian mimed playing the violin and everyone laughed.

Gradually the subject of the conversation changed and Julian began talking about his illness. Paul realised for the first time that Julian didn't just have Hepatitis C, but that he had liver cancer as well. He was in for a series of tests to see if he was suitable for a liver transplant.

Ursula asked about the waiting list; Julian thought it could be as long as eighteen months. Though it could happen sooner. Julian was hoping to get lucky. Paul hated medical conversations, and the ease with which some people rattled off medical terms baffled him. But he tried to listen carefully. The news that Julian's tumour had doubled in size in the last month sounded very serious.

Paul nodded and did his best to model interest and empathy, but he felt his mind wandering back to the conversation about the screen kiss.

He noticed Ursula's lips, how wide they were, how kissable, how she was wearing this rich, red shade of lipstick. And before he could stop himself, he saw himself kissing her under a single spot in the centre of a darkened stage. They were lying on a couch that creaked under their weight, and as he leant into the kiss, her tongue slid past his lips until all he could feel was her ravenous tongue and the warmth of the spot on his cheek, and the kiss went on and on as the stage lights became brighter and brighter.

Paul was dimly aware that Julian had yawned, that Ursula had said he needed to rest, and that Ursula had risen to leave. Paul stood too, quickly said goodbye to Julian and thoughtfully left Ursula and Julian alone. At least it appeared to be thoughtful, though it was more out of his desire to not see the two of them kiss.

'Wait for me,' Ursula called after him. 'I won't be long.'

Paul waited at the lifts. He felt sorry for Julian, really sorry, but he couldn't help wishing that he was prostrate on the bed and being attended to by Ursula. It occurred to him that he had come to hospital hoping to see Ursula, not Julian. Ashamed of himself, he decided to leave at once and not wait for Ursula. But before he could act on this decision, Ursula arrived at the lifts.

The lift was crowded and they wedged themselves in. Despite the crush, the hospital odour of reheated food and heavy grade antiseptic was strong. In the foyer they passed the gift shop with its gaudy pink balloons and rows of white bears with red bowties, then dodged the smokers lingering around the entrance. Outside, an assertive wind tugged at Ursula's hair and blew Paul's jacket so that it threatened to turn inside out.

'Fancy a drink?' Ursula asked. 'I could certainly do with one.'

So they headed for the Marlborough together, a day after Paul had searched the White Pages for Ursula's number. At the door of the hotel Ursula stepped forward at the same time as Paul and they almost bumped together, and like two improvising actors they repeated the blunder in a slightly different manner until they were talking about the time they studied *lazzi* with the Commedia dell'Arte teacher, and how all the routines of the Marx Brothers and the Three Stooges and countless other comics were made to seem so simple.

Paul suggested Guinness and Ursula agreed. It had been a favourite of theirs at NIDA and with a black schooner in each hand, Paul momentarily felt young again. At least with Ursula he would not feel defensive about his fluctuating, struggling career, would not feel he was a failure because he wasn't Heath Ledger or David Wenham.

He put the schooners down on the table and smiled.

'You look happy,' Ursula said, 'but then you always did.'

'Makes a change. I came here yesterday after seeing Julian. I felt so down, seeing him like that…'

'Yeah. I know. But let's not talk about Julian, if you don't mind. I need a break.' Ursula took a sip of Guinness, then licked the white foam off her upper lip. 'I've been meaning to ask you about Jack. What's he up to?'

'He's at uni studying environmental science. Thank God he didn't follow me into acting. He's having a ball. Majoring in geography. Seems like he spends half the time down at the beach, studying the coastline, apparently. Good work if you can get it. I met him down at Coogee the other day and we had a drink.'

'He's moved out?'

'No. Still with his Mum. You remember Leeanna.'

'Yeah. I heard about the break-up.'

'We don't even fight any more. And now that Jack's an adult there's no way we can use him to score points… I'm ashamed when I think back to what we did…'

Ursula nodded. She told him how her sister's marriage had ended when her husband met another woman while walking the dog. Ursula no longer expected people to stay together… But she hated the way people tried to hurt and maim the person they used to hold hands with. She admired the people who were still friends, who treated their ex-lovers like adults, not trolls.

Paul laughed at the mention of trolls. He asked Ursula what she thought of the troll in the *Lord of the Rings* and they spent a few minutes discussing the trilogy.

'Pity that Tolkien didn't write more female characters,' Ursula suggested. 'After all, there's only Galadriel, Arwen and that great big spider…'

'There's Eowyn,' Paul added. 'But you're right, not much to audition for. Though you could have played the spider!'

'Careful! If I was smaller and younger I might have played a hobbit wench. But who'd want that as their last big credit? Yeah, I've just finished playing Samwise Gamgee's wife… Whose wife? You can barn dance like a hobbit? Great!'

They were well onto their second schooner and Paul excused himself to go to the toilet. It was going well, he thought, very well. He paused at the mirrors, flicked his hair into place and grinned. He had just made it to the urinal in time, breathing out as the relief swept through his body.

He glanced up at the wall and saw it, the condom vending machine. No, he thought, she wouldn't. But then another voice in his head took over, saying why not, you might as well be prepared, you never know when your luck's going to change. He remembered how he had once gone home with a woman and she wouldn't do it with him because neither of them had a condom. And here was a condom machine that only needed a $2 coin to operate it. 'Ultra Protection', read one of the advertisements. The other one read 'XXXtra Ribbing for her XXXtra Pleasure'. Right, he thought. Ursula will be impressed with that, really impressed. But he already had his wallet out and a $2 coin in his hand. He had to hurry back; there was no point hesitating and the last thing he wanted was for someone to come in while he was standing there, coin in hand, in front of the machine. It would be like your mother walking in on you while you were masturbating.

Paul tried to put the coin in the slot and dropped it. It bounced on the step, rolled towards the urinal and clanked into the tray. Damn it, he thought. He hated the thought of losing $2, but he didn't want to get down on his knees to extract the coin from the urine-soaked tray. Would his hand fit through the bars? No, he wasn't going to try. He had this vision of his hand wedged into the grille, stuck there with his fingers a few centimetres short of the coin. He turned away, fished in his pocket and found another $2 coin.

This time Paul managed to put the coin in the slot. He pushed it in and the coin disappeared, but there was no sign of any condom. 'Fuck!' he cried loudly and his voice echoed around the cubicles and came back to him. He pushed the coin slot in again, then slammed the condom machine with his fist, just as Fonz had punched the pinball machine in *Happy Days*. Or was it the jukebox? Whatever it was, he was no Fonz, for the little cranny where the condom was meant to appear was still empty. Feeling very frustrated, feeling very foolish, he turned and kicked the door open, walked past the mirrors without glancing up – how could he look himself in the eye now? – pushed the next door open violently, and headed back towards Ursula.

'Sorry,' he said as he sat down, noticing that Ursula had finished her drink. 'Can I get you another?'

'No. Actually I have to go in a minute. I'm working at Cellarmasters tonight. You know the ropes. Have to make ends meet and all that.'

Paul knew all about Cellarmasters, one of the refuges for out-of-work actors. He had worked there once, but he preferred waiting on tables to telephone sales. He sipped on his Guinness and made small talk.

But although he tried to distract himself, the elusive condom was still in the forefront of his mind. He could feel his cheeks reddening, even though Ursula could not have known, would never know. He wondered if he'd become the sort of man he despised: overweight, middle-aged, obsessed with sex. He hated all the male stereotypes in circulation – the commitment-phobic bastard, the absent father, the emotional cripple, the power hungry suit. Then again, why worry? Sexual urges are healthy, aren't they? And surely now that he was past forty he could give up on the Catholic guilt. What he wanted, everyone wanted, especially if they'd been drinking.

Yet why did he think that Ursula would sleep with him? Either she had someone already, or she was involved with Julian. Except that she never mentioned anyone else. And although she was close to Julian, Paul had a hunch they were friends, not lovers. Paul didn't know what to think. Ursula had stopped talking and was getting up, he realised suddenly. Must listen better, he reminded himself as he followed her through the bar.

He caught up with her at the door and made as if to bump into her again.

'Now, now, Curly,' she said and strode ahead.

'Thanks,' she said when they were both out on the street. 'I needed that.' And to Paul's surprise, she threw her arms around his neck, hugged him, then kissed him lightly on each cheek.

'Give me a ring,' she said over her shoulder as she hailed a taxi and jumped inside.

But I don't have your number, Paul thought, as he watched the amber lights on the roof of the cab cut into the traffic and speed away.

* * *

Paul spent the next week in the studio narrating a fantasy novel. It was tiring work, but at least it was work that was related to acting. He liked the challenge of juggling different voices and maintaining their consistency: the airy lightness of the elves; the gruff, earnest dwarves; the wheedling, sonorous necromancer. It was easy to lose yourself in this world of quests and mortal dangers, Paul said to his producer during one of their eye breaks. It might not be Tolkien, but you could still escape into a story where the ordinary person mattered. No wonder people liked reading these books. The threat and tension was such a contrast to Vegemite on toast, the train trip to work, an evening of television. The story allowed you to fly, when normally you had to be content with crawling. The producer gazed at Paul and made a reassuring grunt, but Paul had the feeling that she didn't get it at all. She was far too young to have experienced a life of crawling.

Paul was too tired after work to visit Julian or track down Ursula's number. He stopped at the Canterbury pool on the way home and swam laps, letting the strain of concentrating on the novel's fine print seep away as he battled against the water. He swam in the centre of the lane, over the black line of tiles, finding its certainty soothing. The black line was dependable and straight and suggested a journey.

Actors were always talking about their character's journeys, but even the journeys of the best-written characters were finite and manageable. The biggest problem for the actor was that you knew the end point before you started. It was hard to prevent that knowledge from infecting the performance. You had to play each moment as if you didn't know what was coming next, play it without foresight. It was difficult to perform a scene again and again, yet perform it as if you were experiencing it for the first time. The best actors, the ones Paul admired, created their character moment by moment, without any indication that they had done this a hundred times already.

That Friday, just after Paul arrived home from the pool, Ursula rang. He walked around the flat talking to her, running his hand through his wet hair. She told him that Julian wanted to have a barbecue at the hospital and that the nurse in charge on Saturdays had agreed. This seemed to be the reason for the call.

'Have you got a barbecue, Paul?' she asked.

'Yep. A Weber.'

'Perfect. Can you bring it in tomorrow, around six?'

'Sure. Can I bring some food? Kebabs? Sausages? Fish?'

'No. I'll take care of that. The barbie's perfect. Look, I'm working again tonight so I have to fly. See you tomorrow.'

'See you then.'

Paul put the phone down on the table and thought back over the call. She had seemed so friendly at first, so interested in the fantasy novel, the swimming, how he was getting on. He wasn't making it up, was he, the warmth he heard in her voice, the genuine interest and affection? He had started thinking dates himself, was just about to suggest a movie or a drink, when she had brought up the barbecue. It was good to be included, but thinking back, there didn't seem to be one single occasion when he had seen Ursula in the last couple of weeks that hadn't involved Julian. Even the drinks at the Marlborough were straight after a visit to the hospital. Was he being too sensitive? Or just plain jealous? He didn't know. For an actor who had spent his career playing subtext, he couldn't read the subtext in his own life. He guessed that there was nothing to do but order fish and chips, have a quiet meal and sleep on it. And then clean the Weber, check the state of the heat beads and see if he needed any Little Lucifers.

The following afternoon Paul sat on the bus holding the barbecue drum on his knees. He didn't have a car because cars ate money – it was one of the ways he had survived for so long as an actor. He had stashed the stand and his bag in the luggage area and grabbed the closest seat. Holding the Weber was like holding a fat child, except that the Weber didn't squirm and wriggle. The other passengers gave him odd looks, and he remembered how he'd been on buses in Bali when people got on with live chickens, or squealing pigs with their feet trussed together, or sacks of coconuts that they'd been collecting all day. And here he was in Newtown, cradling a barbecue. Maybe the First World and the Third World weren't that far apart, after all. He felt rather fond of his Weber. The next time someone asked him that dreaded question, 'So what do you do?' he would say, 'I barbecue. I'm a barbecue man.' No explanations, no further details. Just 'I barbecue'.

At the hospital, the party was already underway. Julian was sitting up in bed talking to his sister. Ursula was fixing drinks, while an old school friend of Julian's was setting up a food table. Paul greeted everyone, took the barbecue out onto the balcony and assembled it. He filled the kettle with heat beads, and spread the Little Lucifers out strategically, arranging them like the four points of a compass. The accelerators were easy to light and he soon had them fizzing and spluttering around the beads. It sure beat rubbing sticks together. He watched them take, added another, and then put the grille down. Once the beads were hot, he'd be ready to cook.

Ursula brought him out a beer and they stood looking out over the hospital grounds. In the distance the spire of a university college rose into the trees. The sun was sinking slowly, bathing the courtyard in a serene, late afternoon light.

'This is my favourite time of day,' Ursula said and Paul nodded.

They stood there without talking. Paul didn't want to be the first to break the silence. He listened to the birds chattering; he watched a currawong perched on a telegraph pole. He listened for Ursula's breathing, but he couldn't hear it over the whooshing of the traffic. It was enough to stand next to her and not do anything, not think anything, just stand there. It wasn't an experience he wanted to find words for. He sipped on his beer and stood there until she suggested that they rejoin the party.

Someone had draped streamers off the curtain rails and a couple of the nurses were blowing up balloons. Paul chatted for a few minutes then went back out onto the balcony to cook the meat. He started the sausages first – long Italian sausages with an attractive marbled appearance. They were good quality; the skins held and they browned quickly, only spitting a little. Poorer quality sausages tended to ooze and flare, sending flames up towards your face.

He liked standing close to the heat, watching the flames lift dramatically, then die. It was a link to an outdoor life, to cavemen who sat around fires cooking the game that they had trapped and killed themselves. It must be in the blood, Paul thought, this thing with fires; it must be some sort of evolutionary link with primeval man. You only had to go to a camping ground to find people gathered around fires, staring into the flames and losing some of their pretensions, their armour. Turn the sausages, flip the steaks, let the heat warm your face as you sip a cold one. It was the best place to think. When he first started barbecuing he had blackened everything, but now he had a feel for timing, he knew how to find the hot spots and the cooler areas. He was at ease with calamari, chicken and cobs of corn. Forget metrosexuals, he said to himself, what every woman needs is a barbecue man.

Soon Paul took a full tray of meat inside. He served Julian a rare steak, picked out a charcoaled sausage on request and added some salad and a slice of bread. Everyone else got up to help themselves. Paul sat down at the foot of the bed and listened to the conversation.

'I can't believe that Howard's won four elections,' said Julian's friend. 'It's enough to make you want to emigrate.'

'I wouldn't do that,' replied Chelsea, one of the nurses. 'There's nothing for it but to party and party hard. Things will only get worse, so I'm going to enjoy myself while I can.'

Paul ate his steak, mopping up the oozing blood with a slice of bread. He wasn't as disappointed as the others, for as far as he could see politics didn't affect his life. They couldn't legislate away the taste of potato salad, they couldn't stop him from picking out the blackest sausage, wrapping it up in bread and smothering it with tomato sauce. He enjoyed listening to passion and fervour, habitually making a note of people's excited expressions and rising inflections in case he ever needed to act out a similar scene.

'The steak's great,' Julian said when the whingeing had run its course. 'Actually I think it's probably the best meal that's been cooked on the premises. Thanks Ursula, Paul, and everyone else who had a hand in it. I'm glad you could all come, for I'm going home in a day or two.'

'Are you sure you're well enough?' Ursula asked. 'Maybe you should go to a nursing home first.'

'I'll manage. I'll be back once they've found me a new liver. Actually, as soon as I'm out I'm going to pop into DJ's and put one on lay-by. I've always been a big fan of lay-by.'

Typical of Julian, Paul thought, to turn everything into a joke. If Julian was afraid or angry he never showed it. He seemed to be able to get on with it, to accept his illness and avoid wallowing in despair or self-pity. Though maybe like everyone else he did have his low points, the times that seemed hopeless and beyond fixing.

Once the main course was finished, Ursula cut up a lime and co-conut cake and distributed the extra slices around the ward. Paul went back out onto the balcony to dismantle the barbecue. He wasn't look-ing forward to carrying it home on the bus and was relieved when Ursula poked her head out and offered him a lift.

The party was breaking up and people were saying goodbye to Julian. Tomato sauce and meat juices had spilt on the sheets. 'I'll sleep well tonight,' Julian said, pointing to the stains. 'This place smells better already, less antiseptic, less like a morgue.'

'Don't say that,' Ursula replied.

Julian laughed. 'Don't worry. They might have wheeled me in here, but I'm planning on walking out.'

Paul hugged Julian goodbye, then picked up the Weber and his backpack. He walked with Ursula to the lifts.

'I don't think he'll cope on his own,' she said, as the doors closed. 'I can help for a while, but I'm off touring in February. Still it's only December now… All I want for Christmas is a new liver.'

As the doors opened at the next floor, Paul said, 'Hearts, lungs, new and used livers.'

'If only it was that easy,' Ursula said and sighed.

Walking to the car, Ursula talked about how much Julian had deterio-rated. She was investigating nursing options and herbal remedies, and had suggested to Julian that he visit a faith healer, though he hadn't shown the slightest interest in the idea. 'You have to make miracles happen,' she said as they searched for her car.

When they finally found it, Paul loaded the barbecue into the boot.

'Join me for a drink?' she asked, as he slid his seatbelt on.

'Sure, I don't have to be anywhere.'

'My flatmate's away for the weekend and I don't want to be alone. Not at the moment.'

Paul couldn't help but register the use of the term flatmate, but he stopped himself there. He wasn't going to indulge in any more wishful thinking; his last performance before the condom machine had been enough. He had this feeling that Ursula would talk and talk and it would be his role to listen.

Her flat was on the third floor of an old-style red brick building. It was set right at the back, away from the street, with views over a park and the river. The door opened into a living room with polished floors and hardly any furniture. The only sign of clutter was on the walls, which were crammed with theatrical posters. A TV cabinet sat in the middle of one wall, a maroon couch placed directly opposite it.

'Time to chill out,' Ursula said. 'I feel like a G and T. Do you want one? I don't have any beer.'

'Sure. I'm partial to gin. I haven't had any for yonks. I love the taste of quinine in the tonic. If I had malaria I'd overdose on quinine.'

'Have a seat and I'll fix them.'

But Paul didn't sit down. He walked around and studied the posters. Plays, an occasional film, musicals and cabaret. He hadn't realised how much work Ursula had done. Name a theatre company in Australia and she'd worked for them, right round the country. Black Swan in Perth, Smiling Gecko in Cairns, La Boite in Bris-bane, Playbox and Griffin, as well as the mainstream ones in the southern capitals. And such an impressive body of work: *Angels in America, Night on Bald Mountain, Titus Andronicus, Tis a Pity She's A Whore*. He was standing in front of a poster for *Top Girls* when she returned.

She handed him the glass and stood next to him, looking at the poster. 'I played Pope Joan in that. One of the best monologues I've ever delivered. Do you know the play?'

'Yeah. Doesn't she get pregnant to one of the cardinals and have a baby?'

'That's right. She's stoned to death during a procession, just after she goes into labour. I loved the first act. This manager gets a promotion at work. She breaks through the glass ceiling and invites six famous women to dinner to help her celebrate. We sat there on the stage, eating fabulous food off white porcelain and white tablecloths, talking over each other, as you do. But the play peaks too early and the second half's a let down. Who'd have thought back at NIDA that one of my favourite roles would have been Pope Joan?' Ursula put a hand on his head and made the sign of the cross over him with her gin glass. 'Go my son and sin no more.'

'I feel like a new man,' Paul said.

'Come on,' Ursula beckoned, 'let's sit down.'

Paul sat on one end of the couch. Ursula gave him her glass to hold and went to fetch a small table. She placed it within easy reach and sat down. They drank and talked about the plays they'd been in, the directors they'd worked with, the highs and lows of acting. It was easy and comforting, talking shop.

Paul encouraged Ursula to talk. She had this way of holding the glass out in front of her as if she was going to drink, her forearm and wrist turned towards him. She's not capable, Paul thought, of doing anything that isn't graceful. When she drank, she drank lustily, and was soon on to her second, then her third.

She drained the last of her gin, put the glass down, draped her arm along the couch and wriggled close.

Paul hadn't been expecting this. Her breast pushed into his shoulder as she leant over and kissed his cheek. He turned towards her and she took his chin in her long fingers and kissed his lips. Paul could smell the alcohol on her breath, but he kissed her back. Should I say something? he thought. Should I suggest that she's a little drunk and might regret it later? No, don't be an idiot. When a chance like this comes along, you take it. There might not be another.

And with that thought he kissed her back. He put a hand behind her head, feeling the heat of the skin there, below the hairline. Outside a car door slammed and a bird called *curragh, curragh, kwong*. The last sound rose in inflection and pealed like a bell.

His fingers slipped down her neck, inside her shirt. Her eyes were closed, her kisses greedy. What was that line of Slessor's? How Sydney girls were angry-tongued. Or was it Tahitian girls? Or was it both?

Didn't I recite it at NIDA? For voice class. In front of Ursula and Julian and everyone. Damn, there I go again. Can't seem to get rid of the idea that this is about Julian, that somehow I'm an escape for her, a crutch, a replacement. That she really wants him and not me. Amazing really, how you can kiss someone and not even be thinking about them, how your mind can be in one place and your body another. Except every time she moves her hand I'm wondering where she'll put it next, I'm willing it lower, I'm starting to wish she'd undo my shirt or invite me to undo hers. I've always loved undressing; I hate it when women rush that stage. It should be slow, with plenty of kisses and maybe a little ripping. Though not my best shirt. This is the longest kiss. I like her tongue, it's angry alright. Angry is the right word for sure, as angry as... What? Can't think. Can't think anymore. Just her name. Just think Ursula and remind yourself you're not dreaming...

I think the kiss is ending. Wonder if it would make the *Guinness Book of Records*. No, probably not. They shoot horses, don't they? Someone must have done a kissing marathon already. Blisters. Cold sores. Probably a couple of gay guys hold the record. Or transsexuals. Kiss a trannie and feel his erection up against you. No thanks. Not for me. Ah, she's smiling at me. Such a lovely smile.

Ursula stood up and motioned for Paul to follow. She walked towards the bedroom. He followed her to the middle of the room then stopped, struck by a poster he hadn't noticed before. A single match flaring in a darkened room. And the words 'Burn This' across the bottom. His stared at the flame. What actually happened in that play? He couldn't quite remember.

Ursula didn't seem to be in the bedroom. The blankets and top sheet on the bed had been turned back. Then he saw her coming out of the ensuite. She had taken off her trousers and perhaps her knickers as well, though he couldn't be sure. Feigning modesty, he lifted his hands to his eyes and turned his back to her. She grabbed him from behind and kissed him on the side of the neck. As she kissed, she fumbled with his belt. Not so fast, he thought, but he didn't say anything.

Ursula shuffled him towards the bed with a sideways movement like a crab crawl, until they both fell onto the bed, laughing. She tugged at his belt again and this time undid the buckle. She pushed the button through, unzipped his fly and pulled down his trousers and boxer shorts, until they bunched up and caught on one leg. Now they were both naked from the waist down.

Paul unbuttoned her shirt, found the clip of her bra, and for once, managed to unclip it without a prolonged, embarrassing struggle. He pulled the bra forward and along her arms. Ursula reached over him and began to drag at his bunched trousers. The fullness of her breasts as they swung free excited him. He steadied one breast with his hand and took the nipple into his mouth. He loved breasts, their whiteness, their softness. He had often wondered if this went back to childhood, to being breastfed. Or was it a function of the flow of images, the constant media bombardment of chest and cleavage? Did a day ever pass without him seeing photographs of women in bras or bikinis? Or just passing in the street, their breasts looming up at him. Breasts were good to look at, but how much nicer to wobble them in your hands, to hide them in your mouth. He sucked and kissed, pushed his tongue against her sternum and pressed both breasts against his face.

Paul could feel her hand reaching across his stomach and suddenly he thought – condoms. I don't have a single condom.

As if in response, Ursula pushed him onto his back, draped herself across him and opened a drawer by the side of the bed. She found what she was looking for and flopped back down beside him. She ripped at the condom wrapper with her teeth and drew out the condom. Ursula reached down and kissed him on the tummy, below the navel. Then she flicked at his penis with her finger so it bounced back and forwards, like some sort of elasticised skittle. She laughed and rolled the condom down onto him. Paul couldn't see her do it, but he felt her fingers on him, then the rubber. He studied the bumpy outline of her spine, the fineness of her shoulders. Then Ursula lay back down and kissed him. They kissed for a long time. Somehow Paul sensed that she was struggling with something, some issue that was bothering her.

This uncertainty spurred Paul on and he gently rolled onto Ursula. He took his penis in his hand, directed it to where he thought her vagina was, and pushed. He felt her give slightly and pushed some more. He glanced at Ursula, but her eyes were closed so he pushed again, brushing her forehead with his lips as he slipped inside her. It was one of the moments he loved best about sex – always surprising, always joyous.

But no sooner was he inside her and beginning to draw back and push again, beginning to grind pelvic bone against pelvic bone, when he realised that Ursula was crying. He held his hips still and lifted himself up on his arms, so that their bodies were barely touching. But he was still inside her and he was aware of that sensation as much as the tears that were spilling out of her eyes.

'What's the matter?' he asked.

She frowned. 'I don't know.'

'Do you want me to stop?'

'Yes. No. I don't know. I don't know what I want anymore.'

Paul wanted to keep going, but she looked so anguished, so confused. The tears were coming quicker now, running down her cheeks and collecting on her beautiful neck. Paul wished he could wind back the tape to the moment when he was undoing her bra and find a different way of proceeding. But he knew he would regret it later if there was even the slightest suggestion that he had pressured Ursula.

She was still sobbing. 'I think you'd better stop,' Ursula said, and Paul put his fingers around the base of the condom and drew himself out.

He lay down beside her and sighed. 'What is it?' he asked.

'I can't explain,' she said slowly. 'Not now. If ever. I'm all mixed up.'

'Should I go?'

'Yes, I think so. But can you hold me first?'

She rolled onto her side with her back to him. Paul reached down and pulled a sheet up over them, then cuddled up against her. He held her around the waist and over a shoulder, trying not to make a thing about her breasts. They lay like that for five minutes, maybe longer, and Paul felt her sobbing subside and her breathing deepen. He wondered if she was going to sleep.

Just my luck, he thought. But he wasn't angry, he realised; just frustrated. Sex was so delicate, so tricky that even grown people didn't understand it. Not completely. He couldn't imagine discussing this with anyone. Ursula perhaps, but they'd probably never talk about it. And he certainly wouldn't be telling Julian, lying in hospital with his stuffed liver and his jaundiced skin. Thinking of Julian, he felt glad that it hadn't happened. Yet it had happened, too. Ursula had mauled him on the couch and mauled him in the bedroom. He was frustrated, yet elated.

Ursula turned and looked at him. She hadn't gone to sleep at all. Her eyelids were still wet. She stroked his forehead and said, 'I'm sorry'. Then she kissed him on the lips. It was a kiss of friendship and genuine gratitude, and Paul knew it was time to go.

He got up and dressed quickly, without saying anything. He felt decent and chivalrous, but he knew that if he stayed for long he'd be tempted to tell Ursula off for coming onto him, then drawing away.

He didn't trust himself to keep quiet. He didn't want to say anything he might later regret.

Once he was dressed, Paul fetched his backpack and came back into the bedroom. Suddenly he remembered the barbecue in Ursula's boot. 'What about the Weber?' he asked.

'Don't worry. I'll drop it around.'

Paul nodded, walked over to the bed and kissed her on each cheek. Ursula smiled ruefully at him and held her hands up in the air, as if to say, who can explain this, who can explain life?

The sheet slipped and he glimpsed her breasts again and with that image fixed in his mind he turned, called goodbye over his shoulder and let himself out of the flat.

* * *

As soon as Paul stepped out of the taxi, the hot northerly flayed his hair and tugged at his coat. He squinted, put his hand up to shield his eyes and hurried towards the chapel. He hadn't meant to be late – it was the trains, the consistently unreliable trains.

What a relief to be inside, out of the heat. The service had already started and there were no seats left. He found a spot to stand, leaning against the doorway where he could see over the woman in front of him. The coffin had been placed at the centre of the aisle at the edge of a raised platform. Paul found it hard to imagine Julian lying inside it; he didn't want to think of Julian as still and cold.

A man finished reading from the bible and Julian's sister made her way to the lectern. She was four years older than Julian and just from the way she talked, it was clear that they had been close. She described Julian's school years, briefly mentioned his time at NIDA and went on to his business achievements. Paul learnt that Julian had developed and patented the stock-counting device that was used by stackers in supermarkets. Apparently, it had made Julian very wealthy.

This is typical, Paul thought, another account of a man's life according to his occupation, his career. He remembered the first improvisation workshop at NIDA, how Julian had played a door-to-door salesman selling God, and how Paul had almost lost it when Julian went through his spiel. Julian had been so convincing, so spontaneous and inventive. But tuning in again, Paul realised that Julian's sister was talking about other aspects of Julian's life – how he loved body-boarding, how he had been active in the Big Brother scheme that befriended troubled teenagers, how he hosted dinner parties where he cooked lamb shanks and cheesecake.

These anecdotes surprised Paul; he realised that the Julian he knew was contained by the two-and-a-half years at NIDA.

At the end of second year, they had taken a trip up the coast. They had gone for a drink the night before and on the way home they had stolen a garden gnome from someone's front yard. A typical enough gnome with a red hat, a full beard and a somewhat faded blue coat. It was standing at the edge of a pond holding a wooden fishing line out over the water.

Julian picked up the gnome, took one look at it and christened it Mac, after the Head of Acting.

'What are you doing?' Paul asked.

'We're taking Mac on a holiday. He looks like he needs it.'

'You're nicking a garden gnome?'

'No, we're just borrowing it. And I'll make sure he writes home so these good people don't worry about him.'

And so despite Leeanna's protests that this was a bad example for Jack, the four of them set off on their trip up the coast with the garden gnome in the middle of the back seat. They took the first photo of Mac in front of the Big Banana at Coffs Harbour. Paul put sunglasses on Mac for the photo, while Julian wrote, 'Top banana milkshakes here. Missing you, XXX' on the back. At Lennox Head they had great fun balancing Mac on a surfboard just as the waves were about to break. They chose a photo that made Mac look like he was hanging five. At Nimbin they put a joint in the gnome's mouth and a bag of marijuana in his hand. In a bar on the Gold Coast they photographed Mac surrounded by gorgeous young women drinking schooners of beer. Finally they put him on a beach towel with Kerouac's *On the Road* on one side and a bottle of Johnson's Baby Oil on the other. Julian's last note was deadpan: 'Flying home Saturday. See you at the airport. Love Mac'. If the owners hadn't previously named their gnome, then Julian had done it for them.

Paul could remember it all vividly, despite the twenty years that had passed: Julian sitting in the back seat of the station wagon with Mac on his knee singing along to the country standard, 'Stand By Your Man', and each time replacing the word 'man' with 'gnome'. You had to be there, Paul thought, but the memory seemed like a good way to send off Julian. His sister had finished talking and everyone was singing a hymn. Paul wanted to sing, 'Stand By Your Gnome'; he wanted to lean over a grave and toss in a copy of Stanislavsky; he longed to drive and drive up the coast, only stopping to bury his head in the breaking surf. He wanted Julian back; he wanted his own youth back. The tears welled up in his eyes and he could not stop them.

He saw the back of Ursula's head, three rows from the front. After the evening in her flat he had tried to ring her a couple of times but had only managed to get the answering machine. Then Ursula had rung him to tell him that Julian had died and to pass on the funeral details. They just couldn't find another liver in time, she said. Paul could hear the pain in her voice. She spoke slowly and hesitated a lot, as if she hadn't found a set of words to make it easier on herself. Paul had wanted to talk for longer, but Ursula said she had other calls to make and hung up quickly.

The service ended and the coffin disappeared behind a sliding partition. Later that day, Julian's body would burn in a serious fire. Though not in the coffin. They would recycle that, or at the very least remove the mock gold handles. With burials you saw what happened, you were able to toss a handful of dirt on the coffin, you could linger by the grave and return later to see the mound covered in marble or grass. Somehow it seemed easier than watching the coffin disappear behind a partition, easier to say goodbye.

People were trailing past Paul, leaving the chapel. He turned and made his way outside and was assaulted at once by the heat and the wind. Looking around he couldn't see anyone he knew, couldn't see where Ursula was. Someone was pointing out a woman in a black dress and saying that was Julian's ex-wife, Melanie. She stood with her arm around her ten-year-old son. Paul looked at the boy – his blond hair, his shoulders beginning to thicken, the way he was standing with his head down as if he didn't want to talk to anyone. Julian had mentioned Chris at the hospital, but never Melanie.

'Paul.' Ursula's voice came from behind him. She was wearing a charcoal suit and a white blouse. Her eyes were red. She wrapped Paul up in a hug and held him for what seemed like ten seconds, maybe longer. 'I'm so glad you could come,' she said.

'I nearly didn't make it,' he said. 'The train was late, I couldn't get a taxi—'

'Why didn't you ring me? I would have picked you up. Sometimes Paul, I just don't... Well, let me drop you home, anyway.'

'Thanks, Ursula. That'd be good.'

The wind blew Ursula's hair across her face. She flicked it back into place, took Paul by the arm and turned their backs into the wind.

'I can't believe he's gone,' Paul said.

'I know. I kept telling him to hang in there, that they'd get him a new liver, but he wasn't lucky. And you know he only shared needles once or twice before giving up drugs for good.'

Paul shrugged. It was one of the things he had liked about Julian, his recklessness, his lack of fear.

'Look,' Ursula said, 'I want to give my condolences to Melanie and Chris and then I'm off. I can't face the wake. Not today.'

Paul thought that he should follow Ursula and do the same, but he didn't know what he'd say. And he hadn't met either of them. He watched Ursula weave through the crowd and greet them. She was talking to Julian's son and he was looking up at her, and although Paul couldn't hear what she said, her hand seemed to spin a web of comfort around Chris. It wasn't long before Ursula had hugged the boy, kissed Melanie and turned back towards Paul.

She said something to Paul and he answered back, but he wasn't really listening. He was thinking how Julian's life was over too quickly and how there was nothing that could change that now, nothing that he or anyone else could do about it.

Ursula opened the car and Paul sat down in the front seat. It was like entering a furnace. Paul's mouth felt dry. He could feel the sweat trickling down his back. He glanced at Ursula but she seemed preoccupied.

They were at the gates of the crematorium before either of them spoke. 'Oh God, I hate funerals,' Ursula said.

'But you're good at it. I never know what to say. I feel like I'm acting without a single bloody rehearsal.'

'You don't have to be good. Bumbling works. Sincerity helps. But no one notices anyway.'

'Yeah, I know. But saying you're sorry just seems so inadequate.'

They were back on Concord Road. The traffic was flowing smoothly; the air conditioning had kicked in. Paul wondered why he hadn't taken his coat off. He tugged at his tie and undid the top button.

They stopped at a set of traffic lights. 'I'll miss him,' Ursula said, staring straight ahead. 'God, I'll miss him.'

Paul stopped himself from asking about Julian and her. What difference would it make if he could classify their relationship? If he could say yes, tick, they were lovers, or yes, tick, they were close friends. It was none of his business, really. If Ursula told him he'd listen, but somehow he preferred not knowing.

But Ursula began to talk about the Williamson play she was touring in next year. Rehearsals started straight after Christmas. She was glad.

Glad to have the work, glad to be leaving Sydney for a while. She was looking forward to the routine, the way her life would build towards those two hours in front of an audience. She was ready for flyblown verandahs and drafty changing rooms. And the splendour of the new regional theatres that had sprung up in marginal seats. Perhaps she had Romany blood, she speculated, a distant ancestor who had plied his trade in market places and village greens, who had filled his life with costumes, fooling and the exhilarating sound of applause.

Paul listened jealously to the details of the tour. But he wasn't insanely jealous, for he had just received a call back for a second reading. It was a contemporary play about the waterfront strike. He was auditioning for the role of an investigative journalist, a role well suited to his talent, his range. It wasn't a major theatre company, but a cooperative venture. Still, if the houses were good he'd do well. The director wouldn't have called him back if she hadn't liked what she'd seen. As the second reading was the following day, he only had the rest of the day to work on the detail of the piece, to get it right.

'You're playing a man seeking the truth,' Ursula said with a knowing grin.

'That's me,' Paul agreed. 'An actor after the truth.'

They had stopped outside Paul's flat. 'Do you want to come in?' Paul asked.

Ursula shook her head. 'Right now I think I'll go home and run a cool bath. I keep seeing Julian in little things, thinking of him... I guess I need to be alone. But after twelve weeks on the road, I should have my head together again. You understand, don't you?'

'I think so.' Paul leant over and kissed Ursula. He thought he saw pain and longing in her eyes, but maybe that was just what he felt himself. He shut the car door, blew Ursula an impulsive kiss, then walked up the driveway towards his flat.

The wind was still brutal. He slipped off his coat and slung it over his shoulder. He loosened his tie a little more. I have a character to create, he thought, and I'm already dressed for the part.

The journalist was the sort of man he could relate to, one who appeared to have everything together, but whose personal life was a shambles. He was too busy to spend time at home, yet he was having an affair with a merchant banker, a woman he'd met while researching a feature on women in business.

The scene that Paul was rehearsing was set in a cafe. The journalist told the banker that he loved her, only to have her laugh at him.

'You're just a bit of jam tart on the side,' she says. 'A floozy. Men have always had floozies, and now it's our turn. It's time you caught up with the modern world, learnt to hang loose and chill out.'

'What does that mean?' Paul's character says. 'Hang loose? Chill out? Why do you sound like my daughter? This is serious.'

'No it isn't,' she replies. 'You're just a tape-carrying bore with a beer gut that tends to get in the way. And you know what else?' she asks as she gets up to leave. 'You're not even a good lay. You're just one big disappointment from start to finish.'

The journalist watches the banker walk out of the cafe. First he gets up to go after her, then he says 'hell' and sits down again. He orders a coffee and stares at the table. He picks up her wine glass and examines the lipstick stain on the rim. Without knowing why, the stage directions read, he takes her wine glass and hides it in his briefcase. It's as if that's all he has, the mark of her lips on a crystal flute. It's a hard moment to play, but Paul does it again and again, changing the way he says hell, until he discovers that the quieter the delivery, the more impact the word has.

That makes sense, he thinks. Contemporary drama rarely deals in grand gestures or flamboyant spectacle. Acting is a diminished thing: the art of the tiny detail, of making your eyes speak, of keeping the overtly theatrical in chains. He imagines Ursula playing his lover, imagines what she would do with her hands, how she'd stand up to tell him that he doesn't measure up.

When he picks up the glass to study the stain, he thinks of Ursula and feels the emotion coming from within and flowing through his actions. He works and works on the scene until he's confident he doesn't have to think about anything, until he has committed every word, every moment, every pause to memory. He keeps on at it until his body aches and his energy is spent. Until he can do no more.

'Hell,' Paul says to himself, 'I might just get this part.'

HEADSHRINKING?

At its present stage of development, the entire Australian press resembles, in content and manner, the New York tabloid press, except that for the racy sophistication of, say, the *Daily News* it substitutes either serious ecstasy or serious sulkiness. Some Australian critics have accused Australian newspapers in general of practising on the public the barbarous rite of headshrinking, but personally I doubt whether these papers deliberately belittle their audience. I think their tone is the result of a certain callow gravity and lack of experience, which may in time be mellowed by examples and pressures from outside the country.'

From *The New Yorker*, December 15, 1956– quoted in *Meanjin*, June 1957 (an issue that also contains a couple of poems by Chris Wallace-Crabbe).

Her ____ ___-stained Eyes
Sean Condon

The next day I got on a plane and several hours later knocked on Judy's front door in Topanga Canyon, feeling buoyant and confident; I'd lost quite a bit of weight since Judy last saw me and accidentally remarked on the fact as soon as she opened the door. She greeted me with a grimace, a sigh full of cigarette smoke and a tart, dry snap on the cheek, then said that she hoped that I wasn't there just to talk about and display my waistline.

'Of course not,' I told her and breathed in a little bit. 'I'm not some sort of vainglorious idiot. I love the weather you have down here. It's absolutely freezing back in New York.' I absently fluttered some fingers over my stomach – not rock hard, but firm. 'I should move out here.'

'No you shouldn't.' Judy looked at me for a long moment and then said, 'Don't say "vainglorious". Nobody speaks like that. If you have to say anything along those lines just say "vain".'

I still loved her.

Sentimentality glinted from my left hand and caught her eye. She glanced at my hand, then at me, dismayed.

'Why do you have a suitcase with you?' she asked, dropping her cigarette onto the pebbled porch and staring at it awhile before mashing it beneath the pointed toe of her boot. I could picture her employing the same considered ruthlessness when she dealt with the scorpions and spiders that scuttled around her property. 'You're not staying with me.'

Judy hadn't always treated me with such derision and scorn; when we first met she was merely disinterested, and occasionally bored. But I fell in love with her as soon as I saw her and did everything I possibly could to ensure that she'd fight through the tedium I radiated like halitosis and fall right back in love with me.

Judy was, as I've mentioned, one of the few people who had written back to me after receiving the letter of apology for my first novel. In her letter she had been generous, lenient and witty; reading between the lines, it was clear to me that she'd forgiven me for my book. I wrote back immediately and suggested that if she was ever in New York we might get together for a drink or a hansom cab ride through Central Park (a little joke of mine). Judy replied promptly, telling me that as a matter or fact she would be in Manhattan on an assignment the following week but was not interested in meeting with me (or taking a hansom cab ride through Central Park with anyone at all) and that she'd only written in the first place out of politeness.

I sent her a telegram: AM VERY INTERESTING IN REAL LIFE STOP NOVEL NOT A REPRESENTATION OF AUTHOR STOP DITTO JACKET PHOTO STOP BAD LIGHTING STOP.

When I didn't hear from Judy after two days I began to worry that she was dead – hit by a car or by some falling masonry as she passed beneath the scaffolding on a building site, like that guy in *The Maltese Falcon* who briefly changes his life when he is almost killed the same way, and who afterwards feels as though somebody has taken the lid off life and allowed him to see the works; I believe his name was Flitcraft – and for a while I considered hopping on a plane to see if she was alright. But it would have been wildly inappropriate – I was not insane; I hadn't forgotten that we hadn't even met – so I sent her another telegram, a letter, a postcard, a bunch of flowers and a couriered package containing a copy of the telegram, a copy of the letter, a copy of the postcard and a photograph of the floral arrangement I'd ordered at InterFlora. I was desperate, crazed, excited and, most of all, very lonely; I wanted to lift the lid off myself and let Judy see the works, or perhaps to determine whether there was in fact anything there to see. When I told my friend Fraser Smith about the situation he said that in his opinion there was plenty to see but I might not want to show it all at once, like some kind of 'emotional flasher'.

Judy wrote me agreeing to have a drink – *one drink*, she underlined – at the Four Seasons on the Friday night she was in town, and asked me to calm down and stop clogging up her mailbox. *PS*, she added, *thanks for the flowers, which I have immersed. And thanks for the picture of the flowers which is stuck to my refrigerator. By the way, my last name is not Flitcraft.*

I'd thought about nothing else on the day of my appointment with Judy, and in my nervous eagerness I arrived a half-hour early. She was already there, sitting on a stool at the bar swirling ice cubes in a lowball filled with scotch and a drop of water. There was something almost lost and mournful about the way she was staring into the heavy dark glass, and, for a moment, I struggled with a reluctance to intrude upon her introspection. She seemed unaware of anything around her, hunched like a brooding war veteran or a jazz pianist in search of the next chord. What propelled me toward her – and into her life – was the idea of her catching me staring at her like some kind of ex-con just out of prison rather than the ex-nut just out of psychiatric hospital that I actually was. I ordered a drink then sat down on the stool next to her and introduced myself, sounding appropriately ashamed of the words 'Michael' and 'Sherwood' when preceded by the statement 'I am'. It sounded as though I was reading a name off a tombstone.

Judy laughed and as she turned to face me, I noticed the angular bulge at the top of her right leg. I didn't know what to make of it – my first idiotic thought was that she'd had a botched hip replacement – and quickly shifted my gaze, settling on her face.

She was not beautiful – not in the immediately apprehensible manner that most people prefer to see as beautiful, anyway – but she was stunning. Her features were distinct and, with the exception of her much-broken nose, fine, but all were placed slightly too far apart, giving the impression that she'd been rather carelessly put together by somebody who'd meant to get around to correcting the details later on but never had. It was a first draft of a face; the lower lids of her pale blue eyes were full, as though at any moment she might spill a welter of tears down her cheeks, not the result of any kind of emotion, but simple overflow. She had a slight overbite and shy freckles which appeared if she'd spent too long in the sun or became embarrassed about something (an extremely rare occurrence, I would soon learn). She accentuated her strong and broad forehead by wearing her blonde hair pulled back in a ponytail, an oddly girlish – but very charming – touch in someone I would come to think of as never really having had a girlhood.

Judy was the daughter of a career military man and the career military man's long-suffering, cancer-incubating wife who died the day before Judy's tenth birthday. Her father, Jim, was a marine brigadier-general, and she and her two older brothers had had a peripatetic upbringing not unlike my own, the critical difference being that her experience of the world beyond America – endured rather than enjoyed – was of military bases in Germany, Japan, Iceland and the Philippines. No matter where in the world she was, the other children she knew were all Americans, all displaced and unhappy, as Judy was, and she gave up even trying to make friends after being uprooted three times in as many months when she was twelve years old. Withdrawing from other children – even her brothers – she began to mould herself in her beloved father's image; tough, taciturn, physical. She became an enthusiastic runner, a first-class marksman and a devotee of several martial arts, having her nose broken for the first time when she failed to block a flying jujitsu fist. She was a committed student at the base schools, excelling in history, mathematics and languages. At sixteen, her father began schooling her in whisky and cigars, allowing her to begin his smokes and finish his drinks as he sat in an armchair listening to the classical music which reduced him to a state of such rigid attentiveness that it often seemed to Judy a kind of ecstatic fury, until he was released and slackened – undone – by his fourth or fifth glass of whisky. She developed a crush on a bearded Frenchman and began reading the *Paris Review*, drinking espresso and smoking filterless cigarettes. She earnestly discussed Alain Robbe-Grillet, Nathalie Sarraute, and various –isms; the Frenchman explained exactly what was wrong with her face, why she could never be pretty, only 'terribly beautiful'. When she was seventeen Jim requested and received a posting in DC, where Judy enrolled at George Washington University, majoring in criminal justice, hoping eventually to mete out plenty of it in a professional capacity, although what form such a calling would take she was not then sure.

I knew none of this as, with my eyes firmly locked on her own, I told her about how my father had brought me here to the Four Seasons when I was nineteen and then left me to get drunk on my own after he'd spotted some production executives from United Artists lunching on one of the tiers of the grillroom, whom he went and sat with for three or four hours and by the time he came back I'd racked up a bill of close to $500, all of it single malt whisky; I told her how he'd laughed gruffly and loudly and shaken my hand as though one of us or both of us was Hemingway and we'd just made our first kill or had our first fuck or written our first novel, and I didn't stop talking to Judy until we'd both downed four martinis, by which time I'd become certain of two things: that I'd developed a brain tumour (there was a warm and buzzing feeling on the right side of my head); and that Judy was a little bit in love with me. I knew it, and said something along those lines.

'Uh huh,' she said, then swallowed the last oily drops of her drink. 'Actually, I'm not sure I even like you.' She delicately dropped an olive pit back into the glass, her soft pink tongue nudging the little black lump between two heavy lips, showing hints of imperfect white teeth. 'You talk too much. I'm sure you think it's charming and quirky, but it's not. It's irritating.'

I shut up for a while and stared at her, trying to figure out which actress she resembled and whether she really was falling in love with me but doing an incredible job of hiding it. Of course, I knew in my heart that she was not, but I was drunk and hopeful enough to dream and to attempt some ham-fisted flattery.

'You know who you look like?' As soon as I said the words, Judy snatched her pack of cigarettes off the bar and stood up. 'No one,' I added quickly. 'You don't look like anyone else. You only look like you.'

She breathed out smokily, thought for a moment and sat down again. 'Get the check,' she said. 'We're leaving.'

'Where are we going?'

'Back to my hotel room.'

'Why?'

'You want to sit here and talk about it or you want to come with me and see what happens?'

Not much happened that night – we played a very long game of Monopoly Judy ordered from room service before traipsing up to the roof of the hotel where she listened as I rashly opened heart and mouth and told her of my phenothiazine horrors in Pennsylvania, and we looked at the cityscape through a starlight scope, an old battery-operated night-vision device her father had brought back from Vietnam, and which made the Manhattan skyline appear lumpy and ghostly green, like a convoy of container ships and submarine periscopes frozen on a foggy sea – but six weeks later we were married.

Less than a year afterward, just before our divorce was finalised, as we were sorting through our things and deciding who would keep what, I asked Judy why she'd married me in the first place.

'Various reasons,' she said, not wistfully or regretfully. 'But I guess part of it was because that first night in my hotel room, when I took off my jacket and holster, you didn't ask why I was carrying a gun. Every man I've ever known, as soon as they see it they start carrying on like complete assholes about it. Calling me a "firecracker" or something stupid. You didn't. I guess I was impressed.'

That was about as informative and emotional as Judy ever got – she treated reticence with great reverence, as though our life together was some sort of secret I was trying to eavesdrop on – but that never really bothered me; I loved her for different reasons. I loved her both because of and despite the fact that she bears only a passing resemblance – both in physicality and character – to the woman I have described thus far.

In addition to not using her real name, Judy has also asked me not to include any revealing details of her actual personality or history, a request (bordering on demand) that I've tried to respect, and one which means that some of what I've written about her here is not particularly Judy-like at all.*

The real Judy, as I have mentioned, has a different name and is very ____, incredibly ____, spectacularly gifted in the art (or pastime) of _____ and _____ (although she would ___ _____ such a claim); further, she's highly _____ toward _____ but not _____, which she ____ in the extreme. (I remember one particular occasion when we were _____ along _____ and Judy saw a _____ and immediately took out her _____ and _____ the ____, which provoked a riotous and at times frightening mixture of _____ and _____ from all who were ____ enough to ____ it.)

She is a slender, _____-breasted woman, with an _____ carriage, which she accentuates by throwing her ____ backward at the _____ ___ like a _____ _____. Her ____ ___-stained eyes look ____ at __ with polite _____ curiosity out of a ___, _____, _____ _____ face.

Politically, she claimed to be non-partisan but I once stumbled upon some ___ in her _____ which confirmed what I'd always suspected: that she was a _____ _____ with strong _____ tendencies. Musically, she would always prefer ___ over _____, and only when _____. Her favourite expression, when shocked or surprised is, '_____ _____!' When deeply displeased, she will _____ and then mutter. She believes that _____ were smarter and more important than _____, that ____ was better than _____ and, if it came to it, that _____ could whip ____. When she's in a hurry, Judy ____ with her _____ to one side and _____ (which seems like a physical characteristic rather than an emotional one until you learn that the reason she _____ that way is because when she was

---

* I should mention that the description of her house in Topanga is accurate except for the fact that it is not located in Topanga Canyon – however it *is* located high in a canyon above Los Angeles.

___ a ___ ____ her and ever since she's been _____. Of course, I didn't believe her until she showed me the __ on her ____). The real Judy counts among her close friends such ____ as _____ _____, _ _ ____, former- _____s _____ _ _____, and _____ (I had doubted that particular claim at first until the three of us _____ at _____ in _____ of _____ and I was _____ly convinced); her ex-lovers, she always _____ in telling me, included (but were not limited to) _____ _____, _ _, _____ ____-_____, ___ __ (before he was crippled), _____ (before he was famous), a beard-less Frenchman named Jean-Loup_____, and _____ ____ (before she was executed in ____ for _____).

Finally, in the whole time I was married to her, Judy never _____ __. Not even once.

The great irony of all this is that Judy's actual details are freely available from any number of sources: there are several dozen other books about this whole incident (two of which were *New York Times* bestsellers), a dreadful telemovie (which starred Sonya Walger as Judy, which I felt was superb casting; Judy herself claimed it was '_____ _____ by _____ and _____. Not to mention that Walger woman's English'), hundreds of websites, thousands of yards of newspaper column inches, magazines including a *Newsweek* cover.

'I'm aware of the irony, Michael,' she told me recently, when I pressed her on this very point. 'But it's not so much that I want my former, anonymous life back, so much as I don't want *you* writing about me or us. You shouldn't be writing, Michael. Quit while you're ahead.' I reminded her that I was never ahead, that I was a failure from the gate. 'Then just quit,' she said.*

---

* Of course, this being the very work (or a very work) she was referring to, the above statement actually went like this: 'Michael, I _____ and _____ ___ _____ __ _ _ ___ which makes ____ more ____.' (Laughter) 'But, having said that, _____ I still ___ that you _____ _____ _ _____ or I'll _____ ___ _ _____, you _____! ____?' I knew she meant it, and that's why under no circumstances will I fill in these gaps. She'd ____ me. Well, _____ me first, then ____ me.

Notes and sources
• The two sentences beginning 'She is a slender…' are adapted from *The Great Gatsby* by F. Scott Fitzgerald, published by Scribner's Sons, 1925, p15. Although taken from Fitzgerald's novel (forsaking the descriptors) the description is entirely apt.
• A *Newsweek* cover, November 16, 2008

Etchings
Luke Menzel

1.

**in hospitals the clocks tend to be connected
so that they all show exactly the same time**

Watch me for a moment. I'm the guy in the green station wagon pulling into a car park on Flemington Road. Across from the Children's Hospital.

It's just on dusk. Maybe three weeks ago? Not sure. I'm making my-self go back there, to the hospital I mean, because all of a sudden I want to write about it. Nine years of not wanting to write about it. Now I want to. Go figure. I don't get out of the car straight away. I haven't had any sleep, was up all last night working, and my mind is wander-ing dangerously... spider webs... I shake my head, trying to physically derail the train of thought. I look across the traffic – the building looms large, dominates the landscape. Or just my mind? The traffic passes, heedless. The cyclists swoop by my door. I sit in the gloom, watching. Waiting for a break in the traffic.

I'm writing this in a cafe in Albion Street in Brunswick. A Minor Place. They named it after a song. Neil Young maybe? I can't remember. I haven't gotten around to getting into Neil Young yet. It's only been here for four years or so. It used to be a share house, then they decided to start a little breakfast place in the front room. It's all polished floorboards and big windows and trendy food and beautiful people (lots of stubble and tight stripes). The subsection of Brunswick's population that is into those things pounced. The renters and renovators. A Minor Place ended up being a big deal. They had to kick out the guy who lived in the front bedroom to expand the dining area. He was kind of pissed off, but they ended up giving him a job – apparently that placated him. I don't know if any of this is true. No firsthand accounts I'm afraid, just reporting the myths passed down from one generation of coffee addicts to another. It's funny how quickly a place can acquire its own mythology. The supple threads of story that hang in the air like spider webs… sometimes you can't walk into a place without getting covered with them. I come down here to write when I can't get anything done at home, when I need to focus. Works a treat. So anyway… three weeks ago.

2.
it's all bureaucracy of course
co-ordinated clocks avoid the complications
of pronouncing the time of death at 5:24
when it is really 5:27
practical, don't you think?

after a while, they started to shit me

That's me, still sitting in the car. Gazing across Flemington Road at the entrance to the Children's. They put in a McDonald's at some point, maybe fifteen years ago, and simultaneously tacked on a functionally pointless, angular plate glass foyer by way of justification. It makes no sense because it's too narrow, and doesn't contain anything that couldn't be housed in the real foyer a little further in. However, I have no comment to make on the appropriateness of a fast food outlet being housed in a children's hospital. In the scheme of things (life, death and whatnot), being concerned about that kind of thing seems a touch trivial. Don't you think? Mind you I am compromised: Ronald McDonald Children's Charities provided several years of subsidised accommodation to my family while my sister was in hospital. You could argue that this has in some way blunted my normally fierce critique of American corporate imperialism. If you wanted.

I'm surprised. From my vantage point in the car, the hospital looks much the same as it did nine years ago. I had imagined (hoped?) that it would be irrevocably transformed, half-a-dozen times maybe, renovation upon pointless renovation. Given the propensity of politicians to throw money at sick kids, the place should be unrecognisable. But it seems the same from the outside. Perhaps the money has been spent on the interior? I cling onto some vague hope that time has altered this building as it has altered me, that I won't really have to walk those same corridors again.

Some nights, when Sarah had gone to sleep, I would burrow down to the foundations of that building over there, down where they burn

the shit and detritus of young bodies in distress. No one took any notice, they were used to me, or at least used to my type – a bit player in
the dramas upstairs, walking the corridors in the middle of the night
because, well, what else were you meant to do? So this one night, I got
sick of that and decided to head back to where my family was staying
and pretend to sleep. The quickest way from the basement is to cut
through the emergency entrance and walk up the long drive that con-
nects it with the road.

Except once I got outside I decided to run it. I don't really know
why. The drive had high rendered concrete walls on each side, a dead
tunnel with stars. It was 2:00a.m., crisp. I sprinted the few hundred
metres down the driveway to the street, shocked stagnant blood surging through my veins, the nightmares of the day streaking behind me.
The wall ended, I was in the open, crossing the footpath…

The cyclist slammed into me from the left. He'd been careening
down the footpath while I'd been sprinting down the drive. The walls
of the driveway had made it impossible for us to see one another. Our
paths intersected at right angles, and we cleaned each other up. What
are the chances? The city was dead. It was two in the morning, for
Christ's sake! A second either way, a single second out of the dozen
frozen hours of that winter night, and we would never have collided.
We were both OK, a little bruised maybe, I can't remember really…
but that's not the point. What are the chances?

Three weeks ago it's rush hour, there is no break in the traffic, and
I am stalling. I open the door and plunge into the maelstrom of car
fumes and kamikaze cyclists.

3.
as the months ground away
I realised that there is nowhere that isn't now
no deviation from the devastation of the present

I started to find places where they didn't bother putting clocks
(because no one tended to die there I guess)

Can you see me? Still crossing Flemington Road. Ignoring the pedestrian crossing just twenty metres down the street. Over the median strip,
threading my way through the brakelights. The automatic doors slide
open and I am in the foyer. McDonald's to my left, information booth
to my right. The stark primary colours of the booth and burger joint

duke it out with the institutional greys that dominate the rest of the building. Kids like bright colours. They are tacked on ad hoc, bringing joy to the ailing young folk… or something.

It is all exactly the same. Exactly. I run up some stairs, leaving the plate glass appendage behind and entering the real foyer, the one that was there in the first place. The gift shop, well stocked with puzzles of puppies and tulips, Enid Blytons, *Simpsons* merchandise, and those fucking lame balloons. The dilapidated old cafe still holding out in the face of Ronald's decade-old siege – it's all the same. Hell, the trading card machine is not only still there, it hasn't moved an inch. The mulleted footballers and blow-dried tennis players plastered on its front were dated in the mid-nineties; they are veritable museum pieces now. This is out of control. What on earth has the hospital administration been up to? The state government? I was so sure it would be different. I don't know if I'm pleased or horrified. Nothing has changed.

Not even me. As I poke around I begin to feel myself settling into my old demeanour. I know this building. I own this building. Me and my brothers ruled it for a couple of years. I'd be here during the week with Mum, giving her a hand, keeping her and Sarah company. Then each weekend my two brothers would come up from Gippsland with Dad. We'd leave my parents to it and map out every back passage of this place, every crevice and hidey-hole. The emergency staircases that scaffolded the side of the building were the key, giving us access to places we should never really have been. We conquered the hospital the same way that we used to conquer the paddocks across from our house, the bush down the road, the pine plantations out past the back lane. Except where there used to be a gang of four, now there was a jagged three.

So I'm feeling this strange recognition, a sense of homecoming that I never expected. I pass through the foyer, tracing the stippling in the wall before I even know I'm doing it, before I remember that I've done it a hundred times before. I reach the lifts, step through the doors and take up my habitual position leaning against the stainless steel rail. The familiarity is kind of exhilarating now. The lift clicks through the floors. 'First floor… going up!' I intone the mantra along with the American woman, complete with the inflection on up. The recording is a little scratchier, that's all.

Tracing the submerged outlines in my mind.
Reading the hieroglyphics etched on the inside of my skull.

4.
once she'd gone to sleep
I'd slip away from my sister's bed
and walk the stairs
that scaffolded the side of the building
I'd stop when I got tired
and stare out the windows
at the street lights
that stretched to the horizon

The lift deposits me outside 6 East, the oncology ward. I go no further.
I have rights to the hospital, the public places, the thoroughfares. I
have no rights to the old ward. I feel some dim sense of respect for its
current occupants. It's not a game for them, not a scab of a memory to
be picked at when it pleases them. I stand on the threshold, chastened.
At length I take a seat on the bench opposite the lifts, and watch.

A couple of administrators streak past in sensible skirts, one showing
the other around. They emerge from the lift talking government investment in infrastructure and disappear into the ward without thinking
twice. I guess it's their job, not sacred ground. I'm not sure if I envy the
confidence of their intrusion, or pity the ignorance of their presumption.
I imagine the barely concealed disdain of the nurses as they humour their
visitors. Nurses are brilliant at barely concealed disdain; I think they can
take it as an elective as part of their training. The administrators emerge
from the ward talking square metres of space, and how much extra room
there will be in the new facility. I remember hearing during last year's
election campaign that Bracksy wants to knock down this building and
build a brand spanking new one next door. I don't like the thought of
that much… My newfound nostalgia for this place unsettles me.

The parents pass by, in and out of the lifts, grey-faced, rumpled and
resigned for the most part. The exception to this rule is the odd dad
who prefers to cultivate either anger at the world and its injustices or
a facade of excessive optimism. Depends on the side of the bed, you
know. A mother, thin, agitated, waits in front of the lift for a while,
hands clasped around her chest, fingers rapping her ribs impatiently.
She has her back to me, but I imagine her staring into space. After a
couple of minutes she swears, then a tired laugh; she has forgotten to
press the button. She looks around, apologises to me – unnecessary, but
she's embarrassed – and disappears down the stairwell.

An emaciated kid, body lost in clothes that predate the cancer, lingers in front of the lifts with his mum for a while. Big tote bag sits between them on the floor. Home for a couple of days between chemo, I guess. She spits on a tissue and crouches, goes to wipe his face by way of ritual preparation for the world, suddenly withdrawing her hand when she remembers the fragility of her son's immune system. He grins at me, laughs at her, and his luck (incredible – leukaemia is good for something!) She's disconcerted, but she smiles too. Hugs him instead. I wonder if this is the first time he has been home since he was diagnosed. The lift arrives and they are gone.

The parents look at me, don't register my face, but think they recognise my demeanour, the role I slipped into when I walked through the doors of this place. They think I am one of them. Bound to them by a shared burden, by a lived awareness of the daily grind of coping with the unthinkable. But it's a mistake – I am not who they think. I am just the flotsam of a possible future, the one they don't want.

I share small smiles of acknowledgement with these people.

I feel like a ghost.

5.
or I'd burrow down
to the foundations
down where they burned
the shit and detritus of
young bodies in distress
and laundered sheets
stained with sweat and blood
so that the nurses
could make her bed again
in lieu of making her body again

can you see me?

Watch me for a moment. Slumped on the bench outside the lifts. I am tired, and I am getting over this now. I lie on the bench, close my eyes, end up asleep in front of the lifts. I am left alone. They assume I belong here. They are right. I do. Or I did. I am an insider and an outsider, I am nine years ago and I am now. Later, after I've woken up, I'll struggle down the stairs. By then the magic of this place will be utterly spent. By then it will just be a carcase. The memories will have begun to fester, to fill my nostrils and lungs and cling to my clothes and I'll be gagging to get out. I'll go over to my girlfriend's place in Fitzroy, stand in the middle of her kitchen while she does something useful, and tell her there is no way I can write about this. That I've changed my mind. That I don't want to any more. I thought I could. But I can't.

The Untouchables
Bronwyn Mehan

Driving through Booderee National Park, I'm in my first ever brand new set of wheels. A Toyota HiAce, five-speed manual, power steering and a radio that works. Richard Aedy is telling Fran Kelly about the terrific guests he has lined up for today's *Life Matters*. Being paid to drive around listening to the radio – I can't believe my luck. Maybe one day I'll even pull over and call in. *Hi Richard, Rhonda here. I'm a long-time listener but a first-time caller…*

It's Monday morning and I'm heading for Murrays Beach. I should be there by the end of the news and with any luck back in the van by the time Richard is introducing his first guest.

The landscape here is schizophrenic. On the right are the shimmering sandy saltbush flats that stretch away to the ocean beaches of Wreck Bay and Cave Beach. On the left, closely packed rainforests of tree ferns and paperbarks lead down to the more sheltered bays of Green Patch, Bristol Point and Hole in the Wall. Dotted throughout are camping grounds ranging from the well-equipped with electric barbecues and camp kitchens to the 'walk ins' where you leave your car, hot water and other mod cons behind.

Not far along from the turn-off to Hole in the Wall I see two pencil pines – remnants, I suppose, of earlier European inhabitants. They stand about a house-width apart. I imagine a white two storey place that the owner of the quarry near Murrays Beach has built to house wife, children and housekeeper. I have an urge to pull over and go hunting in the undergrowth for a sandstone step, a shard of willow-patterned china, a rusted tank spout.

Thinking about the old house reminds me of the white picket-fenced grave that lies near the ablutions block at Green Patch. How bizarre to see the heart-shaped headstone among the tents and holiday-makers.

An anodised information plaque tells of an inquest. The nineteen-year-old daughter of the lighthouse keeper was shot by her sixteen-year-old friend.

In my mind, the shooter is the daughter of the quarry owner. Or is that a detail I actually read? Maybe working alone is going to send me nuts. I better go and read it again. Maybe I'll ask the Green Patch ranger if I see her today.

Exactly a week ago, on my first day, the very first stop I made as a Touch-Free Sanolink lady was at the Green Patch camping area. What a sight. I've seen a lot of carnage in my life, what with years of watching *CSI* and *Law and Order SVU*. But nothing prepared me for what I saw in the toilet cubicles at Green Patch.

According to the Touch-Free Sanolink website, the average woman will use 11,000 tampons in her lifetime. Personally, I think that statistic is on the conservative side. What with school holidays and peak tourist season, there had to have been over 200 women and girls camping at or visiting Green Patch on any given day. One quarter of them would be menstruating and going through any-where from two to four tampons each, plus the odd pad. Now your standard sanitary disposal unit holds twenty-five litres and I can confidently say that an additional ten-litre capacity is required for peak periods. Pun intended.

That night, after my gruesome Green Patch clean-up, I went to bed fearing nightmares. It wasn't my usual axe-murderer nightmare that I dreaded. It was all those embarrassing scenes that Mr Comb-Over had euphemisms for. The ones that we Touch-Free Sanolink ladies-in-training all knew he had never had to experience.

That look of horror, for instance, on my brothers' faces when the plumber held up a handful of the grisly matter that had been block-ing the family toilet. That combination of self-hatred, humiliation and fear when I discovered mid-match the state of my tennis whites. That forgotten stash of used pads that my mother found under my bed. I was twelve years old and yet to learn about India's caste system at school, but I knew in my heart that I was a *Harijan*. My brothers were in such fear of contamination from me that they ran from my shadow. The smell, the shame, the stigma. To have visitors, to be on your rags, to have the painters in. These were every teenage girl's nightmare. The untouchable's unmentionables.

As it turned out I slept peacefully and woke up refreshed and ready to hit the road.

Now I'm a week into the job and loving it. With the schools back there've been no repeats of that ghastly first day. I picked up some heavy duty garbage bags and rubber gloves from the guys at the depot so that next time I have to do a manual clean-up, I'll be ready for it.

Pam, who has been on the Crookhaven run for five years now, says she keeps a long-handled scoop in her van for what she calls the copy-cat numbers.

'Like lemmings they are, sometimes.' We were waiting in line at the drinks machine. 'All it takes is one person to leave a sanitary item on top of a bin and not in it, and all bets are off. Breaks your heart to see. One of our bins, totally empty, sitting in a pile of used pads and tampons.'

All in all, the job is fairly much like it sounded on the website and how Mr Comb-Over promised at training. *Ladies, this is the Touch-Free Disposal System. A virtual revolution in sanitary hygiene.*

There is probably quite a lot in Comb-Over's life that is virtual. His head of hair to begin with. In an age of sexy bald men like Peter Garrett, it is hard to see why a person would go through the pain and bother of a hair transplant. The results on my new boss are puncture holes that look like his tacking thread has been pulled out. The half-dozen wispy strands spring from his scalp like question marks in the slightest breeze.

There's nothing virtual about our new HiAce vans, our freshly laundered uniforms or our back-to-base handsets. We are the new breed of Untouchables.

Ladies, said Mr Comb-Over. *Touch-Free Sanolink's clever, infra-red technology means no contamination, for our customers or our staff.*

Elliot Ness and Mr Comb-Over – both in the business of making the world a cleaner, better place. Like our TV counterparts, we have been hand picked. We have throwaway latex gloves. We have bins with wide, non-stick modesty lids. We are incorruptible.

My new job has really opened my eyes to toilet architecture. Take the one I'm heading to now in the Vincentia shopping mall, for instance. It's a circular building of unpainted cement cast to look like corrugated concrete, with a blue roof. Inside, the walls are aubergine, the doors aquamarine and the floor tiles fire-engine red. It's the sort of design you'd expect to see in something called an 'art precinct'. Not alongside the seventies red-brick shops that were built in the era when Laundro-mats and Reditellers were considered cutting edge.

John Howard's always saying that Australians need to learn more about their own history. What better place to start than with toilets? I could run a guided tour: *At Your Convenience*, I'd call it. *A potted history of Australian architecture*. I'd start with the buildings themselves, pointing out the major trends in construction materials, from the ubiquitous Besser block to the rustic clinker brick through to the new, recycled look. For those with an interest in problem-solving design, I'd point out developments, not only in sanitary disposal but in toilet roll dispensary and vandal-proof cisterns. The tour would end with a photo opportunity at the tiny town of Jervis Bay where the best shots of Point Perpendicular can be taken from the disabled toilet at the rear of the police station.

The other great thing about toilets is graffiti. Very educational. Last year I had to hang around one whole Sunday at the University of New South Wales while Dylan competed in the Tournament of Minds. I found a quote in the science block toilet that I liked so much, I wrote it down. There I was, on the loo with my handbag balanced on my knee, scribbling dunny door wisdom on the back of my shopping list.

You don't have to be great to start
but you have to start to be great.

Curiosity got the better of me. I kept washing my hands and fussing with my hair until I was alone and could check out all the other cubicles. Tear-off ads for second-hand textbooks, a room to let to a clean Asian girl, and help with essay writing. One door was scrawled with a long-winded rant about some group called the Raelians. In the last cubicle I found a joke, the sort I really like. Silly but clever.

No more shampoo. We want real poo.

Later, in the train on the way home, I told it to Dylan and his friends and they rolled around laughing.

It was my first ever visit to a campus and I came away thinking that maybe some day, after Dylan finished school, I could go to uni. As a mature age student. I'd do something like social work, probably. Or, if I was good enough, law. When they ask me to make a graduation speech I'll say, *I wouldn't be here today if it weren't for toilet door graffiti.*

It's not so far-fetched. After all I'm here, in a new job with my own wheels, because of a saying I found in a fortune cookie at Fat Puss's cancer lunch.

I was standing with Toula outside Jimmy Fong's Good Luck Chinese Restaurant. We'd just finished our farewell lunch for Doreen, who everyone called Fat Puss because she looked just like the big, jolly picture book character. Toula and I were grabbing a ciggie (my last, as it turned out) while we waited for the bill. It was stinking hot. One-thirty on Parramatta Road and it seemed like every semi in Sydney had decided to drive past and shift down a gear right as it reached Jimmy's. It probably wasn't a great idea to be lighting up, given why we were there. But surrounded by all those exhaust fumes, you had to smoke to prove your lungs still worked.

'Off to the shops.'

'What?' I said.

Toula gestured with her head towards the traffic. Then I saw them. In between the trucks and cars and buses that streamed down the highway in dots and dashes, two Indian women in saris and holding black umbrellas moved like brightly-coloured stop motion dolls towards the bus stop.

'Fabulous,' I said, marvelling at their cooling midriffs, loose skirts and toe ring sandals. By comparison, in our call centre uniform of black nylon pants and white blouse, we looked like dusty town-dump magpies. 'They look almost regal.'

'Wish I was swanning off to the shops,' said Toula.

'Instead of back to the salt mine, me too.'

'What's that you've got, Rhonda?'

I showed her the cookie I'd pulled from my pocket. 'I didn't want to open mine at the table,' I said. 'It didn't seem right.'

'Yeah. Poor Fat Puss. Bit like a last supper, wasn't it?'

I cracked open the curled pastry shell and fished around in the shards for the paper fortune in my hand as my mouth filled with sugary vanilla sweetness.

'So, what's it say?'

'"The sooner you fall behind, the more time you have to catch up".'

'Typical,' said Toula, blowing out a lungful of blue smoke as she ground the butt with the toe of her shoe then flicked it into the gutter. 'Those things never make sense.'

On the way home from work, I took out the fortune and stared at it, willing it to give me some direction. By the time the train pulled into Redfern, I'd made my decision.

'It's a bit rash, love,' Mum had said. 'Why not just go there for a holiday? By yourself. Dylan'll be right with me.'

Mum couldn't understand why I'd give up a good steady job and cheap rent with her. She hadn't been down south since we were all still at school and she and Dad would take us camping once a year. Telling her I wanted to move there was like saying I was going to run the knock 'em down stall at the fun park and pull Dylan out of school to work on the dodgems.

On the way into town, I have to drive past Dylan's school. As I hit the 40km zone, a Chinese dragon of school kids, stick-thin legs beneath bulging backpacks, is heading out of the gates. Off to the council library, perhaps. They are all lively and jostling, glad to be out in the sun and under the blue sky, with the prospect of lunch from the takeaway. I'm scanning the heads for Dylan. He should be easy to spot. His hair is mousy, like mine, not bleached blond like the local kids. And he wears it brushed forward in a Beatles mop as acne cover.

I can't see him. Maybe he has seen the van and is skulking. All fifteen-year-olds are ashamed of their mothers, I know that. But I've given my son additional incentive to disown me. Think about it. You have a mother, covered in patches and chomping on Nicorettes like a camel, who takes it into her head to drag you out of school and away from the few friends you have to a place she's always talked about but you've never seen, so she can drive around in a hot pink van filled with used tampons.

'I'm not riding in that van, you can't make me.'

'Nobody's forcing you to. And anyway, what have you got against my van?'

'It stinks.'

'That new-car smell? I thought you liked new things.'

'Those bins in the back. They're disgusting.'

'Well, that's where you're wrong, Mr Wuss. Those bins have been to the depot. They've been washed in a purpose-built machine, using recycled water that's very, very hot. Once they've been double-checked, they are deodorised and repacked with anti-bacterial granules. So whenever the van's here at our place, it won't smell. OK?'

I watched his face redden and his eyes tear up.

'What? What more can I do, Dylan?'

'When can we get a car of our own?'

'We don't need a car. We've got the bikes.'

'What about when it rains?'

He had me there. My great plan of us doing without a car had been completely discredited on the day we had the interview with the principal.

When we left home it had looked a little overcast but as we rode to the shopping centre the storm broke and we were soaked. We sat in the Laundromat, covering ourselves in copies of *Time* magazine while our pants dried. I spent my only change on the dryer and had to borrow money for the taxi from the school office ladies. Far from arriving at Dylan's new school looking like a health-conscious sea changer, I looked like I'd slept rough and spent my child allowance on heroin.

Once we were home and dry, Dylan quizzed me about my rounds.

'You're not doing the dunnies at school, are you?'

'Nah,' I said. 'The education department uses another company.'

It was a flat out lie. I leave the schools for after 3:30. My secret will be safe so long as Dylan avoids after-school sports and detention.

Dylan has started to thaw a little. Coming from the big smoke has given him playground cred and he has joined a *Dungeons and Dragons* group. They don't meet after school but at lunch times, so I'm thrilled. It also helped that we brought a dog home on the weekend from the RSPCA.

Richard Aedy is signing off now. *Until tomorrow, Richard.* I resisted the temptation to phone in. It wasn't hard. Corporate responsibility is not something I've given much thought to. I could probably have a good spit about James Hardie, but it wouldn't be at the intellectual level expected of Radio National listeners.

Maybe I'd be more suited to Adam Spencer's *Breakfast Show*. I could become one of those regulars out on the road that he speaks to. I could be Rhonda the Sano Lady who calls in each day, before the eight o'clock news, for a chat.

'Hey, Rhonda,' Adam would say. 'What's the haps?'

I could tell him about life as a single mother of a teenager. Like the fiasco this morning when Tex brought in a dead bird and plonked it on Dylan's pillow.

'That's disgusting.'

'He's an animal, Dylan. That's what they do.'

'He's got bird blood on him. Yuck. I'm not touching him.'

'OK. I'll hose him down if you get brekkie.'

I could tell Adam about the grave at Green Patch, maybe do a bit of research about the lighthouse girls. I could become the human face of sanitary disposal systems. Well, the voice anyway.

'I bet your listeners don't realise, Adam,' I could say, 'that it takes about six months for a tampon to biodegrade.'

'Get out. Is that right?'

'Yep. And something like two million sea birds and one hundred thousand marine mammals die every year as a result of contamination by plastic debris from things like the backing strips on panty liners.'

'Sano bins can save the whale, eh Rhonda?'

And, after a while, maybe Mr Comb-Over will call me into his office. *You've exceeded expectations, Rhonda*, he'll say, and make me a sales rep. Then I'll have a laptop, a mobile, an expense allowance and keys to a brand new Bug. Who knows what else might happen?

Escargot Postel
Chloe Walker

The first letter is a surprise. Ellie is reading through her mail over breakfast when a handwritten envelope interrupts the flow of bills and invoices. A blue *par avion* sticker and a French stamp make Ellie's heart skip a beat. It is from Luc.

It's been more than a month since she ate with Luc, but the thought of him is still delicious. Trust the only proper French chef on her books to have such a dishy younger brother. Trust the tasty one to have an early morning flight back to Europe the next day. Ellie had accepted his dinner invitation anyway, making the most of the few hours of drinking in his features and imagining what his hair would feel like between her fingers. After one of Henri's superlative dessert soufflés Ellie gave Luc her business card, took advantage of the European custom of cheek to cheek kisses, as close to his mouth as decorum would allow, and made the hour-long drive back to the farm much later than usual. She cursed the stars the whole way for teasing her yet again. And that was that, she had thought. But now there's a letter.

She slides a fingernail underneath the flap of the envelope and pulls out a cream-coloured note card. Its edges are like nibbled lettuce leaves.

'Lovely Ellie,' it reads. 'It was such a pleasure to share my last meal in Australia with you. Once again, my compliments on your excellent produce. What a shame we met just as I was about to depart – I would have liked the chance to visit your farm, and to show you what I can do with escargot in my own kitchen. Luc.'

Ellie screws up her nose. She doesn't eat snails; she just breeds them for restaurateurs like Henri. She is, however, quite partial to red wine, cheese and soufflés. Perhaps she could win a trip to Europe. She reads over the letter a few more times, soaking up the arcs and sweeps of Luc's pen. Then she puts it back in the envelope, tucks it behind the wooden chessboard on the side table, and pulls on her gumboots at the door.

On the way to the pens a Cibo Matto song lyric tumbles around inside Ellie's head: 'He stared me up and down, as if I was a restaurant menu'. The ground is soft from last night's rain but overhead the sky is empty of clouds. Her charges are always happiest in this type of weather, moist but warm. She pulls open the gate to the enclosure and walks over to the first row of densely planted vegetables. Time to begin the day's work.

The snails are in good spirits today, happily sliding over silver beet leaves and each other. Ellie gently picks one off a leaf and watches as it recoils back into its shell. Despite her job, Ellie is still fascinated with snails. As a kid she would keep them as pets, closing them into margarine containers in her bedroom and feeding them lettuce. Sometimes she would forget about them for weeks on end and their poor tiny bodies would shrivel back into their shells. The stench of decaying mucous and bacteria when she finally remembered, to her, smelt like guilt. An echo of that smell lingered in the tanks she used in the farm's first incarnation. Now her flock of thousands of single-footed farm animals roam in free-range enclosures, surrounded by foliage. Both the snails and her customers seem happier this way.

Ellie reaches over the black netting and pulls out yesterday's uneaten food, lest bacteria grow and her herd falls ill. She drops the food into a bucket for composting, slowly filling it with nibbled slices of cucumber covered with silvery trails. She leaves fresh cucumber and some oats, and eggshells for calcium. She finds new babies in the reproduction area and transfers some teenagers out of it for fattening up.

In the afternoon Ellie works in the greenhouses, cleaning old food from the purging bins and replacing it with fresh oats. The snails that are in for purging are fed a strict fibre diet to cleanse their gullets of dirt. At the end of the week Ellie will end their slithery journeys through life with an enormous pot of boiling water, a task that still elicits a small pang of guilt. At least her snails are allowed a last meal, unlike their Italian cousins who are piled into cages and left to starve for a week, or worse, covered live with sea salt and flour.

That evening Ellie reads Luc's letter again and scribbles a reply. 'I'm pleased that you enjoyed my snails. Thanks again for a lovely evening. If I ever visit France I would love to let you make me dinner. Perhaps I could bring dessert – a nice chocolate tart? Or maybe a good old Aussie pavlova? (Look it up. It's like a giant meringue.) Yours truly, Ellie.'

The second letter is even shorter than the first. Ellie reads it straight from the letterbox. She wants it fresh.

'I hope after our pavlova that you will stay long enough for coffee. Because what I really want is to kiss you. Luc.'

Ellie returns to the house and plucks the first letter from behind the chessboard. The pieces have been halted mid-game, their positions etched into her memory. She met her English grandfather only once as a child, but they kept up a healthy exchange of mail and played many games of chess by correspondence. Some games took years to finish, and her grandfather only lost once. Then he passed away before he'd had the chance to make his next move.

Ellie carefully removes the chessboard lid and puts the two envelopes in the cavity that would ordinarily house the pieces. She knows this game. One move at a time. She goes to her desk and writes a reply.

Slowly, over weeks and months, the little pile of letters in the chessboard box gets bigger. Each one contains a kiss, a touch, a glance. 'I am running my thumb along your eyebrow and down your cheek.' With each note they explore another inch of each other. 'The skin of your neck tastes like honey.' Sometimes Luc's response is too quick, a mere eight or nine days, and Ellie leaves it on the side table for a while to catch her breath and slow things down. She invests in a pack of airmail envelopes and an expensive pen, trying to train her handwriting from beetle tracks into something more resemblant of Luc's calligraphy. She writes slowly, carefully, crafting the shape of her alphabet. Luc's hand slips from the small of her back to caress her buttocks. Ellie undoes the top button of his shirt.

One morning, by the letterbox, Luc slips off Ellie's dress. 'Slowly, I slide the zip of your dress down your back,' his letter reads. 'As I brush the fabric from your shoulders it falls to the floor.' Ellie's skin tingles from her neck and down her sides as she stands there, nearly naked, in her gumboots, old jeans and work shirt.

At the farm the snails are feeling sensual, lustfully sliding over each other's shells, touching mouths and rubbing wrinkly skin. Ellie goes through the routine, removing old food, replacing it with fresh stuff, all the while imagining her zip unzipping and her dress being removed by a French man.

That night she dashes off a reply. 'One by one I unfasten the buttons of your shirt. My hands follow as it slips off your shoulders and down your back.' Overeager, Ellie checks the letterbox daily after sending her mail, half believing that lust and romance will somehow transcend the realities of the postal system. But nothing comes.

A week goes past, then two. At three the snails become restless, and Ellie agitated. Her agonising wait is punctuated by the ghastly task of preparing her produce for sale. She removes the greenhouse snails from their bins and takes them to the second kitchen, the one designed to meet food safety standards. Surrounded by stainless steel, Ellie tips batch after batch of her babies into a giant saucepan, which she then brings to the boil, slowly, so as not to crack the shells. At first the snails make languid attempts at escape, crawling underwater up the sides of the pot, only to lose footing at the top and plop back into the soup. As the temperature rises their efforts become more frantic, until their protesting bodies give in and come free of their protective shells. Ellie drains the foamy water and boils the now-lifeless coils of meat a second time to remove any remaining slimy residue. Despite years of practice she still finds the process disturbing; this time, her mood is made darker as she remembers the shapes on her French date's plate.

Luc leaves Ellie standing in her underwear for five, six, seven weeks. Just when she resolves to pull her clothes and the last of her dignity back on and go home in a huff, another red, white and blue edged envelope appears.

'Your tongue is like an oyster, your breasts like bon bons waiting to be unwrapped,' he writes. As if nothing is wrong.

Ellie makes him wait. The snails keep their heads held high in indignation. Finally, she relents and writes her response. One sentence. A command; an effort to regain control.

'Take off your pants.'

Addressed, stamped, posted. The next move had better be good.

Another few weeks go by. Business peaks and Ellie finds herself rushing to fill orders. In a morning crammed with errands she shoves the mail into her handbag on her way to the car. In town she hurriedly tries to catch up with the shopping and appointments and friends she has been neglecting. Her last stop is the supermarket. She grabs a basket and heads for the fresh food section. No time for the proper market today.

Stopping for breath, Ellie reaches into her handbag, groping for her shopping list. Instead her fingers trace the outline of a familiar blue sticker. She puts down the basket and slides her fingernail under the opening.

'Dear Ellie, I can't help but run my hands over your delicious skin. Your breath is hot and heavy. I pull the lace away from your chest and feel the weight of your breasts in my hands.'

Ellie's hand moves up and cups the underside of her breast. She can feel the lace of her bra through the t-shirt fabric. 'Your bra falls away from your body and I lean down to curl my tongue around your nipple.' Luc signs off and Ellie exhales. She looks up, realising that she is touching her breast in a supermarket. Embarrassed, she looks down, and the nectarines are blushing.

In the fruit and vegie aisle she can't stop squeezing. She squeezes the peaches, running her finger around the tiny bumps at their bases and feeling the microscopic hairs on their skin. She squeezes the eggplant. She squeezes an orange so hard that a drop of juice leaks from its navel. She squeezes the potatoes and dirt comes off on her hands. She squeezes a zucchini knowing that it will be as firm and hard as a ripe zucchini can ever be. She squeezes her thighs together.

It's Wednesday so everything is fresh. Some of the displays have been sprayed with water so they glisten. Ellie loads up her basket until the handle strains and bows and she wonders how she will carry it at all after she has visited the canned goods aisle.

At home she drops the shopping bags onto the kitchen table and takes out the letter. As she reads it again her mouth gets dry and she swallows. It makes a gulping sound inside her ears. Dropping the white pages to the table she takes a peach and lifts it to her face. Breathing in its scent she feels the tiny hairs against her lips. Slowly she brushes it over the skin of her cheek, down her throat and across her collarbone. Her hand snakes up the back of her top to unfasten her bra, but then she remembers the rules. She cuts up the peach with honey and yoghurt and eats it instead before putting on her gumboots.

Like chess players taking out their opponent's pieces, one move at a time Ellie and Luc undress each other and explore. The herd of hermaphrodites at the farm practice free love. New eggs are laid and hatched regularly. Responses are written as quickly as possible as Ellie and Luc touch and grope and taste. At the farm there is a population explosion of Lilliputian proportions, and Ellie is forced to plant out the last remaining row in the growing area to avoid overcrowding.

On damp mornings Ellie is sometimes forced to pull a hungry garden snail's mouth from one of Luc's love notes. One eats right through the layers of airmail weight paper, leaving scars across his words. Her father once told her of a workmate who, upon retirement, left snails in the desk drawer as a parting joke. They ruined invoices and cheque books, but what they really seemed to love was the stamps. Something in the adhesive, which so offends human tastebuds, was, to them, a delicacy.

In the garden, Ellie crushes the common snails that try to eat the tips of her basil plants. Mashing them under her boot, she leaves their vital organs glistening and exposed to the air and sun. Technically they are the same species as her farm animals, but the love and care with which Ellie tends to her *helix aspersa* is equalled by the violence turned upon the common garden snails. They lack the glamour and refinement of her breeding stock – they are an underclass to be crushed beneath her mighty boot.

In the letterbox, things get steamy. Luc rolls on top of Ellie and she cries out in pleasure. Through ten, twenty letters they make passionate love. Luc's hands move all over Ellie's body; she pulls at his hair and bucks her hips. Ellie rips open envelopes and reads with trembling hands; she writes furiously and with an urgency that makes her cross her legs tightly. With every thrust and stroke and roll on their bed of language Ellie's heart and breathing quickens, until finally their act begins to reach its climax. In big, hurried letters Ellie writes, 'Luc, I'm coming. I'm coming.' She shoves the note into an envelope and rushes to the post office, driving erratically. Then she waits, on the edge.

Ellie waits. Her anticipation turns to frustration, as day after day the letterbox yields nothing more than bills and junk mail. Weeks pass, and then months. Errant molluscs found invading the letterbox are flung over the fence to become French feasts for the birds; in particularly dark moods Ellie pokes their eye stalks and watches with satisfaction as they shrivel back into their puckered heads. At the farm, the real snails are pining and refusing to eat. Ellie finds herself using more and more water to try and make them move. There have been no new babies for weeks even though hibernation is months away.

And then, one evening after a long day in the city, Ellie returns home to find an envelope waiting for her. Flushed with excitement she rushes into the house, dropping the letter onto the couch. She brews a proper cup of coffee and hastily removes the chessboard from the box, sending several pieces toppling. Arranging herself on the couch, Ellie rereads each letter one by one, from the beginning. With each page the pressure builds. She runs her fingers down her neck. Her skin gets hot and prickly and her heartbeat and breathing quicken. She undoes her bra and pulls it out through her sleeve, kneading her breast and imagining her French lover moving on top of her. Finally Ellie reaches the unopened envelope. She rips it apart and pulls out the pages. Her eyesight has become blurry in her excitement but soon it registers. The sight of her own handwriting brings her shuddering to a halt.

As her arousal turns to anger, Ellie flips over the envelope. *Return to sender*, lightly stamped in silvery tracks. With a sweep of her arm Ellie sends the chess pieces flying, gathers the letters and storms out of the house.

The wet grass soaks her feet and the cuffs of her jeans. As she marches and staggers towards the greenhouses, Ellie shreds the paper with her teeth and hands. When she arrives she brings white lids crashing from their containers, and she hurls the letters, all those delectable and divine and dirty words, into the purging bins.

A slow motion swarm of brown spiral shells descends upon the pile of letters as the hundreds of snails begin to eat up the words and sentences carefully created by the lovers. Their gullets fill with ink and paper and envelope glue as they slide over the correspondence, dissolving it and covering it with silver lines. Ellie stands and watches her stock spoil, imagining that she can hear a munching sound coming from her minions. For hours she watches as they dutifully destroy her love affair, along with her sales.

A sliver of moon has inched its way into the black sky overhead when Ellie finally hoists her shivering body from the wet greenhouse floor. She closes the bins on her stampeding snails and trudges back up to the house. In the shower she washes dirt from her feet and elbows; a fragment of air-weight paper dislodges from her tangled hair and swirls down the drain. With hair still wet, Ellie crawls into her bed and draws the blanket tight around her like a shell. Exhausted, she slides her legs up to her chest and coils her body against the cold.

365 Birds
Jeremy Ohlback

One morning I pulled open the curtain and there was a stork on the balcony. It was standing there, stark black and white, with its orange beak pulled down against its feathers. Behind it the sky was grey and I think it was raining. I didn't know why it was there – the balcony was just a square of concrete that looked over the cluttered suburbs around Sydney Harbour.

'Hey there,' I said. 'What are you? Silly bird, why are you here? Have you brought me a baby?'

After a while I went to the kitchen and turned on the kettle. When I came back the stork was still standing there on its long legs, looking into my bedroom. We looked at each other until I heard the kettle bubble up and then click off at the back of the apartment. Then the stork raised its bill and sort of awkwardly flapped up onto the railing in a mess of feathers and flew away.

It was a Sunday and I stayed at home, in my pyjamas, because it was cold and wet outside. I didn't tell anyone about the stork that day, but I thought about it a lot. I thought about it while I sat on the couch with my feet on the coffee table next to the pile of rented DVDs I was watching. I thought about it while I spooned oily tuna onto two slices of toast. I thought about it while I called Hazel and listened to her voicemail message. I wasn't really sure what to say so I left ten seconds of silence before hanging up.

I would have told her about the stork first thing when we met at the food court the next day, but something else came up. I took her hand in mine and kissed her on the cheek.

'Guess what?' I asked.

'What?' she asked.

'There was a condor on my balcony this morning,' I told her. 'A real condor.'

She looked blank.

'Like, a big bird. A condor. And yesterday there was a stork. For about five minutes. It just stood there on the balcony in front of my bedroom.'

'No,' she said. 'Are you making fun of me, Randall?'

'No, totally serious,' I said. 'Two really strange birds have been on my balcony in two days. What do you want to eat?' I squeezed her fingers as we zigzagged through the crowd of men and women wearing business clothes, all holding trays of noodles or fish and chips. 'It was perched on the rail with its big bald head and white collar. It was there for about thirty seconds.'

'I thought they were extinct or something?'

'Not extinct,' I said. We stopped. 'Just very, very endangered. But yeah. They are. Soup? Sandwich? Anything?'

'I don't know,' she said. 'I've kind of gone blank now.'

'Yeah,' I said, 'Me too.'

The next morning there was a superb fairy-wren twittering about on the balcony. I'd seen them on the coast before, but never this close to the city. On Wednesday there was a kind of jay usually found on the western coast of North America. On Thursday I thought that the whole thing had stopped because the balcony was empty all morning. There was nothing in the afternoon, either. I pulled the curtains back down and went to bed, but as I was drifting off I heard a hoot-hoot, hoot-hoot just outside the glass. I slipped out of bed and peeked through the edge of the curtain and there was a white owl watching over the suburbs from the railing. He blinked a couple of times and swivelled his head about. I watched him for as long as I'd watched any of the other birds and then finally decided that he might not leave until morning, so I got back in bed. I didn't sleep very well because he'd always hoot-hoot, hoot-hoot just as I was drifting off.

'What bird did you have this morning?' Hazel asked me on the phone. It was Saturday. I was lying with my legs over the arm of the couch, the television off.

'A pigeon. It's been there all day.'

'A pigeon? That's not very exciting. I bet you get pigeons up there every day.'

'No, never.' I said. 'Anyway it wasn't a normal pigeon. It was… it looked clean. And it had a big fanned tail.'

'Right,' said Hazel. 'Sounds exotic.'

'Hey,' I said. 'Gimme a break. It's a cool pigeon.'

'You know, I bet there's an aviary or a zoo around here that closed down or something. I bet they just released all the birds because they didn't know what to do with them. Let them loose. It's sad, really, all these birds out of their natural habitat.'

'No,' I said. 'I don't think so.'

'You don't think it's sad?'

'No, I don't think they're from a zoo.'

'Then why are they there?'

'I don't know,' I said. 'Does it matter?'

'I guess not,' she said. 'Anyway, are you coming to breakfast tomorrow morning? We're going with Ashley and her new boyfriend, I forget his name.'

'Vaughan,' I said.

'Yeah. We're going with Ashley and Vaughan. Do you want to come?'

'Sure,' I said. 'Though I guess it depends what kind of bird turns up, heh,'

She didn't laugh.

I was late to the cafe and the others had already finished their first coffees. I kissed Hazel and sat down.

'What took you?' she asked.

'Oh, nothing.' I didn't really want to talk about the hawk right away. The waitress came over and asked if we were ready for food. I ordered a vanilla milkshake and a big breakfast with extra bacon.

'Hey, hungry guy we've got here,' said Hazel.

'It's a fine morning,' I replied. 'It's going to be a good day.'

I told the others about the birds. Ashley seemed very interested and leant over her plate with her elbows on the table as I described them. Vaughan was rocking back on his chair, taking off his sunglasses, looking into them, then putting them back on every now and then.

'So this morning there was a big fat hawk with a mouse hanging out of its mouth,' I said. 'He ate the whole thing right there. I don't know what kind of hawk it was, they all look pretty similar. But you don't get to see that kind of thing happening so close, at least not very often.'

'That's amazing,' said Ashley. 'I've never heard of anything like that. Is it the time of year? All those birds. There's gotta be a reason, an explanation, or something.'

'We can't work it out,' said Hazel.

I shrugged. 'You're right, it is amazing. But I'm happy to just appreciate it, you know? I'm happy to let it be.'

'Have you seen these birds?' Ashley asked Hazel.

'One,' said Hazel. 'I forget what it was, um, a sparrow?'

'A finch,' I said.

'Right,' she said, 'A finch. Some kind of rare finch, I guess. It was very colourful.'

'Oh, I have to come stay at your place,' said Ashley.

'They're just birds,' said Vaughan. He put his sunglasses down on the table. 'What's the big deal?'

'Jesus, Vaughan,' said Ashley. 'They aren't just birds. They're from all over.'

'Birds can fly. It's not really anything special. I mean if there was a crocodile on your balcony I'd be impressed.' He leant back on his chair and looked satisfied.

'So you wouldn't be surprised if there was a puffin at your window tomorrow morning?' asked Ashley.

'What the hell is a puffin?' said Vaughan.

'Forget it,' said Ashley.

A couple of weeks later I invited Ashley to my apartment in North Sydney, to help put together some benches for the balcony and to see one of the birds. By lunchtime we were red and sweaty, with pieces of wood and Ikea tools spread over the concrete floor.

'Hungry?' I asked. Ashley nodded. Hazel had just come back from the chicken place with lunch so I went inside to bring out the food. When Hazel and I came back to the balcony, plates piled with burgers and fries, Ashley was standing still with a screwdriver in her hand, watching a kingfisher that had landed on the railing.

'Shhh,' she said. The bird was blue and white with gold feathers on its belly. It was preening the underside of its wing. After a moment it looked back towards us, looked at Ashley, then flew away.

'Ah, bugger,' I said. 'Oh well. There won't be another bird today.'

'No, it's…' said Ashley. 'I haven't seen one of those since I was a kid.'

'I broke up with Vaughan,' said Ashley. We were sitting on the unassembled benches and picking at the last fries on our plates.

'What?' asked Hazel. 'How come? You seemed to be happy with him.'

'No, it's a good thing,' said Ashley. 'We both had different ideas about things, I guess.'

Hazel looked at me. I looked at the chips on my plate.

By summer the new benches were being well used and I had also strung some paper box lights from the roof. I was spending most of my nights after work there, eating dinner and resting my beer bottles on an up-turned barrel that I bought from a garden store. The birds started to come in the evening, too. They were never the same, and there was always only one. Sometimes they stayed all night. One night a duck managed to fly in and I don't think it knew how to get back out. It waddled around as I ate my dinner, and pecked at the bits of food I threw to it. Eventually I picked it up and lifted it, flapping madly, to the edge of the balcony and let it go. It turned sharply and went straight for somewhere it must have been thinking about for a while.

Another afternoon, in March, I called Hazel because there was a bird I wanted her to see. She came in on her way home from work, wearing a tapered black skirt, a collared shirt and lipstick. She kissed me on the cheek.

'What's the matter?' she asked, as she ran herself a glass of water in the kitchen. 'I've got to go to the shops tonight, so I really can't stay long.'

'Here,' I said. 'Out the front,'

She followed me through and we stood in front of the sliding glass door to the balcony. There was nothing there.

'What?' she asked.

'Oh, damn,' I said. 'It's gone.'

'Is this… was this about a bird?'

'Well, yeah. It was a lovebird.'

'A lovebird? You called me over for a lovebird? God, Randall,' she used my name, 'I just don't get you sometimes. Is that all? Can I go?'

She turned to leave and I quickly grabbed her wrist.

'Hey,' I said. 'Wait.'

'What?' she asked.

'I,' I stopped. 'I was going to ask if you wanted to move in.'

I looked at her and her eyes changed, for a moment – I saw the kind of love between us that I hadn't seen for a while, not that day at least. But then she frowned and turned away.

'No,' she said. 'Not like this. Not because of another bird.'

'It's not because of the bird,' I said. 'It just made me think of you, that's all.'

'Well,' she said. 'Maybe you have to stop thinking about these bloody… birds.'

'But,' I asked, 'don't you think they're special? At all?'

'No,' she said. 'They stopped being special a while ago. I still don't understand it – I don't think you do either. But you don't have to let this control your life.'

'They don't,' I said.

'They do,' Hazel said. She let out a long breath. 'Listen, I have to get to the shops before they close. Alright? I'll give you a call when I get home, or something.'

Hazel left. I drew closed the curtains and sat on the edge of the bed for a long time.

For a week I didn't lift the curtain but I always heard the birds. On Friday morning a kookaburra woke me before the sun had come up. The next night there was a gull that cried out across the city as I read in bed. I finally pulled the curtain up to shoo off what I thought was a crow cawing incessantly during a movie, but it turned out to be a little grey bird with a faded band across its neck and I didn't dare open the door in case it was scared away.

One night, while sitting on the balcony with a beer, my phone beeped inside. I went to get it from the bedside table and then listened to Ashley's message asking me why she hadn't seen me out for the last couple of weekends.

'Anyway,' she continued, 'I was wondering, if, uh, you could return that favour. Remember when I helped with the Ikea stuff? Anyway I have this sink that, well it's broken and… Could you gimme a call back? Hope you're doing alright.'

I listened to it once again and took the phone back out to the balcony. I stared at the screen for a while, then pressed a button to delete the message. I swapped the phone for a beer bottle that was sitting on the upturned barrel, but it was empty, so I put it back down and started picking at the label.

The whole thing lasted a year. When it was starting to get cold again I was sent a notification by mail that the real estate agent would not be renewing my lease. The letter said that part of the street was being rezoned and they would be developing the property into office suites. I folded up the letter and put it in the recycling bin but my heart felt hollow at the thought of having to leave. After that, most nights I would drink lots of beers and leave the bottles scattered across the floor of the balcony. I hardly noticed the birds.

I met Hazel at the beer garden of a pub to tell her. We sat under a tall gas heater and sipped drinks in small glasses.

'You look like a bit of a mess,' she said. 'When was the last time you shaved?'

'They, uh,' I said. 'I have to move out in a few months.'

'They what?'

'They're building offices.'

'Honey,' she said. She took my hand under the table. 'I'm sorry.'

'I'm OK,' I said. 'Just, I like that place, you know?'

'It's a nice apartment.'

'Yeah.' I picked up my glass and swirled the ice cubes around in the bottom.

'Hey,' she said. 'Don't worry. Things change, don't you think? We always have to move on. We have to move on so we can start new things.'

I looked up at her. I thought about all the times I'd dreamt of walking home with our hands together, one of us holding a bag of groceries and the other a bottle of wine. I thought about all the times I wished she was there when a new bird flew down and perched on the railing next to me as I was eating dinner on the balcony. Then I looked at the table.

'I know,' I said. 'But I still love my house.'

'I know you do,' she said, then, 'And you still love your birds.'

'Will you come home with me tonight?' I asked. 'To my place?'

Hazel lifted her glass, tilted it, and looked at the watery remnants of vodka and cranberry juice.

'Alright,' she said after a moment. 'But let me have one more drink.'

We were woken by a bird singing. We lay together in bed for a while, her head on my chest, then Hazel stood up to open the curtain, with the sheet draped from her shoulders.

'Oh,' she said.

'What is it?' I asked, tilting my head.

'A nightingale, I think,' she said.

'Ah,' I said. 'I've never seen one.'

'I have,' she said. 'In England. Gosh, that was a long time ago.'

'How old were you, again?'

'Shh,' she said. 'Listen.'

We listened to its song for a bit longer and then it must have flown away.

'That was stunning,' she said.

'Yeah,' I said. 'Come back to bed, I'm getting cold in here.'

She stood there for a while, looking out at the morning sky. I reached over and pulled the sheet off her and curled it up under my chin.

'I'll move in with you,' she said.

'What? Really?' I asked. 'But I have to move out soon.'

'I know,' she said. 'It doesn't matter.'

'You really want to?' I asked.

She nodded.

'OK,' I said. 'Can we have breakfast first?'

She laughed and came back to bed because there wasn't any breakfast in the house at all.

That weekend she started bringing her things over. We slept together most nights. When she'd sold most of her furniture and put the rest away in storage, she came over with her last suitcase and a wrapped present. She dropped it heavily on the coffee table.

'There,' she said. 'A housewarming present.'

'What is it?' I asked and pulled away the bow and silver paper. Inside was a big book titled *Birds of the World*. I turned to her and kissed her. 'It's perfect.'

We snuggled together on the couch and I slowly turned through the pages of the book, pointing out all the birds that had been on my balcony over the past year. She started filing her nails and we sat there for at least an hour.

'Oh,' I said, looking at a picture. 'This was a Flicker. I didn't know what this one was. See it?'

She squeezed my shoulder.

'I saw one of these, too,' I said. 'Apparently it's really rare.'

'I hope none of these rare specimens get hurt,' said Hazel.

'What?' I asked.

'When they do all that development,' she said.

'Oh I don't think so,' I said. 'I'm not worried about it.'

'No?' she asked. 'What will happen to them when we move out?'
I shrugged, and turned another page of the book.

One night at the supermarket we were carrying two red baskets filled with bread and vegetables and we happened to walk past the aisle that starts with cleaning products and ends with baby supplies, pet food wedged in the middle. There was a rack of bird feeders wrapped in plastic and I took one and showed it to Hazel.

'Should have got one sooner,' she said. 'We're moving out soon.'

'We could take it to our new place,' I said.

'I don't think so,' said Hazel. 'My parents had one. The only things it attracted were magpies and mynas. Yucky birds.'

'But look,' I said. I pointed at the bird illustrated on the cardboard insert. It had green feathers and little pink cheeks. 'This guy likes it.'

'Forget it, Randall.'

I put the feeder back and wondered what was wrong with magpies and mynas anyway.

The day that we moved out was exactly a year after the stork had started everything by visiting me in the morning. All our stuff was packed up in boxes and I had cleared out the balcony so that the professional cleaners could wash it down. Hazel and her father were taking things to the new house in a truck. All the corners of the house were exposed and the place seemed a lot bigger than it had before. It was dusty so I walked around and wiped the windowpanes and the tops of cupboards and I pulled down the curtain to wipe that, too.

When I pulled it back up there was a big bird standing in the middle of the grey, square balcony. It looked a bit like the stork but it had much darker feathers which were ruffled, a pink bald head and a dirty beak. It stared at me with its black bead eyes.

'What are you, a marabou?' I said. I was glad the sliding door was closed. We looked at each other for a minute. 'Scary bird.'

The marabou lowered its head and raised it as if nodding, then clacked its big dirty beak twice. It stretched its wings and hopped up onto the railing, then soared off over the suburbs. I watched it until it disappeared.

Rearrangement in the Travel Section
Eddie Paterson

Move Wales.
Move Wales closer to Britain, &
Ireland down.
I'm not sure about Istanbul.
Don't worry about Istanbul,
but put Britain into
Wales with Ireland,
or is that too radical?

Best Medicine
Steven Amsterdam

I leave them badgering the nurse in the cafeteria. All I want is to appreciate the volcano alone, without the whole needy crowd thing.

My niche is the last-hurrah set, folks with at least two major cancers or a primary ailment, but still sporty enough to manage a little adventure. I enjoy working with this segment. They're up for anything. Usually in their final stages before the real rattle begins, they don't have a lot of hang-ups. No protective gear when they go in the sun, they drink water right from the taps. They just walk around free, hungry for everything, like last-minute shoppers trying to take home the whole store. Part of the deal – and my biggest, most worthwhile expense – is the nurse who comes along, making sure they're dosed with their proper medicines, hydrated, and pumped full of enough steroids so they can stay vertical, climb the steps, brave the rapids. Each one a little star, burning out brightly. The whole thing is kind of Zen, if you buy into that.

What I'm trying to wrap my mind around is why this particular group has been giving me trouble. I've got my little cancers too, I'm managing my own care regimen, so I have a decent idea of what they're going through. It's what makes me a good guide. Still, this crowd second-guesses me more as each day passes. Just now, when I came out here, the Octopus, whose powers of social insinuation have up until now been appreciated, grabs me at the elbow – so tenderly, as if I'm the weak one – to ask if maybe the group shouldn't skip the two-rope rappel down the cliff after lunch. *Yes, it's on the itinerary you all signed up for. Yes, you're all well enough to do it.*

At least the valley here has the authentic terrain they want. After the floods, the government went overboard trying to make the place look temperate, despite the new facts. They reintroduced all these native oaks, but the warm wind from the ocean blew them back into crazy angles toward the volcano, like they're praying to it. Finally, everyone gave in and started planting palms. For all the planning, what they forgot to add is some human-scale structure that could show you how big the volcano really is. Give the scene a little more wow.

Three times a year, I stand on this promenade and point to the iconic volcano, point to the fierce waves pounding into its base. *This,* I tell my faux-interested charges, *is called a destructive plate margin.* They ask, *How long since the last eruption? Thirty-two years,* then I give my joking smile: *You're safe.* That's when they each quietly wish they'd splurged for the extra day to see a live one on Hawaii. No matter what, everyone wants an explosion, especially when you're going to die. This rock pile here releases all of its pressure in cute, white wisps.

I could look at it as an engaging subject for contemplation and relaxation. An off-center pile, with that slinky volcanic curve up to kiss the sky. An innocent symbol of destruction, like a baby's cough or the sun. My doctor encourages me to meditate on the structure of the natural world. *Get lost in it and find yourself,* like she's selling me a three-week safari. I humour her every now and then by trying one of these exercises because she also prescribes real meds when I need them.

So I study the hill, let it tell me the earth is round, filled with elaborate, molten plumbing. All this will allegedly lead to inner reliance and, eventually, clean detachment from the body – just what the doctor. I close my eyes and project myself into the pale puffs, *to heal each of my cells with love,* just for her.

I attempt to erase the two weeks I've been jetting these desperates around and the two weeks we've got before our last night of big fun, before they all scatter home to die. Why do I bother? Their cliques have been established, the subtle competitions are in place, their impressions of my skills are set. It's not like I'm banking on repeat business. For all practical purposes, I could deliver them home tomorrow. But the money I'm taking is criminal. So we've got the mountain adventure, the rafting adventure, and the ski adventure to look forward to. Yee and hah.

I open my eyes. The volcano is still there, telling me nothing. What a joke. I've only succeeded in creating more cancerous adrenaline. I could sleep for a week.

Someone's there, on the edge of the crater, amid the clouds of hydrogen sulfide. It looks like a man dancing. He's got no details, he's practically made of smoke. The clouds blow in front and behind and all I can make out is this unlikely guy doing his jig. He looks like an ant, as if the mountain just rose up under him. Now, *he* gives you some sense of the scale.

I think I should visit my father.

Standing feels provisional. I spread my feet slightly for support, like you would on the back of a whale.

'That volcano is alright.' It's the Pregnant Teen, carrying some health drink in a giant bottle. She's suddenly next to me, terrorising my space with an unsolicited pat on the shoulder. Wherever we go, she can be relied upon to alternate this kind of breathtaking insight with, 'Would you look at that?'

She points her bottle at the volcano and says, 'I see something like that and, I gotta say, I know exactly how it feels. You know what I'm saying?' She's due in two months. They think the baby will make it.

I'm tempted to bestow a courtesy smile but, weighing that kindness against the prospect of being her only friend for the rest of the trip, I say, 'Would you mind staying with the group?' She goes back inside, undoubtedly with a report to all that I'm moody. Fine, they can keep their distance.

I look back and the wind's changed, the steam is blowing in the other direction. The man on the crater is now exposed, a pile of rocks.

Still, I'm resolved about seeing Dad. It will dovetail nicely. In the last few days there's been a flurry of requests to squeeze an alternative healer onto the schedule. I'm sure Dad can play the part. We'll dump the cliff walk, which they've been complaining about anyway, and fly out this afternoon. We'll see him in the morning, then fly to base camp for the hike. It'll be good. The group will provide maximum deflection. He can preach to them. The old freak will adore the attention.

No one seems sorry to miss the cliff, but I'm sure I'll get a nasty comment card at the end of this. Some of them perk up when I promise them a real-live shaman tomorrow. The prospect of getting on the plane though, sinks them all into doubt. *Can't we find another healer nearby? Today?* Fortunately, the nurse convinces them the treated air will be good for all of us even as she pushes them up the stairs to the jet.

Now they're settled and we're flying into a cloud, which always feels enchanted, like whatever happens here isn't real.

Dad had been a doctor, but lost it when he started getting cancers himself. He'd seen the cures he'd been handing out and wasn't ready to take them. He quit, got us reclassified so we could live outside the city, bought ten acres in the mountains and started building his outpost, with safe water, safe air and an underground garden. A kind of paradise, really. Mum had been gone three years and, in some ways, so had he. I was fifteen and didn't want to get stuck out there. He more than understood, told me we would each make the journeys we had to. He was already talking like that. I'm not complaining, I wanted to go. He would be the tough guy staying behind to die. Looking back, I think I just didn't want to have to hold his hand when he did.

The Octopus comes over to my seat behind the pilot and relates that she once produced a web segment on 'fabricated shamans' – generally middle-aged white guys who pay someone for a vision quest and get themselves ordained without authentic experience. She leans in close with her toxic breath, and says, 'Honestly, no one worth their salt calls themselves shaman anymore. Even the few native tribes left have let it go. Maybe we could visit one of those plant labs, where they're really advancing *effective* therapies?' I look behind her and see she's already shared this nugget with everyone else on the plane.

I clear my throat and cough a little to show I know they're all against me. It turns into a hack which, after ten seconds really gets their attention. The nurse comes at me with her syrup. I keep her back. 'OK: I used *shaman* as shorthand. He doesn't call himself that so much. The land there is beautiful. You'll see another kind of lifestyle. You'll all be entertained, don't worry.' I cough again, emphasising finality, but again it continues till I'm wheezing. The Octopus backs off, throwing her hands up at the others. I realise I'm drenched in sweat. Lately flying has been giving me a flush. The nurse quietly hands me a towel to dry my face. They all watch. Super.

Dad used 'shaman' only once to me. I'd started really making money so I flew out for a visit. He was already well on his way – the hair, the fingernails, feral. An old crazy man who didn't know he was old or crazy. He lived off the land and practiced whatever he practiced on the locals for barter. I was having my first cancer then. He tried to take my meds away, swore he owed his health to renouncing devil pharmaceuticals. He looked well enough. He hadn't died out there after all; he'd got through five cancers before he was fifty. He was sorry he'd ever let me go, promised I would survive long enough for him to heal me. I tried to take him to the city, take him shopping. He wouldn't have it, wouldn't even let me leave any money. Said he wouldn't know what to do with it.

I should have told them he was a wizard, which, by his reckoning, he probably is by now. I don't care. Even if he's only ranting, he'll be something to see, and probably appreciate the attention of a son who seems to be honouring his delusions. Doctors like respect.

The Shaky Widow asks if the detour is going to cost extra because she knows of an excellent healing clinic right near the base camp we're going to tomorrow. She struggles to pose this as an accounting concern when it's so nakedly a matter of her not quite being able to swing this trip in the first place. She's clearly got some sort of bet going as to which is going to give out first, her health or her money. Let's hope it's neither for now. I'm not remotely interested in organising an airlift from the mountain.

'No extra cost,' I assure her. 'I'll spring for this flight.'

Once we're cruising, I make the call from the back of the plane.

'Dad?'

'Who calls me Dad?' That old smile's in his voice.

'Only one person I know of.'

'I wanted you to call me.'

'And here I am.'

'I mean I willed you to call me.' So much for sane. I lean against the emergency door and see if anyone's paying attention. The nurse is forcing cups of antiviral water on everyone. I motion for her to turn up the air; I'm freezing all of a sudden. Down the aisle, my group is all plugged in to their viewers, watching trade data come in from all over. I lower my voice, as if it will do any good. I'm sure at least one of them has a monitor on.

'I'm still doing tours, Dad.'

'That's a surprise.'

The plane bumps twice and we drop out of a cloud. All is visible again.

'I'm seeing so much, meeting all kinds of people. Every day I'm travelling. I work with the dying, Dad. I'm helping people.'

'No explanation needed. Just glad to hear your voice. My surprise is only conceptual, that there are still tours, still sites to see. Still people to pay. But someone always has the money, right? You worked that out a long time ago, didn't you?'

'Are you still practising?'

'I've stopped practising and started doing,' he gives a cluck of that know-it-all laugh of his. 'You're coming by?'

'Depends on you.'

'A child's presence is a perpetual blessing.'

'I think the group would like to have an audience.'

'What? For the hocus-pocus? No more magic. I'm way past that now; all the power comes through my body.'

'That's great, Dad.'

'Are they chemically medicated?'

'They have their regimes, sure, but, come on, they're cornered, they're plenty curious about natural approaches.'

I can hear him struggling to find an open mind about this. 'If it means seeing my son, I'll meet these drugged little barons.'

'How's tomorrow morning? I'm actually calling from the plane.'

'I was ready before the phone rang.'

'Perfect.'

I close the phone and look at them. From the back of the plane, I deliver the good news, 'I've secured the visit.'

There is some immediate grumbling, as I should have expected, but I walk through the plane to give directions to the pilot.

The nurse stops me first, no doubt to ask if I've taken my meds. As much as I appreciate her fraternising with the crowd, I don't cherish her coming at me like a union organiser every time I'm near. I accept a cup of water and squeeze past her before she can even start. I notice a spot on her neck she should probably have looked at.

While I'm talking to the pilot, the nurse faces to the muttering throng and I hear her say, disobeying every bit of protocol, 'The man is his father. We should just go'. I'm not hiring her again.

Machiavelli leans out of the aisle to tell me, 'I don't care if he is your father, if he's the genuine article, he won't agree to see us en masse.'

The Miserable Couple says, almost in unison, 'And certainly not at the hotel'.

Machiavelli adds, 'We're already up, why not keep flying and visit one of the clinics just over the border? They're doing some amazing work.'

Everyone loves this idea. I raise my open hands.

'Because this isn't a medical tour. We've all seen enough clinics. You've had enough experiments, haven't you? I'm trying to expose us to something a little different. Look: Tonight we'll have a hearty meal. I think we could all use a little meat – steak anyone? Then, before bed, let's get you all into the pool. Hog the spa jets, they'll do you good. In the morning – my gift to you – we'll go see him. At minimum, he'll give us a blessing for our trip. At most, what? We're all cured.' This breaks it open, everyone has a nice nervous chuckle.

Having already done her damage, the nurse works the crowd. 'After all, we have the time, maybe the man is a healer of some sort, and since he hasn't seen his son in a while, it could be important.'

They seem to listen to her but I don't want it to be too much about me so I seal it right there. 'Remember: We all need to get a good night's sleep. You're putting packs on those backs tomorrow afternoon.'

On the bus in the morning, I sit next to Magellan, who is enjoying the rare privilege of taking his third tour with me. Some experimental drug cured his cancer but muted half his vision and hearing. His trick is to feel his way to the best vantage point of a site – the edge of a waterfall, the bottom of a canyon – and announce, 'Hey, at least I'm still here'.

It's not till we're cruising around a curve that I realise he's resting his hand on mine. We're both blistered, raw and, apparently, insensate from our respective prescriptions. For a moment, I can't tell which scarred bit of flesh is mine. This sucks. I'm not even thirty and I look like the rest of them. I disengage our skin. I get out my cover-up cream to smooth down the dark orange patches. Dad's going to have some words to say about this. Undoubtedly, he'll reach for something he's ground together from the back of the garden. Or not. Now all he has to do is touch me.

The bus turns left at the mailbox. We climb up the gravel road with steady power. The path is decorated with all sorts of tribal hoo-hahs. Sticks are tied to rocks (with silver hair from my father's ridiculous mane, no doubt) and stuck in the ground to ward off evil, welcome friends, whatever he's in the mood for.

We get up to the driveway and the house is gone. A big red cabin, gone. The original beams still stand in a Stonehenge silence with all sorts of colored fabric pinned to them. Flags for his fort, hanging there with no breeze. Three army tents are set up on dark blue tarp where the front lawn was. Dad stands in front of one of them, authoritatively directing the coach into the only unplanted space on the property. We pull onto a pebbled driveway where the garage used to be.

Dad's not wearing anything protective. In fact, he's only wearing what looks like a batik diaper. His hair and eyebrows are gone, but his skin is clear and his body is muscled, his eyes still healthy and gleaming, so it's not from medicine. There's a cut on the side of his head, a thin line of blood over one ear. What a host. He shaved off all his hair for us. Excellent, the group will get their live freak show and I'll get the points for visiting.

Dad shoves his grinning face next to the window, trying to see through the mirrored glass. All bald men look like chimps, and he's no exception. He walks up to the front, taps on the door and I unlock the seal. The air that escapes seems to knock him back. He covers his face with his arm.

'What are you people breathing in there?'

The Young Man of Independent Means, who sits in the front any chance he gets, tells him, 'It's pumped for immunity'.

I wish that hadn't been the opening salvo. Dad regains composure enough to come back at us with a tense smile, continuing to fan the air.

'Come outside and get a breath of what we've got here.' He inhales deeply and his eyes roll to white. The air is apparently so magnificent that he loses words and holds his arms out to the heavens. It's that good. He stands with his hands in prayer position, awaiting our collective rush to hug him.

Magellan tilts his head like a bird at the others. 'What are you all waiting on?' He heaves up, steadies himself on each chair back, and pulls his way through the aisle. His fingers nearly turn purple as he clutches the railing going down. Dad catches him and Magellan grins like a child. He would gladly spend the rest of his days in Dad's arms.

The others turn to me with concern. I don't move, I'm not ready.

'Don't you want to say hello?' the Pregnant Teen asks, dabbing my face with a napkin. Suddenly I realise how kind she's been to me this whole trip and I feel my guts drop, like everything is going to fall out of me.

'Not yet. Go ahead,' I say, ushering everyone off. Steadying myself on the arm rails, I watch him greet them all, rubbing them in the right places, making them comfortable, learning their names. The group is breathing it all in as deeply as they can. The still, natural air; the smell of his body. When was the last time any of these people were touched like this? Soon the scene becomes one enormous love-in, everyone reaching around and gently feeling each other's bodies. I watch from the top steps of the bus, proud. No, the group won't complain about this stop. And Dad looks happy. He turns to the bus.

'I think there's one more in there!'

I'm stuck on the second step. Before I can come down, he leaps in and surrounds me.

'I'm sick too, Dad.'

'I know,' he says, supporting my head, 'We'll get you fixed up. Come outside.'

'I don't know if I can.'

He yells out, 'We need some help here'.

Suddenly I'm being carried down the steps of the bus by my arms and legs. I look up into my father's eyes. You've never seen a colour like this, like a bucket of summer peas. I relax into it, like my doctor told me to. For a moment, I feel that space she's always going on about, like

I'm attached to this world by a string. I hold it and let it go, hold it and let it go. When I let it go, when I close my eyes, I drift, but when I open them he's looking at me with the sun behind him.

Everyone supports a different limb so the skin won't tear. We've all learned so much about treatment from each other. They carry me across the land that used to be a house and place me on the tarp. A twig underneath pokes my shoulder. I try to shift from it, but can't. I can't tell them, can't talk. They're standing all around now, looking nervous, except for Dad. He kneels down next to me, kisses my forehead in three places, tells me I'm going to be fine.

The nurse says, 'His medication completely stopped working three days ago'.

All I know is I'm looking up into this green that's looking back at me, this green that I've heard about my whole life because I have it too. People meet me and have to comment on it – as if I didn't know the colour of my own eyes. I always think, *You ought to meet my father.*

He looks up at the sky as he feels the pulse on each side of my neck. I count too, like he taught me, feeling the pulse in his fingers. He rubs his healing hands together, then lays them on my scalp, my forehead, my chin.

The nurse says, 'I knew it. It's too late.' Such a worrier.

I don't care who's talking now, but someone says, 'Shhh! Let him work.'

A clear drop falls from my father's cheek. He sees my lips move, tasting the salt. I must be dehydrated. I attempt a smile to comfort him, but I'm not sure what comes out.

'Let me try,' my father says. The group takes a step back.

He rubs his hands together again and separates them over my face so I'm looking at the lines on his palms. Poor man. He's been working hard.

He inhales deeply, summoning his powers. His hands come slowly down to me, hovering from my forehead to my mouth, pressing a current of air tight between us. I can see it rushing across my face. Slowly, with a wizard's precision, he lowers his fingertips nearer my skin till I can feel their heat on my cheeks. Then, without a sound, without the slightest incantation, he closes my eyes.

Remember Sleepy Creek
Virginia Peters

As we wind our way over the ridge we can feel the wind muscling in against the side of the car. Above, dark cloud fits tightly over the layers of green and blue landscape, like the curved seal of a lid. We are a tiny bubble in this watery light, and I am grateful this is the last leg of the eight-hour journey – less than an hour to go. At least the lightning has stopped.

'Jeeesus,' you say suddenly, as we round another bend and the rain fires horizontal nails at our windscreen.

I know what that means. It means, 'Whose bloody idea was this?' but you don't say that bit. We're thinking pleasant thoughts, smiley thoughts, aren't we? Somewhere in these hills our new friends are waiting for us, and we are going to have a wonderful, wonderful week away with them, despite this weather, despite our mood.

'What's his name again?' you ask me.

'You *know* his name. Why are you doing this?'

'Francis, isn't it?'

'Yes,' I say, and I feel the corners of my mouth lift a little. 'It's Francis.' I like priggish names.

In all the time we've been driving we've avoided saying anything about them, up until now. All of the friends *you* have are old school friends, and I imagine you feel I'm tugging you away from your famil-iar circle. Your sandpit. This will be a good test for you. I'm trying to feel ebullient, to make up for you, but I guess it's making me testy.

'Francis and Margo.' You interrupt the silence with this.

'Yes,' I reply. 'Francis and Margo. Is there anything wrong with that?'

'I can see why the other people dropped out. You'd have to be an absolute nong to drive this far for just a few days' break.' You say this as you pivot us around another bend.

'They were going to fly, not drive. So *we're* the nongs. And they didn't drop out – her father was ill. It's fate. I'll admit it's all a bit last-minute, but Margo didn't even know us three months ago, when they made the booking.' I pause, expecting you to say, 'She barely knows us now,' but you don't – you're off form. So I keep going – 'I like adventure,' I say. 'I like the impromptu-ness of it.'

'Impromptu-ness?'

'Yes. And I like seren*dipity*.'

'Serendipitydoo.' You shake your head.

'You know, our lives will be over before we know it – we'll have died of boredom. Seriously. These guys *do* stuff.' You're smirking, so I look out the window on my side.

Margo, I guess you could say, is my new best friend. Yes, I know I'm smitten, but so is she. You do like to tease me about that. You have made me blush at times. And I have to say, I don't mind that nice feeling of blood warming on the surface of my cheeks. I think the last time I ever felt such a feeling was with you. Strange, isn't it. I feel exhilarated all over again. You've told me I'm becoming a lesbian – sleazy you. I've told you you're ridiculous, that in fact we're more like sisters – we've just clicked, and we both have the snapshots on our fridges to prove it: *Year One mothers at Vera Cruz* – significantly, we're in the middle of the shot, our heads touching at the temples, rosy with champagne.

'Have you got the address?' you ask, gruffly.

'Shit!' I hiss as I rifle through my bag. 'Yes, I've got the bloody address.'

We have to backtrack. It's very confusing on these little country lanes, isn't it? I'm about to say that, but I skip it – your nose is screwed up and you're leaning over the wheel like a hawk.

Then suddenly you announce, 'This is it,' and you swing the wheel sharply.

Yes, there is the sign nailed to a gnarly tree trunk, a grubby white sign, its font like the masthead of a newspaper, but with the letters having started to grow together with some sort of fungus. It reads: Sleepy Creek.

'What do you think?'

'Well we can't tell yet, can we?' you say. You drive us over a ridged metal grate and down, down, down into trees and scrub which in places have grown together to form an intestine. We dip, we climb and turn. They're not exactly manicured gardens, and the surface of the drive is chucking us about with its potholes – rustic – you pay for those holes – but we're not paying, are we? – but you did say you were going to offer half, it would only be right, as it would only be right they don't accept. Margo has already stated emphatically, *We simply wouldn't hear of it.* She actually put her hands over her ears to shut me up. Dear Margo.

We come up over another rise only to discover yet another fall in the drive, and I start to laugh. Nerves. And now you're laughing, too. We're uptight and practising at being light-hearted.

Now we arrive at a wall of trees and we stop, and you go, 'Mmmmm'.

And I go, 'Mmmmm,' too. Bunches of bright yellow flowers clump in the trees and a wonderful vine of purple bells weaves through the tangle of green, everything's juicy wet with rain. Fat, full drops as big as ball bearings explode on the windscreen. I feel excited. We start again, following the curve round, crushing stones beneath our wheels.

Now I remember they'd called it a villa. Before us is a two-storey house rendered in the mottled grey of a plover's plumage; wooden shutters in plain timber are fitted to the windows – authentic ones, I can see the hooks. In the gravel courtyard Margo and Francis's red rental car is parked like a tethered horse with its nose to the old stone wall – they'd flown up.

'Oh, isn't it pretty?' I say.

'Who needs to go to France?' you say shrewdly.

'Exactly.' And I find your hand and squeeze, but you're all action, I can almost see the electrons sparking off your reddened face.

'Come on, what're we waiting for?' you say. 'Let's go.'

'There's *Mar-go*.' It escapes me like a wonderful sigh as I get out of the car.

'Yes, here's Margo. *Jacqui.* You made it.' Her cheeks are as fresh as crushed strawberry against the black shine of her hair, crinkles gather at the corners of her eyes – small, keen eyes that glitter like black sequins. She is wearing that finely-striped navy boat neck with the shaping – oh dear – and a small loop of pearls around her neck – very old-fashioned. Her hair sweeps far left like a salute and mushrooms neatly beneath her ears, but strangely it does seem to suit her. She's just Margo. My Margo.

She opens her arms wide. 'Welcome to Sleepy Creek.'

We fold into one another quite naturally, like utensils, no fat between us. 'I was worried about you, driving all that way,' she says, her breath shooting hot in my ear.

'Don't be silly. It was a good drive, wasn't it Morton?' I look back to include you.

'Yeah. Apart from a bit of weather. Great to see you Margo.' Your voice glows, warmed with sincerity, and you kiss her cheek with a big sucking sound. 'Thank you so much for thinking to invite us. We're really chuffed you thought of us.' You touch her arm and smile, almost shyly.

'It's a pleasure,' she's saying. 'It's worked out for the best, actually.' I notice Margo's eyes are wet, probably from the smiling. Mine feel a bit leaky, too.

'Now, this place is fantastic,' you say, breaking into up-tempo. 'What a find!' you boom. You really know how to say all the right things. I'm proud of you.

'Yes, isn't it gorgeous? This is our second time here. We just *love* it. Now come and see inside. I've got Champagne chilling in the freezer – don't let me forget.'

'Where's Francis?'

'Oh, he's gone for a walk over the hill. Filling his lungs with cow dung.' We all laugh.

I notice Margo is very proud, moving through rooms with the long slow legs of an owner rather than a holiday renter. I get all excited over the thick slab of table in the kitchen and the odd assortment of old dining chairs, and the Aga – I just love the curved corners and that milky-coloured enamel, and the still life paintings on the walls, little chunky ones with thick daubs of paint.

'Naive,' you say as you inspect them, and Margo and I make discerning sounds, agreeing with you. The owner collected everything from absolutely everywhere, Margo tells us. Even the doors and window frames have been recycled from old homes.

'The house is a puzzle of pieces. How clever,' you say. And I think you are glad you've come.

'And this is the lounge, or the hunter's den,' Margo says, with a wry smile. There is a fire crackling in a soot-blackened recess, there are mounted deer too, and leather sofas with saggy seat cushions and strapping ends like shiny rumps – I watch you as you sink into one of them and buttress your back and neck with two cushions.

'*Ahhhhgh.*' You sound like a horse, so we leave you to rest. We steal away – Margo, in a conspiratorial whisper, saying it would be sensible if we emptied the car for ourselves.

She leads me up the stairs. The steps are smooth in the centre where feet have polished the wood to stone, and I feel reassured by this almost sensual curve, as if I've walked these steps many times before. In my nose, dank stone air hitting hard as I lug my case. I notice the light hangs limply at the stair window – outside a rainy sky, although none falls now. The pane looks as cool as cold water, making me feel snug inside myself. Margo carries your sausage bag and your tweed jacket on its hanger. I'm looking at her bottom – you're right, it's flat, tucked away neatly into her long thighs and narrow hips.

She flicks a switch and we are standing in a hallway, red walls and lantern lights, the floorboards are blackened with stain and at the end is an oriental-looking cabinet with a painting above it.

'Fresh towels are in there,' Margo says, pointing to the cabinet, but I'm looking at the painting; it is of a woman with her back turned, a bowl of water in the foreground, her arm is raised and her head tilted down as she touches a white cloth to her side – a basin wash. My eye is drawn to the palest tinge of mauve worked into the creamy paint, a suggestion of where the breast begins to fill with tissue.

'Beautiful, isn't it?' Margo says.

'Yes it is, isn't it?' I almost whisper.

'Now, that room is ours,' Margo is explaining, 'and I've put you in next door, as I think this is much nicer than the one on the other side. So, I hope you don't mind, I've made it all up for you.' She is telling me this as we wait at the door, instilling the moment with a touch of suspense. I play along, my eyes wide with curiosity.

'Your boudoir,' she says, and she flings the door open so that I may walk through first. She's right, it's too romantic to be called a bedroom. I go straight to the white curly-haired cow skin in the centre of the room, and I turn in a spiral under what might be a tasteless chandelier anywhere else. It is a room full of its own grace.

'Oh, the colour. It's divine,' I say.

'It's sort of "ballet pink".'

'Yes, you're right. It *is* ballet pink. Did you make up the bed—oh Margo. And look at those beautiful flowers.'

'We were in town yesterday. I just thought I'd brighten it up for you.'

'You're the dearest.'

'I'm so glad you like the place,' she says, almost shyly, as she puts your things so carefully down on the chair, draping your jacket so that it doesn't crease.

Now she sits on the edge of the bed, and she is smoothing a circle around herself with her palm.

I hear her sigh. 'Still, it's nice to get away isn't it? Away from kids.' Her voice dwindles as if she is suddenly weary. Then, 'Hey,' she says. 'I've got something for you. Sit down here,' she says, patting the mattress next to her, 'and *don't* move.'

I do as she says, taking pleasure in my girlish obedience. When she returns she's holding a neat little turquoise paper bag between her fingers.

'For you,' she says, sitting down next to me. She watches as my fingers ruffle the tissue.

'Oh my God,' I breathe. Inside is a ring, woven from tiny green glass beads, mostly forest green with specks of teal and lime, and set in the centre is a large baroque-style pearl, shimmering with iridescence. It really is beautiful.

'But why?' I say, as she takes the ring from me, sliding it onto my middle finger.

'Because you liked mine.' She holds up her finger to show me her own ring, which is in amber tones. 'They're made by a French woman,' she says. 'Quite exotic really, aren't they? I can always change it, if you don't like the colour.'

'No. It's gorgeous. I'm going to treasure it.' Then I think she might say something else, but suddenly she is practical, suggesting I need time to get myself all organised. But after she is gone I lie there for quite a while, the bedside lamp on, holding my hand up every so often, altering its angle in the light.

Margo is vigorous in the kitchen. She is practical and efficient. A real mother type. You, me and Francis watch, happy we're in her good hands. Francis slouches in a carver chair, making his legs appear longer than they really are. He is a man who sits with his ankle on top of his knee – I do like that – there's an arrogance about it. Francis is smart, he cuts people open, he saves lives, but his auburn hair is short, like an adolescent's. You are sitting squarely in your kitchen chair, upright, your legs apart, a grin like a sickle.

Francis is pissed off he has forgotten to bring his CDs. Have we heard of Otis Oberon? What about Spearhead? The worst thing to happen in the music world this decade was the death of Jeff Buckley.

'*Really?* You haven't heard him? He's phenomenal. Seriously, you have to hear him. Tomorrow, Morton. We'll go downtown and pick up some CDs. If I'm right, he'll blow your brain. Beautiful stuff.' He kisses the tips of his fingers.

'Sounds good,' you say, and I'm glad you look amused by his enthusiasm.

The air is thick with lamb. Margo opens the Aga, her face glowing as she lifts out the oven tray. She doesn't know I detest lamb, how could she? I find myself smiling lovingly at the slab of meat as I place the vegetables I've chopped around it. Now Francis is up out of his chair to fill our glasses – but you tell him to sit down, insisting you'll do it. Chipping in already – I like that. You're so considerate.

Now you are at the fridge with Margo, jostling her out of the way with your elbow, and she is giggling and telling you to nick off, that she was there first. I can't tell you how happy I am. I feel so warm. I turn to look at Francis – when he smiles back I see his jawbone, it's strong and follows the exact curve of his smile. He swallows and a lump in his throat undulates – I have to look away. I look for you, holding my glass out to you.

'There you go,' you say as you pour. And your cheeks are full and soft as you look down at me, and you give me a cutie-pie smile.

Over dinner we talk about movies. Francis is very intense about Russell Crowe.

'Yeah, the guy can act, but he's too much of an arsehole,' you say.

'But he's a genius,' says Francis.

I decide to support you and I work out what I'm going to say before I open my mouth.

'My theory,' I begin, 'is that you don't watch a movie with Russell Crowe in it. You watch Russell Crowe.' It doesn't sound as good as it did in my head, so I try to elaborate. 'His reputation has destroyed his ability to—'

Francis cuts me off. 'I'm sorry, but there comes a point as a viewer where you have to contextualise. We all know actors are only acting, and he is the most outstanding acting talent in the world today.' Francis squares his jaw at me.

'But you can't argue that,' I say, matching his insistence. 'It's a matter of taste. Opinion. And I don't like him. Neither does Morton.' I look over at you, but you couldn't care less now. You and Margo are talking about something else and you're making zigzag movements with your hands as you explain something – probably your next fishing trip with your old school buddies.

'I think you're wrong.' Francis leans his head towards mine. 'I think acting talent can be quantified.' He says it in a low nasal voice as if it's a dirty secret no one else is to know about, and I can see a nerve jiggling on the sharp edge of his jaw. He's serious. I laugh out bubbles of light fluffy air, because it seems nothing to do with Russell Crowe anymore.

Margo looks over at me. She winks. Her face is flush with red wine and she looks soft and pretty, so I tell her so.

'Yes she does, doesn't she,' Francis affirms, and he looks very pleased

– so must I, because you're raising your eyebrows at me.

'You girls are as sticky as glue,' you say, suspiciously. And Margo doubles her chin, and I shake my head at you as if you're really quite odd. Then we smile – not at you, but at each other.

Over dessert, stewed apple and vanilla ice-cream, Margo complains about the attitude of so-called 'working' women.

'I'm sick of being patronised. I don't have to make *money* to be considered useful. I make *babies*, I make *food*, I make a home, I make—'

'*Lurve*,' Francis interrupts.

'Yes, that too,' she smiles up at Francis who is now standing, excusing himself from the table.

'And just because nothing we do can be quantified in dollars,' she continues after he has left the room.

'No disrespect to you, Margo,' you interrupt. We wait for you to clear your throat. 'But your worth is equated with the cost of a full-time nanny-slash-housekeeper. An insurance company would probably set your worth between sixty and eighty thousand a year, at best. *Hey, don't shoot!* I'm not saying I'd pay that. I reckon around forty, 'cos you guys have got cleaners.' You're laughing as Margo and I bark you down.

'We're not keeping house or nannying, we're mothering – that's an art.'

'We represent an institution.'

'I can't believe we're having this—'

'OK, OK. How about this – mothers are worth their weight in gold.' You attempt to flutter your foreshortened eyelashes.

'You,' says Margo, with a jab at your chest, 'don't know how lucky you are.'

Then Francis sticks his head in the door.

'Hey dudes! I have some A-grade shit here. I'm just gonna roll a couple of nice little spliffs in front of the fire, if you care to join me…' His voice is groggy with suggestion.

You look at me, a grin on your face.

'Why not?' you say, raising your eyebrows.

Francis is sitting cross-legged on a shaggy rug, back as straight as a Buddhist – magazine for a flat surface, with a little plastic pillow of green mulch and a packet of papers. He smiles up at me, 'You smoke?' I'm sure his eyes are already dilated.

'I have done.' I try to sound nonchalant. Then I add, 'But a while ago now.' Margo takes a position behind Francis on the armchair. Legs apart, she starts to dig her fingers and thumbs into his shoulders – I notice the pearls still gleaming at her neck. You and I are on a sofa opposite, as snug as a pair of thick socks, watching her as she slinks her arms down his chest and runs her cheek adoringly over his hair – for us I think. She looks up, breathes a smile through her nose. Then Francis starts to suck, cheeks hollowing like a drug-fucked malcontent in one of those nineties fashion shoots. I go to nudge your ribs, but you are already beginning to lean forward, reaching as he passes the joint, palm up like a precious offering.

'You guys have this one.' His voice sounds dry and pinched. 'I'll light one for Margo and me.'

We smoke, and everyone coughs, except for Francis who inhales cleanly, with medical expertise. When I finally turn to you I see your eyes are hooded. It has been a long day for you. I remember, we'd agreed marijuana sends us to sleep.

'We should go to bed,' I say to you, and I smile at them way, way across the rug. Margo smiles back, and Francis nods his head, very slowly. I haul you up with two hands and then I slowly travel across the rug, and I lean down and press my lips to Margo's, a goodnight kiss, a thankyou kiss, on the lips – it's the drugs I suppose, but it feels so natural. She puts her hand up to my cheek and cups my face, and I wait for a moment, until the hand drops.

Not sure what to do with Francis, I touch my hand to the top of his head. He looks up at me, his eyelashes quivering – I see the pale stretch of his throat, the knot in the centre poking out, almost painfully, and I turn away.

There you are, waiting, my sentry, your palm held up to say goodbye – and they respond with palms too, and you click your heels, wobble and laugh.

'He's an unusual boy,' you whisper across your pillow.

'How do you mean?'

'A bit of a master of the universe.'

'Do you think?'

'Do *you*?'

'Dunno. Are you glad we came?' I make my voice sound sooky.

'*Yeah*,' you say, but you're not sure, are you?

'You're a team player,' I say, encouragingly, and I stroke your brow.

Now I hear the knob on their bedroom door turn – how did they get up those stairs without me hearing? My heart starts to gallop ridiculously and I have to put my hand over your mouth as if the sound of hooves might take a circuitous route through you. We wait. We wait quietly, until we hear their bed creak.

Now your hand feels like a paw between my legs, but I'm lying there thinking of *them*. I can still hear them, very faintly, but nevertheless they are there, they are there.

'I can't,' I whisper. 'Wait until morning.'

In the morning I wake up to Francis's groan. It is very dramatic. I open my eyes and see you, just as your eyes open too, for the first time this morning I think, because your lips are a softly crumpled 'W'. You swallow, and then your eyes droop shut. But there goes Francis again. He has one of those voices that carries – it's trapped inside a fresh coconut, pubescent and woody. I close my eyes with you, and wait, half expecting them to stick their heads around the door.

There is a tang of bacon in the air. Margo is sitting at the kitchen table, still in her dressing gown – a Mother's Day present I seem to recall, cream velour. Francis is in camouflage board shorts at the Aga, a pair of tongs pointing in the air, poised like an artist's paintbrush. A quick glance, and I note his legs are athletic; the hairs are not apishly dark, thank God, but a light fuzzy felt, like yours. For some reason I find this reassuring.

I smile and say, 'Hi guys,' and they're grinning at me and I'm grinning back. It's as if we're all *in* on something – last night I guess – this is how they are, they're a club, we're a club – I see it gleaming in Margo's eyes as she looks up at me.

'So guys, what can I do?' I say, suddenly guilty that I've only wiped a few plates since I've been here, but they tell me to sit down and relax, there's nothing *to* do, apparently. So I sit opposite Margo, and we both lean forward on our elbows, like girls do, pretending Francis is not there.

'Did you have just the *best* sleep?' Her hand is on top of mine.

'The best.'

'There's no noise here. Absolute dead silence. And no kids jumping on you at 6:00a.m. It's unreal, isn't it?' And I tell her I love it, too, and I tell her again we are so glad we've come to Sleepy Creek. We're as happy as pigs in mud.

Now she is asking me if I heard anything last night.

'Um, no?'

'Blow job,' she mouths, and she shakes her head and rolls her eyes.

'He's so noisy,' she mouths again – and at the same time you barge through the door and a sort of hiccup yelps between my shoulder-blades.

We look at you. You pretend to click your heels, but you're wearing socks, but we get the idea.

'*Guten tag,* playmates.' They laugh at you, and although I don't, I'm happy they're growing fond of you. I'm still busy thinking about what Margo just said. I know what *you'd* say – you'd say she was showing off. But if I know Margo, I'd say she's letting me know the barriers between us have completely dropped.

You're diplomatic, moving straight into a collaborative arrangement with Francis on the bacon and eggs. And I'm watching, remembering that you normally wield the tongs, but not this time; he is the surgeon after all. You're crashing the cupboards and drawers as you look for plates and things.

'No, no mate, up there. Next one along,' I hear Francis say. Then he has you chopping frantic sprigs of parsley.

What next? This is a question that often preys on my mind, even now. Not yours I think. You're happy for *nothing,* next.

You're saying, 'No, you two go. I actually need to make a few business calls this morning.' And I can sense what Margo is going to say next, before she even says it – yes, I'm on a downhill slide.

'Look. I did it yesterday,' she's saying. 'And I'm happy to just potter around here this morning. I've got three chapters left in my book.'

Francis is looking at me with amusement as I look from you to Margo, to you again, and then back to him. I'd made the mistake of saying I felt like exploring, and now it seems it's just Francis and me.

The truth is, you're the only man I've ever walked with in ten years, and prior to you, I can't actually recall any male with whom I've shared a perambulatory relationship. Walking is very personal, don't you think? Your conversation should move with your limbs, flowing, without thought. Individually, I actually have nothing to say to Francis. Our relationship is structured on a square. With two struts removed we become a couple of pointless sticks; either that or two pillars, which must by all rights rise to the occasion, support, carry, uphold a fascinating conversation. Certainly, I'm not capable of that. Not with him, anyway. We will be lopsided. We will limp in awkward silence.

'Make your damn calls when you get back.' I'm suddenly gruff with you. 'This is supposed to be a holiday.' But you're not taking the hint, are you?

'Take her right out to the point,' Margo is instructing Francis, her face flush with such goodwill. 'You'll be blown away,' her voice whooshes as she turns to me. 'It's so beautiful.'

Francis smiles at me, 'You're happy with that?'

Not quite. I tell him I'll be ready in a minute and I run up the staircase. I'm stalling. I'm rubbing blobs of thick sunblock into my cheeks when you come into the bathroom. I shut the door behind you – because of course you don't.

'Thanks a lot.'

'Oh go and enjoy yourself.'

I threaten you with a scornful look, a finger against my lips to shut you up.

We're taking the bright red rental car. Francis is tweaking buttons and dials on the radio, an expression of scientific accuracy set in his jaw. His ear is finally satisfied.

'It's surprising how well you can get Triple J up here,' he says, and I notice his voice has that nasal quality again, the intrigued wonderment of a connoisseur.

'Really?' I say. 'You're a Triple J listener? That's funny, I was thinking more Radio National.' We reverse out of the turning area of the courtyard, the engine screaming like a high-powered drill as we cut the gravel.

'Oh, I don't mind a bit of national program,' he's saying as we set off. 'I stumble on a few interesting interviews, now and then. But Triple J's got its finger on the pulse, musically – and I'm also partial to a bit of leftist shit-stirring.' He glances the side of my face with his eyes, then tightens the wheel to meet the bend, his palm whacking the gear shift down. Our back chassis flares out. Now he thrusts the gear stick up, and I can hear we're spitting stone out the back like some ludicrous cartoon. I catch him in the corner of my eye. He looks deadpan, so I take it he sees this as normal. This is the way Francis drives. We change down, another bend, and I have to use the muscles in my legs to pinion myself to the seat.

We don't talk for a while. I'm concentrating on the road, and I'm angrily thinking about the light, feathery consistency of the word 'farce', and of course, its obvious rhyming potential. But then we reach the ridgeline, and my heart lifts.

When you and I came along here the other day, the sky was leaden, and a mist clouded the shape of the land, but today its mood is changed – it's drenched in clarity, and every colour dazzles as we enter into the diorama; the fields and hills are luminous greens with fuzzy clumps of camphor laurel and caramel velvet cows; closer in there are little dots of yellow buttercups, and clusters of flamboyant palms celebrating their hairdos in the thermal lift. We can see for miles up here, absolutely miles; the subtle variegation of blue sky and deeper blue sea, the streak of sand and diaphanous salt haze, swatches of silver for township. Further away, rising out of the sea is the promontory, appropriately a shade of almost-navy – I can even see the lighthouse, its whiteness, its solitary tip. This is where we are going. You should be here with us.

'Pretty damn fantastic, isn't it?' he announces over the top of the radio. 'I love this place. We're actually driving along the rim of a volcano, right now,' and then he points across my face. 'It sweeps all the way to the rocks out there – Julian Rocks.'

'Yeah? Wow. It really is beautiful.' But I'm uncomfortable agreeing with him. I'm thinking that maybe friends' husbands are meant to be a bit like brothers. You have to treat them with disdain. That's what I'm thinking at this moment, anyway. And the thought helps me to relax.

Ten minutes later, we come scooting down a steep hill to a sandy little beach, and we stop next to a clump of flax with a lurch. I see the sign: Cape Byron Lighthouse walking track, 2km.

'Well let's do it,' he says, slapping his thighs. I take a big, wide-eyed breath.

'What's the matter?' he says.

'*Nothing*,' I say, and then I'm out the door, clasping my hands and stretching them down the length of my back.

'Gotta hat?' he says. 'Sun's a scorcher. Even in winter. Better chuck this on.'

I catch it. It's Margo's, a wide-brimmed straw hat. I put it on my head, but it makes me feel like Miss Daisy. I must look doubtful.

'Don't worry. It looks *really* noice.' He's smirking at me, a soft floppy surfie hat on his head.

'I'll swap you.'

'No bloody way mate,' he says, and he leaps away from me as I make a swipe at his head.

We attack the steep cobbled steps like mountain goats. He's vigorous. So am I. We focus on keeping a good pace. He makes the odd observation, and I second it with a breathless, *Yeah*. Like you say, nothing is as bad as I imagine. You're always right, aren't you?

'OK,' he's saying, and I can see his forehead is prickled with sweat. 'We can either keep going, or divert down here and join back later.'

'Let's divert then,' I say.

So we set off down the narrow stone steps, Francis in front. The steps are deep and we have to watch our feet as we stumble down, feeling the thump of our feet shuddering in our thighs.

At the bottom we take in the shape of the point: it's long and curled like a thumb resting on the sea; the grass is bright, synthetic green against the foaming white of waves. I can just pick out the white railings of a lookout. We walk along the crest, taking in both sides – it's a cusp of yin and yang – on one side the water is sparkling against a gentle rim of fawn sand, on the other side there are vicious crags of black rock and great hurls of sea spray – this is the side to which we are drawn.

We lean our forearms against the railing and watch with great concentration as the sea bursts its foaming guts against the might of the rocks. I push Margo's ridiculous hat from my head and let it hang down my back.

We stand there for quite a while, not talking, then he leans into me, and he says, 'See how there's a washing machine churning at the base? Those are opposing currents and they're being sucked together into this relatively small nook.'

I like the sound of that, and each time the currents smash against the rocks I can feel my heart lift and groan with pleasure. You should have come.

Francis is saying, 'Come on. I'll race you to the top.'

You know me. I can't help myself. I'm flying along behind him, and as soon as he realises I'm right on his tail, he turns to catch me in the corner of his eye, and I catch the corner of his grin as he makes for another burst of speed. When we get to the top of those damn stairs our lungs are thumping and whistling with thin needles of laughter. We have to hold our knees and let it all spill out.

'Jesus, you put up a mean fight,' he tells me. As you can probably imagine, I'm glowing, smiling and panting, and he's doing the same.

It's kind of embarrassing, so I say, 'Well, what are we waiting for? *Come on*.'

We head back up the main track again, climbing our way to the lighthouse. A little slower now, in tandem. We talk about you and

Margo missing all this, how silly you are, we've got *carpe diem, joie de vivre* and all that stuff happening in our hearts. It puts a spring in our calves.

At one point, Francis reaches over and puts Margo's hat back on my head. I say nothing, but I feel a little smile weaken my mouth.

Now we can see the lighthouse. We're right out on the point now, cutting across the cliff above the Pacific Ocean, and no longer alone – the path is an itsy-bitsy snake of Japanese tourists heading in the opposite direction. Francis is nodding and saying, *Ohayo gozaimasu.* I join in, and I feel a little silly because I feel oddly proud, like I'm an ambassador to Australia. Francis mutters little asides with a Japanese accent, and I blow smiles through my nose, although I have no idea what he is saying. I feel so happy.

As they pass us I consider it's a little weird, you know, the way you see yourself reflected in the faces of other people – their eyes are blinking like camera shutters, and they take an image of us, they think we are a couple, and they shoot it back at us in their smiles – the picture is as tiny as a pinprick on their pupils, but I can see it, I can see it. Francis and Jacqui. Like two pools of water slowly merging.

We squeeze together to let them pass and I feel the back of my hand glance his thigh, and now I feel his palm between my shoulderblades, hesitantly soft. It makes my breath catch in the base of my throat, and then my nerves are hitting a sudden chord.

I remember this feeling. It makes me think of you. I let myself go closer, so I can feel my shoulder nudge into his arm. Now he steps in behind, letting a larger group of Japanese pass by. I can feel him inching behind me like a phantom, and I'm considering how nice it would be if I were to suddenly fall backwards, heavily – how he would suddenly materialise, a human cup all round me.

But now he's in front, he's overtaking me, racing up the final set of steps like a greyhound. And I scamper up behind, distracted by my new and exciting thoughts.

'Made it.' He turns to smile at me, a look of breathlessness freshening his face. 'Isn't it a beauty?' He's looking up now at the lighthouse, full of man's universal admiration for tall construction. I start making noises about the tessellated brick surround, and *look*, how lovely it was that they left a ring of natural sandstone around the top. Yes, I'm gabbling.

'Come and look at the view from this side,' he says. And we lean on the rail looking out across the district and to the hills from where we came. 'See that sharp point, there?' I tilt my head so he can see I am following his finger. 'That's Mount Warning. They say that when Cook came into the bay the needle on his compass went haywire. He couldn't get a reading. They say it's something to do with Mount Warning. According to local lore, it radiates some sort of magnetic field that draws people into the area. It's meant to be hypnotic.'

'How do you know all this?'

'I know lots of things.' He looks sideways. I do, too, and although we're not quite looking at each other as we lean into the rail, I know we're inhaling from the same well of air. Deliberately. It's as if he's sucking me slowly up his nose and into his head and his lungs, and something inside my ears starts to warm and melt, making liquid pool beneath my tongue. I have to look away, for I don't want him to see me swallow or hear me gulp. When I look back, he's looking at me, right in my face.

'So, what next?' he whispers, and I see his eyelashes, they are chestnut, and they seem to be sprinkling his cheekbones with tiny freckles as they quiver… and I'm so close I feel my breath might blow the chestnut dust away.

When we get back, we find you and Margo around the back, lying on deckchairs in a spill of sun. You're drowsy and content.

'I hope he's been good company, Margo?' I say, mocking you with a disapproving tone.

'He's been absolutely lovely. We're great mates now, aren't we, Morton? Not that we weren't before,' she says, with a little cackle.

'Yes, Margo is my new best friend. We know everything about each other now.'

I smile drily at you.

Back in the kitchen, Margo puts her hands on my shoulders.

'Morton's a sweetheart.'

She says it with such sincerity I have to say, 'He's OK,' and I clasp her shoulders too, so that we're balanced.

'Was Francis fun?'

'He was *great*.'

'*Really?*'

'Yeah, really. He's a blast.' And she squeezes my bones.

We decide to go out for dinner that night. They pick an awfully expensive restaurant.

'Let's make it special,' Margo says, and she suggests we girls get dressed up. But I've only got jeans – perhaps I'll just wear them with high heels. But she's doubtful, it would be better if I borrow something of hers.

She wears a red shantung silk dress with a Chinese collar and lots of powder pressed onto the pink of her cheeks, and a black blazer and formal black shoes. The little black shift dress is not quite me she agrees. I'm not tall enough for such an elegant dress, I say – but I can see she's disappointed.

I wear jeans, high heels and a long fake fur coat, and I feel comfortable, and uncomfortable. In the back of the car, I show her the ring on my finger, and she holds up her finger, too. We don't have to say a word.

It's the sort of restaurant you and I would go to for a special occasion, but I'm just loving the spontaneity of such extravagance. We're silent as each plate arrives, looking down our noses at the food, our faces bathing in the sticky aroma of meat jus. And we chew in a circular fashion, round and round, like *Herald* critics. I notice you and Francis make quite a performance of swirling and sniffing the wine before you wash it around your mouths with your tongues. You're both being terribly conceited, and Margo and I smile at each other, amused and strangely proud of you both as though you are children and we two, matriarchs.

Later that night in bed, you slide across the pillow up to my ear.

'Did you notice the way Margo spoke to the waitress?'

'You mean over the water spilling?'

'Not just that. *Everything*. She couldn't speak to her without her lip curling. *Strange girl*,' you say with long vowels. Then you are silent for a moment, and then – 'What about jug ears. Did you see him turn scarlet when I asked him to let me finish my sentence?'

'On tax.'

'No. *Iraq*.' You inhale a little cry.

'*Jug* ears?' I whisper.

'You haven't noticed?' And then you add, 'I reckon he's got a dirty little temper. She's terrified of him.'

'Jesus. Where do you get this stuff from?'

'I observe.'

I stick my mouth up to your ear: 'I bet they're not lying in bed saying things about us.'

'Oh,' you say, not even bothering to whisper. 'I bet they're saying plenty, m'dear,' and you roll over.

But I'm angry with you, and I'm rolling right behind you, and I'm up on my elbow and in your ear.

'Why can't you just think they're *fabulous,* and *ordinary*? Why do you have to complicate them, and turn them into freaks?'

In the morning you announce you're going on a drive. It sounds very bold. When I ask you if you want me to come, you say of course you do – in fact you *expect* me to. So I decide to wait for you before heading down the stairs – you can break the news to them.

It's agreed that toast is all we need, and a glass of orange juice to replace any vitamin loss from last night's intake of wine. And while I'm doing the toast, thanking God it's nothing as harrowing as my famous rubbery eggs, I hear you tell Margo we thought we might go for a drive. Oh God, I'm glad you said *thought.* I'm not looking yet. I can't bring myself to. But now you're asking them if they'd like to come with us.

'Oh no. You two go. It'll be nice for you to have some time to-gether,' says Margo. It sounds faintly ironic.

When I turn to look at her I can see she's pale with a light flush in the centre of her cheeks; her colour goes with her voice, which is pastel. She bruises easily, and I think you know this as you're saying, rather unctuously, 'You know, you're both *most* welcome to come'.

'Oh, come *on*,' I say. But the atmosphere does not lend itself to jolly persuasion.

We settle for breakfast, like the little family we are not. Jam, Vegemite, butter, teapots and a TV antenna of toast. Very civilised.

You're talking enthusiastically about fishing, and Margo is doing an admirable job of showing interest, asking you dull questions about the speed of trout, their extreme sensitivity, and how it is they're able to change colour in different circumstances. You don't know the answer to that one. Perhaps it's related to heat, I suggest.

And Francis. Oh, Francis is quietly sipping his tea, his eyes darting over me, occasionally. I have to look the other way – it's almost em-barrassing – their newness has rubbed off, already. And yes, I already know what you're going to say to me later, when we're heading off up the road. You're going to say it very gently, because you'll notice I'm looking despondent.

'They're not really my cup of tea, but it doesn't mean we can't still be friends. Perhaps just in small doses, though.' Or something like that. A judgement of sorts. And you'll be right. I know I would have let them envelop us, let them sweep us along in their fast current until we washed up downstream. But it's the novelty Morton – it's almost worth it. Wouldn't it be wonderful if life was just one big long beginning?

We leave the next day, a day early. I look blandly on as you tell them in your pragmatic voice we've decided to break up the journey with a night in a country town. We must be rubbing off on them, for they agree it is sensible, they completely understand.

That night under the low stippled ceiling of our motel in Port Macquarie you kiss me. I'm not sure what moved you to do that, my quietness perhaps, intuitively reclaiming me, for it's been such an awfully long time since we've kissed. It usually happens when our faces get in the way of each other, when our lips graze, and out of respect for something lost we are moved to recall those early days. Your tongue is so cool though – it doesn't even seem to fit, and we writhe and lash against each other's teeth.

Remember how we used to kiss? There really is nothing quite like the first kiss.

Prussian Blue
Jane Wallace-Mitchell

'Right. You're done.'

'Thanks, Anna.' Libby stretched and closed her novel.

'Hold still and I'll release you from these trappings.' Anna held the tube with one hand and peeled the tape away with the other. Libby never watched when they pulled the needle out. 'There you go. I'll just put a bit of tape over it. Not too long this time. You were in at ten, weren't you?'

Libby nodded. She wasn't sure she was ready to brave the madness, the ugliness, of the outside world yet. This ward was peaceful in its own way, as long as you didn't get too caught up in thinking about why you were all here in the first place. Within these walls there was a respect for life that she'd never come across anywhere else. She couldn't place whether it was a certain vulnerability that she felt and liked, or just an absence of the usual facades people wore to protect themselves out there in the real world. It was the fear, she guessed, that levelled them all in the end. Either way, Libby felt as though she'd never really looked at a person until the first time she'd come into this room. She loved this room – and dreaded it. This room was her nightmare, and yet the only place she'd ever felt alive, accepted.

'It's only 2:30 now.' Anna slid the pillow out from beneath Libby's arm. 'Still got the best part of the day ahead of you.'

'Yeah, might run that marathon after all.'

'Well, leave me those gorgeous shoes then, will you? I think they're just about my size.'

'They're seven-and-a-halfs.' Libby pushed herself forward on her chair, testing her balance before she stood. 'And you can't have them. I'm taking them with me.'

As she said it she caught the eye of the woman in the next chair, who raised an eyebrow and smirked. 'That's right, sweetheart. Don't surrender a thing, least of all good shoes.'

Anna put her hands in the air. 'OK, I know when I'm outnumbered. See you next time.'

Libby laughed and turned back to the woman. 'I'm Libby. Sorry, I've been antisocial today. Should have introduced myself hours ago.'

'Lois. Pleased to meet you, and don't apologise. We all have our days.'

They talked as though they'd just met in a shop or on the tram, as though a fluorescent red cocktail wasn't seeping, hissing, through tubes and into Lois's left arm, into her arteries and bloodstream, threatening her heart, attacking her very life force.

They'd never spoken before, just smiled in passing, but it was because of Lois that Libby made an effort to dress well when she came. Over the past month, Libby had observed this woman like a guilty spy; she'd never really noticed anyone else.

Lois was in her early seventies, Libby guessed, and always presented as though she was stopping by on her way to somewhere better. Her clothing was draped over her, rather than zipped and buttoned like Libby's, and clearly celebrated a love of colour. She looked soothing, peaceful today in all her blues, right down to the paisley headscarf. Showy rings banded Lois's fingers. Her thin wrist bore a chunky gold chain clasped with a heart-shaped lock. She read fashion magazines and spoke over the top of her pale blue bifocals.

Lois's forearms and the tops of her hands were covered in age spots; they reminded Libby, achingly, of her long-dead grandmother, of being smothered in talcum-scented hugs as a child, of the brush of her skin against cool cottons. In a shock of regression she felt the abandonment all over again. The space a person left when they died was enormous, unspeakable. Libby couldn't imagine leaving any kind of space at all.

Lois was always chatting and laughing with the nurses, swapping recipes, telling them about films she'd seen, making them smile. She nodded towards Libby's plate. 'You didn't eat your greens.'

Libby had eaten her lunch, though: an avocado and turkey sandwich. 'It's only parsley.' She picked it off the plate and chewed. 'Happy?'

'Quite.' And Lois looked it, too, in spite of everything.

There was something so true about the look of a face with no embellishment of hair – no lashes, no brows. Libby doubted she'd find the same beauty in herself in the coming weeks when baldness stared rudely back at her from the bathroom mirror. Brittle hairs were deposited in greater quantities each morning now when she woke. If she dared to pull it, it might come out in chunks.

It was a sweltering summer, oppressive and dry as all hell. Heat leaped up from the footpath and smacked Libby in the face, inhibiting her breath as she walked. She coaxed herself along the street, pausing under each protective canopy of leaves. It was all about perspective wasn't it, these days: whether she was a morbid, bleak-horizoned, glass-half-empty pessimist, or a sanguine, bright-eyed, glass-always-gettin'-fuller optimist? It was a stinking, putrid, shocker of a day… but at least there were promising ponds of shade about… at least when she reached the supermarket there would be air conditioning… at least she was here.

Half full? The jury was still out.

Libby had given up trolleys long ago, tired of the close-to-tears battles she'd had when she chose one direction and they, inevitably, chose another. She'd always found supermarkets depressing, even this little independent struggler. They reminded her that she was just another sucker, just another shampoo, bread, tea, coffee, tinned-tomato consumer. She bought the Italian tinned tomatoes, convinced of their superiority, and shrugged disdainfully at the smattering of local brands. But, even as she basked in the minute glow of her discernment, it was obvious the choice was limited. There were only two Italian brands, weren't there? They lured you, in these places, into a head space where you thought there was freedom of choice: dangled three, five, seven variations of the one product before your eyes, and you thought you were an individual, thought you had power.

Take baked beans, for example, spread before you in all their glory: curried, cheesy, no salt (God forbid), ham flavoured – in small, average, bulk, super-bulk – and you stepped back, pulled your trolley to the side of the aisle, and considered. It was an important choice. A simple slip-up, a misread of the label, could devastate when you unpacked that can at home.

What most people neglected to consider, as they beheld those cans of beans, was that around the world in millions of supermarkets, in millions of suburbs, millions of powerful, discerning shoppers were claiming the same right to their particular flavour of beans. Or breads. Or shampoos. One of seven choices in one of four sizes. But Libby never forgot. Libby was reminded, every time she walked into a supermarket, that Big Brother – and not the reality television kind – had her beaten.

This time she grabbed the bare essentials and put off the rest for another day. There was only one mouth to feed, after all, besides Boris.

She'd been starving him anyway, enticing him into being the brute of a hunter he was meant to be. A nasty, germy, little mouse had taken up residence in the kitchen and Boris, in his self-satisfied, well-fed ginger-ness, had refused to oblige. Now *there* was a creature that knew he had choices. The mouse traps and bait Libby had set were proving useless. Starvation, releasing the inner beast of Boris, was her only option.

Nicki's aisle was free when Libby unloaded her salt, tin of beans, soft toothbrush and four-ply, floral-embossed, gardenia-scented toilet pa-per onto the ramp. Some things you just couldn't surrender to save the earth and, in recent times, Libby's sensitive posterior came first.

Nicki was always smiling. Half full, then? Nearly overflowing. Some people were just like that.

'You OK, darling? How they treating you round there?'

They were all darlings, Nicky's customers, and all faithful. It was the gold tooth that had first attracted Libby, though. She'd always wanted one; loved their sleazy, sinister connotation. But Madonna had put her off in the end, in her gold-toothed stage, and ruined it for all the gold tooth coveters of the world.

'I'm fine. It's fine. They're good people. Just knocks the wind out of you a bit, you know?'

'How's your family taking it? They helping you out? Cooking meals?'

'I haven't told them.'

'What? What d'you mean, you haven't told them, darling? You have to tell them. They're your flesh and blood. That's what families are for.'

'You don't know my family.'

'That's no good.' Nicki picked up a peach and a knife. She always had fruit under the counter. She sliced a piece and handed it to Libby. 'Here. It's beautiful. Juicy. That's twelve-fifty, darling.'

'Thanks, Nicki.'

'S'alright, my love. Here, take another piece. Go and treat yourself. It's a hot day. There's that nice new cafe round the corner. Have a rest. You look tired.'

The peach juice trickled through Libby's fingers as she left the super-market. She knew not to be seduced by its lush flesh: it represented acidity and the mouth ulcers she was losing the battle against. Instead, her tastebuds had a date with a saltwater wash. She flicked the fruit into the closest bin.

The thought of telling her family had, of course, occurred to Libby but every time she reached for the phone she heard her mother, Hortense's, inevitable response, her *this never would have happened, Elizabeth, if you weren't such a stubborn girl… you always were – even as a child. If you'd only learnt to meditate, loosened up, if you'd only let a nice man into your life…*

As she dialled Virginia's number Libby heard the signature sighs, the way her sister would – always did – bring it around to be about herself. She'd be rushing off to have breast tests, self-diagnosing her way to hell and back. Or there'd be the *I told you so*'s, the *you know this would never have happened if you'd lived in a nice, leafy suburb like ours instead of breathing in that foul smog, if you'd made something of yourself and weren't so bitter… you always were bitter, Lib, even when we were little. I used to wonder what it would be like to have a happy little sister… but I've told you all that, haven't I? Of course, an analyst would do wonders… and natural therapies… I'll ask Marianna. Her mother's best friend had cancer and she's fine now…*

Libby saw her brother-in-law, Charles, poor Charlie, absorb her burden as though it were somehow his fault she had cancer, his responsibility to save her from the cruel fate of rudely multiplying blood cells. She couldn't bear the responsibility of making his life even worse.

And her nephew, David? Well, he wouldn't say much – never did. She'd never really found out who he was, couldn't even be sure of his age these days.

Libby always hung up before she finished dialling.

Cancer was a dirty word, wasn't it? And people who had 'issues' grew it, didn't they? All those squashed up little irks from the past, all that bitterness and anger packed up too tightly in your brain had to eventually pulsate and breed of its own accord, didn't it? And then suddenly it had the life force of a demon, conquered the bloods, the organs, the muscles and glands, until you were left a seeping, bed-sored, dying bag of bones. And Virginia: loving, perfect, tight, clipped, bitchsister – and Hortense: self-interested, overpowering, freak-on-wheels mother – would never hold back on an opinion anyway, would never consider Libby's feelings, would never think beyond themselves, never really had.

Fucking 'family' did her head in – always had, always would. Libby had learned to stay away; distance was her salvation. She'd taught herself to ignore their interfering, their superiority, exhausted by the self-doubt they seeded and nurtured into her sponge-like, pathetic excuse-for-an-ego.

She could do what she wanted, now that she kept away, and what she wanted was a fucking strong coffee, side effects or not. She hadn't had a coffee for weeks. You couldn't give up goddam everything. There had to be something besides plush toilet paper to look forward to in life. Otherwise, what was the point? What she needed now was a brain-flush of caffeine to power-cleanse the grimy stain of family from her thoughts.

Libby visualised her sister and mother leaving her head as she gathered a fistful of them with her hand and metaphorically flung them under the wheels of passing traffic – no: floating, drifting off into the never-never, NEVER again of her future.

Two scrubby youths smirked as they passed and she flung. The taller, pimplier, more tragic of the two obviously couldn't resist verbalising his extreme wit. 'Loco lady!'

His plump, dripgreased companion snorted in collusion.

Libby stopped flicking off her family and glared. 'Fuck off, you sad little jerks.' It just made them laugh harder when you fought back. Better to concentrate on growing that leathery skin, that layer of invincibility, than to react in any way at all.

The cafe, a European-style study in understated chic, seemed – thankfully – to be occupied by only one other customer. A waiter washed dishes behind the bar. Libby avoided all eye contact and chose a table in a corner. And then a disturbingly familiar screech, a not quite identifiable niggle from the ugly past.

'Lizz-ee? That's not our Lizzie Proctor?'

Evidently, there had been two customers in the cafe. Clickety-clack heels approached, along with the horror of recognition.

Libby tried not to wince through her smile. 'Ka-thy San-der-son. Hi. I haven't seen you in years. What a nice surprise.' Libby hated the word 'nice'. It was bland and noncommittal – like the colour beige, which Kathy was wearing in abundance. 'You look great. I didn't know you lived around here.'

'Me? Never! Oh, sorry. This is obviously your haunt, though, Lizzie. You always were the alternative kind.' She held her quotation fingers up as she said it. Libby could see the 'I'll call you' hand mimes coming her way in the very near future. It was one of her pet hates. Libby loved her pet hates; they were her dearest companions. She brought them out at every opportunity – or people brought them out for her. Katherine Sanderson was doing an excellent job.

'Yes, Kathy. I live around here. You always were good at placing people, weren't you? Made an art of it, really. What are you up to these days?' Libby dumped her bag down. She didn't bother to mention that no one had called her Lizzie for the last twenty years. She was tired. She didn't need this shit. Half empty and draining to the bottom. She could hear the straw slurping out the dregs.

'Oh… ha! I've moved on to other things now. You know me, Lizzie. Gone a bit corporate these days.' She indicated her outfit as evidence: tight skirt, tailored jacket, glimpse of a French bra, heels, Malibu Barbie foundation. She had the look, anyway, but then Kathy always did. She even smelled corporate. 'This is my friend, Philippa.' She called across the cafe as though she owned it. 'Lizzie – Philippa – Philippa – Lizzie.' She swept her hand as she said it. Next she'd be a game show girlie.

Philippa flickered Libby a cat snarl; the kind where the back of the mouth opens while the front holds its ground.

That was it. 'Oh, Christ. I'm sorry. I can't do this. It's not you, Katherine. I'm sorry, Philippa. I'm glad you're looking so *up*, Katherine. I'm sure you're on top of the world. I'm sure your glass is flowing fucking over, but I just can't…'

Philippa said, 'Well!'

Katherine gasped.

Libby grabbed her shopping bag and left.

There'd be no 'I'll call you' hand mimes then, no promises of keeping in touch, diary entries, invitations to dinner. The glass was empty with a nasty little dried stain at the bottom if Katherine Sanderson was the best prospect on the horizon.

Libby thundered towards home visualising ice cubes bundled up in a face towel soothing across her forehead. She was in desperate need of that fucking meditation tape her mother had given her.

Ice cubes worked wonders. And an old brick house that fought off the heat like a superhero.

And Prussian blue.

She tossed off meditation in favour of paint. She covered a sheet of heavy paper with a wash of blue-black sky, a haunting midnight seascape, the dark soul of her favourite colour. Libby leaned back in her chair, swam in the Prussian blue, and let all the crap dissolve away…

Something snapped in the kitchen and the peace was spliced by weeny, shrill whimperings. Libby dumped her brush in the water jar, disregarding the delicate sable – an act, in anyone else, punishable by death. The brush could wait – the mouse couldn't.

'Boris, you're pathetic!' Boris eyed Libby briefly from his lounge chair and tucked his chin back under his paw.

In the cupboard under the sink Libby found her tiny intruder. He was trapped horribly, his back legs pinned by the snap of the metal rod. His front legs quivered in frenzy. His head reached towards Libby as though she might help, as though she wasn't his grim reaper at all, but a saviour.

'You poor little thing. You're just a little mouse, for God's sake.'

It had to be done – and quickly.

Libby picked up her victim and its trap and ran into the garden. 'I'm so sorry, little mouse… I'm so sorry.' She chose a heavy rock, one that would do the job. She put the mouse down on the ground, dropped the rock right on top of it 'Ohhh!' and shuddered. She lifted the rock but the mouse was still alive. 'Oh, Christ… oh, God!' She raised the rock high and this time crashed it down with force.

It was dead, the poor, tiny, little grey-brown critter. She'd murdered it, stopped its heart, played God, all because it had trespassed into her holy fucking kitchen.

Libby left the mess in the garden and went inside. She sat down at her desk. Her hands shook as she washed the paint out of her brush and set it down. She had grit from the rock on her hands. She wiped it on her skirt. A wave of nausea rushed up her throat and stung at her nostrils. She arched forward and emptied her stomach onto the paper and contemplated, as tears streamed down her cheeks, her new landscape – a bilespill of avocado green and turkey flesh on a still, deep, moody sea of Prussian blue.

Dingbats
Darryn King

☞ **Design Tip:**
Consider your page layout!
When laying up a piece, make sure the text is spaced evenly over the pages! There's NOTHING WORSE than finding a page with only ONE WORD on it! Except maybe being stood up by your boyfriend.

* * *

I'm by myself, drunk, and wondering, could I ever *really* love a guy who uses **Comic Sans**?

And then I see **Marilyn**. She's at the other end of the backyard, letting herself get chatted up by **Spider-Man**.

Unbelievable. I mean, hello? It's *Spider-Man*.

Like that. You don't need Freud to decipher that one. But in case you do, he's over there, doing karaoke.

God, I hate these fucking stockings. Where the hell is my boyfriend?

I pour another Baileys on the rocks. Only, the rocks have melted. That is to say, the ice has melted.

Obviously,
       I'm
           starting
               to
                 lose
                   it.

'What?'

Oh. Wow. I didn't realise I was saying these things out loud. 'I'm starting to lose it, I said,' I say.

The guy, collapsing into the seat next to me, nods – once, slowly. He's got a nice jacket.

Somewhere underneath the empty glasses and bottles and booze, there's the table. I've been sitting at it for probably years now, just drinking my Baileys, watching guy after guy after guy after guy after guy after guy flock to *Marilyn*, talk to *Marilyn*, crack jokes at *Marilyn*, HA HA HA.

'You're a friend of Marilyn's, aren't you?'

Oh, fuck it all. 'Apparently,' I offer, in 8 point font.

The guy ponders this, and then asks, 'Is that Baileys? Can I have a bit?'

I consider, at length. 'Alright,' I murmur eventually, and pour some for the guy. He takes a tentative sip. Then he drinks the whole lot in about a second. I shake my head. That's not how you're supposed to drink Baileys. 'That's not how you're supposed to drink Baileys,' I tell him. 'Who are you supposed to be, anyway?' I ask, probably a bit too sternly.

He pauses to remember. '**Ted Bundy**.' He gestures at his top under his jacket, which, as I focus and refocus my eyes, I notice is splattered with red food colouring.

'Oh,' I say, pausing thoughtfully. 'You smell like cake.' It's true. I also notice, in Ted's pocket:

I'm trying to work out if it's plastic or what when Ted says, 'And who are you supposed to be?'

'**Alice**,' I tell him. 'From *Alice in Wonderland*.' I accidentally nudge my drink off the table and it smashes in a glorious fashion, with splinters of glass going everywhere, very dramatic. Except it doesn't do that at all, on account of it being a plastic cup. Anyway, no way am I cleaning it up.

'I'm in your graphic design class,' he says.

'?' I say, except I don't really say that as such.

'We were doing page layout the other day.'

'Ah, oh, OK,' I say. I'm failing the subject big-time. I suddenly become animated: 'In a four page essay, he fails me on the layout of the LAST FUCKING PAGE, because – he actually said this – there was ONLY ONE WORD ON IT. How ANAL is that? It wasn't like it was actually a design assessment or anything. I mean, that would make sense, but it wasn't a design assessment, it was a FOUR PAGE ESSAY. *Can you believe that anal retentive shit?* A FOUR. PAGE. ESSAY.' (I am drunk.)

Ted is silent for a while. Then he says, 'The book or the cartoon?'

Suddenly, I realise I'm crouched over uncomfortably like I've had *too many italics*, and I need to go to the toilet and I have no idea what we were talking about. 'Huh?'

'Alice from the book, or Alice from the cartoon?'

I get up from my seat. 'Is there a difference?'

He sits back in his seat and says, 'Absolutely,' and I stumble off.

* * *

☞ **Design Tip:**
Choose a font that suits the personality of your piece! Though slower to read, sans serif fonts, like Arial or Helvetica, are great for creating that casual, just-got-out-of-bed look!

Serif fonts, such as the ever reliable Times New Roman or Book Antiqua, are best for a professional, classy touch. Generally speaking, they are easier to read, but sometimes they worry about being too fat.

* * *

When I get to the bathroom, Marilyn Monroe is there, waiting outside the door, except it's really Marilyn *Parkinson*, channelling the spirit of Marilyn *Monroe*, but they have the SAME FIRST NAME. IT'S **GENIUS**.

She says, 'Hiii…'

The teeth in her smile match the white of her dress. It's unbearable.

'Hey,' I say, because there is actually nothing else to say.

She asks – squeaks – 'Are you enjoying the party?'

I shrug. 'I'm hammered,' I say, which doesn't really answer her question either way. I don't particularly want to talk to Marilyn. I just want to use the bathroom.

She points to the door. 'He's been in there for about five minutes.'

'Who?'

'Julius Caesar. He must've pissed all over his toga or something!'
Marilyn titters to herself, and I just look at her.

Because I'm drunk, and I don't care, and I'm not even listening any
more, I'm finding it hard to concentrate on what Marilyn is going on
about.

'Orheurr dlt hrink fronn dlt dlt mbrpt blmpt...'

So I eventually have to say, 'What?' and she says, 'I was just talking
about Batman.'

'I thought you were into Spider-Man.'

'Tee hee!' (She actually says 'tee hee', I swear it.) 'Oh, he says he's
spoken for!'

'Right.'

'But, so, anyway, Batman, he goes to me, Can I get on the ground
and blow up your dress? You know, like in the movie,' says Marilyn
and, again, she's tittering like a mouse. 'Oh I just LOVE him! He's just
so warm, you know?' Tittering is the perfect word for it.

'Yeah,' I say, but what I'm looking at is the golden crucifix that's
practically in her cleavage:

Except it's really this.

And I'm thinking, Jesus is probably rolling in his grave about now, or
else he's jerking off over Marilyn too. God have mercy on our souls.
Our souls, oursouls, arseholes.

'Ha,' I cough.

Marilyn says, 'Um, so where's—'

'He's on his way.'

* * *

☞ **Design Tip:**
Think visually! There's nothing more boring than a page crammed with text text text!
Remember, there are a shitload of ways to turn a potentially boring piece into something eye-catching and interesting to read! Use capital letters! Use pictures! Use italics! (Not too often, that's pretentious.)

* * *

My boyfriend still hasn't arrived – so I go back to the table and collapse in my seat. Marcel Marceau is doing karaoke, which sounds terrible. The Arts students are gathered round him, laughing ^{HA} _{HA} ^{HA} and carrying on and congratulating themselves for being so fucking ironic. And Marilyn is back in the corner again. There's a Ghostbuster sliding his hands up her thighs, presumably to search for ectoplasm ^{HA} _{HA} ^{HA}.

I must be scowling because Ted says, 'You don't like Marilyn very much, do you?' He has a beer in his hand now.

'Pfft,' I pfft. Ted raises his eyebrows. I sag in my seat. 'She looks like an angel.' I pour myself some more Baileys and turn away from Marilyn. There's a fight starting over by the buffet table. Seems Sigmund Freud said something about someone's mother. H-i-l-a-r-i-o-u-s.

'You're jealous?'

'Piss off,' I say, slurring. 'I have a **boyfriend**.'

I look at the screen of my mobile phone. *Where are you, dumbarse?*

'But are you *jealous*?'

'What? I just told you, I have a **boyfriend**.'

'Do you resent her for being attractive?'

'What is this, twenty questions? I don't need this shit.' I want to get up and storm off but I can't really be fucked. Need. More. Drink.

'Just trying to help,' says the psychopathic killer, and he goes to get another beer.

God have mercy on arseholes, that's good.

I look over at Marilyn again. She has Osama Bin Laden's tongue down her throat. 'This is obviously some kind of nightmare,' I find myself saying, out loud. I pinch myself.

I watch Ted coming back, smoothing the creases in his bloodied shirt, and I think, oh why the fuck not.

'Slut.' I push my glass across the table. 'She's a slut.'

Ted sits down, looking interested. 'Go on.'

I reach for my handbag, and I take out my notepad and pencil, because I don't want to look him in the eye, I don't want to feel like I'm at a psychiatrist's. I scribble drunkenly as I talk, to help me think. 'Can't you see it? She turns up to any party and in five minutes every guy in the place is literally hanging off her. Well... not *literally*.'

$$Marilyn$$

'That annoys you.'

'It's just – well, yeah. I mean, if I got that kind of attention...' (Ha.) 'I mean, she's bound to catch some sort of disease sooner or later.'

'This happens a lot?'

'Oh, oh, you have no idea. Do you have any idea... how much of an idea you... don't have?'

Ted watches me write. I find myself mouthing Marilyn's name as I write it, overandoverandoverandover.

$$Marilyn \quad Marilyn \quad Marilyn \quad Marilyn$$

$$Marilyn \quad Marilyn \quad Marilyn \quad Marilyn$$

$$Marilyn \quad Marilyn \quad Marilyn \quad Marilyn$$

Then I start rearranging the letters.

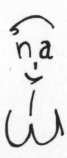

'I think you've got a serious problem,' says Ted.

Fuck. Even her name has great breasts. 'God.' I blunt the pencil. 'Get me a drink.'

'The Baileys is right there.'

'Get me a real drink.'

'I don't think you should be mixing drinks.'

'I'm not – *fuck* – I'm not going to fucking *mix* it.' I look up through eyes blurry with booze and point my finger for emphasis. 'I'm going to drink it.'

* * *

☞ **Design Tip:**
Remember, the Undo function is your friend! Press Ctrl+Z to get rid of nasty mistakes! It'll be like the horrible event never happened at all! There must be no witnesses!

* * *

Ted is going to get me a drink, has gone to get me a drink, has been gone to get me a drink for some time. Here come Marilyn's breasts, and Marilyn some way behind them.

'Hey, who's that guy?' she asks me.

'That what?'

'That guy you've been talking to for, like, the whole night!'

She's talking about Ted. 'I don't know what you're talking about.'

'Uh huh. So, umm, how's your boyfriend?'

Jesus. She has a fucking beauty spot. A beauty spot. There, at the corner of her mouth, by her airbrushed cheek. A beauty spot. A full stop. Like she's eaten an exclamation mark.

'Is everything alright?' Marilyn leans in and touches me on the arm.

'I'm great.' I pull away from her.

'No, I mean, with you and—'

'Great!'

Marilyn just watches me for a bit. Finally gets up and leaves.

I sort through the assorted junk in my handbag and take out my mobile phone. **You have 0 missed calls from your sonofabitch boyfriend**, the screen might as well say but it doesn't, of course. One has to read between the lines. This is where double spacing comes in handy.

I punch in my **boyfriend**'s number and hold my phone to my ear. Then I hear his ringtone.

I hear his ringtone? Not through my phone but here, at the party, somewhere or other. He's here. It's definitely his ringtone. But he doesn't pick up. In fact, it suddenly stops – just like that – as if he… No, he couldn't have… Why would he *hang up*?

I try the number again. The phone is switched off.

'Your drink,' says Ted, holding a… something… out for me.

I put my phone in my bag and do a thankyou nod because I can't pull off a thankyou smile, not right now, and take the bottle of whatever it is and take a long swig of it. Ergh. It's horrible. Glug glug.

Ted takes his seat and watches me drink and doesn't say anything. I'm not sure how long we sit like this – time is playing stupid childish tricks ^{HA} _{HA} ^{HA} – but I get fed up with the silence, so I kick him under the table, and he says, 'Ow,' and we can talk again. 'I thought you wanted to talk about Marilyn,' he goes on.

It's almost like he's… what's the word? I forget. 'What exactly are you playing at?' I half-heartedly jab a finger at the air in front of him.

Ted just raises his hands defensively.

I take my mouth off the bottle. 'Listen, sorry, I'm not really… I don't normally act like such a… like this.'

Ted nods.

'Really, I know I must seem like…' Then something catches in my peripheral vision. Jesus. Actually *Jesus*. She's making out with Jesus. This is… I don't even know what this is any more. How can one girl be so—

'So you're sure you don't want to talk about it?'

It's getting harder and harder to breathe, the margins are too tight, and getting tighter. My fingernails are digging into my thighs. My huge, white, ugly, boyfriend- and god-forsaken thighs.

Now I know I'm starting to lose it.

'Look. Over there. Just look at her. Seriously, just look at her.'

Ted eventually adjusts himself in his seat, and follows my gaze. 'I'm looking at her.'

'Don't you see it?' For a moment I feel like I'm swallowing a jagged-edged upper case letter X. I'm already blinking back tears. 'She's just… she's just so…'

'So what?'

'Symmetrical!' I blurt out.

'Symmetrical?'

'You're a design student, you… know what I'm… talking about.' I'm choking on my words. Fucking Marilyn.

'Maybe you shouldn't—'

I slam the underside of the bottle of whatsit on the table, grinding my teeth. 'She… successfully… directs the viewer's attention,' I manage. 'And… effectively… enhances… content.' And suddenly I've buried my face in the tablecloth, and I'm crying, and I hate myself for it, I must look like such a, such a whatever, but I can't stop, just can't, can't stop for the life of me.

'Alice,' says Ted, reaching over.

'That's… not… my *real NAME*…' I grab Ted's knife, kick the chair aside, and stand up so fast that it hurts my brain. Ted backs off in about a second.

'Marilyn!' I scream, from across the yard. Never use more than one exclamation mark – it looks tacky.

Marilyn freezes, eyes swapping between me and the knife in my hand. 'W-w-what are you…' Everyone at the party is looking at me now and, for once, *it feels good*.

I could do it, I think, contemplating Marilyn through narrowed eyes. You know red looks *so good* on white? It's *wonderful*.

'Please, what are you—'

'Off with her head!' I scream, and lunge towards her, knife glinting in the Cheshire Cat moon ^{HA} _{HA} ^{HA}.

Something grabs onto me. 'Ted! Let! Go! Of! ME!'

He doesn't. I kick and I shove, but he won't budge. 'LET! GO!' Marilyn has run out of sight, and the knife is yanked violently from my hand and I almost want to throw up. I bite into Ted's arm, hard.

'!' he says, but he doesn't say that really, and he loosens his grip just long enough for me to slip out and run into the house. The way is cleared for me, and it's like Alice's coronation ceremony for a moment, except it isn't like that at all, and I slam the bathroom door shut behind me, and hold myself,

    and weep

        and weep

                and weep.

It's not fair.

I just… wanted to leave my mark on a work of art…

There is an uncertain sounding knock at the door, and it creaks open.

It's Spider-Man. Perfect.

I turn away from him, to the mirror. 'What the fuck do *you* want?'

Spider-Man just looks at me with his beady insect eyes. Arachnid eyes, whatever.

'*What the fuck do you want*, I said!' I say.

Spider-Man takes off his Spider-Man mask and says, 'I think I should take you home.'

* * *

There is nothing to say.

I exchange glances with Alice in the looking glass. It *is* Alice. Only a bit torn and ragged at the edges.

She looks furious.

Determined.

Psychotic, even.

Actually, you know… I think I have a pretty good aesthetic going here.

Eighteen
Eleanor Elliott Thomas

I think I'd better kiss you, he says, and leans in and presses his mouth up against hers, the taste of hazelnut on his tongue and the heat of his hand on the curve where her shoulder meets her neck, and what do you think? *Of course* she kisses him back. It's the beginning of summer, she's incandescent and she's just eighteen, and what she feels right now is only bliss and desire. But even now, with the sense of his mouth coursing through her like water and sunshine, like her own blood, the first time she has ever felt this way – even now, she is thinking: I don't want to feel this way. From the very beginning, she concedes afterwards, it seemed like a bad idea. Like the best bad idea she had ever had.

In the very beginning, she takes him to a party. Early on she's talking to some boy, too young for her, and he walks over and interrupts, ignoring the boy and taking her hand, pulling her over on the couch and he kisses her again, and again she lets him, again she kisses him back. Then he's gone and she's alone while on the other side of the room he puts his hand on another girl's thigh, and he makes the girl laugh, and she watches, stricken, thinking: Jesus, not so *soon*! Could he be *tired* of her so soon? And then it's nearly dawn and they're still at the party, and as he stands huddled against her in the wet black morning air, he's telling her not to worry. *I'm a flirt, I'll always flirt* – this is what he says – *but I won't ever betray you.*

She doesn't believe it. She's just eighteen, but she's not *stupid*, remember – she knows better than to trust a man like him. But she is helpless under the weight of her desire. She says nothing, and he kisses the back of her neck.

When she finishes school, she has lunch with him, late lunch at some shitty restaurant in a part of town that after it's all over she'll never want to go to again, and she's changed out of her uniform for the last time, and he jokes, feigning disappointment that she's not trussed up in a short skirt and knee-high socks (although she can see he really is disappointed). She orders soup, but she can barely taste it, barely manage to swallow. The feeling that swims through her body as they talk and her knee rests against his is so right, she doesn't want her senses interrupted by anything but him. On the way home she sits on the pavement next to his car while he has a cigarette, the smell of smoke and sun, his hands large, casual, and he talks about something she'll never remember, because she's looking at him and she's thinking: I will never stop loving you.

Their first fight is quiet, cold. He walks out on her at a pub when he sees her talking to another man, a man who's taken the seat beside her and who she's too young and too polite to ignore. *I'm leaving,* he says, and although he doesn't invite her to she follows him out of the bar, confused. *What's wrong?* she asks, panicked, but all he'll say is *Why don't you go home and work it out.*

A few months in, on a Monday morning soon after Christmas, it's much too hot and she's sitting outside near his pool, and he's lying between her legs, his head heavy between her breasts, and she's roughing up his hair, stroking it back into place and thinking: this is love. And he doesn't love me, she's thinking, and as her hand strokes his hair and as his body lies against her she thinks: this is love and I will never be happier or more unhappy than I am right now, ever again.

Can we still be friends? she asks, when she breaks up with him, and – oh, thank god, she thinks – he's keen to stay in touch, really, he quite likes her. This, saying these words, is the bravest thing she has ever done, possibly the bravest thing she will ever do. *Can we still be friends?* she says, but oh, she wants more than that. Even as the words slip from her mouth: *I don't want to be with you any more, you see,* this, *this is not what I want, what we have is not what I want, but I – but we –* but can we still be friends? Even then, she is thinking of the skin of his chest, the slow beat of his heart. But it had to be done, she can't stand being near him, waking with his arm on her waist, knowing what it means to her and what it doesn't mean to him. Leaving someone you love, she's decided, is not as hard as staying.

But six months down the track, around about then, six months since she left him, once again she finds his mouth close to hers and once more his hand is on her neck and she thinks: oh yes, oh no, oh *god.* He wants her back, he wants her comfort, he misses the feel of her body fitting into his, he misses the way she fights, and as for her – well, she misses everything. So when he once more decides that it's time he kiss her, what do you expect? Of course, *of course,* she kisses him back.

When he starts calling her again, she thinks: maybe this time it's different, because – well, he wants her back, doesn't he? There's still something between them, the sharp kick of desire still finds her when they touch, and she's sure it's the same for him. And if he still wants to fuck her, that must mean something, she thinks, surely it must (she's just eighteen, remember). But when he says he's been thinking of her she clings to the words with the worst yearning she has ever known, because of course he's lying, and of course she knows.

Off and on they're lovers, or at least she's in love and he lets her love him: it stays this way for months. In the meantime, in the off time and sometimes in the on, he fucks other people, seduces other women while she waits for him to realise the way they're meant to be. On an icy night in August, so cold the rain leaves splinters in her skin, they go out together and drink and drink until they know they'll remember nothing in the morning, and in the back of the cab as he's taking her home she shivers and he takes her hand. She holds still, afraid that if she moves, if she breathes, he'll take his hand away and all the while she's thinking: this is worth remembering.

It's the night when she's lying on a couch while he's lying on a bed in the same room, fucking someone else, that she realises she has to stop. They've all been out, the three of them, him and her and the girl in the bed, and now they're back at the girl's place, and it's still the three of them. In the bed, he and the girl are trying to be quiet – they think she doesn't know – the only noises are a shuffling blanket, a sigh, the rhythmic slide of wet flesh on wet flesh, but every sound seems so loud to her, a sonic boom, she's sure it's damaging her hearing. She wonders how he can do this, knowing she's there, knowing that she loves him. And then she thinks: but why do I still love him? And as she lies there, her body held rigid with that barren love, she wonders: why am I here?

So she climbs off the couch and goes to the bathroom, she looks at herself in the mirror and is shocked by how lovely she is when she's at her most pathetic, her eyes vast and bleak, her skin sheer, thinned by too much feeling. In the room where he still lies with the other girl, she collects her things and dresses slowly, delicate with herself, knowing the slightest touch will bruise, and as she leaves she looks at him and thinks: this is the last time I will see you, it's the last time I will see you and you are lying against the skin of another woman. She wants to touch him, still wants what he gave her once, when he kissed her that first night, when everything was hot and beautiful and he tasted of hazelnuts. Now she knows him too well to believe a kiss like that, but even now, even as he sleeps against another girl, this is what she thinks: I will never love anyone this much, ever again.

On the way home, leaning her face against the dirty bus window, she cries, and she can't stop, the pain of it soaring through her torso and tumbling out of her mouth, her eyes, her skin. She cries and she thinks: this will never be over.

But she's just eighteen, and this is what you already know: of course, of *course*, she's wrong.

The Russians are Leaving
Emmett Stinson

So I said, 'Tell him, tell him that happy pizzas are all alike, but every unhappy pizza is unhappy in its own way.' Orson repeated my comment quickly in Russian, and Yuri, shaking a limp over-sized slice at me as if it were a shameful finger, responded in slow, solemn syllables.

'What did he say?' I asked.

'He says you're an asshole,' Orson replied, biting into a piece of plain cheese.

They arrived the day the towers fell. All flights cancelled indefinitely. We got the three middle-aged Russian scientists, Alexei, Pavel, and Yuri, through Orson's girlfriend, a Bulgarian émigré. Yuri, the tallest, was a bear of a man, huge and fat. The ringleader. He gesticulated wildly, his hands and arms flailing away from his round belly like they were trying to escape its gravity – his moustache flared up at the ends in curves, a hairy grin permaplastered to his face. The other two I had trouble telling apart. For all I could see, they could've been twins. Both had salt and pepper hair, thin frames complimented by bulging pregnant-man bellies, and a worn look that suggested they were possibly a decade younger then one might initially guess. But one thing was for certain – they didn't look like scientists. There were no Einstein-ish long grey locks, no horn-rimmed glasses, just skinny ties and ill-fitting polyester pants. They could've been salesmen from Iowa. Alexei and Pavel deferred to Yuri because only he spoke English. Unfortunately, his English was one entirely of his own devising. Perhaps I assumed all Russians spoke pristine eighteenth century rhetorical English, like Conrad or Nabokov. Perhaps it was my deep American prejudice that all foreigners should speak and understand our language and that a failure to do so was tantamount to willful barbarism. Regardless, Yuri roared in odd cadences, refusing to slow or repeat himself, as his tongue rolled over our poor, battered language with strange diphthongs and

Slavic consonants. Although he was a man of science, one felt that perhaps he was only recently evolved from the apes.

I had just moved from the suburbs of Northern Virginia, regressing back into the District by default, into a townhouse near 14th and U with Mike and Orson, old college roommates. They were paying double what they had when they moved here six years ago, before the flower shop, dog-groomers, and yuppie furniture store had nestled themselves in between the local punk rock bar, the Whitman-Walker AIDS clinic, and the homeless mission.

Yuri held the pizza slice between his hands, peering at it with a pantomime of disgust, like he was just disciplining a small child. Again he uttered something in his unintelligible pidgin.

'What?' Orson asked.

For once Yuri slowed. 'Kentucky efried cheeken?' he said slowly, his tongue sliding over the syllables like he could taste them, before he rolled his eyes upwards and licked his lips.

By 11:00a.m. on the 11th, the normally placid streets of the midday city were filled with people walking to their homes, turning in shock and terror with the sound of every passing airplane. Though we forget, a plane did crash into the Pentagon, too. This might have been a front-page story on a slow news day. From the District, all we could see were the enormous plumes rising into the air, an indecipherable smoke signal. But this passed and all that was left was a strangeness, a sort of hollowness, the very feeling one got in looking at the New York skyline – that what was present was what was missing. I wondered if TV could erase the whole thing from our collective memory if only the footage of the planes crashing into the twin towers were played back in reverse.

That night, Orson, Mike and I walked to the Pharmacy Bar in Adams Morgan. Its dimness and the cool embrace of air conditioning bit into the heat of early September in a year when summer did not seem to realise it should be ending. I don't recall any conversation on the way up. In the bar, we chugged our beers and drew the cool air into our lungs. We did not talk. We drank. And breathed.

Finally, Orson spoke. 'Man, this is so fucked up?' he said it like a question. He looked around at us, his large eyebrows raised in a vee, his long arms extended skyward in the same gesture.

What more was there to say?

Alexei and Pavel fought over the telephone like two competing lovers.

They never made any calls of their own on it, nor did they pay it the least attention when it sat there quietly. But whenever it rang, they both rushed to pick it up, skittering down the hall in their socks like two kittens, as if they might impress the device by their speedy reflexes and pudgy quickness.

'Khello?' the winner would intone to a very confused person on the other end. To add to the confusion, they did not know any English other than this butchered greeting, and tended to respond in strings of rapid-fire Russian, which usually meant that the listener just hung up, and then called again, starting the whole skittering process over. I tried to get to the phone first, but no matter how close I was, one of the scientists always seemed to make it there faster, as if, by understanding the rules that govern the mechanics of velocity and acceleration, they were able to break them. Usually, I could wrest the phone from the winner's grip in time to hear the click of disconnection, but as I placed the receiver back in its cradle both of them would look at me sadly, almost tearfully. Like I'd just killed their puppy.

Flights resumed on the fourteenth, and Alexei and Pavel, ever the Gemini twins, were lucky enough to be bound on one of the earliest ones out of the country. That night The Cro-Magnon Men were playing down the road. Orson and Mike formed the band shortly after they started their real jobs working at NGOs downtown. Whether it was inspiration or refuge, I'll never know. But they were good. Or I liked them anyway. Mike buried his bass under layers and layers of distortion. And Orson hit the drums so hard he looked like he was in a fistfight. He placed the drum kit at the maximum possible distance from his body. 'It makes it louder,' he had explained. 'The further I extend my arms, the faster the velocity of the stick, so the harder the hit.' Mike wasn't wearing a shirt but he was wearing a gasmask that he had bought second-hand at an army supply store.

I stood in the front, trying to show some support and to negate that social standard wherein a crowd forms a distant arc from the band at under-attended shows. At the start of the first song, Mike bent over and head-butted the pint of beer out of my right hand. It flipped up through the air and smashed on the ground.

I looked over at Yuri's face as Mike dove onto the broken glass. His face still bristled with the same hairy smile as Mike rolled around on the ground, bleeding in several places where he had been cut.

And the Russians liked beer. A lot. This was perhaps not a surprise, but they had no interest in our vodka, our whiskey, or gin – no, just the cheapest, most watery, coldest American beer you could buy, and they swilled it down with relish. They took two cans out of the fridge at a time and barely paused between finishing one and starting in on another. Yuri would extend the can at an arm's length and pull the tab back, sending a small splash of foam skyward before it came to rest on the hardwood floors of our renovated townhouse. '*Na zdorove!*' Yuri would bellow, then he would look over at me, his eyes big and full of hope like a child's, 'Is good?' he would ask. 'Is Good?'

'They three kings of Orient are…' Orson sang.

After the Cro-Magnon Men played, we decided to keep celebrating. Yuri didn't have any money, but Mike and Orson claimed he was their roadie, so he got free beer all night.

I had only been in Northern Virginia for two years, and it's just across the Potomac river, a twenty-five minute drive without the traffic, but it may as well have been a different world: nine to five in a corporate skyrise, early evening at the gym, a quick stop at the organic food shop and video store in the strip mall near my apartment on the way home. This was what constituted the suburbs for me. I still couldn't process the streets of DC, where even the clerks at the liquor store served you behind a half-inch of bulletproof glass. I suppose I liked it out there – lying comfortably in my bed of ease and all that. I didn't want to be here, out drinking beer with sweaty people who probably didn't bathe or use deodorant. Everyone here looked five years younger than me. Thinner. Less haggard. Orson and Mike had already left our table and were making the rounds talking to people I didn't even recognise. I knew I should get up, get reintroduced, but when I saw Orson talking to some little punker girl who looked like she had just traded her prep school uniform for a studded wristband, I knew I wasn't going anywhere. It was Yuri and me.

Yuri babbled enthusiastically about whatever it was he was saying in, allegedly, English. He punctuated his sentences with either a hard pat on my shoulder or else a hardy clinking of glasses that stirred up the foamy beer inside.

'You know what, Yuri,' I said, 'this whole thing, the whole thing, I knew it was going to happen all along, not what happened exactly, but what were people thinking? Did they not know the world was unsafe, that things are terrible? I was relieved, Yuri. Actually relieved.

And awed. Don't listen to what they say. It was beautiful – sublime. When the airplane disappeared into the building and shuddered out in that fireball it was better than any big budget action movie. And if it wasn't why would they replay it 1000 times a day from every angle we have on tape?'

I looked at Yuri. He looked back at me and blinked. I heard Joe Strummer singing something about revolution on the jukebox. Yuri looked at me again, shrugged, and nodded.

Yuri refused the idea that plastic bags were given away freely to anyone who might want them. When I went to throw away four that I had brought back from the Wholefoods down the road, Yuri snatched them out of my hand, eyeing me like I was insane – so shocked that he blubbered on only in Russian instead of his mutant English. Luckily Orson saw the whole thing and intervened, explaining how Russian consumers paid for them, and economics were so tight there that everyone reused them.

No, he told Yuri, we did not mind if he took the bags back to Russia with him.

The next day was Sunday. Since I had left my job, I was used to having the house to myself in the mornings. As I walked into the living room I realised that today I would have both Orson and my hangover to keep me company.

'Where's Yuri?' I asked.

'6:00a.m. flight for Russia. Left at the crack of.'

In the kitchen, I poured a spoon of bargain-brand instant coffee into a cup of hot water I'd heated up in our microwave – a relic of the early eighties, which probably emitted lethal radiation. Everything seemed sinister now. I examined the hairline crack along the side of the coffee cup wondering what insidious germs were hiding there, waiting to infect me.

The cupboard revealed a package of dried fava beans and half a pack of penne pasta. A few pieces of onion peel lay along the flat empty board along with some other unidentifiable crumbs and a few stray flecks of crushed red pepper. I looked down at my coffee, still cooling in my hand, a slight swirl to the black muck. I had no milk to thicken it, no sugar to cut its bitterness. My small savings were almost gone and I was living on credit, on borrowed time. This, finally, was my life.

I consulted Orson and we ordered a mid-morning pizza on my credit card, washing it down with two cans of Coors and a helping of Crossfire. They were discussing the attacks, but all I could think about was Yuri last night, how, after days of begging, we finally walked him to the dingy Kentucky Fried Chicken over on 14th street. It was a combination restaurant, half Kentucky Fried Chicken, half Taco Bell, its floors were sticky and it smelled like Kool-Aid and vomit. We got him a three-piece, all dark meat (apparently Russians don't like the white meat), with a coke and buttermilk biscuits.

Back home, we all gathered around him. As he picked up the deep fried chicken leg, we watched him bite into it and then pause, raising his eyes to heaven, swallowing slowly. He spoke.

'What did he say?' I asked.

'He said,' Orson paused, looking like he was going to both laugh and cry, 'he said, "It's like a fairy tale".'

Yuri just sat there rapt, just looking up at the ceiling like he was waiting for it to fall in on him.

These Russians Aren't
Going Anywhere

White Russian

5 parts vodka
2 parts Kahlua
3 parts fresh cream*

Pour the vodka and Kahlua into an old-fashioned glass, with ice. Stir, and then gently top with cream.
* For the flab-conscious (or soft), substitute milk.

Historically interesting...
The White Russians opposed the Bolsheviks during the Russian Civil War (1918-1921).

Black Russian

2 parts vodka
1 part Kahlua

Build the ingredients in an old-fashioned glass filled with ice. You can also top up with Coke, if you like it like that. Stir.

Eliot's Awakening
Pierz Newton-John

In the car park out the back of Jim's PC World, Eliot was having a smoko with a couple of the part-time gophers. In an attempt to impress J Edgar, they were seeing who could punch a hole in the side of one of the cardboard boxes that were stacked up outside the loading bay. J Edgar was a pretty Greek girl with a single flaw: she had the hugest nostrils Eliot had ever laid eyes on. He was unaware of her real name. She had been J Edgar ever since he'd worked there. If she hated being called this, she never complained, although she did cover herself in a cloak of icy disdain that may or may not have had something to do with the insulting nickname. While the boys puffed out their skinny chests and took turns stepping up to the battered boxes, she leaned against a car ten metres away, staring into space and blowing smoke up, up and away.

When Eliot stepped towards the boxes and made a fist, Donald – a short, fat sixteen-year-old kid with the kind of fine red hair he was sure to lose by twenty-five – laughed out loud. 'Ooh,' he stirred, 'that's *really* threatening.' Eliot flushed and had a momentary impulse to smack him in the lip. He may not have been the most macho of specimens, but there was still something intolerably galling about having his fists mocked by a nerdy gopher two years his junior. In fact, Eliot had been taking *Wing Chun* classes for a year and he rather fancied himself against the boxes, but when he punched, it was a pathetic, un-co flail that only made Donald laugh harder. Embarrassed, he shot a glance at J Edgar, but she was a million miles away, chewing down her pink lacquered fingernails and staring into the shimmery haze that the heat made over the road.

'Hey, we got customers here. Butt your ciggies and get your arses inside.' Nathan, the sales manager, was leaning out of the doorway. Everyone hopped to it and in a moment the car park was empty, except for Eliot who dawdled over the last centimetre of tobacco in his cigarette before finally grinding the butt out on the roof of one of the company cars. It was bloody hot, had been all January. Sweat trickled inside his cheap grey suit. Still, he took his time, leaning back on the car to breathe in the moment of solitude before he went back in to face the customers and their incessant demands.

At Jim's PC World, salesmen were like sharks. They had to remain in perpetual forward motion. Jim had an uncanny radar for stationary employees. As soon as one came to a standstill, he'd appear, demanding to know what they were doing to justify their continued employment. There were times when there was not much to do and, at these moments, the only way Eliot had found to avoid Jim's attentions was to adopt a purposeful, charging gait and do circuits of the showroom, workshop and storeroom. After a while, he settled into a pleasant rhythm and could dream off. In fact, he did a few laps whenever he got tired of serving customers.

He'd watch the clock, baffled by its Einsteinian capacity to slow to a near stop between the hours of three and five. But then, when the moment of freedom arrived, he'd stand at the bus stop wondering what the hell he'd been looking forward to. Eliot's home life was sad. Sad in the loser sense. His dad had split for Queensland with, can you believe it, his *secretary*, and his mum had quickly repartnered with a poker machine. 'What are you looking at?' she'd bark from the mirror, lipstick hovering momentarily away from her mouth.

'Why do you bother? It's not like you're gonna *talk* to anyone,' Eliot would answer, teenage-resentfully.

She'd snort, make a cat's bum of her mouth again and finish the lippy. Then with a final tease of her hair she'd be out the door: 'Dinner's in the freezer.' He'd open the fridge to find a pack of Bird's Eye fish fingers, frozen peas. *Oh yeah, thanks for that Mum.* So he'd order in a pizza. Not that it was much better – all those half-cold worms of ham.

The absence of his parents left him at the mercy of his older brother Troy, who nobody except Eliot seemed to have noticed was turning into a mental case. For weeks the smell of piss in the house had grown – so gradually that, like frogs in a slowly heated beaker, they had adjusted to it without comment. Then came the inevitable moment at which the point of supersaturation was reached, and the stench precipitated at once into their mother's consciousness. Suddenly she was screaming, 'Why must I live in a men's urinal?' and running around sniffing everything like a bloodhound gone berserk. It turned out Troy had been pissing in the pot plant outside his room because he couldn't be bothered making the trip to the toilet at the other end of the house. The plant

– a sensitive, ferny creature – was fading fast. Its feathery hands were upturned in surrender as it prepared to depart this world.

'Are you responsible for this?' she yelled when she discovered the source of the stink. But Troy just leaned insolently in his doorway, a pout of childish defiance on his face. And when she ditched the plant into the compost heap, he kicked his bedroom door so hard he broke the hinge. 'I *needed* that plant!' he shouted.

His mother went gambling, and Troy stuck his head into a plastic bag full of Araldite. Eliot found him in the garage, flaked out on Mitzy's sofa, so-called because it had once belonged to their dog, before she was run over. The vapours were dizzying. 'Bitch,' he slurred, looking straight through Eliot with irises the blue of half-dried glue. 'Dad was right to leave. Stupid fucking bitch and her fucking pokies.'

A few days later, Eliot had caught him trying to give himself a blow job (never was the term more inapt) with their mother's new high-powered vacuum cleaner. As soon as Troy kicked the power on, the thing nearly tore his balls off and he let out a howl alarming enough to drag Eliot away from *Age of Empires*, even though it meant losing the game and a consequent drop in his online rating. Apparently the pain had overwhelmed Troy's problem-solving abilities, because he was still screaming over the unnaturally high whine of the machine when Eliot burst in and pulled the power cord from the socket. He knew better than to laugh at his brother rolling on the floor, crying and clutching his frankfurter-pink cock, swearing Eliot to eternal silence.

Eliot was often kept awake by the sound of gunfire and the screams of dying men. He'd swear and roll over, pressing his pillow around his head to cover his ears. Silence would fall for a while and a sweet dreaminess would creep over him. He'd be sliding deliciously into the pool of sleep when a machine gun would start up, and a cut-off shriek would wrench him back to wakefulness. '*Fuck!*' he'd shout at the wall. '*It's two o'clock!*' The wall would remain obstinately silent, apart from a few muffled pistol shots. Occasionally there'd be a crash and a burst of swearing as Troy threw his joystick against something. This would go on until sheer exhaustion dragged Eliot under.

He was packing shelves in the storeroom, noting with curiosity the new fish tank Jim had installed. Some of the fish were so garish and unusual that it left Eliot feeling quite puzzled. One of them walked on the bottom of the tank like a neon-legged spider. His confusion had a familiarity about it, but he could not quite pin it down.

'Hi Eliot. Need a hand?' J Edgar had appeared in the doorway.

'Sure,' Eliot replied, a little surprised. Normally she was so stand-offish.

She came forward and started putting software onto the shelves, leaning over Eliot as she did, so close that her breasts almost brushed his face.

'J Edgar,' he said lightly.

'Yes honey.'

'Why are you in your underwear?' His suspicions were growing.

'Hmmm?' she said dreamily, her lips brushing his ear, one hand planting itself on his thigh. It was unbearably sweet.

He remembered the weird fish and a light went on, a deeply disappointing one. 'Hang on! I know what's going on. This is a dream, isn't it?'

She looked disbelieving, offended. 'No, honey, I swear.' The bra evaporated.

Ah what the hell, he'd never have another chance; he grabbed her and started kissing her. It was bliss, but then he noticed something was wrong; her breast felt flat and too hard, her arm too strong. He pulled away and with a surge of horror realised it was Nathan the sales manager he was kissing. But it was too late to stop the uncontrollable spurting in his loins that woke him sticky and sweating in his bed.

'Oh *God!*' he moaned. 'Now I'm turning *gay!*'

It was the confirmation he had been dreading ever since their most recent sales meeting. Jim's automated sales tracking and charting software showed the trajectory of each staff member's accumulating sales through the month. The chart was divided into colour-coded 'performance zones'. Nathan's line soared rocket-like far into the blue empyrean at the top of the chart. Way down below it, the other salesmen tracked like droning Cessnas through a band of mediocre grey. Eliot breathed a sigh of relief. He had expected worse.

'Congratulations Nathan,' Jim beamed as the graph appeared. 'Once again, your performance is stratospheric.' Then he turned to Eliot. 'Eliot. Your performance is… to be truthful, it's egregious.'

'Thankyou.'

'It's terrible.'

'Oh.'

Jim fingered the screen, pointing out a line so close to the X-axis that Eliot had failed to notice it before. It beetled almost horizontally across the band of red at the bottom of the screen.

Jim shook his head sadly. 'Let's say a customer comes into the shop and tells you he's looking for a computer for his kids. What's the first thing you say?'

Eliot floundered. He looked at Nathan, who tried to mouth something without moving his lips. It was like trying to lip-read a ventriloquist. 'You're a very generous man?' Eliot ventured.

'NO! *When are you looking to buy!* How many times do I have to tell you this stuff Eliot? There are *three key questions*: How can I help you? When are you looking to buy? How much do you want to spend? Is that really so hard to remember?'

Nathan coughed. 'Err, Jim, if I could just say something here?'

'Certainly Nathan.'

'I think there may be another explanation for Eliot's figures. As far as I can tell, he's actually pretty good with the three key questions.' Eliot gave him a startled look. This was news to him. 'But he's not selfish enough. He's almost made some great sales this month, but then he's left me to close the sale. So to be honest, I don't think the graph represents the true picture.'

That was when Eliot first felt it – the algedonic twang in his chest like someone had just cut a very small piano wire, a feeling of pathetic, embarrassing adoration. And – was it true? Did he really feel it? A prickling in his groin. It was so dreadful. On top of everything else he was turning into a poof.

He'd always thought something like this was going to happen to him. It was just his luck. Ever since Miles Valiant had been struck down suddenly by homosexuality after he left school, Eliot had worried that it might get him too. For ages everyone envied Miles because he was going out with Fiona Willis, the school's second-hottest girl. Then, the year after school finished, he'd broken it off with Fiona, drifted out of contact with everyone, and then Geoff McKinley had seen him outside the Peel, in a white tank top.

After the sales meeting, Nathan drove Eliot home in his hotted-up, turbo-charged Commodore SS. When they turned off Studley Park Road onto the Boulevard, he put his foot to the floor, and the car shot forward with a vicious growl, leaving Eliot's stomach lurching to catch up.

As they went round the first bend at close to 100km, the tyres skittered over the road surface, the rear of the car slewing a little before pulling itself back into line. Eliot clutched the dash, his feet making futile braking motions. He tried closing his eyes, but it only made things worse. He looked at Nathan and saw that he was extracting a cigarette from his pocket with one hand while he took the turns with the other. Once it was in his mouth he started to fumble with the cigarette lighter in the dash. Eliot lost it. 'I'll do it!' he shrieked. 'Just fucking drive!' He batted Nathan's hand away and pulled out the lighter, held it up to the fag hanging from Nathan's mouth.

'Thanks mate,' said Nathan round the side of the cigarette, Humphrey Bogart-style.

'Can I have one too?' Eliot asked.

'Sure.' Nathan chucked the Peter Jacksons into his lap and Eliot plucked one and lit up, sucking in the smoke like an asthmatic with an inhaler. The nicotine rush instantly soothed his mind. Watching the car swallow the road like spaghetti, he felt suddenly detached and sanguine about the prospect of death.

'Hey thanks for today,' he said. 'You didn't need to lie to cover for me.'

'Nah, that's alright. But I can't keep Jim off your back forever you know.'

'Yeah I know. I'm getting better… I think.'

'Hey, look!' Nathan pointed suddenly at two super fit, gym-inflated figures emerging from the trees near the side of the road.

'What?'

'You know what this is along here?'

'What? A jogging track? No, what do you mean?'

'It's a beat.'

'A beat?'

'A *gay* beat.'

'You mean they…'

'Yep.'

Eliot was silent, taking it in, looking at the trees in a whole new sinister light. Suddenly, the previously scenic stretch of road seemed full of cloying, phobic horror. It pullulated invisibly with obscene muscular acts, moustaches, gargantuan penises. He felt a wave of carsickness.

When they pulled up outside his place, Nathan turned to him. 'Say, what you doing Saturday night? You wanna go clubbing with me and some of me mates?'

He felt it again, that pang in his chest, that little chiming note of pathos and something that might have been love. He hated clubbing, but he felt a pitiful gratitude for the invitation.

'Sure. That'd be cool.'

When he got inside, his mother was sitting at the kitchen table. The table was strewn with bills, most of them in colour. Her face was a wreck of dribbling mascara and haggard lines.

'Hi Ellie!' she said with a ghastly smile.

He started to tell her not to call him that, then his shoulders slumped in defeat. 'How much do you need?' he said in a dead voice.

'Only a few hundred sweetie, just to cover the mortgage. You know, it's all your dad's fault. He hasn't paid me a cent of maintenance since he left. If I ever see that bastard again I'll kill him, I swear it.'

'Mum, I'm an *adult* now. He doesn't have to pay maintenance.'

'I had a bad night Ell, that's all. Someone was sitting at my lucky machine. I knew it was a bad idea to play on a different one. So stupid! I broke all my rules. I smoked with my left hand. I didn't even wipe the chair before I sat down…'

'What are you talking about Mum? Listen to yourself!'

'*Please,* Eliot!' She took hold of his sleeve, her eyes looking up at him in such a desperate, beggarly fashion that he felt a surge of confused emotions: disgust, love, hate, pity, fear. He shook off her hand and threw his pay packet onto the kitchen table. As he slammed the door behind him, he heard her voice calling after him, 'I'll pay you back, Ellie! Next pension day, I promise, OK?'

In the darkened corridor outside his room, Troy was lurking, silhouetted against the blue computer-screen light from his room.

'Hey Eliot. Payday today, right?'

'I don't have anything, Troy. I just gave it all to Mum.'

'Bullshit!' The hulking figure came towards him fast. Eliot tried to dodge past him to his room, but Troy caught his arm in a bruising grip. 'Give it!' he snarled. He seemed to be growing more thuggish and stupid by the day. Eliot could smell solvent fumes and body odour.

'I told you…' He tried to shake off his brother's hand, but it was too strong. Troy had inherited genes for muscle bulk that had completely bypassed Eliot. His other hand now began to force its way into the pockets of Eliot's trousers. Eliot fought and kicked, but it only made Troy more violent; he rammed Eliot against the wall with his weight, pinning him there while his hands groped in his pockets for the cash. Eliot began to sob, but it was only when Troy had gone through every pocket that his body went slack and he released him.

'You little shit,' he whined. 'Why'd you go and give *her* the money? Don't you know she'll only blow it on the pokies?'

Eliot swallowed back salt. 'Yeah, and I suppose you were going to invest it in your *super…*' he spat. He retreated into his room and slammed the door.

Eliot had once heard that every moment of our lives is recorded in our memory perfectly, and that it is only our capacity to access those records at will that is limited. If this was true, he figured he had within his internal archives kilometres of the world's dullest archival footage of his father. Dad reading the newspaper. Dad yawning. Dad picking his nose. Dad going down the corridor. Dad mowing the lawn. Dad saying, 'Cathy, what the, uh, what did the weather say? Bugger, looks like I won't be able to work on the shed today after all…' Loads of boring, incoherent rubbish like that. Miles of it, spools and spools all over the cutting room floor of his unconscious. This, he figured, was the true history of his relationship with his father. And yet, out of all these endless, unwatchable reels, there were just a few seconds that for whatever reason got replayed over and over, until the film itself was worn out, faded with overexposure. Perhaps even falsified by subtle distortions and alterations that he unconsciously introduced with each viewing.

One such film clip: his Dad occasionally took him down to the Mornington Peninsula to fish. For some reason that Eliot could no longer recall, Troy was not there. Was he sick? They went out on a pier in the early morning and sat in silence, their lines dangling into the sea that rose and fell sluggishly, gently slapping the rotted pillars. They hardly ever caught anything, and normally Eliot would feel as bored as the few seagulls that stood around in listless hope of a scrap long after the others had flown off. But today he felt a mysterious potency in him, that golden presence so worshipped by the Chinese and which we prosaically call 'luck'. He caught a fish, a magnificent, improbable fish, a pinkie snapper that weighed nearly four kilograms. It came out of the water thrashing, resisting him like all miracles do, a shimmering lode of luck almost too heavy for his arms to reel in. But the moment that he replayed through the projector of his mind over and over, the moment faded almost to transparency but still able to leave a certain singing resonance in his heart, was the look on his father's face when he brought that mighty fish up onto the pier between them.

It was odd, but after that day he could not recall going fishing with him ever again.

Sitting in a corner of the upper lounge at the Metro, sipping a rum and Coke, Eliot remembered why he hated clubbing. The massive amplifiers blasted out a noise so loud it obliterated thought. The beat pounded his head with giant, weightless blows, while a disco ball on the ceiling regularly speared his eyes with migrating shards of light.

He smelled sweat, alcohol, aftershave, perfume. The dance floor below heaved and thumped under rivers of ultraviolet. Nathan and two of his mates, Dave and Andrew, sat opposite him, beers in hand. Nathan leaned towards him.

'Eee ooo aaa aa oh oh ooh ay?'

'What?!' he shouted back.

'Eee ooo aaa aa oh oh ooh ay?'

'Can't HEAR you!'

'Eee ooo aaa dance floor ooh ooh OK?'

'OK, no worries!' He'd already spent half an hour thrashing about to the music like an electrocuted monkey, getting elbowed in the head by an oversized Greek in the throes of Dionysian abandonment and wondering whether anyone was watching him and how stupid he looked. 'I think I'll stay here!'

Nathan and the others got up and squeezed into the crowd, leaving Eliot in the solitary embrace of his lounge chair. Two girls fell into the empty places they left. One was pretty, the other beautiful in a toxic, Los Angeles kind of way. With her perfect little retroussé nose, her plumped-up, golden breasts, her sharky little mouth with its even rows of teeth, she was gorgeous and awful. She flicked her lissotrichous locks over her shoulder every seven seconds. She rolled her eyes in shock horror: *no waaay!* He watched her laugh through the wall of sound that separated her from him as if through glass. The mixed drinks tasted of nothing. He was drinking pure space. His face was numb.

When they spilled down Bourke Street at 2:00a.m., his ears were ringing and deadened, his vision dimmed with alcohol. He heard himself laughing.

'Ooh that girl, dude!' Nathan was saying. 'She *wanted* it Eliot, I'm telling you. The way she looked at you! She wanted to sit on your *face!*' Eliot knew it was bullshit, but the laugh kept hacking out of his throat. 'And she was *hot!* Like fucking seriously!'

'Yeah man,' said Dave. 'Pussy was in the bag. You fuckin' blew it.'

They piled into the Commodore. It smelled of cold and cigarettes.

'You gonna drive me home now?' Eliot asked. It occurred to him that Nathan must be way over the limit, but the thought struck him from a remote distance, as abstractly troubling as someone else's burglar alarm.

'Home? Like shit! The night is yet young.' Nathan spun the car out of its parking spot and fishtailed down the street. He looked at his mates. 'We got a tradition anyway for Saturday nights. Can't go home yet. It wouldn't be right.' They started to laugh. Their three faces turned towards him, expressions expectant but unreadable.

'OK cool, whatever.'

He was too tired, too blind to worry about Nathan's driving. His face fell against the window and the night-life rolled past like a dream. He was almost dozing when he realised they were on Kew Boulevard, not driving at breakneck speed this time, but cruising slowly, almost at a crawl. He came awake suddenly, anxiety coagulating in his guts. Everyone was quiet now, the only sound the predatory rumble of the engine.

He tried to speak, but when he got the words out, they came in a squeaky child's voice. 'What are we doing?'

The silence extended so long he thought no one was going to answer. Then Nathan turned to look at him again. 'How's your *Wing Chun* going?'

Almost as soon as he said it, Andrew started to shout. 'There! There!' He pointed into the headlights. Someone was emerging from the trees. A young man's face, bleached of detail by the halogen headlamps, turned towards them, a hand going up to shelter his eyes against the brilliance. He hesitated, and in that moment the Commodore's doors burst open and Dave and Andrew jumped out. The man turned and ran. Nathan wrenched up the handbrake and, in the split second before he gave chase too, turned to Eliot. 'Come on! There's only one of them. It'll be easy. We'll hold him and you can kick.'

Eliot sat in the car, the doors open, the engine still running, and the cold air blowing through. Saliva flooded his mouth and he rolled out into the gutter and vomited. From his knees, crouched over the sour, stinking puddle, he looked up. He couldn't see anyone, just the trees in the headlights, twisted and ghostly, their exaggerated shadows growing gigantic as they spilled down the empty road.

A cheerful jingle – 'Copacabana' or something – woke Eliot from a deep sleep. He fumbled his phone out of his pocket to see it was an '07' number – Queensland.

'Eliot? Is that you?' It was a bad connection, and it took him a moment to recognise the voice as his father's.

Apparently things hadn't worked out with the secretary. Apparently he realised he'd made a terrible mistake. He wanted Eliot to talk to his mother, find out if she'd have him back. Act as a peace-maker, broker the truce, that kind of thing. He was such a fool. You don't know what you got till it's gone, that's what Joni Mitchell said, and you know what? He never knew how right she was. And anyway, how was everyone? How was Cathy? How was Troy? How was Mitzy?

'They're all fine, Dad, fine. Everything's fine, and all Mum keeps talking about is how much she wants you back. I think you should surprise her. She'd be thrilled to death.'

'Really?' It was all too good to be true. He'd pack his things right away.

'Fine Dad, you do that. Maybe we can have a party.'

He heard just a moment of hesitation in his father's voice at that, a crack in his stupidity quickly plastered over by his excitement. 'You're a good lad Eliot. I knew I could rely on you.'

'Yeah, likewise.' He hung up.

Outside the bus window, brown fields rolled past, a drab spectacle. Perhaps not the shining omen of a bold new future he might have hoped for. Then he saw a green sign up ahead. Sydney, 140. That, at least, gave him cause to smile.

Great Big Baby
Will Eaves

'It's not as bad as all that.' Esther offered her daughter the same glum reassurance with each visit. 'You won't remember the pain afterwards. *I didn't.*'

The goading emphasis made Esther's teeth rattle with pleasure. Ces feared the threat of weakness more than the pain, and wondered, staring past the elfin stoic at the foot of the bed, what she would find in the next six months to sustain her; what books and day-dreams, letters, incidents and friends – what family – could possibly absorb the vacancy of her prospects. The doctor's strict orders were for complete bed rest, which Ces dreaded the way she dreaded long journeys.

Esther was seventy-four, tiny and spry, clad in a pink woollen coat that she never took off. She lived along the road in Malvern Terrace in a house like her daughter's with three rickety floors (one rented out), a sloping lawn, a Singer and treadle, the bed that sounded a minor chord when you lay on it, a few chairs and no heating. To Ces's children, Anne, Lotte and Clive, she gave delicious teas; to their mother, a feast of stony looks. Or rather – stranger – like the coat, a sort of sympathy for all seasons done up to its neck in pride. *Oh, you poor thing. I expect you'll live. How ever did I manage, on my own?*

A threat to survival and nothing less roused Esther's pity. Sometimes, not even then. She came from Tollington Road in North London, where seven families topped and tailed in five-room houses. Her husband had died while she was pregnant with Ces. They were penniless after the birth, unable to pay the hospital bill. Men arrived to take Ces and her brother into care, but Esther's doctor intervened, waiving his fee, saying, 'I'll eat my hat if this woman isn't fit to be a mother'. She took in work, making dresses, sleekly beautiful coats and skirts, sewing hems by evening candlelight until her head nodded and hit the bridge of the machine. At four she rose to scrub floors until eight, then walked up to Drummonds in Dalston for more piecework. Bombs fell. Esther could not afford to stop for them. Besides, Laetitia Voy upstairs had read her leaves and said she'd live to go on a journey West, maybe as far as Basingstoke. The children meanwhile, clutching kitbags and labelled underwear, went to Devon. Esther took them to Paddington Station and returned home to find Miss Voy shaking beneath a tin tray on the edge of a crater two streets long. *Didn't see that one coming, did she? Don't talk to me! You think you've got it bad.*

Cecily thought nothing of the sort, although perhaps she should have done: a seventh pregnancy had placed her in great danger. No matter – in Esther Crocker's world, the instinct for self-preservation cringed before the civilising virtues of self-sacrifice. The right to be distressed, or ever to complain, did not exist. All cries for help went up in smoke.

The ashen residue was sarcasm, a diet of sly belittling designed to toughen Ces and make her grateful, which she was. From Esther, Ces got her wit, know-how and dexterity. She was both educated and practical, a minder and a maker: she stitched and patched and sang and laughed. Made quilts, sold them. Bore kids, raised them. Cooked meals from almost nothing, ate them – standing up.

Her talent to deride was a less certain inheritance. Once only she tried to cow her mother, to pay her back in kind, and the attempt blew up in her face.

When Esther moved to Bath, to Malvern Terrace, to be near the grandchildren, she brought with her the high bed, the Singer, a suitcase with all her clothes in it, and an album of photographs. Somewhere along the line she'd also acquired a brown Hoover that ate the carpet. The sac, fully inflated, bobbed gruesomely. Ces turned it on and nearly lost her toes. 'This thing's dangerous. You should get a new one,' she shouted above the noise. 'We'll *help*.' Her mother winced, wrong-footed by generosity. The monster stowed, they spent the rest of that morning shaking out sheets and stocking a chest of drawers left by the previous owner with Esther's things, light sweaters especially, many of which surprised Ces with their softness and scent of violets. She did not associate her mother with any kind of feminine sensuousness or with the word that sprang to mind as she lifted, unfolded, folded and set down on tissue paper a silver-grey brushed cotton chemise – 'sartorial'.

The scalloped neck belonged to the prewar era and a mother she could not remember. She was willing to bet the shirt had been made, not worn, but the plain fact of its discovery was enough: the long-sought, frail and thrilling proof of Esther's vanity; of fallibility. Ces gave an eagle cry of victory to cover her confused emotions – and then spotted the letters. There was a small bundle of them tucked into one of the suitcase's peach-coloured lid pockets. At this point, Esther was downstairs, investigating the fireplace, snapping kindling. It was January. From the upstairs bedroom window the tiled roofs of the crescent below Malvern Terrace bared themselves at the sun like hardy souls determined to enjoy the fresh air on deck.

The letters were neatly folded into handkerchief-squares, their envelopes tied together with a shoelace. They were from Ces's father, the father she had never met, and – a quick glance told her – they spanned many years.

The top one was from 1926, quite late on, and post-marked Baden-Baden. The hand was evenly spaced but shaky; some of the looped f's and p's did not connect to the next letter. Each sentence, in the manner of the time, heaved with a kind of formalised yearning. Emotions struggled and writhed beneath set phrases, pleasantries, so that the letters as a whole were never simply decorous. For all their awkwardness they communicated things the person writing them would not have been able to say out loud:

We are all well looked after here, my dear Hetty, though it is perishing in the huts at night. There is enough food at least for us, and for which I am thankful. What a carry-on it is for the ordinary people hereabouts. They must push money around all day just to eat, and even then they come up short. Well, the machines are nearly done and then I will come home to you and little Horace. It will not be long now, I think, but I am counting the days, as you may imagine.

Your loving husband, H

Looking up from her father's bottled longings, Ces felt the necessity of a response. So she laughed. And having laughed, immediately sat down on the bed, just as if she had been pushed. The machines would have been aeroplanes, for Lufthansa, she knew that much. Her brother remembered playing with the armfuls of worthless deutschmarks that their father had brought home.

The next letter came from Montreal and was attached to a certificate of demobilisation, granted by the Royal Canadian Expeditionary Force in June 1915. It exuded eagerness. He had been happy. By this point, he had an understanding with Esther and a heart defect. They intended to marry when he got back. Something – his happiness maybe, or her own eavesdropping – struck Ces as a dreadful betrayal. It was like confronting a person with their private habits and making a joke of them. There were things about people you might know, but were not supposed to know: the way they laughed without meaning it, their misshapen feet (Esther had a gnarled green toe), their peculiar sensitivities and coverings-up. Of course there was nothing misshapen about this letter, which was innocent and light-hearted, almost gaseous with hope. But her father had died of pneumonia. He'd been born with a hole in his heart. The adventurous, affectionate husband who'd written this, the letter she was holding, was not that man. A different man had existed. A different father, and a different mother.

'What are you up to?'

She had not known him, and she had not been told the truth about him, if such a thing could even be done; at any rate, no one had tried. It was a double blow.

'*Ces*. What *are* you laughing at?'

The inquiry came from the top of the stairs.

As she held onto the letters, Ces wondered at her own nerve. She was powerfully angry and upset. Terrified, come to that, of who the woman now advancing down the short hallway might turn out to be. But the violent feelings were not enough in themselves. Ces required a witness, as a murderer requires a victim, in order for her passion to enter the world of consequences.

Esther was in the room, smiling. She had glaucoma and needed to be close up to her daughter to understand the source of amusement. When finally she did understand, she gave a meek little shrug, making no attempt to wrest back the bundle of letters, admitting and denying nothing.

Ces read out a few choice endearments, astonished to find herself still laughing between the lines. Her mother listened unembarrassedly. Ces turned again to the letter sent from Baden-Baden. 'Dearest, sweet,' she recited, almost crying with frustration. 'I am counting the days. Your ever loving husband. Dear. *Sweet*.' It wasn't the sentiment in the letters that beggared belief. It was Esther's toleration of them – her weakness for them, one might say. Between what Ces knew for certain of her mother's disdain for romance and the wizened coquette now tutting and giggling at her side, a gulf of implausibility opened up.

'I don't know why I kept them,' Esther said at last.

'Oh, you *liar*, Mum!' Ces exclaimed with real delight. 'You big fibber.'

But as she crowed, she glanced about her – at the bed, the green eiderdown, the half-full chest of drawers, the nets – and saw the room of a woman, a widow, the silent correspondent, whose circumstances had always been reduced. Seen like that, the myth of sacrifice – that comforts had been refused, that there had been the option of refusing them – was one way to a kind of self-respect.

'Well, aren't you clever, being inside my head.'

Now Ces felt weak. They went downstairs and boiled the kettle in a dark kitchen at the back of the house, below street level. Cars drumrolled overhead. Nothing in the kitchen was flush. The yellow Formica tallboy did not fit against the wall – it wobbled if you pushed it – because the floor was uneven. The sink came away from the tiles. The paint bubbled with damp. They took their cups into the front room, which was warmer. It had a number of items picked up from Old Jack's, the junk shop on Walcot Road: two wing-back armchairs, a glass cabinet on splay legs, a drop-leaf dining table. And a coal fire.

Esther sat back with her tea and asked for the letters. 'I just want to see.'

Ces handed them over and her mother re-read the first two or three, carefully, considering. After that she seemed to grow bored. They talked about John going to America and what that would mean, about Clive's splints, Summerfield. Ces said there was no question of her joining John; he hadn't asked her, and anyway she didn't want to go. Esther grunted, listening, and reached for the tongs to open the fire door. She fed the flames one letter at a time, as if to eke out the waste with an equally consuming and purposeful thrift.

The memory of those exploding intimacies made Ces's face warm, so that on his arrival Mr Murison took her temperature.

'Normal enough,' he said, tilting his head back to read the thermometer. 'Though God knows it shouldn't be. It's absolutely freezing in here, Mrs Alden. Have you not got a heater? Of some description?'

Ces explained that the electric heater needed a new element, without adding that she did not know what an element might be (she was simply repeating her husband's diagnosis) and that in any case it cost too much to run.

'And I'm only up here for a couple of hours in the afternoon. It'll be warm soon. It hardly seems worth it.'

Mr Murison, who was younger than he looked, smiled and sat on the bed. In the doorway Esther opened the clasp on her handbag and started fingering drily through its meagre contents – stamps, small change, her pension book.

'I won't stay, Doctor. I just popped in to give my daughter this.'

She took out a postal order for five shillings.

'This is for Clive, Ces. He wanted to get a book, he said, and I've an idea he wanted to choose it for himself. He told me the title.'

'Five shillings! Oh, Mum, you are good.'

Esther was quiet a moment, looking a little enviously at Mr Murison and his patient. The vow of silence she observed with most visitors, anyone who was not family, could be relaxed in the doctor's favour, but the opposing discretion with which he listened made her nervous.

'He's a one, isn't he, Ces,' she broke out. 'Little monkey. But he does read beautifully. I quite look forward to it.'

'He must enjoy it or he wouldn't run along so eagerly.'

Mr Murison smiled. He was looking down at his lap, hands folded, entranced by awkwardness – a short, rather solid man, in whom a combination of shyness, soft-spoken professional competence and a surprising delicacy of movement and touch suggested sadness. His eyes were forget-me-not blue – too eerie against the dark stain of his cheeks. Others said that he drank.

As if in response to some unvoiced dissent, Esther added unexpectedly: 'They'll all be after him, you mark my words.'

'He's only just nine,' Ces objected. 'Give him a chance. I *am* sorry, Doctor. Anyway, what about the girls? Ann's going to have a nice figure.'

'Ann?' Esther sounded irritated. She viewed opinions, even her own, with suspicion. 'Ann's like you. Lotte's pretty. Was there anything else, Ces? If not, I'll be off.'

When she had gone, Mr Murison asked how Cecily was, and how Clive was getting on with the splints and the spectacles, and Cecily was relieved to report that she was feeling quite alright and Clive was being brave and Ann was already such a help in the house—

'Have you and your husband discussed the letter, Mrs Alden? Have you looked at the forms? You do know that you'll have to decide very soon.' Dr Murison shut his eyes as he marked the words with pauses.

'Yes I do. We have, John and I have read the… papers.'

Mr Murison nodded.

'And I'm so grateful to you for everything. I understand everything you've told me – and I just can't bring myself to sign them.'

'You're aware of the risks?'

'John has said it's my decision. He backs me up.'

Downstairs, the front door opened and the noise of traffic roared into the passage along with the children back from school, arguing.

'It's WILL,' Clive was saying furiously, his phlegmy treble charged with adult exasperation, 'not "shall". Shall is weaker than will. It's feminine and the last line is masculine. It's WILL never be slaves, Ann, you *moron*.'

'I know what you must think, Doctor. But I can't do it.'

'"Britons never, never, ne-ver WILL be slaves."'

'Have it your own way,' a girl sighed. 'But it's still "shall". Mr Leyshon said.' And with that Ann took Lotte, who was crying, downstairs to peel potatoes while Clive began his painful, expostulatory ascent to the bedroom.

'He'll be alright,' Ces assured the doctor. 'He likes to do it on his own. It takes him a while.' She raised herself onto her elbows. 'Are you managing, Clive? Dr Murison is here. Do you want him—'

'Mr Leyshon said. Mr *Leyshon* said. Who CARES what that fat oaf thinks? He's not a proper Briton. He's from Swansea.'

'Clive?'

A gulp interrupted the flow of invective at the bottom of the stairs. 'How would HE know?'

Clive was really her favourite child. The idea of having a favourite horrified her, but there it was. Many years later, when he returned to visit her and she could barely mumble his name – when names no longer meant anything – a part of Ces still knew this, and though by middle-age Clive himself stank and fumed with neglect, nevertheless she clung to him. In the chill passageway beneath the framed butterflies, she turned to her other grown-up children, saying, 'I love this one. I can't help it. It's true.'

The same part of her tried to concentrate, now, as Neil Murison told her all about placental insufficiency, but it was no use. Cecily heard only the short-breathed stagger of her son in the background. Clive had been born blue, with the umbilical cord round his neck. Every day when he clambered up the stairs, her heart leapt at his restoration, the joy of knowing that he had survived and she had not been left on her own. Because that was the worst thing by far about a stillbirth. Worse than the fact of it was the stillness and isolation of the room they put you in, the unmarked afterthought with a lone bulb in which you were abandoned to get on with things. And the dead two had been hard deliveries, and she had screamed for hours, probably. When it was over, the nurses were never kind enough. They took the baby away, shut the door and let you have a good cry. Two days later, you were dressed and sent home with antibiotics. And you always felt you'd failed, no matter what people said, which wasn't much. Clive had nearly died on the way out, but not quite, so he had to be lucky.

'I'm lucky, I know.'

Mr Murison was saying, 'You have three lovely children,' and seemed prepared to leave it at that, then changed his mind. Some gear of impassivity slipped as the boy stumped nearer.

'You will be in this bed for the next twenty weeks, all day and night except for one hour or two at the most, and you could still lose the child, or it will be born with defects, or it will die shortly after birth. Or you will. Having this baby could kill you, Mrs Alden – Cecily. I mean it, and I wouldn't be much of a doctor if I left here feeling I hadn't, well, got this across to you. Do you understand?'

Cecily looked at her hands.

'You could die from any number of complications that we mightn't be able to detect until—'

Clive came in, elated. 'Beast!'

He saw Mr Murison and stopped.

'Oh, *Clive*. You did it all on your own again, didn't you?'

The little boy, thin as a seed, held himself against the edge of the door, his head angled away from the doctor and his mother. He moved his jaw around, stuck for words in front of the man sitting where he, the hero, would normally sit at this time of day. The doctor smiled and checked Clive's legs, tapping the shinbone and the clamps, asking if anything he did hurt any more than usual. Clive looked at his mother out of the corner of his eyes.

Mr Murison left and Ann, the capable one, cooked dinner. At eight she put Lotte to bed, checked on Cecily, and ran Clive's bath. John had gone back to work. Between tasks, Ann walked about the house on her hands.

The next morning, after his father had left for the day, Clive returned to his parents' bedroom and gave Ces his glasses to clean. 'Beastie not getting up no more? Beastie staying flat for ever and *ever*?'

A posture went with the nasal voice – shoulders hunched and arms locked straight down by his sides.

'Maybe not for ever,' Ces laughed, spat and polished. 'Here.'

'Beastie continue to pretend she's alive by being brought tea and toast in morning which Beastie can't eat because Beastie stiff as a post?'

John had brought her some breakfast on a tray.

'Is that what you'd like?' she said.

Clive chewed the insides of his cheeks and gave her his sideways stare. He went to the toilet next door and steadied himself. It was a fine day and from the top of the house you could see small birds speed-boating across the open sky. He was full of exciting title music and fast getaways.

The possibility of a defective birth had not occurred to Cecily until Mr Murison mentioned it. Whatever the risks involved with this pregnancy, for some reason Ces took them to be of the all-or-nothing variety. She could not imagine an alternative or compromised outcome, a state between absolute loss and complete gain – which was strange, considering her job at Summerfield and considerable experience in such matters. Summerfield was the school behind the cypresses behind the approach golf course – a joke and a threat to dim kids elsewhere in the city. The children in her care were all Educationally Sub-Normal, with a range of incapacities, from the merely slow to the bawlingly disturbed. She minded them with great compassion: there were pictures to cut out, collages to be made, chaotic trips – occasionally – to parks and gardens to be survived. Ces thought it a shame that they suffered their imperfections as they did, but her sympathy couldn't extend to real empathy because she did not for a moment question the necessity of their segregation from the rest of infant society. Assessments had been made and that was that. Only now in the empty house, after Ann had led Clive away, did she consider that assessments were indeed *made* – by someone, somewhere – and that, as a result, of all the children born equal, or not obviously deformed, there were a minority who passed from the Eden of normality into a world of certified inadequacy, for ever. They were a separate concern.

But her brother was blind in one eye. Her grandfather had had a cleft palate. Cousin Phyllis, in Edgware, could not be trusted to go to the shops and still depended on her mum for everything. And Barbara Molton, Cecily's best friend over the road, who played the saxophone with one lung, smoked as though she had three to spare. Was anyone the full shilling?

She heard Esther's words, repeated with a prophetic insistence: *you won't remember the pain afterwards.* The pain that was fear and threat and dire uncertainty, a sum of conditions only secondarily, historically, physical. Her mother had carried her despite the shock of bereavement, and they had both lived. Perhaps she was right. Perhaps it was all or nothing in the end.

The thought reoccurred to Ces on several future occasions, each time with a rush of adrenaline and woozy relief. The first was when the Gas Board finally installed a heater – downstairs – on William's sixth birthday.

The gas fire had three upright bars, each the size of a large Cadbury's, and a dial at the side with two settings: Super Heat (all three bars) and Miser Rate (one). There was a turning-on tea ceremony-cum-birthday party at No. 2 – this in the middle of the Energy Crisis – and as the weak flame leapt Esther had an inspiration. 'Take off your clothes, William,' she quavered, from deep within her pink fastness, 'or you *won't feel the benefit.*'

William did as he was told, and eagerly stripped. He'd seen, besides, something in his grandmother's comical, indulgent eye that his mother might have missed. It was fun, nudity, and the idea stayed with him. Spring and summer of that year were both hot, so one blistering day William decided to walk home from school, naked. It started as a dare with his school friend Daniel and turned into a demonstration. Daniel needed a lot of persuading just to unbutton his shirt and then refused outright to take off his trousers. William sighed pityingly. If he had to take the lead, he would.

He arrived at the front door with his clothes tucked under one arm.

'D'you see your Willum, then?' gasped a neighbour.

'You won't be able to do this when you're grown up,' Ces said, and sent him back to look for the sock he'd dropped along the main road. God forgive her, but she was proud. William was precocious, and he was all there.

John and Ces eventually got a new element for the heater in their bedroom, but it smelled funny, and on balance, and because they were the children of their generation, they preferred to do without. Nothing was safer, too. Not long after the gas fire had been fitted in the front room, someone left it on unlit. The hiss was scarcely detectable beneath Clive's own hum of concentration as he settled down to watch TV, shivered a bit, got up and struck a match.

Ces heard the *whoomph!* from the kitchen and was by her son's side before he had recovered himself enough to cry out. His forehead was the colour of Empire; the air smelled of burned hair. Clive shuddered and brushed away his scorched specs. Little black filings – eyebrows – tickled his cheeks.

'See?' Cecily cried, shaking the teenager, who had a notorious temper. 'You're still in one piece, aren't you? See? *There* now. Oh, Clive!'

Her emotion caught up with her. She fought it back.

Clive's eyes had started to leak meanwhile and Cecily, noticing, reacted as though robbed of her own fear. She almost snapped: 'Would you believe it? Clive Alden, you great big baby. It's never as bad as all that.'

BONFIRE OF THE VANITY UNITS

Paul Oslo Davis

The Reluctant Adventurer
Eddy Burger

Pan and I wandered onto the bridge. It was as wide as a highway and strewn with odd bits of trash.

'I've never seen this bridge before,' Pan said.

'Me neither.'

We passed some driftwood that had obviously once been a table. And there was an odd thing, hard to describe, but it looked something like a cross between a trombone and a watering can.

'It's an odd looking thing, don't you think, Pan?'

'I don't care.' He stepped up to the railing and looked over. 'I'd like to know what's down there.'

'It's the bridge *I'm* interested in. It must lead somewhere important.'

We continued along the bridge, though Pan was lagging further and further behind. He was swaying as if he were struggling with the wind, although there wasn't any.

'Come on, Pan.'

'This is boring.'

'But think where this bridge might lead.'

There was a dilapidated armchair, bunched together with other things, beside the railing. Pan sat in it. 'Let me know if you find anything interesting,' he said.

I continued alone, walking at a brisk pace. I walked for a while but there was still no end in sight. The only thing of interest was something that looked somewhat like a cross between a chest of drawers and an umbrella. I couldn't imagine anyone being strong enough to carry it.

I didn't know what to make of these contraptions. Were they the products of a civilisation that had advanced till there was no room left for innovation but for the creation of useless absurdities? Or was there some external influence that corrupted the minds of their creators to favour the nonsensical over the practical?

In any case, it was all the more reason to find out what lay at the other end of the bridge. Pan wouldn't agree with me but I wasn't about to leave him behind. I made my way back to where I left him. He wasn't in the chair anymore. I looked around and called out but couldn't find him. Then I noticed a break in the railing on the opposite side. I went over and saw there were stairs spiralling down into the mist below. It was like being above the clouds. It was impossible to tell what was beneath it all – probably some untamed, wild land, full of beasts and savages.

As loath as I was to leave the vestiges of civilisation behind, I descended the stairs and soon found myself amidst a forest of pines. There was no sign of Pan. I sought him here, I sought him there, I sought that demmed elusive Pan everywhere. 'Where the hell are you, dammit!' I screamed. Yet I heard not a peep. It was very quiet around these parts. Too quiet.

I headed back to the bridge but I couldn't find the stairs. Just that great expanse stretching out in both directions. I called out again, and then Pan's head popped over the railing a little way along. He was still on the bridge!

'Where were you?!'

'What!'

I walked over till I was directly under him. 'Where were you?!'

'I can't hear you! Where are you?'

'Down here!'

'What!'

It was strange that Pan couldn't see or hear me. I could see him as clear as anything. That bridge cut a swath through the mist like it was repellent.

'Can you see where the stairs are?' I yelled.

'What!'

'The stairs!'

'What!'

'Oh never mind.'

'What!'

Well, I chose a direction and started heading that way. I spotted a few flowers that had been ground into the ground, probably by my feet, so I assumed I was on track. I glanced back at Pan. He was still leaning over the railing and he was pointing hysterically in the direction of the trees. I couldn't see anything untoward. Still he was pointing like a madman. I quickened my pace, but then I came upon a lot of rabbits. They were sitting on either side of my route, facing in my direction but looking beyond me, like they were expecting something of great import to come this way. I started to run, but then all the rabbits turned to face the direction I was heading to. I stopped and tried to see through the mist. The rabbits turned towards me again.

'What is it, you stupid animals?'

I turned around again – and then I saw it. A huge shape moving through the mist. I couldn't make it out at all but it made me think of a really big elephant or something. It was coming towards me. I was transfixed by the enormity of the monstrosity. Then it disappeared into the foul mist from whence it came.

From behind me came the sound of twigs being crushed underfoot. I spun around. It was Pan.

'It's very pretty down here, isn't it,' he said.

'Never mind that! What about that bloody great big elephant or whatever it was!'

'Elephant?'

'I got a glimpse of this really big thing that reminded me of an exceptionally oversized elephant or something. There was too much mist to see it properly. And all the rabbits were acting very queer.'

'What rabbits?'

'There were a lot of rabbits here a moment ago. They were waiting to see it.'

'Sounds to me like we'd better find out what this big thing is.'

'I'm not going anywhere. I only came down here because I thought you were down here. Where did you go when you left the chair, anyway?'

'I found a big box to sit in. It was too windy up there. But it's nice down here.'

'I don't think so. I think we ought to get back to the bridge.'

'Don't tell me you're afraid of a little elephant?'

'It could probably kill you just by breathing at you!'

'Then we'll have to be sure not to get too close.'

'Off you go then.'

'Come on.' Pan grabbed me by the arm and we headed after it. Eventually, we caught sight of a *huge* elephant, ten times bigger than I had ever seen, sitting on its belly, wedged under the bridge. It was almost as if it was supporting the bridge. Come to think of it, I hadn't seen any bridge supports. There was only this elephant.

'So where are you headed?' came a nearby voice.

There was a man standing beside a bus parked under the bridge.

'Who are you?' I asked.

'The bus driver. I drive around, giving people lifts.'

'You must be familiar with this place, then. Where in God's name are we?'

'Some place. It's nice don't you think?'

'I need to go to the toilet,' said Pan.

'There's a Portaloo behind the bus. It's a bit smelly though.'

'I haven't seen one of those in ages,' Pan said. He headed for the loo.

'What's the story with this big elephant,' I asked.

'You call it an elephant? Most folks call them Bridge Supports.'

'How many people come through here?'

'Same as anywhere.'

'So how many's that?'

'Were you born yesterday?!'

'Of course not! It's just that there are more people in some places than in others. For instance, I was by myself a little while ago, and now there's you and this Bridge Support, and my friend who's in the loo.'

'And me!' said a girl's voice. She leapt out the bus. She was wearing a cape and a black mask like Zorro's.

'I am the masked avenger! Hail stranger, well met.'

'Er... hi. My name's Edward. So what's your real name?'

'The masked avenger! Be ye friend, then all is well, but be ye foe, beware!'

She had quite a vocabulary for such a pipsqueak.

'But you can't be sure he's in there,' interjected the bus driver.

'What?'

'How can you be sure your friend's still in the loo?'

'What's that go to do with anything?'

'Well, you just said that before, you were by yourself, but now there's me, this Bridge Support *and your friend who's in the loo.*'

'I didn't see him come out.'

'But you were distracted just now.'

'True, but anyway, you're referring to a statement I made before this young'un appeared.'

'I am the masked avenger!'

'Are you? So what are you an avenger of?' I asked.

'I am an avenger of cruelty and injustice.'

'You've been reading too many comics.'

'But like I said,' said the bus driver, 'how can you be sure your friend's still in there?'

'I'm getting sick of this.'

But then the bus driver raised his eyebrows in a queer way. They went almost vertical. He was a pretty queer guy all round. I haven't even mentioned his life jacket and the hat adorned with an elephant's ears and trunk. But his eyebrows really unsettled me.

I walked over to the loo and listened by the door. It was completely quiet. I slowly pushed open the door.

'Fuck off! The toilet's taken!' Pan slammed the door closed.

'It's only me! Just checking to see if you were still in there.'

'Sorry Edward. I didn't know it was you. The toilet seat just feels so good. I haven't sat on one of these in ages.'

I went back to the bus driver. 'So where are you headed?' I asked.

'That's what I asked you.'

'When?'

'Before.'

'Can you please answer the question!'

'I'll probably be going along the bridge route – that is, unless there's a great catastrophe.'

'What kind of catastrophe?'

'Same as anywhere. Were you born yesterday?!'

'Of course not! Some places can be prone to earthquakes, for instance, while others are prone to tornadoes, hurricanes, volcanic eruptions, bushfires, droughts or floods.'

'Gadzooks! I wouldn't want to go to one of those places.'

'All those things wouldn't happen to just one place.'

'Just as well.'

'Look, just tell me – what kind of catastrophe might happen here?'

'Well, there could be a flood or the bridge could collapse.'

'But if there was a flood and the bridge didn't collapse, then the bridge route would still be safe, wouldn't it?'

'Don't be daft. Everything would get washed away!'

'What's the point of making the bridge, then? They should have built it higher.'

'Why should they build it higher?'

'In case it floods!'

'Don't be daft. The water would never reach that high.'

'But you just said it would!'

'No I didn't.'

'Yes you did!'

'I didn't. Anyway, it hasn't flooded here for a long time.'

'Why mention it then?! Look, tell me this – assuming there isn't a catastrophe, in what direction will you be heading?'

'That way,' he said, pointing in the direction in which Pan and I had been heading on the bridge. This was perfect. Once Pan returned, we decided to give the bus a try. We all entered the bus, including the avenger, and headed off.

The avenger didn't like Pan. Pan was a big man and I guess the avenger saw him as a threat.

'Will you stop looking at me,' said Pan.

The situation was rather laughable. We were like some hotchpotch crew on a wacky adventure, just like in a movie. It was disgusting. I was leaving the moment we reached the other end of the bridge.

We didn't get onto the bridge straight away. We were driving under it. We came to another big elephant – I mean Bridge Support – and then we pulled over. There was a bunch of people gathered beside the elephant. They each had leafy branches stuck to them, like camouflage. The bus driver got up to leave the bus.

'How far to the bridge entrance?' I asked.

'What end are you talking about?'

'Isn't there a ramp or something halfway?'

'No.'

'I thought we were going onto the bridge.'

'Don't know what gave you that idea. I follow the bridge from the underside. That's my route. You'll find a lot of folk and other things under it.'

'What other things?'

'Bridge Supports, trees and grass, as well as a few trampled flowers.'

The driver left and started chatting with the tree people. The avenger went out also and I could hear her introducing herself.

'I don't want to hang around with this weird bunch,' I said to Pan. 'I want to get back to the bridge.'

'I want to get away from that kid.'

'Bridges are like arteries that serve, bind and sustain great civilisations,' I said. 'They were built to bypass in-between places such as this, and for good reason. It must go somewhere important.'

'But it's deserted. At least here there are things to see and do.'

'Well I'm getting out of here!'

But just as I was getting up, all the tree folk entered the bus. There must have been a dozen of them. They remained standing in the aisle. I guess they couldn't sit down because of all those branches. Then the bus took off. I hadn't even seen the driver with the branches in the way.

'Where are you headed?' I asked the tree folk. They didn't answer. Their leaves were rustling a lot but I couldn't tell if it was merely due to the bus vibrating.

'Trees don't talk and neither do they,' said the driver. The tree folk made no reaction. They were emotionless. Yet they definitely were people. Their faces were human and their branches were stitched onto clothing that looked like it was made of hessian.

Pan was completely absorbed by the spectacle. He ignored the avenger, who had managed to squeeze past the trees into the seat opposite us.

'So, avenger,' I said. 'What do you think of all this?'

'These are goodly tree folk. Many a time have I encountered them in the woods. They are the guardians of all things natural.'

'Why did you introduce yourself if you'd met them before?'

'I know them only as a species. There is little to distinguish them apart, and their foliage changes with the seasons. In spring they are arrayed with the most exquisite flowers, and thou might then discern greater differentiation between them, but alas I am no botanist.'

The bus soon came to a halt and the tree folk began to disembark.

'I want to go with them,' said Pan.

'Are you alright? You're not bewitched or anything?'

'I just find them interesting.'

Pan and I left the bus and walked after them. 'Do you mind if we come with you for a way?' I asked.

'They don't mind,' said Pan.

'How do you know? You *are* bewitched.'

'I'm not. They just seem very friendly.'

'I guess it beats hanging around in that bus.'

I looked back to the bus. It was heading off again, but then I noticed the avenger leaning out the window and pointing hysterically at the trees.

'That's just how you looked when you were pointing over the bridge railing.'

'When?'

'Just after we were yelling at each other but you couldn't hear me.'

'Oh, that.'

'You were pointing at the big elephant, weren't you?'

'No.'

'Well what were you pointing at?'

'Nothing. A bloody big ant was biting my finger and I was trying to shake it off.'

'Oh.'

'Yet I did happen to notice something moving through the mist. I couldn't make any details but it was much bigger than one of those elephants. I think it was heading in this direction.'

'Do you think it's dangerous?!'

'Don't know.'

'Maybe these tree folk are going to fight it! Or maybe they're friends with it and are leading us to it so it can eat us!'

'These tree folk are friendly. I'm sure of it.'

'Well, we'd better find out what they know – better warn them, at least.'

'Excuse me, tree people! Can you stop a moment!'

They continued walking.

'Excuse me! I think you should know, in case you don't already, that we think there's a really big thing heading this way!'

All the tree folk stopped and looked around in great agitation. Their branches were trembling like mad and they started making high-pitched squealing sounds. Then they sped off in all directions. In an instant, there wasn't a trace of them.

'Shit! What do we do now?' I said. I looked around me, trying to see through the mist, expecting that huge thing to appear at any moment.

'This way,' Pan said. 'We should go this way.'

I followed Pan in the direction he suggested. We walked at a hurried pace for a while. And then Pan had one of his more lucid moments. Or perhaps I just paid more attention because he was talking about me.

'How would you describe yourself, Edward?'

'Do you mean physically?'

'No! I can see what you look like. I mean what do you feel? *How do you feel about me?*'

'I thought we were supposed to be talking about me!'

'We are. If you think highly of me, then you are a wise and virtuous person. But if you don't, then you are blinkered and untrustworthy.'

'You know, Pan. You really are an odd fellow.'

'I'm odd? You're the one who can't decide what gender you are.'

Pan tripped over something. I almost tripped over it myself. It was a small dog. It looked like a show poodle, but instead of pompoms, it had lollipops on its head, ears, feet and tail.

'Lick me,' it said.

'This is ridiculous!'

'What's ridiculous?' it said.

'A talking lollipop-poodle.'

'You could evidently do with some sweetening.'

'There's no way I'm going to lick your toes or anywhere else.'

'Can I try?' asked Pan.

'Suck my ears.'

Just then, the avenger came swinging by on a vine and plonked herself down beside Pan and me. 'No further may ye venture till this brute has proven his virtue.'

'Are you referring to my friend Pan?'

'Yes!'

The avenger stood eyeing Pan suspiciously.

'That's no way to treat my friend. You're not even old enough to have accumulated such virtue as my friend here is bursting with. That's why he's so large, you know. Anyway, what's all this business about venturing no further? Are you referring to walking or sucking a poodle's ears?'

'What poodle?'

'Eat me,' said the poodle.

'Oh, hello. From whence did you spring, sweet thing?' The avenger crouched beside the dog, untied her hair, and her blond locks tumbled over her shoulders and back. (Strange that she would untie her hair just as she was going to eat a lollipop.)

'I've seen enough. Let's get out of here, Pan,' I said.

'But I haven't had a lollipop in ages.'

'You wouldn't want to try one of those. They're probably covered in dog hair.'

'But poodles don't shed hair.'

'Come on!'

Pan and I set off again. We had been walking for a while when the sound of drums and ringing reached our ears. It seemed to be coming from the top of a small hill. I was keen to avoid the hill at all costs but Pan started running up the bloody thing.

'I wonder what interesting characters we'll meet this time!' he called in an overly excited fashion.

I caught up with him on the summit, overlooking a pit. It's an odd thing, when you think about it, something that's both a hill and a hole, like a bellybutton that's both an innie and an outie. But it was also like a volcano. It even had steam coming from it.

In the pit was a seated woman wearing a tight yellow Lycra jumpsuit, all one piece from the shoulders to the soles. She looked rather fetching, particularly as she was surrounded by all that steam. She appeared to be playing an instrument that looked somewhat like a cross between a drum kit and a telephone. It was the most discordant racket I'd ever heard.

'You're a lousy musician!' I yelled.

But it wasn't the woman who responded. It was the instrument, yelling to the beat of its own drums. 'When you're born an instrument, you can't always hear what other people are thinking!'

'What are you talking about?!'

'Though a lousy musician I may be, we should not waste celery unnecessarily!'

I was convinced the instrument had lost its mind, only I wasn't sure it had one. And the woman continued to make such a racket, I couldn't even hear *myself* think, let alone others. I wanted celery to plug my ears. Either she was deaf or she couldn't take a hint.

'I'm sure the fault lies not with you, my good instrument,' I yelled, 'but rather with the WOMAN IN THE YELLOW LYCRA JUMPSUIT!'

'But Trying To Keep From Being Squashed didn't make me!'

'What?!'

'Trying To Keep From Being Squashed! It's the woman's name!'

'Are you saying that she isn't making you play?'

'I never said she was!'

'You're the one who brought it up!'

'No I didn't!'

'Yes you did!'

'Oh… I see what you mean. No, what I actually meant was that Trying To Keep From Being Squashed did not manufacture me!'

'I didn't say she did!'

'You're blaming her for this racket.'

'Well, she is the one who's playing you.'

'What are you talking about? I always play by myself!'

'Really? That sounds very lonely.'

Suddenly the noise stopped.

'What makes you say that?' The instrument's voice was wavering. It was trying its darnedest not to cry. Fluid was welling from the rim of each drum, just like tears.

'Don't tell me she's been hitting your eyeballs? No wonder you're crying.'

'Trying To Keep From Being Squashed would never hit me!'

It was then I noticed that she was still moving as if she were playing the instrument. She'd never been playing it in the first place.

'Why is she moving like that?'

'Her jumpsuit was made for a much shorter woman. It's all she can do to keep from being squashed.'

'Why doesn't she take it off?'

'Don't you think she looks good in it?'

'Well… yeah.'

'There you are.'

It was an odd thing to see, this voiceless, steaming woman jerking her arms and torso around. 'Is she mute?'

'No. She's just eccentric.' Then, with a wink, the instrument said, 'But she's not as eccentric as I.'

'I'm much more eccentric!' she yelled.

In an instant, she adopted the character of a maid to an aristocratic family. 'Good evening, Madam. Can I take your coat? How would you like your brussels sprouts?'

'But I'm not wearing a—'

'I can top that,' said the instrument. 'Listen to this.' It began to produce bangs and rings of a most harmonious composition.

'This is ridiculous. Let's get out of here, Pan,' I said.

'Wouldn't you like to hear a story?' asked the instrument. 'It's quite preposterous.'

'Yes please,' Pan said.

The Instrument's Retelling of the Aardvark and the Organ Grinder's Tale of the Two Giraffes and the Ladder

Once there lived two giraffes who were strolling across a bridge.
Bridges are commonly used for linking members of a civilisation
to other parts of itself in the shortest possible time,
ignoring everything that lies between.
Well, by chance, the two giraffes strayed from the bridge
and journeyed through the in-between land.
One of the giraffes was keen to adventure
and explore this land that was full of surprises
but the other was very inhibited
and wanted to go back to the bridge straight away
because it needed to have direction and hated wasting time.

But the inhibited giraffe stayed with the adventurous one
because they were good friends.
They met lots of interesting characters
and had some terrific adventures
but the inhibited one couldn't see the interestingness or terrificness
because it was so blinkered and deluded.
It couldn't see that aimlessness was the greatest aim of all.

But Pan and I didn't stay to hear the story. I don't know why the instrument chose to tell it with bangs and rings instead of just speaking it – it was impossible to understand. Anyway, there was something in the tone of it I didn't like. Must have been in the wrong key.

'All this wandering seems so pointless,' I said to Pan.

'You have no sense of adventure. You're blinkered and deluded.'

'That's not true. I'm keen to know what's at the end of the bridge.'

'Oh, you know it's going to be familiar and comfortable, where you can busy yourself doing the same old routine chores that instil you with the illusion of productivity and progression, when all you're really building up to is your own death. That's all a career is – the road to death.'

'Huh! You're a loony. This whole place is an illusion. Everything is mixed up and everyone is silly.'

'Yet you're still here and you've been everywhere I have. You're as much an adventurer as I am.'

'Then I'm a reluctant adventurer. This place pushes you along from one ludicrous, irritating scenario to the next. I am a victim of its peculiarities.'

'I'm no victim.'

'I can't even remember where we came from.'

'We came from the bridge.'

'I mean before that.'

'Who cares? Why can't you appreciate the world around you for its own sake? Can't you see that aimlessness is the greatest aim of all?'

'What a load of crap!'

'No it's not!'

'Aimlessness can't be your aim, because if it was your aim, you wouldn't have an aim since to aim to not have an aim is to not have an aim.'

'Oh yes, I forgot that one – progress, productivity, purpose *and* logic.'

'But they are all central to human society. Everyone needs a purpose, everyone wants to better themselves, and everyone wants to taste of the pleasures and luxuries that only hard work can buy. And without logic they'd be floundering around picking daisies. You can't tell me that these people don't rely on some kind of industry, at least, to occupy and provide for them. Who grows the food, who makes the furniture and who makes the clothing, like that Lycra jumpsuit? They'd have to have machines to make Lycra. I bet there's a great industrial area somewhere. We just haven't seen it yet. I bet the workers work like slaves. Their methods are sure to be barbaric, I'll bet.'

'But everyone we've met are goodly folk! They'd never support such a system! There might be some among them who work part-time at a trade, with the aid of perhaps one or two very well-treated apprentices. One might operate a spinning wheel or loom, another might run a smithy or small smelter, another might have a vegetable patch, and another might give massages in exchange for vegetables, for instance, or perhaps a teapot or some thatching for the roof.'

Just then, Pan and I stumbled upon a small clearing where yellow jumpsuits were in the process of being manufactured. A little old woman was sitting in a rocking chair and stitching one of the jumpsuits, which was being modelled by someone who was much shorter than Trying To Keep From Being Squashed and who had the head of a cat. Another old woman in a rocking chair was weaving the material in a loom, and another was operating a spinning wheel – well, she was using it as a spinning wheel, but it looked somewhat like a cross between a small helicopter and a tea set. These old women were laughing a lot about nothing. They were cackling. And there was also a giant slug. It was the size of a one-tonne van, only longer, and the yellow stuff being spun was oozing from its mouth in a thick, lumpy strand.

'Is that vomit?' asked Pan.

'I'd rather liken it to a spider's thread. Better to be coming out of something's mouth than its arse.'

'So that's where Lycra comes from.'

'It can't be Lycra exactly. Lycra's a brand name and I never heard of any big company using giant slugs.'

'Maybe they kept it secret. This miracle fibre suddenly appears, super-elastic and as strong as leather. Sounds like just the sort of thing to come out of a spider or slug.'

'I see you're admiring our Herbert (cackle cackle),' said the first old woman.

'He's taken a shining to you, young man (cackle cackle),' said the second. She appeared to be referring to me.

'No he ain't! None of them deserve our Herbert's respect!' said the third.

'I'm sorry to intrude,' I said. 'We really should—'

Suddenly my face and body were covered with thick gobs of the yellow stuff. I managed to scrape it from my eyes long enough to see Herbert galumphing his way towards me, then I was blinded by more of the stuff.

'Edward!' cried Pan as he tried to lead me away, but the slug knocked me flat and writhed on top of me with its masses of slimy blubber. 'Leave him alone, you bully!'

'Don't you worry,' said the first old woman. 'Herbert ain't gonna hurt your friend (cackle cackle).'

'Hurting ain't exactly what he's got in mind (cackle cackle),' said the second.

'Killing's what's on his mind,' said the third, 'and I can't say you don't deserve it (cackle cackle)!'

Then the slug's weight lifted till only my legs were trapped. I cleared my eyes and could see Pan beside me, pushing with his back against the slug. He was covered in goo.

'Quick Edward! Free yourself!'

'Don't do that, young man,' said the first old woman. 'Herbert ain't finished yet.'

'It's rude to interrupt him while he's doing his thing,' said the second.

'Now you've done it!' said the third. 'He's so angry he'll kill you both (cackle cackle)!'

But I pulled my legs free and leapt to my feet. 'Come on Pan!'

Pan jumped away from the slug and collapsed to the ground. His legs were bound and he couldn't see. 'Help me!'

I pulled him to his feet, but the slug was almost upon us. I started to run, but Pan could only hop.

'Hop faster, Pan!'

'I can't!'

'Hop faster!'

Just then, the avenger came swinging by on a vine and plonked herself down between Pan and me and the slug. The avenger looked tiny against the great mass of advancing blubber.

'Halt, foolish creature!' commanded the avenger. 'Canst thou not see that these are noble folk, not to be subject to your wayward tendencies? Begone unto your labours!'

The slug turned around and galumphed back towards the old women.

'He was only playing, ma'am,' said the first old woman.

'He just gets a little excited sometimes,' said the second.

'He would never have done anything to harm such nice young men,' said the third.

'Just make sure he behaves himself in future,' said the avenger.

'Yes ma'am.'

The avenger turned to face Pan and me. 'Hail friends, well met!'

'Thankyou for your help, avenger,' I said.

'It is your companion you should thank. He has proven himself of most virtuous character.'

'Yes, thankyou Pan,' I said. But he was still covered in goo. 'Let me help you get that stuff off.'

I dug my fingers into the goo caking his head and managed to get it off. But the goo between his legs was extra thick, particularly around his groin where it had accumulated before setting.

'I can manage to clean that part myself, Edward.'

'Let me.'

'Don't touch me there!'

'You never minded before.'

'What are you talking about? We've never been friends in that way!'

'You know, you really are very odd sometimes Pan.'

'I'm odd? You're the one who keeps changing your accent – Irish one moment, American the next, then cockney, Indian, Mexican, Chinese, Ethiopian. What next?'

'I don't know what you're talking about.'

'See what I mean!'

But the avenger interjected. 'Excuse me, good fellows. The time is nigh for me to depart.'

'Oh. Yes, well, thanks again for your help,' I said.

'I am happy I could be of service. May good fortune shine upon you both.'

'And you,' said Pan.

But there was something that was nagging me. When the avenger had appeared, she certainly looked small compared with the great blubbery slug, but when the slug had gone, she still looked small. Granted, she was a pipsqueak, yet I was sure she had been a whole head taller before.

'Excuse me, avenger,' I said as she was turning to leave. 'Have you shrunk?'

'Shrunk? Well… I don't know. I thought the two of you had grown.'

'I think I've shrunk,' said Pan. 'I haven't eaten anything in ages.'

'Yes. It's funny, that,' I said. 'I can't remember the last time I ate. But the avenger had some of the poodle's lollipops.'

The avenger blushed and looked down in embarrassment. 'The lollipops were very nice. Well… till we meet again.' Then she swiftly strode off and disappeared into the trees.

'She was acting odd,' I remarked.

'She's odd? You're the one who—'

'Oh, shut up.'

Pan and I stripped off the remaining goo from our bodies and headed back into the forest.

'Are we heading in the right direction, Pan?'

'I think so.'

'Why did you choose this direction, anyway?'

'It's the direction we were headed before we met that slug.'

'But why this direction in the first place? When the tree folk abandoned us and we had to escape from the big monster, you said we should go this way.'

'Oh. Well, I don't really know which way is north or south, but let's say the monster was coming from the north and we and the tree folk were heading east. Now, if we had continued east or gone back towards the west, it still might have crossed our path, and if we had gone south, it might have caught up with us, so the best ways to go were either south-east or south-west.'

'So you think it would have come from the north?'

'Yes.'

'But we've been heading north!'

'Have we?'

At that moment, a horde of about twenty small armour-clad creatures stepped out from the trees and encircled us. They looked like a very small species of otter.

'What business do you have here?' asked one of them. It was the only one that *didn't* have a feather sticking out of its helmet.

'We are merely travellers passing through,' I said.

'You can't go any further in this direction.'

'Why not?'

'Because of the bloody great big wall, that's why not.'

There was a massive wall rising up from behind the trees. It was made from tall tree trunks stuck together. It was so big I hadn't noticed it. Pan was looking up at it and began swaying. It was that high.

'You and your friend better come with us,' the featherless otter said. 'You'll want to rest before we fearless warriors drive you back from whence you came.'

'Yeah, whatever.'

They led us to a small building that backed onto the wall.

'This is our great hall. Our forebears built it when they built the wall.'

'Are you telling me that relations of yours built the wall?'

'Yep. They certainly did.'

By human standards, the hall was more like a hut. The otters sat down on small sacks on the floor, beside little logs that lined the wall, which they were using as benches. But what really caught my eye was the human-sized table in the middle of the room with human-sized chairs around it.

'Do you mind if we sit down?' Pan asked.

'No, of course not. Put your feet up,' it said, pointing to a couple of sacks.

There was a whole pile of sacks stacked against the wall, so I grabbed those instead and sat next to the featherless otter. But Pan pulled out a chair and sat down at the table. All the otters stared.

'Well, I'll be! Is that what they're for?' said the featherless otter. 'Our forebears must have been bigger than we thought.'

The other otters all exclaimed in wonder.

'You're otters, aren't you?' I said.

'Yep.'

'But these are humans' chairs.'

'Why would our forebears build chairs for humans?'

'You tell me. Anyway, I thought otters were water dwellers. I've not seen a river or anything in this place. What's the bridge for if not to span water or some great chasm?'

'Well,' said the otter, 'it could serve to create a shortcut, or bypass a ghetto, bypass lowlands, highlands, in-between lands or stupid lands.'

'The bridge was built over a wide river,' said Pan. 'The whole forest is growing on an old riverbed.'

'The humans sucked it all up,' said the otter.

'There must have been a lot of them,' I said.

'The city's full of them.'

'City! What city?'

'Behind the wall. That's what it's for. To keep the humans out.'

'Is there any way in?'

'Only the bridge.'

'The bridge? But it looks so deserted. Is the city still inhabited?'

'Do you think we'd waste our time guarding a wall if there were no humans on the other side?'

'But they can still come down from the bridge.'

'It's too high.'

'We came from the bridge. There's some stairs leading down.'

'Stairs! We've never seen any stairs. And we've never seen any humans either… Say, you're not humans, are you?'

'Oh no, no, no. Definitely not.'

'Yes we are,' said Pan.

'What did he say?'

'Oh don't mind him. He just burped.'

'Burped? Why, thankyou, sir.'

The otter burped, which was followed by a chorus of burps from the other otters. They all looked at me expectantly.

'I'm sorry but I can't burp.'

'Can't burp?!'

'No.'

The featherless otter eyed me suspiciously. How ridiculous. They were all so silly, burping to be polite, and guarding against humans yet not knowing what they look like. Why wasn't this featherless one wearing a feather, anyway?

'You're the leader of these guards, right?'

'These warriors – yes.'

'Well why are you the only one without a feather? It's normally the other way around.'

All the otters burst out laughing. Pan started laughing too.

'What's so funny, Pan?'

'What you said! Ha ha ha! How silly! Ha ha haaaaa!'

I had to wait a while for the laughter to abate. Then the featherless otter said, 'Allow our jester to educate you. He shall tell you the why and wherefore.'

One of the guards got up and took from a chest a stick with bells and a jester's hat that it placed upon its head. Then it danced around in front of me, jingling its stick in a very annoying fashion as it sang a song.

The Warrior-Jester's Song of the Fearless and Featherless

So fearless is the warrior
but how fearless is the most fearless
when all have feathers upon their heads
for fearless less the 'less'
would leave the warrior with 'fear'
and a warrior who was a worrier
would be afeared by none

What if the fearless was without the 'fear'
Then 'less' would be left this warrior
less of fear and less the warrior
less of all would then be she
who was called no more than less

But why not take away that feather
worn by so many with equal pride
Could not the most fearless of the fearless
be best distinguished if featherless were she
for fea*the*rless without the 'the'
would make this warrior fearless
thus the 'the' thee find in fea*the*r
would the warrior be best with less.

For an otter, its grasp of the English language wasn't bad. But that wasn't what I said.

'That's the dumbest thing I ever heard.'

'I hope you're jesting,' said the featherless otter. 'That song has been handed down—'

'Look, just tell me about these humans. Have you ever heard—'

'Why are you so keen to find out?'

'Er… because we want to fight them. We hate them!'

'No we don't.'

'Shut up, Pan.'

'What did he say?'

'Oh, he just burped again.'

This was followed by another chorus of burps.

'Look! I'm just saying that if there were still—'

'Humans still have those Bridge Supports in place so they must still be there!'

'That doesn't prove a thing.'

'The Bridge Supports are their last line of defence,' said Pan. 'If anything tries to come over the bridge, the Supports stand up and it becomes too steep to get over. But if something does get through, then all those Supports come out and defend the city.'

'You seem to know a lot, Pan. Were you able to sense all this?'

'It's all in this book that's on the table.'

'Why didn't you say you were reading from a book?'

'Well how else could I have known?'

'You really are an odd fellow, Pan.'

'I'm odd? You're the one who dresses so weirdly.'

'But I'm not wearing anything!'

'I mean the way you groom yourself. You're such a freak.'

Then the featherless otter interjected. 'The only thing this side of the wall worth making a fuss over is that big critter, What The Wall Is For.'

'What the what?'

'What The Wall Is For. There are the Bridge Supports who lie around all day, there's Trying To Keep From Being Squashed who for some reason is always jerking her arms and torso around, and there's What The Wall Is For. It's a huge creature, much bigger than the Bridge Supports. You don't see it about much. No one knows where it actually lives.'

'So the wall was built not to keep the humans in but to keep this creature out of the city,' I said.

'Why would our forebears go to the effort of building this great wall just to keep that creature away from humans?'

'Because that's what the wall is for.'

'That's what the what?'

'That's what the wall is for.'

The otters were dumbfounded. One of them fainted.

'So what does What The Wall Is For look like?' I asked.

'What does what?'

'What does the huge creature look like?'

'It looks like a giant mole.'

'A mole! So the wall was built to keep out a mole! You're all mad!'

I stood up and made for the door. 'Come on, Pan. Let's get out of here.'

'But we have to escort you!'

'Escort my arse! We're humans, d'ya hear! We'll come and go as we please.'

'Humans! To arms, warriors! Stop them! Chop off their heads!'

'Our heads? You'd be lucky to reach our knees.'

'Chop off their knees! Chop off their knees!'

I probably should have left my announcement till we were outside. They came at us like a swarm of small otters, all brandishing small twigs and trying to hit our knees. We had to kick our way through. By the time we were outside, there was such a battle going on, I wasn't paying attention to where I was walking. I almost fell into a huge hole. It was a hundred metres across. There were hundreds of rabbits that formed a great avenue leading to the hole. They were just beginning to disperse. It was like they had been spectators to a royal procession or something.

We all stopped fighting and listened. Through the hole came sounds of breaking glass and twisting metal. Buildings were being demolished. Then through the woods came the sound of elephants trumpeting. You could see the backs of the huge elephants rise above the trees as they entered the city. Others were coming this way. The ground was shaking so much, Pan and I dropped to our knees and all the little otters hid behind us. From out of the trees the huge elephants charged. By this stage, the rabbits had formed themselves into a wall in an attempt to stop the elephants. They weren't successful. One by one the elephants ran into the hole.

There must have been a dozen elephants come this way. I don't know how many entered from the bridge, but there was a great racket coming from the hole, with all their trumpeting and the sound of buildings being demolished.

'Do you suppose there are still people in there?' asked Pan.

'If there are, they must have made another entrance, unless they became self-sufficient and isolated themselves. Or perhaps there's only a few people left.'

'I haven't heard any screams.'

'You wouldn't hear them above this racket.'

'They could all be mute.'

'Mute? Well… I guess anything's possible in this place.'

'At least the elephants won't be slaves to the bridge any more.'

'What else are they good for?'

'They can stampede through things and wreck everything.'

'Whoever's idea it was to use giant elephants as a means of defence was an idiot.'

Yet it was a city, a melting pot of progress, a symbol of civilisation at its peak. I looked at the hole entrance wistfully. 'It's a shame it's full of giant fighting monsters.'

Pan and I returned to the hall with the otters. They gave us beer to drink as well as some rather large meatballs. Just one, they said, was enough to feed them all. I didn't usually eat meat but I was too hungry to worry about what they were. Could have been giant slug's testicles.

'So you think humans built the wall to keep out that big burrowing thing,' said the featherless otter.

'Yes,' I said.

'And you're a human.'

'Yes.'

'Ha ha ha haaa!'

'Well you didn't even know what the wall is for.'

'What the what?'

'Never mind.'

'So, where will you go now?' asked the otter.

'On an adventure!' said Pan.

'Can we come with you?'

'Er… well…'

'That would be marvellous,' said Pan. 'You are most welcome.'

Soon we were on our way, walking through the grassy woods. We were just like a family going on an outing – two adults and twenty children. The otters even wore little backpacks. They were so cute it made me sick.

Eventually we came to a large paved area, about 200 metres across. It was a lot like a square, except that it was circular. In the centre stood two giraffes that were ten times bigger than normal giraffes, and they were supporting a ladder that extended all the way up to the clouds.

The scene was very similar to that of the bridge, really, but without all the rubbish – unless one encountered it on the way up. Perhaps there was a cable car instead of a bus. Not that I had any intention of going up there.

But then Pan stepped up to the ladder. 'Come on, little otters,' he said. Half the otters climbed onto his back and then the other half climbed onto my back. Just as I was going to protest, someone else climbed onto me.

'Hark ye, friend!'

It was the avenger. She stuck her head over my shoulder. She was tiny.

'Be so good as to be my ride for this leg of our journey. Those rungs are too far apart for my little legs.'

'Yeah, whatever.'

And so began another wacky adventure.

Bitter Medicine
Julie Milland

Susan demonstrates to Rachel the most efficient way to kill a mouse.

She places the cage on the bench without a noise. The mice appear relaxed, running around sniffing each other, whiskers twitching as they sense their environment. They have that fluffy look that most mammals have when they are young. These mice are light brown. The tag on the box reads '5 x ♂, C57/brown, Animal Ethics Number K267/06'. One mouse is on his hind legs drinking from the metal teat as Susan removes the water bottle from the cage lid. He sits on his back paws, snout in midair for a second, and then runs towards the bedding at the other end of the cage.

Susan lifts the lid of the cage with her left hand, quickly grabs the tail of the closest mouse with her right hand, replaces the lid and lets the mouse rest on the wire. His grip on the wire is tight. He urinates. His head swivels in both directions as he tries to see his tail. Susan swings him to a towel on the bench, holds his head down by placing the thumb and forefinger of her left hand behind his neck and pulls his tail backwards in an elegant motion. A graceful dislocation of his cervical spine. She pulls on his tail once more to ensure death and lays him on the towel. His body twitches. Especially his whiskers and paws.

Rachel's fingers rake through her hair. The smiling cartoon mice in lectures last year now seem like a cruel joke.

'Your major task in this project will be to prepare spleen cells from mice and analyse them by flow cytometry. OK. Now you've watched me do it, you have a go,' Susan says.

Rachel doubts her ability to make a good impression on Susan. It seems that she worked for Professor Sullivan since he was Dr Sullivan and still had a full head of hair. Information about Rachel's performance will definitely move upwards.

This is Rachel's third day at the university. She had applied for fourteen research assistant positions in six months while working part-time at a bakery, but didn't make the cut in her six interviews. The ad for the job with Professor Sullivan mentioned 'small animal models'. Rachel had hoped to avoid working with animals but a foot in the wrong door seemed better than one caked in baker's flour. And, as her mother reminds her every week, that chemistry set was her favourite toy when she was twelve.

Rachel stretches powderless latex gloves over her hands. Susan stands beside her. Watching. The heat of the lamp and the closeness of Susan make Rachel feel trapped. She doesn't have the full range of movement in the small gloves, her hands restricted and suffocated. Just her luck that they are between sizes. The medium gloves had left chunks of rubber flapping at the ends of her fingers.

'Those gloves look too small for you, Rachel,' says Susan.

'But the others were too big.'

Susan shrugs.

Rachel faces the bench. It seems so random. The mice are doing what mice in cages usually do, and then a big rubbery hand plucks one from the box and ends his life. Their little whiskery brown snouts remind her of poor Fonzy sniffing her hand, tail wagging. She lifts the lid from the box. The water bottle clatters to the floor. The mice all jump in unison and run for the bedding. A pool of liquid forms in the corner of the lab.

'Shit! Sorry.'

'It's OK. You need to remember to remove the water bottle,' says Susan. Her voice is even.

The mice now scurry around the box. They're fast and Rachel can't grasp a tail.

Susan remains calm. 'Just wait a few seconds. Then pick one up by the tail and let it rest on the lid of the box.'

It sounds so easy. Rachel's trembling hands are wet inside the gloves. Underneath the lab gown, her shirt sticks to her back. She lifts the lid of the box again. Her hand darts around. The mice are alarmed. She grabs a tail. In a rush, she swings the mouse out and he urinates in midair. She slams the lid down and lets him cling to the wire. Rachel and the mouse rest and catch their breath. She wiggles her back, trying to scratch an itch between her shoulder blades.

'OK. Now bear down on the neck with one hand and pull firmly on the tail with your other hand.'

Rachel tenses every muscle in her body. The itch fights for her attention. She lifts the mouse onto the bench and puts two fingers of her left hand on his neck.

Susan's words explode in her ear. 'You're not trying to flatten it. Just hold it in place. Try to be gentle but firm.'

Rachel holds her breath. She pulls on the tail and releases the mouse. The air rushes from her lungs. Is he dead? His back legs seem to be moving. Susan ensures death and dislocates his spine again.

Rachel flops onto a lab stool. Sorry, mouse.

Susan smiles. 'OK. That wasn't too bad. You need to get back on that horse. Everyone finds it tough at first. When I started out, I was nervous too.'

All Rachel wants is a slug of vodka. 'Shouldn't I wipe the water off the floor first?'

Anything to put it off.

'We'll fix that up later. Don't forget to remove the water bottle this time.' Susan looks directly into Rachel's eyes. Waiting.

'Yes. Of course. You're right.'

Rachel recites in her mind the mantra of logic. She can do this. This isn't as cruel as putting out mouse bait around a house. A mouse that eats that stuff suffers for days, blood dripping from its anus. At least for these guys it's quick. And the research might lead to a cure for breast cancer. Just get it right. Don't hesitate. Do not muck it up with a half-arsed attempt. A dead mouse feels no pain.

Rachel stands with purpose, strides to the cage and with a swipe, grabs a tail.

She holds the mouse on the bench. She quickly puts her fingers behind his head and pulls back on his tail. Hard.

'Good work. The mouse is dead.'

The outer layers of the mouse's tail hang from Rachel's fingers, stuck to her gloves. The mouse twitches; each bone of its tail is visible between disks of pink flesh. She shakes the tail skin from her fingers.

'What have I done?'

Susan picks up the remnants of tail and the dead mouse and places him neatly on his side, next to the first one. 'You've de-sheathed the tail. That's all. We can do better next time.'

Next time? Rachel's stomach turns. She rips off her gloves. 'Excuse me a moment.'

She lurches down the corridor and into the women's toilet. Slamming the door of the cubicle and lifting the seat at the same time, she heaves the contents of her stomach – Weet-Bix she now remembers – into the toilet. She flushes and leans against the wall. A flash of the deconstructed tail invades her mind. Tears of sweat trickle from her forehead. She shakes her shoulders and kills the itch on her back against the wall. She hopes no one has heard anything.

As she leaves, she smiles at a woman from another lab who has entered. Rachel doesn't know her.

The woman returns a half-smile. 'Perhaps you don't realise, but it's against the occupational health policy to wear lab gowns in the toilets.'

'Are you chewing gum?' Susan says.

'I just grabbed some.'

'Well, you can't chew in lab areas.'

Rachel spits the gum into the bin, detecting a partial roll of Susan's eyes. 'Sorry.'

'OK. This time you'll nail it. Hold the tail firmly, closer to the base. That way you're less likely to de-sheathe it.'

Her stomach jumps at the mention of that word again.

The smell of lamp-warmed mouse bedding fills the room. Rachel sneezes.

She lifts a mouse by the tail. This one turns on her. She gasps. Before his teeth are anywhere near her finger, she drops him back into the box.

'Can we do this later, Susan? I need a break.'

Susan reads her watch. 'No. Once they've been taken from the Clean Room in the Animal House and brought to the lab, they can't go back. And once we've killed them we need to tease the cells from their spleens as soon as possible.'

Rachel completes the task. She kills her third mouse, its tail intact. The little whiskers twitch. Susan makes it easier for both of them and kills the last mouse in the cage.

The five little bodies are arranged in a neat row, one with a skeletal tail. They look like sorted corpses from a mass murder.

On the bench in front of the two scientists, mice are pinned through their paws to a plastic board, bellies exposed. Rachel had avoided selecting the mouse with the skeletal tail for her board. A waft of dead mouse fills her nostrils. At least they can't feel anything now.

'We're going to grow the splenic cells in culture and analyse them by flow cytometry, so we need to use sterile technique. There's nothing more frustrating than killing mice, doing all the work to isolate the cells and when you look the next day you find the culture infected with fungus, yeast or bacteria. OK. Sit beside me at the cabinet and we'll do a mouse each together.'

The laminar flow cabinet has a stainless steel surface, sides and ceiling, not unlike a kitchen bench, and at the back of a hood is steel mesh through which sterile, filtered air blows directly forwards at a rate of four metres per second. As Rachel sits at the cabinet, the noise of the churning motors assaults her ears and the warm air dries her eyes. Between the women, a Bunsen burner flame struggles to remain upright in the sterile wind.

'To sterilise the body we douse it in seventy per cent ethanol. All our surgical equipment will soak in this beaker of ethanol and we'll flame each item before we use it. This keeps the entire procedure as clean as possible.'

She picks up a squeeze bottle. 'Watch me.'

She squirts the ethanol over the mouse. It looks like a victim of drowning now, except for the fact it's pinned down. The smell of ethanol overwhelms all the other odours; Rachel is one step closer to that shot of vodka. Susan picks up a pair of forceps and scissors and jabs them towards the Bunsen burner. Blue flames burn any living organisms on the instruments, sterilising them. She lifts the skin of the belly with the forceps, cuts down the midline and folds back the flaps of skin so that the ribs and intestines are exposed. Drenched fur on one side, pink and smooth on the other.

'If you pull the intestines back like this, you can see the spleen is lying underneath. Can you see it? It's the large, deep red, almost purple organ.'

Rachel moves her head closer. A wave of heat, the stench of guts engulf her. She holds her breath and nods.

'Dunk and flame the instruments again and remove the spleen by cutting here and pulling away the connective tissue.' Susan snips as she speaks.

The spleen plops into a dish of orange cell culture medium.

Such a rapid transition. One moment he is running around urinating with brothers, the next he is sliced open, his guts dragged to the side and sticking to a piece of paper towelling while his spleen soaks in a dish.

'OK. Now you try.'

'Sorry. I just need to change these.'

Rachel's hands are drenched. Again. She rips her gloves from her hands, dries them. They're still clammy as she tries to drag the latex of a fresh pair over her skin. It sticks and pulls. Her fingers are nowhere near the tips of the gloves, trapped near the latex palm. The right glove tears.

Susan sighs and gives an ever so slight purse of the lips. 'Try a larger size.'

Rachel grabs the larger gloves. Now the gloves want to slide off her hands and she has to pull on the latex to keep her fingers flush against the rubbery tips. At least she can stretch her hands now.

Rachel gives the mouse on her board a good long soak in a stream of ethanol. The fumes hit her in the face. Liquid spills onto the stainless steel bench. That should be sterile.

She picks up a pair of forceps and fine scissors from the beaker and flames them. She waves them around to extinguish the flames. The tips of her fingers are hidden beneath flaps of rubber. Lifting the skin of the mouse's belly with the forceps, she cuts down the midline, snips on either side of the main cut and pulls back the skin. The intestines are sagging inside the abdomen and look a little grey. This mouse must have been the first one to die, the pink, the oxygen, gone from its tissues.

She swizzles the instruments in ethanol. Eddies of fur circle the beaker. Rachel drags at her gloves again. She straightens the board on the bench.

'We need to move on, Rachel. It's better to tease the spleens when they're fresh.' Susan's voice is sharp.

Rachel pulls the instruments from the beaker and plunges them into the flame. She gives them a shake in the sterile breeze. Leaning forward for better vision, she touches the intestines of the mouse with the forceps.

A blast of heat hits the corneas of her eyes. She smells burning hair and jumps back, dropping the instruments. Her fingers burn, searing, and she rips a partially melted glove from her right hand.

'Shit!' Rachel blows on her hand and then scans it for stray pieces of latex.

The mouse, the board and the bench are sizzling.

Susan shuts off the gas tap feeding the Bunsen burner, grabs the bottle of ethanol and moves it to the sink. 'Just stand back.'

Susan runs out of the room.

Rachel watches the mouse burn, smells the mouse burn. A blaze of fur and flesh fed by the rush of sterile air. The din of the hood crowds her brain. She could vomit into the waste bin, but only bitter bile remains in her stomach. She swallows the urge. Susan runs back into the room carrying a jar of water and a fire extinguisher. She throws the water onto the mouse and board. A hiss. The flames are gone.

Susan shoves the fire extinguisher in the corner and swings around to face Rachel. 'This whole day has got to be the biggest fiasco that I have ever witnessed in the lab.' She pushes a strand of hair from her eyes and doesn't wait for a response. 'For God's sake. You need to make sure the instruments are not flaming when you touch the mouse or they'll ignite the ethanol.'

Wordless. Rachel can't understand why she has become such a total loser.

To make it worse, Susan would have heard Rachel swallowing her sobs as she ran into the hallway.

Quiet at last. Rachel sits at her desk with her right hand soaking in a beaker of water. Her head is throbbing. She dries her hand and picks up the pack of paracetamol Susan gave her. If she takes these, she contributes to the death of thousands of lab animals. Thousands of little brown bodies lying neatly on their sides, snouts and whiskers all pointing in the same direction. A lump forms in her throat. Rachel throws two tablets into her mouth and manages to swallow some water.

Blood
Karen Hitchcock

They were sharpshooters. They hunted rabbits and wood duck. They shot wild pigs, goats and kangaroos. They went away camping and came back sunburnt, with wild-man grins and an Esky packed with carcasses. A deep freezer the size of a car growled against the wall in their kitchen, filled with headless animals in transparent bags: goose-bumped duck, kangaroo, pale pink rabbits striped with rivulets of frozen black blood.

> *There are twenty-six polar bears in Australia.*
> *Half of them are alive.*
> *Half of them are stuffed.*

Bob shot his first animal in a paddock of high, dry grass when he was five. Rabbits were still in plague proportions, before myxomatosis made their eyes gummy and their little mouths bleed, before it was even thinkable they might one day be scarce. The shot rang out and the rabbit dropped. Bob's father ruffled his hair.

At about the same time, Anne took to removing the steel wool her mother had put behind the cupboards to block the mouse holes. Anne would push in cubes of yellow cheese and bottle tops of water. She couldn't just let them starve to death, trapped inside the wall. It wasn't their fault they were a plague.

> *There are approximately 25,000 wild polar bears in the world. Most live in the uppermost reaches of Canada, but they can also be found in Greenland, Alaska, Norway's Svalbard archipelago and Russia. In most places their numbers are stable or expanding, and the bear is now classified as a threatened rather than endangered species.*
> *Since 1973 polar bears have been protected from indiscriminate slaughter by the Oslo Agreement, and since 2000 by a further treaty*

between the USA and Russia. Hunting polar bear in most countries is an activity restricted to indigenous communities.

At one time or another they kept dogs, cats, guinea pigs, rabbits, budgies, quails, finches, chickens, a duck named Rufus, lizards, black mice, a white rat, a lamb, poddy calves and fish. There were, at times, many insects. Bob had bad luck with his pets. His fat brown chickens were found dead in their coop, white tissues stuffed down their throats. His lamb was frozen stiff behind the lemon tree. A horse kicked his dog to death. The neighbour broke his crow's squawking neck. His caterpillars ran away. In her bedroom Anne had fish breaking longevity records. Bob's pets broke his heart.

After the death of each pet Bob would have a sort of fit in the back yard. He would scream: *Why can't I keep anything alive?*

A polar bear's fur is not white. Each strand is transparent, with a hollowed-out core, just like a thin glass straw. Polar bears look white because the space inside each strand of fur reflects and disperses visible light, in much the same way as ice and snow and a fine-cut diamond can. Having hollow fur has its problems: there have been at least two reports of bears in captivity turning bright green from algae colonising the cores of their fur.

By high school the plague of mice had taken over. Anne's mother laid out rat baits. Anne heard from a boy at school that rat poison makes mice bleed from their stomach and their ears. They vomit blood, he said. They piss blood, he said. Their brains are destroyed, by their own spurting blood. Anne found a glove, collected all the poison in a plastic bag, and buried it at the bottom of the rubbish.

At thirteen Bob decided that he wanted to be a taxidermist when he grew up. A taxidermist their father knew from the pub gave him a weekend job. The taxidermist's shop was like a zoo: he had a buffalo head, a Bengal tiger and a brightly coloured, $980 toucan that Bob especially coveted.

On Saturdays Bob would skin fifty refrigerated bats and stuff a few dozen cane toads. The market for them was immense.

At home he started stuffing the animals he killed. The first was a ratty orange fox. He only stuffed the head. Its triangular face looked slightly wonky, mounted on a square jarrah plaque. He saved his pocket money to buy shiny glass eyes.

It was around this time that Anne turned vegetarian.

Viking hunters killed polar bear mothers, skinned them and lay the bloody pelts flat out on the snow. The cubs crawled back to lie in their mother's soft white fur. From there they were simply plucked up and stuffed into sacks.

The polar bear's only real enemy is the human. Apart from humans, the polar bear stands at the very top of the Arctic's food chain; they even eat small whales marooned in the ice.

The garage was turned into a workshop for skinning, gutting, preserving and stuffing. Anne was haunted by images of Bob prying out brains, of him ripping out intestines. How did he cut through the necks? Where did he stash the refuse? She called her father and brother 'The Great White Hunters'. They laughed and said: *Ah, so you're speaking to us now.*

In the West, the polar bear is considered to be the father of all hunting trophies.

The father looked like a cross between Walter Matthau and Robert DeNiro. Tall and dark, but droopy around the cheeks. Sharp, but a little eccentric.

He could make mouse hutches, fish tanks, aviaries, anything. When he made the chicken run he hammered a nail through his forefinger. Anne held her stomach and ran to call the ambulance. Her father walked calmly to the kitchen and pulled the nail out with a tea towel. He sat at the kitchen table and smiled at the look on Anne's face. He said: *I thought you were going to be a doctor?* Anne told him again: *I'm going to be a veterinarian.*

Vets, he said, examining his finger, *perform operations too.*

The only legal way for an Australian to kill a polar bear is to purchase a quota-limited permit from a Canadian traditional hunter. The use of aircraft, icebreakers, traps and snares is banned, as is the killing of female bears with cubs younger than a year old. It is illegal to hunt near bear dens.

The house they lived in was a brick cottage surrounded by dirt paddocks, in the hopeful suburb called Deer Park. There were no deer. There were no parks. But they had a sunroom.

The sunroom walls were dark brick, with a few aluminium windows and an eight-foot high, wood-panel ceiling. By the time Anne moved out the walls held over seventy stuffed animals, with very little space between them. One wall housed a wild boar, a woolly black bison, four ducks in flight, a pair of buffalo heads, a kangaroo from the neck up, a pet guinea pig, a fox, Peter their old blue budgie and a pheasant with a brilliant yellow and green tail. Another wall held the Pacific Deer Grand Slam.

When Anne walked into the room, the effect of all this crowded taxidermy was overwhelming: such a deathly silent racket in her eyes.

Taxidermy preserves animals, at most, for a little over a human lifetime. You can tell the disintegration process has begun when the animal's hair leaves a halo, like snow, on the floor. Museums struggle against this disintegration: they control temperature, light and humidity; they condition and disinfect the air.

In 1991 Damien Hirst suspended a four-metre tiger shark in a tank of formaldehyde. He titled the work The Physical Impossibility of Death in the Mind of Someone Living. *To the consternation of the curators, that 23-million dollar shark is slowly dissolving.*

The father was diagnosed with leukaemia. The specialist wore a suit, an expensive tie and shiny hard shoes. There was no need for a stethoscope. He held a family meeting so he could tell them, without once blinking, that their father had too many white blood cells. Anne imagined dots of pure white floating through her dad's blood, as if it was snowing inside his veins, turning him into winter. *In the future*, the specialist told them, *we'll have to try a little chemotherapy. But for now, we'll treat conservatively.* They all stopped blinking. They all nodded in sync.

The father still looked the same. He still went hunting with Bob. Years passed and he simply had a blood test and saw the specialist every three months. Years passed and he still pretty much looked like a cross between Matthau and DeNiro. He was sometimes tired, but he still stood pretty tall.

You hunt polar bear from dog sleds led by guides. You spend your nights in a tent. You will need clothing that will keep you protected in temperatures that can drop to minus-fifty degrees Celsius.

Bob became a panelbeater, got married to a girl with honey-brown hair and moved into a house not so far from Deer Park. Anne memorised the writings of Peter Singer, joined the RSPCA and PETA. She donated most of her pocket money. But after year twelve exams, when faced with the university application form, her hand ticked medicine over veterinary science; her hand ticked medicine over zoology; it ticked medicine over animal husbandry.

Your rifle must be utterly dry. Any moisture in the barrel, action, bolt, chamber or magazine will freeze solid and render the gun useless. Ask a gunsmith to remove all trace of oil from your rifle. Ask him to pay particular attention to the inside of the bolt, the firing pin and the firing pin spring. You don't want to find yourself face to face with the king of the Arctic food chain, holding a rifle that has seized.

There is a suspicious, meaty smell in the sunroom. The air in there is thick and dusty, and there is that smell… Anne suspected the wiry old billy goat. His ancient, indelible piss. But it is the silence in that room that is most striking. All of those animals with their mouths open wide and not a peep to be heard. It's as terrifying and as unrelenting as the silence in a stethoscope held against a dead man's cold white chest.

Bodies are full of the tiniest flaws: flaws in the tissues, flaws in the organs, flaws in the walls of the blood vessels. You are simply an amalgam of threatened permeation; a haemorrhage held gently at bay.

Blood is made up of red blood cells, white blood cells and little fragments called platelets. Platelets are the plasterers: they march around and patch up all the flaws. Platelets stop you from leaking. Platelets hold back your haemorrhage.

Anne had stopped feeling faint at the sight of blood when she graduated. And with that stethoscope around her neck she felt she could probably conquer anything. She bought a dilapidated apartment and her dad helped her fix it up. There were cavities in the plaster and stains on the ceiling. None of the plumbing would work. They'd stand before some gaping hole and her father would say: *Don't worry, we'll patch that up easy.* Anne watched him sit down sometimes and slump against his knees.

If you want to kill well you must aim for the heart. You could aim for the head but then you'll ruin your trophy. Anywhere else and the poor beast will just bleed to death. You must know how to send your bullet directly through the heart.

Anne visited her father in hospital when he received the first course of chemotherapy. Her father, in his pyjamas, in a starched white hospital bed. She bought him his favourite, an apple pie from Myer, but he couldn't even look at it. She fiddled with the IV line and explained that the doctors were attacking his white blood cells. He asked her if they were using a bomb, and laughed before he dry retched. She put her hand on his shoulder. He wiped his mouth and said: *You want that red deer, Doc?*

Polar bears are the most prestigious of animal trophies.

The fact that other hunters have access to guns and to bullets mostly makes Anne nervous. They all look the same, sound the same, act the same. She feels sure there is something a little bit out of control about them, something needing compensation.

And there are those stories about duck-shooting season: the bands of drunks around a lake shooting every bird that moves, in an orgy of imprecision.

Once you have successfully killed your polar bear, you have to get its carcass back to Australia. To do so you will need import permits from the Department of Agriculture, Fisheries and Forestry, from Australian Customs and from the Department of the Environment and Heritage. To get these permits you must produce an Australian and a Canadian hunting licence, a CITES permit and an export permit. The latter two documents will not be issued until you have killed the bear.

You can, as an alternative, hire a customs broker who specialises in the importation of animal trophies, and he will arrange the whole thing – except for the aim, except for the kill – for a single fee.

Regardless of who arranges it, the issuing of permits takes up to three months, during which time your dead bear must be stored in a Canadian refrigerator.

Anne holds a dinner party and unveils the red deer. Her friends laugh and raise eyebrows. One wipes her napkin over her lips and says: *Oh you have got to be kidding.*

Polar bears give off no detectable heat. They are so well insulated with blubber and fur that they do not even show up in infrared photographs. An infrared photograph of a polar bear looks just like a small puff of red – the bear's warm exhalation.

Bob showed Anne photographs. The father hunting for the red deer, in camouflage gear, black stubble on his jaw and a gun slung over his shoulder. He'd camped for two weeks waiting. They were at one of those family dinners feeling dazed and raw and numb. The world was vertiginous, not altogether real. And then someone pulled out a box of old photographs. And they peered into shards of clarity.

Polar bears are the toughest animals on earth to bring down. Only the most skilled hunters even attempt it. Less than ten per cent get their bear.

Bob reads about the polar bear in the Deer Park newspaper. The article, illustrated with a picture of the white bear, announces the auction of a deceased estate. The polar bear, its forefeet outstretched and its mouth open wide, towers in someone's lounge room next to a small framed print.

He calls Anne without thinking, his voice wavery and excited like when they were kids, after too many lollies. *Can you believe it?* he asks her. *A polar bear. Only ten k's from here!*

On the day of the auction Anne goes to work and keeps her phone in her pocket. She investigates fevers, shortness of breath, an exacerbation of the pain in one man's chest. She adds and subtracts medicines with a hopeful precision. When her brother rings in the afternoon she holds her phone with both hands, presses it to her ear: *Did you get it?*

She imagines being able to wrap her arms around its massive body and bury her face in its soft fur.

For a while they hold on to their phones in silence.

Anne hears Bob take in a long, jagged breath.

Grief is the way you keep a lost object present in your world. In exchange for some pain, grieving keeps them with you for just a little longer.
   Grief is preservation.

Anne writes to an Arctic safari operator in Canada.

Rick, she writes, *I would like to arrange for my brother to hunt a polar bear.*

Soon. In a few years. When I am some kind of specialist.

She imagines what it must be like to shoot a gun. The weight of it, the power. To have that metal up close to her face, and the trigger beneath her finger. To squint through the scope and see only the animal she wants to kill.

The Arctic is so white. It's as white as the corner of a young girl's eye. As white as sharp, bright light. As the after-flash of loneliness.

The chemotherapy slipped into the father's bone marrow and wiped out everything that moved. White blood cells, red blood cells, platelets, everything. When he ran out of platelets, he started to bleed. Like a glass full of warm blood, shattering.

Now Anne has a thought about what happened to her father. The thought barges in like a redneck, and guts her with its arrival: *I let them use a bomb.*

And the Arctic is blue. As blue as wind. As cold deep water. As pale pale blue as a melancholy thought that follows you like vapour.

She closes her eyes and he looms up large. He fills her mind and leaks out between her eyelids like fine-cut diamonds, like ice, like snow.

Past Voiceworks Editors:
WHERE ARE THEY NOW?

Voiceworks is a national quarterly magazine that features writing by young Australian writers. Run by Express Media, and produced entirely by young people, it is an opportunity for writers and artists who are under twenty-five to publish their poetry, articles, short stories, comics, illustrations and photos. It began life as a newsletter and wasn't credited with an editor until its tenth issue, in July 1992. Interested in life after *Voiceworks*, Sleepers asked the past editors, where are you now?

Philippa Burne: issue 10 to issue 26
'I am currently looking after some cats in Amsterdam before heading back to Croatia for a few months. After six years writing television in Australia (yes, I did *Neighbours*), around Europe (Poland, Slovakia, Croatia, Holland) and in the USA, I am trying to get my soul back by working on another book. Finally, a follow up to *Fishnets*, which was published by Allen and Unwin in 1997. They made me a Young Adult novelist, probably so they could market me à la *Voiceworks* (even though I am much, much older than that…) Given the ten-year gap, this one is likely to be a very different book.

I am also writing travel blogs for the website Viator.com, which makes me feel less like a spoilt princess during all the current travel (television paid well…) and more like a legitimate travelling writer. The latest is on climbing every mountain in Salzburg. Writers should not spend all their time at their desks…'

Adam Ford: issue 26 to issue 33
'These days I live outside Melbourne in a small country town in Central Victoria. I live in a 1950s weatherboard house on half an acre of poorly mown grass with my wife, our daughter, our cat and our chickens. I still work in Melbourne, so I catch the train a lot, which lets me do a lot of reading, sleeping or writing, depending on my mood.

These days I'm writing a novel. I'm writing poems and short stories. I'm reviewing comics and poetry books for websites and radio. I'm making zines and comics and running two websites of my own: my personal site (www.labyrinth.net.au/~adamford) and a more esoteric beast called Monkey Punch Dinosaur (www.monkeypunchdinosaur. blogspot.com).

These days I'm the Content Editor of youthcentral (www.youth-central.vic.gov.au), a Victorian Government website for young people. I write and edit articles about things like jobs and careers, study, health issues and government policy. I work with a team of forty people under twenty-five who write articles for us as well. I train them to write for the web and they write about everything from their life stories to reviews of movies and CDs. It's not very different from what I used to do at *Voice-works*. There's heaps of editing, a bit of writing, regular deadlines, the joy of working with a team of talented young writers… no, it's not very different at all.'

Craig Garrett: issue 34 to issue 43

'Editing *Voiceworks* was joyous and horrendous. On the joyous side, many people who I've met and worked with have become good friends, and their honesty, passion and professionalism is an enduring legacy. On the horrendous side, I produced what was described by someone close to *Voiceworks* as, "the worst *Voiceworks* ever". I was devastated and resigned to do better. So – on the joyous side again – when the next edition was published that same person said I'd produced, "one of the five best *Voiceworks*". I was so proud.

I do remember thinking, many times, "It's all up to me! If I don't do it it'll collapse!" To a degree that's true, because the editor has to get the mag out there, but *Voiceworks* existed before me and continues well after, and wouldn't have collapsed if I didn't "do it", whatever "it" was. It's far more robust than that. Being part of something bigger than me, and watching subsequent editors take *Voiceworks* places I never could, or would have thought to take it, is heartening.

Speaking of unexpected places, I remember speaking to a woman about ordering more copies of the 'Fashion' edition because hers kept getting stolen. She used it as a resource for counselling teenage girls with eating disorders because it gave alternative views of fashion compared to mainstream magazines. For me, that sums up *Voiceworks*: it has positive impacts, speaks to people on its own terms, is honest, and it can't be pigeonholed or easily defined. Same can be said about the editors.

There's also a hipflask that has everybody's name and tenure engraved on it. Each new editor gets the hipflask to look after when they begin their tenure. (I started it in 2000 and backdated Adam's and Philippa's tenures, so it looked like it'd been around for ages. Now, I don't think it's the original flask. It's been lost a couple of times and re-engraved. It's kinda nice that the flask now has a chequered history of its own.)'

Aren Aizura (formerly Aizura Hankin): issue 43 to issue 49
'After editing *Voiceworks*, I took some time off to rethink my direction. I changed my name and my gender, and I decided to change 'career' too, although 'career' is an odd word to apply to the piecemeal working life people construct nowadays. I took the typical solution: back to study. In July 2007 I'm nearly finished writing a PhD about transgender people who travel, and I hope to keep doing academic research here or overseas when I finish. I've continued to edit and write short fiction and essays, published in some small press publications.

I miss the thrills and spills of *Voiceworks*: being part of a creative hub with lots of spokes; discovering extreme talent lurking in the submissions tray; drinking a longneck in the gutter after putting the magazine to bed. I especially miss working with some of the most talented designers in Australia – *Voiceworks* has always been about making a beautiful object, not just the words. But I never had the time to write or think enough as a 'full-time' editor. Now I cherish the freedom to make my own words/ ideas, rather than being the editor who constantly polishes other people's. Of late, I've been making themed mixtapes with covers that approximate small, personalised zines. Write to me – alchemic@optusnet.com.au – I might make you one!'

Kelly Chandler: issue 49 to issue 58
'I left the country after *Voiceworks*. Couldn't stay in Melbourne knowing there were editorial committee meetings going on without me and figured getting paid to live in paradise might take the edge off.

Using borrowed keywords like 'sustainable development', 'capacity building' and 'skills transfer', I talked my way into an AusAID gig in Vanuatu at *The Independent* newspaper, where I was meant to train journalists but really drank kava, found stories at the market, lost command of English and learned some beautiful Bislama.

From there, I found a travel angle on eye surgery in the Solomon Islands and eventually made it to the place where writing 'forced to flee a war-torn homeland' feels really good the first time.

Mostly I bear witness to the horrible things people do to each other, and sentences, at a non-government organisation, and as a tonic find beauty in things like riding past the State Library and noticing Dale standing next to the bike into which he built his nan's oil heater.

"Does it keep you warm?" I ask.

"Only when I pedal fast," he says, adjusting his tracksuit pants.'

Tom Doig: issue 58 to issue 66

'Right now I am sitting in the kitchen of former *Voiceworks* editor Kel Chandler, listening to a 'Best of Madonna' CD on my laptop.

I am staying at Kel's house while I look for a new sharehouse, having recently returned from four months in Europe, where I was ostensibly doing research for a creative writing MA about David Hasselhoff and Adolf Hitler. I was actually chasing a girl called Alice Rose Gunn Swing.

I first discovered Alice after we published one of her poems in *Voiceworks*, although she didn't reply to my flirtatious emails until I stopped mentioning experimental free verse.

I am also working like a protestant on the National Young Writers' Festival, sending out emails to gazillions of amazing wordsmiths and deviants across the country, many of whom I first met through *Voiceworks*.

Basically, I owe every aspect of my current life, every one of my challenges and triumphs, to *Voiceworks*. If it wasn't for *Voiceworks*, I'd probably be a sake-addicted ESL teacher, sleeping in a capsule hotel in Tokyo and collecting underpants from vending machines.'

Ryan Paine is the current editor of *Voiceworks*, which thrives. Check out the latest edition at www.expressmedia.org.au/voiceworks

Where are YOU now?

Score yourself according to the Robert A Heinlein personal assessment test:

'A human being should be able to:
change a diaper ☐
plan an invasion ☐
butcher a hog ☐
captain a ship ☐
design a building ☐
write a sonnet ☐
balance accounts ☐
build a wall ☐
set a bone ☐
comfort the dying ☐
take orders ☐
give orders ☐
cooperate ☐
act alone ☐
solve equations ☐
analyse a new problem ☐
pitch manure ☐
program a computer ☐
cook a tasty meal ☐
fight efficiently ☐
die gallantly. ☐
Specialisation is for insects.'

- Robert A Heinlein, *Time Enough for Love*, 1973

Do you disagree? What would you say?
A human being should be able to…

....

....

....

....

....

....

So Much Author So
Close to Home...

Steven Amsterdam
Steven grew up on West 82 Street in Manhattan, and that's why he's nervous. He now lives on Charles Street in Abbotsford, Victoria, and can hear kookaburras from his kitchen.

Kalinda Ashton
Kalinda lives in Melbourne. She is a fiction writer and associate editor of *Overland*. She'd like to thank Laurie Clancy's 'A Full House Beats an Empty House' for inspiration for this story.

David Astle
David has written four books, from fiction to travel with true-crime in between. His dog is called Tim.

Jessica Au
Jessica is drinking cold tea and quietly tapping away on a Blickens-derfer 7.

Max Barry
Max is the author of three novels: *Syrup*, listed by the *LA Times* as one of the Best Books of the Year in 1999, *Jennifer Government*, a *New York Times* Notable Book, and *Company* (Scribe), a bestseller in the US and Australia. He lives in Melbourne. www.maxbarry.com

Jo Bowers
Jo is a Melbourne-based writer and lawyer. Her fiction has been published in national literary journals, including two previous *Sleepers Almanacs*, and has been broadcast on Radio National. She recently completed a term as writer-in-residence in Sydney, working on her first novel.

Eddy Burger
Eddy has writ lots funny and experimental fiction, poetree, play & drawings. Can find in plenty journal, and berry hippy to be in Sleepers Owmyneck agen!!!

John Burnside
John has published five novels, of which the most recent is *The Devil's Footprints* (Jonathan Cape). His memoir, *A Lie About My Father* (Jonathan Cape), won the Saltire Book of the Year and the Scottish Arts Council Non-Fiction Book of the Year awards. He lives on the east coast of Scotland, where the risk of sunburn is almost non-existent.

Steven Carroll
Steven played in bands in the 70s and can't hear as well as he used to. His books are being nominated for awards left, right and centre, including two Miles Franklin Award shortlistings, for *The Art of the Engine Driver* (Harper Collins, 2001) and *The Gift of Speed* (Harper Collins, 2004). *Engine Driver* was also shortlisted for the Prix Femina, 2005, France. His latest novel is *The Time We Have Taken* (Harper Collins, 2007).

Sean Condon
Sean is the author of several books.

Patrick Cullen
Patrick writes short stories and tries to publish them in only the best possible places (a plot that looks to have worked yet again).

Paul Oslo Davis
Paul is a Melbourne illustrator and cartoonist. You can find him at www.pauloslodavis.com

Will Eaves
Will is the author of two novels, *The Oversight* (Picador, 2001) and *Nothing To Be Afraid Of* (Picador, 2005) and a short collection of poetry, *Small Hours* (Brockwell Press, 2006). He is a commissioning editor at the *Times Literary Supplement*, teaches at the University of Warwick, and lives in Brixton, London. www.willeaves.com

Eleanor Elliott Thomas
Eleanor claims to be a writer, but she doesn't even know how to finish this sentenc

David Gibb
David is a retired advertising and marketing copywriter who, having spent four decades meeting other people's unreasonable deadlines, is now writing fiction to his own equally unreasonable deadlines.

Grace Goodfellow
Grace has a guitar called Lucy, a harmonica called Ziggy, and a tiny silver stud in her nose.

Karen Hitchcock
Karen's fiction has been published in *The Best Australian Stories 2006* and *The Best Australian Stories 2007*, *Meanjin*, *Griffith Review*, and *The Sleepers Almanac 2007*.

Jeff Hoogenboom
Jeff is a Melbourne writer who can't be defined in two sentences. He is, however, definitely working on his first novel.

Darby Hudson
Darby writes and draws, and he lives in Melbourne.

Darryn King
Darryn is a writer, insofar as he has written things. He shot a man in Reno just to watch him die.

Andy Kissane
Andy teaches writing at the University of New South Wales.

Scott McDermott
Scott has published stories about elderly women, finned mice, mermaids, traffic lights, invisibility, murder, and gods in exile. He lives in Brunswick.

Russell McGilton
Russell is a writer, playwright, screenwriter and actor. He's written for publications including *The Age* and *The Big Issue*. He recently wrote a radio play, *Seditious Delicious: A Portrait of John Howard*, and he is currently writing a children's book, *How to Play with Bandsaws!*
www.russellmcgilton.com.au

Bronwyn Mehan
Bronwyn has recently moved to Darwin in search of lawn sales and enlightenment.

Luke Menzel
Luke is twenty-seven and lives in Melbourne. He writes poetry and prose.

Julie Milland
Julie was a research scientist who wanted to write. Now she's a writer.

Paul Mitchell
Paul's latest books are a short fiction collection, *Dodging the Bull* (Wakefield Press, 2007), and a poetry collection, *Awake Despite the Hour* (Five Islands Press, 2007). He hopes to soon own a cat.

Paul Morgan
Paul lives in Melbourne with his partner Caroline, his cat, and his beloved Karmann Ghia (not necessarily in that order). His two novels, *The Pelagius Book* (Penguin) and *Turner's Paintbox* (Penguin), have been widely praised, drawing comparisons with David Malouf.

Rose Mulready
Rose suspects she has recently begun sleepwalking. It's the only way to account for certain bizarre events.

Pierz Newton-John
Pierz is a Melbourne-based writer, web developer and psychotherapist. He won the Boroondara Literary Awards open short story competition in 2006, and has had several short stories published, including in the *Sleepers Almanac 2007* and in *Overland*.

Jeremy Ohlback
Jeremy is an MA student from Sydney, who writes because it suits his natural disposition towards broodiness, gin-drinking, and romantic optimism.

Ryan O'Neill
Ryan's latest collection of short stories, *A Famine in Newcastle* (Ginninderra Press) was shortlisted for the Steele Rudd Award in the 2007 Queensland Premier's Literary Awards.

Eddie Paterson
Eddie writes in North Carlton, in Melbourne.

Virginia Peters
Virginia lives in the Northern Rivers region of NSW, and is enrolled in the Masters program at the University of Technology, Sydney.

Andrew Preston
Andrew is a writer whose fiction and non-fiction has appeared in publications such as *Island*, *Australian Book Review* and Vandal Press's *Adventures in Pop Culture*.

Emmett Stinson
Emmett has received the Age Short Story Award, the Arts SA Creative Writing Award, and a Lannan Poetry Fellowship. He serves as Fiction Editor of *Wet Ink: The Magazine of New Writing*.

Jane Wallace-Mitchell
In her next life, Jane intends to be taller and more daunting.

Chloe Walker
Chloe grew up in Colac and now lives in Melbourne. Her short stories have also appeared in *Voiceworks* and *Verandah*.

Tony Wilson
Tony is the author of the satirical novel *Players* (Text), for which he was a 2006 SMH Young Novelist of the Year. He's also written a sporting memoir, *Australia United* (Geoff Slattery Publishing), and four picture books. The piece in this *Almanac* was read out on Radio Triple R's Breakfasters, where he was on the team from 2002 until the end of 2007.

Ephemera

A selection of books we have read in the last twelve months

The Man Who Loved Children, Christina Stead
My Revolutions, Hari Kunzru
What is the What, Dave Eggers
Mother's Milk, Edward St Aubyn
The Gathering, Anne Enright
Special Topics in Calamity Physics, Marisha Pessl
Two Lives: Gertrude and Alice, Janet Malcolm
The Low Road, Chris Womersley
The Sirens of Titan, Kurt Vonnegut
Napoleon's Double, Antoni Jach
The Time We Have Taken, Steven Carroll
Emotionally Weird, Kate Atkinson
Rosencrantz and Guildenstern Are Dead, Tom Stoppard
Aphelion, Emily Ballou
Let the Northern Lights Erase Your Name, Vendela Vida
Dodging the Bull, Paul Mitchell
We Need to Talk About Kevin, Lionel Shriver
Leonard Woolf, Victoria Glendinning
The End of the World, Paddy O'Reilly
Erasure, Percival Everett
The Broken Shore, Peter Temple
The Raw Shark Texts, Steven Hall
Reading Like a Writer, Francine Prose
Turner's Paintbox, Paul Morgan
Restless, William Boyd
Lisey's Story, Stephen King
Omar and Enzo in the Big Talking Book, Colin Batrouney
On Chesil Beach, Ian McEwan
Feather Man, Rhyll McMaster
Rohypnol, Andrew Hutchinson
Love Without Hope, Rodney Hall
And Now You Can Go, Vendela Vida
Company, Max Barry
Unless, Carol Shields
Wake in Fright, Kenneth Cook
The Road, Cormac McCarthy
Three Dog Night, Peter Goldsworthy

The Man of My Dreams, Curtis Sittenfeld
Lucky Jim, Kingsley Amis
The Discomfort Zone, Jonathan Franzen
Helen Garner and the Meaning of Everything, Alex Jones
The Post Birthday World, Lionel Shriver
The Unknown Terrorist, Richard Flanagan
Never Have Your Dog Stuffed, Alan Alda
Disgrace, JM Coetzee
Martin Bauman, David Leavitt

Music that blew/cleared our minds

Rufus Wainwright: Release the Stars; Want Two; Poses
The Yeah Yeah Yeahs: Show Your Bones; Is Is (EP)
Bill Callahan AKA Smog: Woke on a Whaleheart
TISM: The White Albun
CW Stoneking: King Hokum
Cake: Pressure Chief
Antony and the Johnsons: I Am a Bird Now
IQU with Miranda July: Girls on Dates
Devastations: Coal
The Hold Steady: Separation Sunday; Nearly Killed Me
Jarvis Cocker: The Jarvis Cocker Record
Morrissey: Ringleader of the Tormentors
Camera Obscura: Lets Get Out of This Country
Love is All: Nine Times That Same Song

TV that kept us up

The Sopranos
The Chaser's War on Everything
The Eagle
Summer Heights High
Weeds
Spicks and Specks
Rockwiz
Doctor Who
Media Watch
The New Inventors
The Cook and the Chef
Top Gear

Mythbusters
Spooks
Twin Peaks
Flight of the Conchords
'Rank' films shown between 1:00a.m. and 5:00a.m. on the ABC

Sites we've visited
postsecret.com
getup.org.au
abc.net.au
misssnark.blogspot.com
salon.com
thebookgrocer.blogspot.com
darbyhudson.com
scribepublications.com.au/blog
chaser.com.au
jackywinter.com

Printing and typographic details
This *Almanac* was printed by Griffin Press. The body font is Adobe Garamond. The cover font, and title page font, is Century Gothic.

A note on the typeface
Garamond is the name given to a group of fonts that constitute some of the most popular serif fonts in use. They were designed during the 16th century by a French printer named Claude Garamond. There have been lots of variations developed since 1540, like the one used in this book: it has a horizontal bar on the lowercase 'e', a slightly greater contrast between thick and thin strokes, axis curves that are inclined to the left, and bracketed serifs.

Century Gothic comes from the curiously named font group Grotesque, a name coined by the English, who considered the first of these typefaces awkward and unappealing because they lacked the traditional serif.

If you have trouble remembering the difference between serif and sans serif (and let's face it, life's too short to find yourself confused about typefaces),

then think of the word serif as 'feet'. Anyone who's done first grade French should know that 'sans' means 'without'; so if the font is 'sans serif', that means it doesn't have any feet. I hope this little tip has improved your understanding. If you're more confused then you were before, don't worry about it. These things have a way of looking after themselves.

A note on this *Almanac*
This *Almanac* you're reading, *The Sleepers Almanac No. 4*, is the fourth in the series. As you can see, we have altered the name of it slightly. There are reasons for that, but we won't go into them here. The format, the size, has also changed a bit. Oh OK, for those of you who were asking why we changed the name, it's because we realised that bookstores return books that have last year's date on them (outdated) but keep things that run in a series (commitment to serious series action). And even though we know, and you know, that it was all part of a series before, the date-thing was obviously confusing people. Let's face it, it was confusing for us too. Mainly because we did actually create the book the year prior to the date on it. And you know, bookshop people deserve all the help they can get right now, while they are up against the internet, the ebook, and of course the recent propensity of people playing hakki sack all lunch.